STATE OF EXILE

VIRGIL JONES MYSTERY THRILLER
BOOK 5

THOMAS SCOTT

Copyright © 2018 by Thomas Scott. All rights reserved. No part of this book may be reproduced in any form or by any electronic or mechanical means, including photocopying, recording, or by any information storage and retrieval system without written permission from both the publisher and copyright owner of this book.

This book is a work of fiction. No artificial intelligence (commonly referred to as: AI) was used in the conceptualization, creation, or production of this book. Names, characters, places, governmental institutions, venues, and all incidents or events are either the product of the author's imagination or are used fictitiously. Any resemblance to actual persons, living or dead, businesses, companies, events, locales, venues, or government organizations is entirely coincidental.

For information contact: ThomasScottBooks.com

HIGH ROAD PRESS

— **Also by Thomas Scott** —

The Virgil Jones Series In Order

State of Anger - Book 1
State of Betrayal - Book 2
State of Control - Book 3
State of Deception - Book 4
State of Exile - Book 5
State of Freedom - Book 6
State of Genesis - Book 7
State of Humanity - Book 8
State of Impact - Book 9
State of Justice - Book 10
State of Killers - Book 11
State of Life - Book 12
State of Mind - Book 13
State of Need - Book 14
State of One - Book 15
State of Play - Book 16
State of Qualms - Book 17
State of Remains - Book 18
State of Suspense - Book 19

The Jack Bellows Series In Order

Wayward Strangers - Book 1
Brave Strangers - Book 2

Visit ThomasScottBooks.com for further
information regarding future release dates, and more.

*One final time, for my late father, Richard.
Exiled no more - Yet exiled no less.*

ex·ile
eg͵zīl, ek͵sīl

To banish or expel

———————

"Your life is now." —John Mellencamp

———————

"Someting bad coming our way, Virgil Jones. Maybe it already here." —Delroy Rouche

CHAPTER ONE

It was a single, instinctual act, one that demonstrated good and decent men could still do honorable deeds in defense of others, no matter their methods or the consequences that might arise from a future not yet written. After it was over, the harshness of the moment would fade, lost to a false measure of time and the ambient noise that made up their daily lives.

But deep beneath the watery surface of their existence where the pressure was heavy and the light remained dim, something lurked, waiting to strike back. And when it did, its grip could only be defined as relentless and deadly, a hold without borders, one that threatened to pull them all under. Virgil Jones knew it would come back on them one day—he had no doubt in that regard. Except he didn't think it would happen quite so soon.

And even then it didn't happen the way he thought it might.

It rarely did.

Immigrations and Customs Enforcement agent Chris Dobson had long ago mixed in with the wrong crowd, his mistakes based on his own erroneous thoughts and demonstrations by others that gave witness to situations outside his scope of understanding. When shown that wealth and prosperity equated to privileged righteousness—as if the moral high ground was a gift bestowed only to the worthy—it became a drug, no less addictive than those stuck in the unending cycle of despair brought on by chemical escapism that deconstructed lives like reverse evolution. When Dobson put a timeline to it, he discovered it started back in high school with an old buddy named Ken Salter, a guy who'd probably been hit in the head a few too many times out on the football field.

The head-banging buddy had grown up and not only had he taken a position within his father's business empire, he'd managed to get himself elected to the state legislature. No matter. Even as a grown man, he was still a child who followed his father's instructions to the letter. In short, Ken Salter didn't do much thinking for himself. Often his thoughts went no deeper than deciding he'd had a good day based solely on the fact he hadn't accidentally swallowed his own toothbrush or cut his face with an electric razor.

Salter was from the south-central part of Indiana, deep into his second term at the statehouse and looking for a third when he'd recruited Dobson three months ago for a little side job that, in Salter's own words, would be 'a walk in the park.'

"I'm telling you," Salter said, "there's nothing to it." They were in Salter's government office, a closet-sized room in the basement of the statehouse. "All you have to do is be a presence. Pick up this Homeland guy..." Salter shuffled some paper on his desk and found the note with the Homeland agent's name…"Robert Thorpe at the airport and tag along with him."

Despite his wealth and access to all the things that should have made him shine, Salter's bulb didn't burn all that bright. Dobson thought the bulb might shine in the neighborhood of sixty watts, at best.

"Why?" Dobson asked. "Homeland trying to save money on the rental car bill?"

Salter rolled his eyes. "It's called federal inter-agency cooperation. He's looking for one of his own, a guy named Paul Gibson. Gibson is undercover with an MCU detective by the name of Murton Wheeler. I don't care about Gibson. I need to know where Wheeler is so I can shut him down. He's about to mess something up in a big way, something that took a lot of planning. Anyway, you can get to Wheeler through his asshole buddies at that Jamaican bar right here in the city. You know the one?"

"Never been, but yeah, I know of it."

"So pick up Thorpe, point him at the bar, listen to what everyone has to say, and then report back to me."

"And what if we run into trouble?"

Salter held his hands out, palms up. "If you want to run with the big dogs, Chris, you've got to get off the porch once in a while. You're a federal agent, for Christ's sake. How about you start acting like it? If there's trouble, take a Jamaican or two aside and let them know there's always an open seat on the deportation express back to the islands."

"What's this all about?"

"You don't want to know," Salter said. "Trust me, you really don't." He passed an envelope to Dobson.

Dobson peeked at the bills inside the envelope. "Little light for not wanting to know." Then, with a bit of sarcasm,

"Or a big dog." When Salter didn't respond, Dobson put the envelope in his pocket and walked out.

When he arrived at the Indianapolis International airport to pick up Thorpe, a TSA agent tried to tell Dobson he couldn't park his vehicle in the red zone. A Hispanic TSA agent, no less. He badged the TSA spic and told him to get lost. The whole country was swirling down the drain right in front of him. As an ICE agent, he saw it first hand, every single day. Was he the only one who noticed? Didn't anyone else care? What's next? ISIS running the X-ray scanners? Boko Haram handling baggage claims?

Dobson leaned against the side of his car and lit a cigarette. He took a long drag and blew the smoke upward out of the corner of his mouth the way a woman might. The TSA agent glared at him for a beat, then went away. A few minutes later Thorpe stepped outside and Dobson pegged him before he was halfway across the sidewalk. He flicked his cigarette in the gutter, whistled through his teeth, and got Thorpe's attention. He waved him over and both men got in the car.

Thorpe offered his hand and said, "Bob Thorpe, Homeland Security, Portland field office."

Dobson dropped the car in gear and occupied himself by adjusting the rear-view mirrors and monitoring the flow of traffic, ignoring Thorpe's hand in the process. When he pulled away he cut across two lanes of traffic causing another driver to slam on his brakes and lean on his horn. Dobson would have let the horn go for what it was—a coward hiding behind a noisemaker—but the middle finger was over the line. He threw the car in park and left it angled across both lanes, traffic now backed up behind them.

"Hey, what are you doing?" Thorpe asked.

Dobson ignored him. He got out of the car and walked over to the cab. The driver wore a turban, his cab decorated with beads and prayer cards. When the window came down the smell of incense caused Dobson to turn his head to the side. When he tried to read the cab driver the riot act, he gagged and almost vomited in the street. The driver laughed at Dobson, which made him madder than he already was. When he turned to walk away he kicked his heel into the side of the cab, leaving a dent the size of a soccer ball.

He got back in his own car and drove away. "Fucking ragheads." He looked at Thorpe. "If you knew some of the shit I have to put up with in this job you might not have such a superior look on your face right now."

Thorpe held his stare. "You Indiana guys are wound a little tight."

"That's because we love our country and don't cater to a bunch of liberal sissies who think the whole world should be a rainbow of skin tones getting a free ride on the welfare merry-go-round."

"What welfare? It looked to me like a guy making an honest living."

"Yeah, all on the backs of hard-working Americans who can't find a decent job. At least we're finally making some progress on this DACA bullshit. That ought to get the ball rolling in the right direction."

"You mean the Deferred Action for Childhood Arrivals program?"

"That's the one."

"Progress is hardly the word. The whole thing is being ripped to shreds. Personally, I think it's a good program. I wish they'd leave it alone. My son has a friend who's part of it. This is the only country he's ever known. He's worried sick they're going to deport him."

"He should be. In fact, you better tell your boy to let his friend know it might be time to start packing. We've finally got a president who isn't screwing around."

"I don't think you know what you're talking about. The president himself is on record saying net immigration is down."

Dobson wasn't having it. "Whatever. There are facts, and then there are alternative facts. That means you pick a team and play ball. You know what it should stand for? DACA?"

"I'm afraid to ask," Thorpe said.

"Degenerates Are Constantly Arriving."

Enough was enough, Thorpe thought. Time to try a different tactic. "Tell me about your skin condition. My grandfather had the same thing, I think. If not, it was something like it. Is it Vitiligo?"

"That's the technical term. It's a pigmentation issue. Mine's a little more severe than most."

"I can see that."

"If you have a point, it's lost on me."

"I guess maybe I'd be sensitive to other people's skin color too if I wasn't exactly sure of their thoughts regarding my own. How long until we get to this restaurant?"

"It's more of a bar. Probably twenty minutes. Why?"

Dobson had let the skin color remark go unchallenged and Thorpe didn't know why. He didn't care, either. "No reason," Thorpe said. "No reason at all." He turned and looked out the side window and didn't speak for the rest of the ride.

STATE OF EXILE

WHEN THEY ARRIVED DOBSON TURNED INTO THE BACK LOT, pointed out the front window and said, "Hey look, there's our first victim."

Victim? "How about we dial it back a little?" Thorpe said.

"Sounds to me like someone's been riding a desk a little too long. I'll bet you've got hemorrhoids the size of melons. C'mon, I'll show you how we roll in the Midwest."

"I think it's time to slow your motor down, Agent Dobson."

But Dobson wasn't listening. He got out of the car and in less than ten seconds had Delroy Rouche, co-owner and bar manager of Jonesy's Rastabarian up against the exterior wall, his forearm across the Jamaican's throat. "Where's Murton Wheeler?"

Delroy's eyes were wide with surprise and fear. "I don't know, me. I just got here, mon."

"What'd you call me, boy?"

Delroy opened his mouth to respond but Dobson pressed his arm harder against his throat and no words came out.

"You really should make an effort to answer me. Know why? I'm with ICE. If you don't cooperate I can fix it to have you sent back to Tongo-Tongo land or wherever you're from. Know what that means? It means no more land of the free and home of the brave for you. It'll be more like land of the losers and home of the grass huts. How's that sound? Want to help me make America great again? We're doing it one degenerate at a time."

Delroy turned his head enough to get the pressure off his throat so he could speak. "Go ahead and try. I'm an American now, like you. Jamaican too. I got dual citizenship, mon. I'm at home no matter where you try to send me." He smiled when he said it.

"We'll see about that," Dobson said. He spat at Delroy's

feet then turned him around and pushed him through the kitchen and all the way into the bar.

Those were the thoughts that seemed to play on a constant loop in Dobson's head, thoughts from three months ago when he'd lost his shit and let the Jamaican get the better of him with a baseball bat. He'd swung the bat and caught Dobson in the arm, snapping the bone. Since then his life had been one downhill slide after another.

He was at the doctor's office to finally have the cast removed from his arm. When the doctor came in, Dobson looked up at him and closed his eyes, a knot of cartilage forming at the back of his jawline, right below his ears.

"Herrow," the doctor said. "I Dr. Lau. I take off cast now for you."

A chink doctor? No thank you. Dobson stood from the chair, put his hands together, did a little bow and said, "I don't rink so, Hop Sing. Not today." Then he walked out, went home, and removed the cast himself with an old hacksaw blade. It was a little more difficult than he thought it might be.

He only cut himself twice.

Was he the only one willing to make a stand? It certainly looked like it. But where to start? What was the name of the island hump who'd broken his arm with the bat? He rummaged through his old case notes and found the name. Delroy Rouche. That was it. How'd he let some bald-headed Jamaican jerk-water get the better of him? If that wasn't enough, one of the asshole state agents had him arrested and booked like a common criminal. Was everyone out to get him?

His lawyer had managed to get the charges dropped, and his union rep kept the higher-ups from firing him, but after the internal review process was complete his boss said he didn't have a choice. Regulations were regulations. He got a three-month suspension without pay. "Take a vacation," his boss had said. "Cool out a little."

Fuck that, Dobson thought. Time for a little good old-fashion down-home original American justice. He wouldn't go after the Jamaican right away. That'd cause more trouble than he could afford. He'd have to find another way. It took some serious recon, but he eventually figured it out.

CHAPTER TWO

By most any measure, Carlos Ibarra should have been living the American dream. His mother, Lola Ibarra had brought him into the country twenty-three years ago when he was only two years old. Carlos and his mother hadn't crossed the border illegally. They came into the country the way most illegals did—on an airline flight—this one direct to Dallas. It took most of her meager savings to make her way north with her son, all the way to the city of Indianapolis, where she eventually found work as a housekeeper and cook for a wealthy couple who wanted help with the care of their own child but didn't want or need the bother of all the tax implications of an actual documented employee.

The family paid her a fair wage, provided a home for herself and her son and even offered protection by keeping her passport locked in their safe. When she asked why she wouldn't be allowed to maintain possession of her own documentation, the answer was simple. In America, law enforcement was everywhere, and they were to be feared. When her Visa ran out, she could stay and continue to work, or be free to go and live on her own and raise her son with the constant worry of Immigrations knocking on her door and sending them back to a place that held no future other than misery and despair. Lola Ibarra didn't like it, but what choice did she have? She wasn't about to go back to Mexico.

And the wealthy couple seemed so nice, no matter how hard they tried to hide their arguments. They helped get Carlos enrolled in a private school, paid the cost of his tuition, and even had their personal driver drop him off and pick him up every day. Other than not having access to her passport, Lola Ibarra thought she'd hit the jackpot.

But she sensed the unhappiness of the couple, as their arguments grew in both intensity and duration. After only a few weeks of her employment, the couple no longer bothered to hide their disdain for each other. A year later when the wife disappeared, the lawyers helped the police understand that their client had no idea what had happened to his spouse. Lola Ibarra didn't know much about American law enforcement, but she knew that they seemed to accept her employer's word without much unpleasantness at all. After a few meetings that ended with handshakes and smiles, the case went away almost as quickly as the wife had, who in fact, was never heard from again.

Then one night not long after the wife disappeared, Lola Ibarra heard a quiet knock on her door. He closed the door softly behind him and climbed into her bed without saying a word. When she tried to resist, he explained her options in great detail, all the time stroking her thick dark hair and wiping the tears that leaked from the corners of her eyes.

Lola stared at the ceiling and convinced herself it was all for Carlos. She'd do anything to ensure he had a better life than she'd had. Was it such a price to pay? She'd been raped in Mexico on more than one occasion, the last time by a gang that left her beaten and bloody behind an abandoned adobe at the edge of her own hometown, not three blocks from where she lived. If she simply thought of it as part of her job, like doing the cooking and cleaning, it wasn't rape, was it? It was what was expected of her. Like it was part of her job description that somehow got left out of the interview process.

He promised he'd be gentle with her, and he usually was. He told her he'd pay for community college or trade school for Carlos when the time came. And he reminded her of Immigrations...always out there, always on the prowl. He'd protect her and keep her and Carlos safe.

And he did.

But eventually, as Carlos grew older, he began to understand what his mother had been forced to endure for so many years. He was seventeen when he finally confronted her. She told him of the visits that had been a part of her life once or twice a week for more than a decade, Carlos nodded, his face twisted with rage when he showed her the gun. She took it from his hands and slapped him in the face.

The next morning the gun went into the river and when she returned, Carlos was home from school. They argued about what to do. Carlos said he could get a job and take care of them both. His mother told him they had to keep their station in life. It was the way the world worked these days. Did he want to be deported back to a place he didn't know? Maybe someday the world would change, but they wouldn't change it with violence.

"We have to leave this place," he told her.

"And go where?" she replied.

"Anywhere. I won't let that man touch you again."

"We don't have papers. My passport is locked in the safe. You don't have a birth certificate. What about the policía?"

"We will avoid them. It can be done. I have many friends who tell me it is possible."

"And what of your brother?"

"He is not my brother. He is the child of the man who has been abusing you for years. I would kill them both with my bare hands if you would let me."

They talked and argued about it for weeks and eventually Carlos wore his mother down. When they snuck out in the middle of the night with her employer snoring softly in his own bedroom, they left without Lola Ibarra's passport, where it remained locked in the safe.

Almost like a trophy.

Carlos found work as promised and made enough money to rent them a room in a run-down motel that had been converted to small apartments for transients and illegals. True to his word, they stayed clear of the policía until one day when Carlos was walking home from his job he saw his mother speaking to the plain-clothes detectives outside her door. Carlos stopped at the edge of the complex and watched the policía and their crime scene people as they went up and down the stairs above the room where he and his mother lived. Many of them wore white coverings to protect their clothes and the coverings were coated with blood.

Then suddenly a car came screeching around the corner of the building, the driver going much too fast for the maneuver and the amount of room behind the building. She crashed into one of the policía's vehicles and jumped out screaming something about her brother. When everyone turned and looked at the wrecked cars, Carlos locked eyes with his mother from across the lot. She shook her head at him and the message was clear: It is not safe here.

Carlos knew the young woman and her twin brother. They were the Pope twins, Nicholas and his sister Nichole. He covered his head with the hood of his jacket, then turned around and walked away. Nobody stopped him.

When Lola Ibarra was interviewed by the police, she never mentioned her son.

CHAPTER THREE

Virgil Jones, lead detective of Indiana's Major Crimes Unit was a majority owner of a Jamaican-themed bar and restaurant called Jonesy's Rastabarian. He'd bought the bar with his father, Mason Jones, several years ago after Mason had retired as Sheriff for Marion County. Shortly after purchasing the bar and while on vacation, Virgil met and became fast friends with two Jamaican men, Delroy Rouche and Robert Whyte, who ran their own roadside bar and grill in the small town of Lucea, in Jamaica. Delroy served the drinks and befriended the customers, while Robert handled the cooking.

Lucea sat near the halfway point between the resort towns of Montego Bay and Negril. Both men eventually came to the states to work for Virgil and Mason and soon turned Jonesy's place into one of the hottest bars and restaurants in the entire city. When Mason was shot and killed inside the bar, his will stipulated that three other people were to receive his ownership share of the establishment: Delroy and Robert were among them. So was Murton Wheeler, Virgil's long-time friend, adopted brother, and coworker for the MCU.

Virgil walked in through the back kitchen entrance and said hello to Robert and the sous chefs. Robert had a bandana tied around his forehead and it made him look like a Japanese chef. He was working two knives at the same time, their rhythm chattering off the cutting board like a drummer's paradiddle. He set the knives down and tipped his head to the side, an indication for Virgil to follow him.

"What's up?"

"Dat what I'd like to know, me. When do you tink Murton going to stop putting on a show? I feel like I been watching the same play for about tree months now, mon."

Virgil remembered something his mother had told him long ago, shortly before he and Murton left to fight in the first Iraq war. She'd said that almost without exception, the people who would know you longer than anyone else in your life were your siblings. She went on to say that meant they were the ones who would probably know you best.

"It's his way, Robert. It always has been. Murton keeps the battles he fights to himself. He doesn't want anyone else to carry his weight, especially the people he cares for. He's still working through everything that happened with his father. Give him time. He'll get it sorted out."

Robert pushed out his bottom lip with his tongue and nodded in a meaningful way. "Dat not the way we do where I come from." Then, almost as if he didn't want Virgil to miss his point, he asked, "Sandy and da boys irie, mon?"

"You're the best, Robert. You and Delroy both. I don't know what I'd ever do without you guys in my life."

"Murton in the corner booth, by da stage. He need you. Maybe more than you know. Maybe now more than ever."

"I'll see what I can do. Sandy and the boys are fine. Thanks for asking."

"Don't ever have to tank me for asking about the ones I

love, Virgil Jones." Robert handed him a plate of Jerk chicken and two forks rolled tight inside cloth napkins. "You two eat this chicken. Heal you both right up, mon."

For some reason, Robert's remark made Virgil think about the pills.

HE FOUND MURTON RIGHT WHERE ROBERT SAID HE'D BE, sitting alone in a corner booth, near the stage. Virgil set the plate of chicken and silverware in the center of the table and took a seat. Murton made a show of carefully unwrapping his fork, placing his napkin on his lap, arranging the silverware just so, and rolling up the sleeves of his shirt. He glanced at Virgil. "Help yourself. If I try to eat all of this myself two things will happen. One, I will, and two, I'll need a nap."

"Murt?"

Murton put a piece of chicken in his mouth, tucked it into the side of his cheek, and said, "What?" He held Virgil's stare, the look in his eyes intense, almost a challenge.

"Why won't you talk to me?"

Murton tried to keep a measure of normalcy in his voice. "I am talking to you. In case you didn't notice, that's what we're doing right now. C'mon, Jones-man, eat some chicken." He jabbed another piece of chicken with his fork. Virgil grabbed his wrist, ready to say something, but the look on Murton's face kept the words from forming. Then, as if two different people lived inside his skin, Murton winked at him and took another piece of chicken from the plate with his other hand, popped it into his mouth and smiled as he chewed. Virgil let go of his wrist.

They sat quietly for a few minutes, and when Murton looked at Virgil again, his eyes were narrow and fixed. He suddenly stood and tossed his napkin on the table with enough force to scatter the silverware onto the floor. The words he spoke next were without normality and seemed to suck all the air out of the room. The tone of his voice was tight, his words clipped and direct. "Okay, how about this? Try taking your power back from a dead man."

And Virgil thought, *there it is*.

WITH THE CAST OFF, DOBSON THOUGHT HIS ARM LOOKED shriveled and dead. And it stank. The smell reminded him of a middle school locker room. He scrubbed it clean and that took care of the smell. Most of it, anyway. Whatever.

When he walked into the bar the lighting was low and no one seemed to pay him any attention. Delroy, the Jamaican, was busy blending drinks for the customers and the band was cranking out some sort of jungle bunny hip-hop island bullshit that no one in their right mind would refer to as music. The idiot customers were eating it up like maybe the Caribbean had been the birthplace of the Rolling Stones.

What a joke.

A waitress came by and he ordered a beer in a glass. When he reached out to take the drink from her hand he caught her staring at his skin condition. He didn't care. People gave him odd looks all the time. He sipped his beer and watched Delroy flirt with a woman at the end of the bar. She put her feet on top of the brass foot rail and stood on her toes and leaned over the bar top. When she kissed him, Dobson thought, *Bingo*.

Later, when she walked out, Dobson followed her home and over the next three days and nights he watched her every move.

When he was ready, he made a move of his own. He parked his car along the side of the dirt road where the woman lived. He felt relatively safe, the tree line gave him cover and the dead-end portion of the road protected him from the rear. The fog was so thick he couldn't even see the house when he drove past. He went all the way to the dead end, turned around, and killed his headlights. When he was sure no one was watching, he let his car roll forward through the fog until he was close to the end of the drive. He left the engine running and settled in to wait. On the seat next to him was a heavy cloth bag. The bag held a coil of nylon rope, a roll of duct tape, and a single syringe filled with pure China White, topped off with a touch of Fentanyl.

Getting the drugs wasn't a problem. Practically every hump they arrested was bringing drugs over the border and into the US. No wonder the entire country was swimming in smack.

He was letting his mind drift and when he caught the headlights coming toward him he looked at his watch and noticed it was almost two in the morning. The fog was so thick it was hard to judge the distance of the oncoming vehicle, the headlights refracting through the dense layer of condensation. It was, in fact, so difficult to tell the distance that Dobson almost missed his opportunity. The car looked like it was still half a mile away and suddenly it was right there.

He threw the transmission into drive, hit his lights, and stepped on the gas. The other car swerved to avoid the collision and ended up in the ditch on the opposite side of the road.

Dobson killed his headlights, grabbed the bag, and jumped out of his car.

Huma Moon couldn't remember when she'd been happier, or felt more alive. She wasn't quite ready to call it love, but it was certainly close, and it felt good, no matter the label. She'd been spending more and more time with Delroy, and over the past three months they'd taken their relationship beyond the illusion of what could be and turned it into something thrilling and electric, all in a very laid-back, island sort of way. When she tried to define it she decided they simply fit together, like she was a Jamaican soul inside an American body.

And her boss, Sandy Jones, God bless her, had noticed. Not only did she notice, she went out of her way to encourage the relationship. Even Sandy's husband, Virgil—who was mostly quiet on the matter—got a particular look of pleasure on his face whenever she talked about Delroy. Huma worked for Virgil and Sandy Jones as their live-in nanny and housekeeper. With their two sons, Wyatt and Jonas under her care, and the support of Virgil and Sandy, she was beginning to feel like part of a larger family, something she'd never had before. Those were some of the wonderful thoughts going through her head as she crept down the road, searching for the entrance to the driveway through the dense fog.

When the bright lights of the other car suddenly appeared she wasn't prepared. A thought that may have been nothing more complicated than *'What?'* flashed through her mind. Her reaction was instinctual. She cut the wheel hard to the left and slammed on the brakes. But the road was narrow, the surface slick over the loose, damp gravel, and before she knew it the front end of her car was in the ditch. The impact wasn't severe, but it was hard enough she banged her face against the top of the steering wheel. She felt a pain in her eye and it began to water as if she'd been punched. Then all of a sudden the passenger door flew open.

Her first thought was: *Virgil*.

But when she turned and saw the man, his hands gloved, his face covered with a mask that had openings for the eyes and mouth, she knew with sickness in her heart that she was in real trouble. She reached for the door handle and even managed to get the door open, but she'd forgotten about the seatbelt. She stabbed at the release mechanism, but in her panicked state she couldn't get the latch free. Then his hands were on her, pinning her down. When she saw him reach out she felt a severe pinch in the side of her neck and everything seemed to fade, like tentacles of smoke swirling skyward, the panic replaced by a warm glow that felt as smooth and silky as melted chocolate running through her entire body.

Dobson taped her mouth, then killed the headlights on her car, but the interior was still lit up and he couldn't find the switch for the overhead. He made a fist and punched the light. The plastic covering cracked and fell in pieces, but the bulb—some sort of LED—seemed indestructible. He finally managed to kill the damned thing by ripping the fixture half out of the ceiling. He yanked the woman out of the car and threw her over his shoulder, then dumped her into the rear of his vehicle. He put the car into reverse and backed down the road…not an easy task with the thick fog.

He carried her a few yards into the woods, then dropped her on the ground. He tied her hands together around the trunk of a tree with the rope. He put the bag over her head, then without forethought he removed it. She was a fine-looking woman. He pulled the scarf down around her neck and let her hair fall across her shoulders. Why not have a little run at her? It's not like she could say no.

No condoms, that's why, you idiot. He put the bag over her head again, cursing himself over the missed opportunity. He crashed through the brush, made it back to his car and drove away. The fog was so thick he almost collided with her car on the way back. That wouldn't have been good.

He laughed out loud.

CHAPTER FOUR

VIRGIL JONES LIVED OUT IN THE COUNTRY, SOUTH OF THE city of Indianapolis. His house was isolated, nestled back off a dead-end dirt road that connected to highway 37, one of the many feeder routes that hooked into 465, the giant, fifty-three-mile beltway that circled the city.

The faint light of day snuck over the horizon as he began his morning run. He jogged down his driveway, then turned left out onto the road and picked up the pace, headed toward highway 37. A heavy fog had rolled through overnight and the sun sat low and dull in the distance behind him, like an old silver dinner plate hung from a string, its brilliance quiet and tarnished. But the heat would come before long and rip the fog away, the hot, damp, tag end of summer now almost gone.

Virgil's morning run along the gravel pack was a refuge, a sanctum that kept his mind quiet and held his thoughts in abeyance. Still in his forties, healthy and now more physically fit than when he'd served in the army with his best friend and brother, Murton Wheeler, he'd come to not only enjoy his workouts, he discovered he needed them.

Something was happening to him, something not easily explained. When he talked about it with his wife, Sandy, she suggested a visit to their family physician and friend, Dr. Robert Bell. He blew it off until Sandy started to insist. Virgil loved his wife dearly and trusted her opinion and intuition more than anything.

So, Bell...

"It's hard to explain."

"Try," Bell said.

"I feel like there's something wrong with me."

Bell nodded, reading through Virgil's chart at the same time. They were at Bell's home. He was unofficially retired from his medical practice, but kept an office and exam room at his house for a few select patients he couldn't let go of. Those very same patients didn't want to let go of Bell either, Virgil and his family among them. After a moment he looked at Virgil over the tops of his glasses, puffed his cheeks, and let out a sigh. "Ask me about my flying lessons."

Bell had been taking helicopter flight lessons and was near the end of the training process.

"Why?"

Bell, a thin, jolly-looking man, had a balding pate and a full white beard. He wore round John Lennon glasses perched halfway down his nose and his overall appearance made him look like a skinny, out of work mall Santa who might play a little guitar on the side. He tipped his head a little further and said, "Humor me."

Virgil let his face go slack. "Okay. How are the flying lessons going?"

Bell dropped a whiff of sarcasm in his voice. "Thanks for asking." Then his eyes brightened and he said, "They're going well. I take my check ride with the FAA examiner in a few days."

"That's great. I'm sure it'll go just fine."

Bell waved him off. "I'm trying to make a point here, Jonesy."

Virgil rotated his head as if his collar might be too tight. When he finished the roll, he asked, "Who's stopping you?"

Bell waved Virgil's chart in the air. "If you'll pardon the cliché, you're as healthy as a horse, Jonesy. Your blood pressure is perfect, your heart rate is fine, your lungs are clear, the kidney and liver tests came back normal, along with all the blood tests we did, and we did damned near all of them. There's nothing wrong with you."

"First of all, I think there is, and second, what does any of that have to do with your flight test?"

Bell tossed the chart on the counter by his side. "It's stress, Jonesy, plain and simple. I'm so stressed out by this check ride I've got coming up I can hardly sleep."

"I've been under stress before, Bell, and I've never experienced anything like this."

"Walk me through it again."

"Don't you have it in my chart?"

"I need to hear the words. Again. From you. Quit stalling."

Virgil looked down at the floor. Stress? That wasn't what he wanted to hear. He wanted to hear he had some sort of vitamin deficiency or something. "Okay, look, I don't want to be too over-dramatic or anything, but it feels like something is wrong in my head. When I wake up in the morning it's as if my mind isn't my own. I have these weird, disparate thoughts that don't make any sense. It's like they're not even my own thoughts…like they're coming from outside of me. I can't make any sense of it."

"What kind of thoughts, exactly?"

"That's just it, Bell. I don't know. If I had to paint a picture, the thoughts would look like bits of confetti being blown around in the wind. Or maybe more like a junkyard getting tossed down the stairs. There are all these little fragments that don't make any sense or come together in any logical pattern. And instead of coming together they fade away, and once they do I can't get them back."

"And this started when?"

Virgil shrugged. "I don't know, a few months ago, I guess."

Bell shook his head. "Don't give me the easy answer, Jonesy. Think about it."

"I have, goddamn it. A few months ago, all right?"

"Well, at least we can definitely rule out stress."

Virgil held up his hands. "Ah, I'm sorry, Bell. I didn't mean to snap at you. You want the truth? Here it is: It scares me."

"How long do these thoughts last? With you all day? A couple of hours, minutes, what?"

This time Virgil paused, not because he didn't know the answer, but because he wanted Bell to think he was thinking about it even though he didn't have to. "In the big picture of the day they go away pretty quick. A half hour or so. The sooner I occupy myself with someting the better."

"You sounded like Delroy there for a second. You said, 'someting.'"

"There's a lot of that going around these days. When was the last time you spoke with Jonas? He's starting to sound like he was born in Jamaica. Look, here's the scary part of the whole thing, Bell. It's not that I can't make the thoughts go away—because I can—it's that once they're gone, I can't remember what they were. And while it's happening, I'm not aware of myself enough to write them down so I can remember after the fact. It's the inability to remember that bugs me the most."

"Are you functional while it's happening?"

"Functional in what way?"

"You know, the basics. Can you move about, brush your teeth, shave, shower, etcetera?"

"Yes, but it's like I'm on autopilot. I can and do manage those things, but I wouldn't want to drive or anything like that. Half the time I don't remember the things I've done unless I make the effort to check."

Bell was quiet for a few moments. "It's not as uncommon as you think. Psychologists call it a disassociated state."

Virgil leaned forward in his chair. "What causes it?"

Bell let his eyelids droop. "Ask me about my flying lessons."

"So it's stress? Plain and simple."

Bell laughed kindly. "With you? Hardly. I've known you your whole life, Jonesy. I don't think 'plain' or 'simple' are two words anyone would use to describe any part of your life. You're experiencing a disassociated state brought on by acute post-traumatic stress. That's a fancy way of saying you're suffering from PTSD. Look at what you've been through over the last few years." He ticked his fingers as he spoke. "Your father was killed right in front of you. No, no, hear me out on this. Your father was killed right in front of you by the wife of a pedophile. Nichole Pope and her brother took you and the governor over the hurdles and on a ride I don't think you'll soon forget, if ever, mostly because they got away with the whole thing. You watched Ed Donatti, a coworker and friend, die right in front of you. You beat back an addiction to prescription pain killers. You almost lost your wife and unborn son, Wyatt, to a lunatic, then almost lost her again, this time with your adopted son, Jonas. On top of all that you watched Sandy shoot and kill Murton's father. If that wasn't enough, you're trying to manage two thousand acres of land you've inherited, you're the majority owner of one of the most popular bars in the city, and you work a full-time job running across the state fixing the governor's problems." He paused for what was, Virgil thought, nothing more than dramatical effect. "Have I left anything out?"

Virgil opened his mouth wide, trying to take the tension out of his jaw. "You've hit the highlights. What I'd like to know is this: What do I do about it?"

"We'll get to that in a moment. Let me ask you something: How is Sandy feeling after what happened with Murton's dad?"

"She seems fine to me, Bell. She was protecting our son. It's what any parent would do."

"That's true. What's also true is the fact that she's been through a lot herself lately."

"I know, Bell. I was there for most of it. And that's what bugs me. These thoughts I'm having in the morning when I wake up? If they're PTSD like you say they are, then why isn't anyone else having them?"

"You're upset because Sandy isn't suffering from the same level of stress as you, or suffering in the same way?"

Virgil turned away and shook his head. "No, that's not what I'm saying. I'm simply trying to figure out what the hell is wrong with me."

"For starters, you can stop lying to yourself."

He turned back and faced Bell. "Meaning what, exactly?"

"A moment ago I asked you if I left anything out. You said I hit the highlights. But I didn't hit them all and I think you know it. Everything I mentioned is true, except I left something out and you didn't bother to correct me."

Virgil bit into his bottom lip, hard. "What do you want me to say? It happened, I survived, I'm healed, and I'm over it. You said yourself I'm as healthy as a horse."

"You're only seventy-five percent correct there, Jonesy. You're not over it. You almost lost your life when Pate had you strung up on that beam. Then you almost lost it again because of the infection after the surgery, and yet again from the addiction to the pain meds. I'll tell you something, you won't be over it until you address it."

"And how do I do that?"

Bell simply stared at him, as if the answer was obvious. When Virgil didn't say anything, Bell took the initiative. "Don't you still owe your wife a honeymoon? Something about a trip to Jamaica, wasn't it?"

VIRGIL REACHED THE END OF THE ROAD AND STOPPED BEFORE turning around. The air was heavy with the sounds of semi-trucks lumbering down the highway, the smell of diesel and wet rubber a harsh contrast to the aroma of the woods and pond water of his own property only a few miles behind him. He bent over and placed his hands on his knees, his breath coming easily, the words Bell had delivered the other day pounding in his head with the same level of intensity as his heart. Why did everything have to be so complicated? Then he thought maybe it was time to take the advice Bell had given him. He had, after all, not yet delivered on the Jamaican honeymoon promise. And the time...he could feel it. Forever slipping away. He'd talk to Sandy about it when he got home.

He stood up, stretched for a moment, then turned around and headed back. The more he thought about the honeymoon, the more excited he became. What the hell had he been waiting for? The last three months had been slow enough. They could have gone and had the time of their lives. When he thought about his caseload, which was still slower than usual, he was sure now was the time. He knew Sandy would agree in a heartbeat. What better way to get out of his own head and get back on track than spending a couple of weeks in paradise with the woman of your dreams?

He hit it hard on the way back, running fast, his thighs burning, his shins pumping up and down like pistons inside an internal combustion engine. The fog was beginning to clear and Virgil was already mentally packing his bags, but when he reached the end of the drive he saw something that didn't make sense.

Virgil and Sandy's live-in housekeeper and nanny, a wonderful woman named Huma Moon had been out late the previous evening. Virgil knew she'd been out late because he'd been up well past midnight, half afraid to go to sleep because he knew what he'd wake to in the morning…the junkyard of thoughts tumbling down into the basement of his brain. Huma still hadn't returned home by the time he went to bed. She'd been on a date with Delroy Rouche, Virgil's partner and bar manager. They'd been seeing each other with greater and greater frequency over the summer months, both of them as happy and content as Virgil had ever seen.

But what stopped Virgil at the end of the drive and refused to let his heart rate slow even though he'd finished his run was Huma's car. She drove a Subaru, and the small SUV sat about ten yards past the drive, facing away from Virgil on the wrong side of the road. The front of the car was buried in the weeds, its frame resting on the ground, the left front tire completely down in the ditch. Both front doors were open and the engine was still running. The fog had been so thick Virgil hadn't noticed the car when he turned out of the driveway and started his run. He'd been so focused on clearing his head he hadn't heard the engine either.

He ran over to the car and looked in through the right side door. Huma's purse was on the floor in front of the passenger seat, its contents scattered across the carpeted mat. Her cell phone was under the brake pedal. A few pieces of clear broken plastic were scattered across the seats and the top of the dash. When he glanced up he saw that the overhead light had been smashed out with such force that part of the headliner had been torn away, the light fixture dangling by its connecting wires.

He backed away from the vehicle without touching anything and did a quick scan of both side ditches. He ran a few yards past the car toward the dead-end portion of the road and didn't see anything, but with the fog it was hard to tell if she was out there. He yelled out her name and it felt like the pockets of fog trapped his words and left them muffled and dull. He took a few more steps further down the road, then turned around and ran up to the house, the adrenaline pumping through his system, his thoughts and his mind more clear than they'd been in months.

CHAPTER FIVE

When Virgil burst through the kitchen door he scared the hell out of Sandy, who'd just poured herself a cup of coffee. She juggled the mug and managed not to drop it, but had to do a quick little dance away from the hot liquid as she set the cup on the counter. She shook her hands and wiped them on her pajama bottoms. When she looked at Virgil, her face was lined with sleep and twisted with confusion, but her voice held a smile when she spoke. "You being chased or something? If you wake the boys before I'm done with my coffee, you're making breakfast. How was your run?"

Virgil ignored her question. "Where's Huma?" He barked it at her.

Sandy frowned at him...and his tone. "In bed. Sunday's her day off. You know this, Virgil. What's the matter?" She let her eyes slide down the hall toward Huma's room.

"Go check on the boys."

Sandy was a strong woman, both physically and emotionally. She'd proven that to herself and others throughout the course of her entire life. In short, she didn't take attitude from anyone, including her husband, though she'd be the first to admit he rarely gave her any. "How about you toss it into neutral for a minute? The boys are fine. I looked in on them two minutes ago, right before you came barging in here like a mad man. They're still sleeping. At least they were. I wouldn't be surprised if—"

Virgil ran through the kitchen and down the back hall to Huma's room before Sandy could finish her thought. He threw the door open without regard for privacy and when he saw her bed had not been slept in he spun around and almost ran right into Sandy who'd followed him down the hall.

Sandy leaned around Virgil, peeked into the room, then followed her husband as he returned to the kitchen. She was speaking to his back the whole way, her words coming out as fast, their pace matching the speed at which they moved down the hall. "She and Delroy have been seeing a lot of each other, Virgil. You know this. She's an adult. It's not her responsibility to report her whereabouts to us every single moment, especially when she's on her own time. I don't think it's that big of a deal if she didn't come home last night. It's still early."

Virgil turned and grabbed his wife gently by the shoulders. "The front end of her car is in the ditch out in the road, past the end of the drive. Both front doors were open and the overhead light has been smashed out. The contents of her purse were scattered all over. Her cell phone was on the floor under the brake pedal. There may have been a spot of blood on the steering wheel. The engine was still running."

Virgil watched the color drain from Sandy's face. He grabbed his phone off the counter and ripped the charging wire free. He punched in 9-1-1 and looked back at his wife. "Get a hold of Murt and get him out here."

Sandy grabbed the landline. "What about Delroy?"

"Not yet. Not till we know what's going on." Then into his phone. "Yes, this is Detective Virgil Jones with the Major Crimes Unit. Are you showing my location? Good. Get two state units headed this way. I need them blocking civilian access on the road that leads to my house. Notify the MCU that I need crime scene techs out here immediately…right at the end of my driveway." Virgil pulled the phone away from his ear in frustration, then put it right back up. "Please stop talking and listen. I *am* telling you the nature of my emergency. We've got a possible abduction. I'm not certain of the timeline. The victim's name is Huma—H-U-M-A, last name Moon. Say it back to me." Virgil listened, then said, "That's right. I'm going back out there now. I want you to stay on the line until you can confirm everything is on the way. Yeah, yeah, I'll hold. Go, go."

Sandy pulled Virgil's gun and shoulder rig off the top of the fridge and handed it to him. He set the phone down and slipped into the rig. "I don't know who trains emergency dispatchers, but they need to listen more and talk less."

"That's not what I meant," Sandy said.

Virgil had already lost the thread. "What? What didn't you mean?"

"About Delroy. I meant what if he was with her?"

Virgil hadn't considered that, but dismissed the thought. "She was out late, and clearly on her way home. He wouldn't have been with her."

Sandy shook her head. "He might have been, Virgil. Why do you think she was out so late? He's stayed over here a couple of times already."

"What? Here?"

"They're adults, Virgil. She lives here. What if he was with her?"

Virgil could hear the emergency dispatcher coming

through on his phone, trying to get his attention. He put the phone up to his ear and said, "Hold on a minute, will you?" Then back to Sandy: "How is it I didn't know that? This is our home." Then, as if his own question was of little importance and he had no time to entertain an answer he said, "Okay. Call him. If he answers, apologize and tell him you called by mistake."

Sandy had the landline to her ear, waiting for Murton to pick up. "And if he doesn't?"

Virgil visibly swallowed. "Let me know." He brought the phone back up to his ear and said, "Yeah, yeah, I'm here. How long before the units are in place? Good. Let them know Murton Wheeler and the techs are coming. Nobody gets through without a badge. Nobody. Are we clear on that?" He ran out the back door and left Sandy to work the phone.

Out at the end of the drive, Virgil stopped and took in the scene as carefully as possible. Because he lived on a dirt road, the county came out a few times each summer and sprayed a fine layer of oil over the gravel pack to keep the dust down. But they didn't do the entire road, only the portion in front of Virgil and Sandy's yard and about fifty feet past either side of the property line. Virgil knew it wasn't good for the environment and had even said something once to one of the road crews. The crew member chewed on the inside of his lip before saying the spray contained a complex mixture of organic compounds designed to absorb the dust particles and keep them from going airborne when cars and other vehicles traveled over the gravel.

It was, of course, complete bullshit. Virgil knew a

petroleum product when he smelled one. He suspected it was a tanker full of dirty oil collected from oil changes done on county trucks and other equipment—a cost-effective way to legally dump the toxic fluid and save a few bucks at the same time. When he said as much the crew member shrugged and drove away, a grin tugging at the corner of his mouth.

It did keep the dust down though, Virgil had to admit that.

It did something else as well. It helped preserve tire tracks, and to a lesser degree, footprints. The sun was higher now, no longer a tarnished plate as it burned down through the mist. With the fog melting away Virgil got a better look at the road and began to paint a picture in his mind...a dark moonless night, a thick fog, a car parked east of his drive right up against the grass on the wrong side of the road. Huma would have been going slow because of the limited visibility. At the last minute the other vehicle must have pulled forward and when Huma saw it she swerved and ended up in the ditch on the opposite side of the road.

Virgil looked at the tire tracks next to his driveway. He could see exactly where the other car had been parked. He could even see the spot where the gravel had been kicked out from under the tires when the other driver accelerated toward Huma's car. He noticed skid marks in the gravel on the west side of the drive as well, like maybe Huma hadn't reacted fast enough and the other driver had to slam on the brakes to avoid a collision. It was all speculation of course, but it also looked pretty clear to Virgil. He'd spent the early part of his career as an ISP Trooper and had seen enough accident and reconstruction reports to know what he was looking at.

The dead-end portion of the road continued about one hundred yards past Virgil's house. It was wooded on both sides and at the end, a dark tunnel of gravel that went exactly nowhere. Virgil desperately wanted to get a better look at Huma's car, but he also didn't want to contaminate the scene. He stayed on his side of the road and walked through the grass until he was even with the little SUV. With both front doors open, Virgil thought Huma must have tried to escape out the driver's side door, but was somehow incapacitated by the other driver who came at her from the passenger side.

He continued down toward the dead-end section of the road. If he could get far enough past the scene, he could cross over, jump the ditch, and view everything from the other side. He worked his way about ten yards past the oiled section of road, the sun higher now, the woods coming into view and growing brighter by the minute. Virgil stopped in the middle of the road and looked around. Something was lying in the gravel not far from where he stood, the sun sparkling off the thin pieces of metal and glass. When he figured out what he was looking at he ran that way, any thoughts of preserving a crime scene lost to the fear of what he might find.

Huma Moon had a bohemian style that fit her casual, free-flowing personality. She wore large hoop earrings, beaded leather bracelets wrapped around her wrists, and long, wispy, ankle-length dresses that seemed to float about her body instead of resting upon it. Her hair was almost pure white, done in dreads that she normally wore tied up in multi-colored scarves, the dreads poking out the back. She kept a pair of reading glasses on a chain around her neck. If you saw her on the street you might think she was a funky librarian or maybe a barista from Seattle or Portland. Virgil didn't know how old she was but had managed to narrow it down and convince himself she was somewhere between thirty-five and fifty. Not that it mattered…she was part of the family now.

He bent over and looked at the glasses without touching them. They were Huma's. He was certain of it. One of the lenses was shattered and the silver chain had been snapped in half. A faint line of boot prints was visible in the gravel, the oil marking a trail that led toward the woods. He left the glasses and ran toward the tree line, shouting Huma's name over and over.

CHAPTER SIX

He found her not more than ten or fifteen feet past the woods line at the end of the road. Virgil crashed through the brush, the low-lying branches smacking him in the face and snagging his clothes as he pushed his way through the dense foliage. Huma was on her knees, facing away from Virgil, her head tipped back, listing awkwardly to one side and covered with a thick cloth bag, her arms wrapped around the trunk of a tree. Her wrists were tightly bound with nylon rope, her hands swollen and purple from the lack of circulation. When he pulled the cloth bag from her head he saw that her mouth was taped shut and her right eye was swollen, a large bruise already forming around the socket. She had a small cut above her eyebrow.

Virgil carefully peeled the tape away from her mouth. She was unconscious, her breath coming in shallow, ragged gasps. When he checked her pulse it was weak and dangerously slow. Her clothes were a mess, and the scarf she'd used to tie her hair back had fallen around her neck. He went to work on the knots in the nylon rope, saying her name over and over, trying to wake her up. It felt like an eternity before he got the nylon to loosen and give way.

He punched in 9-1-1 again and told the dispatcher he had her and to get an ambulance headed his way. Then he picked her up and carried her out to the road. By the time he stepped through the line of trees he saw the flashers behind the grille of Murton's unmarked Dodge Charger as he pulled to a stop at the end of the drive. When Murton saw him, he hit the gas and a few seconds later slid to a stop in the gravel pack, right next to Virgil.

"I've got an ambulance on the way."

"How bad is she?" Murton asked as he got out of the car. He wore a pair of loose-fitting gray and black plaid pajama pants, flip-flops, and a white V-neck T-shirt with the sleeves cut off. His hair had grown back over the last few months and it stuck out from his head at awkward angles. Sandy's call had likely pulled him out of bed.

"I don't know. She's unconscious and I can't wake her."

"Can't wait on the ambulance," Murton said. "It'll be at least twenty minutes before they make it. Here, let me have her. Take the wheel."

Virgil didn't argue. Murton had basic medical field training from their time in the army, and if anyone could help Huma in the moment it was him. He helped Murton get her into the back, then climbed in the front and got the car turned around. He hit the lights and siren, flew past his house, and headed toward the highway. He grabbed the microphone from the holder and radioed the troopers he was coming their way hard.

The troopers, who'd heard the siren long before they got the call from Virgil had already blocked the northbound traffic at the intersection. Virgil made the right-hand turn off the gravel and onto the pavement and held the accelerator to the floor all the way up to 465. The nearest Level-One trauma hospital was fifteen miles away.

Murton was on his knees on the floor of the back seat, his body twisted awkwardly to the side. "Pull the passenger seat forward. I need more room back here."

Most of 465 that circled the city was three lanes wide on either side of the center divider and Virgil was running in the middle lane, trying to leave as much room as he could on either side for civilian vehicles to clear out of his way. He leaned over and grabbed the mechanism and yanked the seat forward and when he did it caused him to drift out of his lane. A semi-truck driver leaned long and hard on his rig's air horn as they sailed past, the drift a little too close for comfort. When he pulled the Charger back into his own lane he almost overcorrected, a dangerous maneuver with the speed they were running.

"Take it easy, Jones-man. I'm trying to work back here."

When Virgil had a second he reached up and adjusted the rear-view mirror to get a better look and saw Murton performing CPR on Huma. Her face was starting to lose color, the muscles under her skin slack and loose. "How is she? Murt?"

Murton stopped the chest compressions and the mouth-to-mouth to remove the scarf around Huma's neck. It was in the way every time he checked her pulse. That's when he noticed the bruising and the puncture mark below her ear.

"Why are you stopping the CPR, Murt? Keep at it. We're almost there."

"Pull over."

"*What?*"

"Pull over now, Virgil."

Virgil and Murton had known each other since they were kids. They'd grown up together in the same house after Murton's mother had been killed and his dad—an abusive alcoholic—had been run off by Virgil's late father, Mason Jones, who'd been sheriff of Marion County at the time. As both best friends and brothers, Murton only called Virgil by his given name when he needed his total attention.

"Now, Virgil, or I'm going to lose her."

Virgil cut to the right and pulled alongside the barricade that lined the highway and let his speed bleed off. "We're close, man. I think we can make it."

"We'll keep going in a few seconds. I need to get in the trunk."

"Talk to me, Murt."

"She's got a small puncture wound on the side of her neck. Looks like a mark from a needle that went in hard and quick."

Virgil got the car stopped. The siren was still screaming at them. "You're saying she's been drugged?"

Murton threw open the back door. "Pop the trunk."

Virgil released the trunk and Murton scrambled to the rear. He was back in less than ten seconds, a small bag in his hand. He jumped in and shouted, "Go!"

Virgil floored the accelerator and shot them down the highway. He had one eye on the road in front of him and one on the mirror watching Murton work on Huma. He was about to repeat his question when Murton asked one of his own. "What's the most popular street drug these days?"

"You're saying someone gave her a hot-shot?"

Murton ripped open the plastic cover on a pre-filled syringe. The syringe didn't have a needle on the end…it had a soft plastic cone. He stuck the cone up against one of

Huma's nostrils and pressed the plunger, injecting the medicine directly into her nose. "That's what I'm thinking. Naloxone only works on opiates. If it's anything else, I think we're going to lose her."

Virgil knew about Naloxone, the life-saving drug that fire rescue crews, patrol cops, and paramedics carried with them at all times. Apparently Murton did too. Countless lives had been saved because of the drug's ability to almost immediately bring an overdose patient back to life. Virgil didn't carry any, but after this he'd get some as soon as possible. When he looked in the mirror again he saw Murton was still doing chest compressions. "Why isn't it working?"

"She's not breathing and her heart isn't beating on its own. It's either something else or they really loaded her up. Knowing what's out there these days, it was probably laced with Fentanyl."

Virgil gripped the steering wheel so tight his knuckles were white. "Can you give her more?"

Murton stopped the compressions, tipped Huma's head back, pinched her nostrils shut, then breathed into her mouth. When he brought his head back up, he said, "Yeah, but I only have two and this is my last one. If this doesn't do it, we're in real trouble here, Jonesy. How far out are we?"

Virgil was running at one hundred and twenty miles per hour. If he went any faster he risked the vehicles in front of him not getting out of the way in time to let him through. They were out of the fog, but one-twenty was pushing it. "Less than five minutes." He bumped the speed to one-thirty.

Murton ripped open the last package of Naloxone and injected it into the other side of Huma's nose.

Virgil slid into the right-hand lane and made a sweeping right turn onto an exit ramp. He drove with one foot on the gas, the other on the brake. He had to back his speed off, but he still did it going almost eighty miles per hour, both his feet working the pedals at the same time, the tires squealing nearly as loud as the siren, the Charger right on the edge of control. But he hung on to it through the sweeping turn and accelerated up the street, weaving through the traffic, planning his moves well in advance.

Virgil knew how to drive.

HE USED THE POLICE RADIO IN MURTON'S CRUISER AND radioed central dispatch and got patched through directly to the hospital. By the time he got them on the line they were almost there. "Less than thirty seconds now. We're only four blocks away. We'll be coming straight into your emergency bay. Get a gurney and a doc out there right now."

"Tell them she's got eight milligrams of Naloxone on board," Murton shouted from the back. "They need to have more standing by."

Virgil repeated what Murton said, dropped the mic, and put both hands back on the wheel. Less than a minute later they had her on the gurney, Murton riding on top of Huma, his shins on either side of her hips, the muscles in his back and arms rippling with tension as he continued CPR all the way into the Emergency Department. A nurse rode on the front of the gurney, her feet propped awkwardly on the frame's crossmember, bagging Huma to keep the air moving in and out of her lungs. Virgil helped push the gurney and noticed Murton had lost one of his flip-flops somewhere along the way. The sole of his right foot was filthy and his heel had a nasty slice that bled down over the bottom of his foot and seeped between his toes. A large bloodstain was forming on the gurney pad. Virgil realized that Murton probably lost the flip-flop when they'd stopped to access the trunk only a few minutes ago.

The doc hit her again with another dose of Naloxone, this time an injection straight into her bloodstream that finally brought her around.

"Stop the compressions," one of the nurses said. Murton stopped for a moment and the nurse said, "I'm getting a pulse." Then she smiled with relief and said, "Here she comes." One of Huma's eyes was swollen shut, but she managed to get the other open. She looked up and said, "Hi Murton." Her words were thick and slurred. "Are you okay?"

Murton put his hands on the side rails of the gurney and rested his forehead on Huma's chest. He could feel her heart beating on its own, then felt her hand as she rested it on the back of his head. One of the docs put his hand on Murton's shoulder and said, "Let's get you down from there. We'll get you sewn up."

Murton lifted his head and gave the doctor a blank look.

"The bottom of your foot is bleeding. Rather heavily, I'd say. I think there's a piece of glass in there as well. C'mon, let me help you down. The nurse will get the wound cleaned and I'll be in to stitch it in a few minutes."

"Didn't even know I was cut."

"I'm not surprised. You were a little busy." He seemed to take notice for the first time of how Murton was dressed. "I don't know what happened but it looks like you may have been pulled out of bed."

"I was," Murton said as he crawled off the gurney. He stood on one leg, his arm around Virgil's shoulder for support. Blood ran out of the cut on the bottom of his foot and pooled on the floor.

"Well, that's some fine work you did. You saved this woman's life, I'm sure of it. Are you family?"

Murton looked at Huma, then Virgil. When he answered his eyes were red and filmed with moisture. "You better believe it," he said.

His voice cracked when he spoke.

A NURSE USED FORCEPS AND PULLED A SHARD OF GLASS FROM Murton's heel, then pressed a large gauze pad over the bottom of his foot and told him to keep the pressure on it. "I'll be right with you," she said.

He sat in a wheelchair in the corner and pressed the pad against his heel. The doctors and nurses got Huma hooked up to all the electronics, started a couple of lines—one in each arm—then swooshed Virgil and Murton out of the room and told them they'd have more information as soon as possible. "It might be a while," one of the nurses said. "We'll have to do a complete workup. Are one of you the responsible party?"

Virgil, who was pushing Murton's wheelchair was still amped up and not thinking quite as clearly as he normally did. He looked at the nurse and said, "What kind of question is that? We're cops, for Christ's sake. Why would you think one of us is responsible for this?"

Murton gave the nurse an apologetic look, then grabbed Virgil by the arm. He pulled him close, tipped his head back and whispered into his ear. "I think she's speaking from a financial perspective, Jones-man."

Virgil felt his face turn red, then told the nurse he was the responsible party. The nurse looked at him as if she had her doubts, then gave him directions to the admissions desk. Once Virgil was on his way, the nurse wheeled Murton into a different curtained-off area to properly address his foot.

Virgil found the desk and sat down to do the paperwork and got stuck on the second question: Age of patient. Then the adrenaline hit him like a sledgehammer and he began to shake. He covered his mouth with his hand in a way that made him look like a Parkinson's patient with a toothache.

"Are you okay?" the admissions clerk asked.

Virgil looked at her and a rogue thought popped into his head: *Yeah, except it's time for my meds.* Other than the conversation he'd had with Bell a few days ago, he hadn't thought much about his addiction to pain killers since he'd beaten them back two years ago. And never a thought like this one. It scared him.

"Sir?"

He slid the paperwork back to the clerk. "I'll finish this in a minute. I need to get some air." He stood from the chair and walked outside.

CHAPTER SEVEN

VIRGIL SAT ON THE CEMENT HALF-WALL OUTSIDE THE emergency bay and called Sandy. He told her everything he knew and when he finished, Sandy said, "Becky got here a few minutes ago. She's going to watch the boys. I'll be there in thirty minutes or so."

"I don't know what's happening yet. Maybe you should stay home."

"Virgil, there are about twenty cops here, and that's not counting the crime scene people. I don't think you're aware of the kind of support you have from the people in your life. Half of them showed up in their personal vehicles and they aren't even in uniform. They're here on their own time. Becky and the boys are safe. So am I. I'll see you in half an hour."

Virgil knew better than to argue. "What about Delroy?"

Then, like maybe he'd asked the universe instead of his wife he saw Delroy running toward him from the far end of the parking lot. "Never mind. Here he comes. Be safe. I'll see you in a little while."

JAMAICANS TEND TO MOVE WITH A RHYTHM THAT IS AT ONCE melodic and harmonious, as if everything they do is a part of who they are no matter their environment or situation. But in this particular moment, Delroy proved that everyone had, at least on some level, the ability to reach down and acknowledge that fear and panic weren't simple emotions that hid inside the brain, they were living breathing beings who could have their way anytime they wished. All you had to do was open the door and invite them into your life.

He ran toward the hospital entrance, one arm pumping like a sprinter, the other clutching a gold chain that hung from his neck. Attached to the chain was a simple piece of jewelry. It wasn't a cross or a religious medallion…it was a pendant in the shape of the letter H. Virgil had been lucky enough to be present when Huma had given him the gift…

When Delroy opened the box his eyes got wide. He held the necklace up with both hands, the H resting in the palm of his hand, the chain draped over his fingers. "My mother's name was Hazel," he'd said to her.

"I know," Huma said, her face glowing in the soft light of the bar.

"You named Huma, you."

She laughed. "I know that too. Here, let me help you put it on." She leaned forward and fastened the chain around his neck, then kissed him on the lips. "Do you like it?"

He turned and admired the chain in the reflection of the bar mirror. "What you tink, you?" Then a look passed over his face and Huma caught it.

"What?"

"I'm embarrassed to ask, me."

"Delroy, you can ask me anything. And you never have to be embarrassed."

"Is the H for Hazel, or for Huma?"

She brushed the side of his face with her fingertips. "Why can't it be both?"

"You beautiful, Huma Moon. Through and through, you."

He wore black sweat pants cut off at the knees, a lime green dress shirt that he'd inadvertently buttoned crookedly, and a pair of moccasin-style slippers. Virgil had the impression he put on the first items of clothing available when he'd heard about Huma. His bald head was filmed with sweat. His eyes were wide, his mouth a thin, tight line. "What happened? Tell me she okay."

"I think she's going to be okay. We're not exactly sure about the sequence of events."

"You *tink*? Where she at, her?"

Virgil put his arm around Delroy's shoulders. "Come on, let's go find the doctor."

Once inside, a discussion took place regarding who belonged to whom. The medical staff didn't want anyone in Huma's room who wasn't family. Murton, who had earlier answered the doctor's question about family told the staff that they were all family. No one really wanted to argue the point and eventually the three men were all let into the room.

"We've got her on a very mild sedation," the doctor said. "I won't bore you with all the details, but it's something of a delicate balance due to the various combination of drugs. We'll keep her that way for at least another twenty-four hours. Maybe more."

Delroy walked over to the bed and touched her hair and

the side of her face. He turned and looked at the doctor. "Why?"

"We got the initial blood work back. She was loaded up with heroin laced with Fentanyl. Her body needs time to adjust and let the drugs work their way out of her system. Physically it can be, mmm, quite a challenge. By keeping her sedated we can make the transition much more tolerable."

Delroy looked at Virgil. "Like they did with you?"

The doctor raised his eyebrows and Virgil caught it. "I had a little run with pills a couple of years ago."

Murton shot him a look. "*A little?*" The edge in his voice was unmistakable.

Virgil ignored him and looked at Delroy. "Something like that, only not as long, I'm sure."

Delroy looked at the doctor. "But she going to be okay?"

The doctor rotated his head in a noncommittal way that could have been either yes or no. "We'll have more tests to run…we've already started on some of them. Any time you have a situation where the body stops breathing on its own or the heart stops beating, even for a short amount of time, you've got to be careful. The brain gets deprived of oxygen and depending on how long that may have been there could be complications ranging from—"

Virgil interrupted the doctor. "Maybe we don't need to get too deep into the details, Doctor."

Delroy turned and squared off with his friend. "I'm a grown man. Don't you treat me like a child, Virgil Jones."

"The key word here is short," the doctor said. He'd seen these types of reactions before. He didn't know the dynamic between the men in the room, but he knew what was happening. The people who first arrived on behalf of the victim tried to protect any loved ones who showed up after the fact. It wasn't an insult or a power play. They simply wanted to soften the blow. The doctor got Delroy's attention. "She almost didn't make it. She wouldn't have if your friends hadn't gotten her here so quickly." He jerked his thumb at Murton. "This one in particular saved her life. Got her the proper meds and from what I hear he did CPR on her all the way in. I'm confident…not certain, mind you, but confident there won't be any long-term damage. Are you with me, sir? I said she's going to be okay."

Delroy turned to Virgil and Murton. "I'd like a few minutes alone with her, if dat okay with you."

"Sure," Murton said.

They turned to follow the doctor out of the room, but Delroy grabbed Virgil and Murton at the door. "Tank you. Both of you." He wrapped his arms around his friends, his body shaking as if he'd just stepped inside after being caught out in a blizzard without the proper clothing. No adequate description existed for the sounds that emanated from deep within his chest.

THE DOCTOR GOT MURTON'S HEEL STITCHED UP WHILE VIRGIL finished the paperwork at the admissions desk. With that done, they walked outside to get away from the hustle and smell of the hospital's emergency department. Once they were out, Virgil said, "That was pretty amazing, Murt…what you did for Huma. I'm proud of you, man."

Murton shrugged it off. "Basic CPR. Anyone could have done it."

"But you knew to give her the Naloxone. I wouldn't have thought of that. I don't even carry any."

"I never did either until—" Murton's words seemed to

catch in his throat, the darkness behind his eyes conveying the rest of the message.

Virgil saw the look and said it for him. "Until I was on the pills."

He nodded. "You don't know how scared we all were, man. If we couldn't get you to quit, we were at least going to be prepared."

"I'm sorry."

Murton scratched at the side of his head and turned away for a moment. When he turned back around he redirected the conversation to a different track. He poked Virgil in the chest with his index finger, the light back in his eyes. "Anyway, that was some heavy-duty driving you did." Before Virgil could answer he said, "Listen, I'm going to head out, go home and grab a shower, then let's get together and see if we can't get ahead of what's happening here."

Virgil checked his watch. "Becky's at our place and Sandy should be here anytime. Why not head over there? See what the crime scene techs are saying. I'll be there as soon as I can."

Murton thought about it for a moment. "Sure. I'll need to borrow some clothes."

"That's no problem. Drive safe and I'll see you in a while." Virgil clapped him on the back and turned to go back into the hospital. He didn't get very far.

Murton looked around the emergency bay. "Hey, Jonesy?"

Virgil stopped and turned around, "Yeah?"

"Where's my car?"

Virgil turned and pointed. "Right over there, next to the —" When Virgil looked where he was pointing all he saw was an empty parking slot. He spun around and looked at the entrance doors of the hospital to get his bearings, then turned back. "It's right…it was right over…"

Murton looked at the empty spot where his car had been. Then he looked at Virgil and said, "Where are the keys, Jonesy?"

Virgil began frantically patting his pockets, searching for the keys he knew he didn't have. In the frantic rush to get Huma out of the car and onto the gurney, he'd left the keys in the ignition. The more he thought about it, he couldn't even remember if he turned the engine off or not.

Either way, Murton's car was nowhere in sight.

They went inside and asked the admissions attendant if they could speak with one of the hospital's security personnel. She made a call and twenty minutes later—after speaking to three different hospital security people—they finally located Murton's car.

"I'm sorry about the mix-up," the security guard said. He handed the keys to Murton. "It was blocking the entrance to the ambulance bays. After I moved it to the parking garage I got sidetracked with something else and then I couldn't find you."

"No problem," Murton said. "They had me behind the curtain. I was getting my foot stitched. Anyway, I'm glad to get it back. The state owns it, not me. The paperwork would have been a drag."

"Hell of a nice ride, I'll say that. I thought of taking the long way around to the garage."

Murton kept the expression off his face. "Why didn't you?"

"I don't think you understand. By long way, I meant back

around 465." The guard looked down at the ground in an attempt to hide the grin on his face, and when he did he saw Murton's foot. "I think you might have sprung a leak, partner."

Murton's foot was wrapped with a heavy pad and covered with a blue paper cover, the kind medical staff use in operating rooms. Virgil looked behind them and said, "You're leaving a trail, Murt. You probably popped a stitch. We better go back inside and get it looked at."

"Ah, they're busy. I'll do it myself."

"Bad idea, brother."

"Let me know when you're ready to go," the security guy said. "I'll bring your car around if you like."

Murton dropped the keys in his pocket. "I think we can manage. Thanks for the help, though."

The security guy shrugged. "A guy's gotta try."

"A guy sure does," Murton said. He was looking at Virgil when he spoke. They walked back inside to find the doctor and get Murton's foot re-stitched.

CHAPTER EIGHT

THE NEXT TWENTY-FOUR HOURS WERE FILLED WITH THE SORT of activities no one likes to think about, let alone address. Even though the doctors had said Huma would be fine, the entire ordeal reminded Virgil of the type of occurrences that take place when someone has died. In short, there was plenty to do and everyone wanted to help, but no one had an exact path to follow. The problem was, whoever had attacked and tried to kill Huma had been careful. Mimi Phillips, the lead crime scene investigator told everyone that they'd found no fingerprints or DNA in Huma's vehicle, on the road, or in the woods. "We've got nothing. Not a scrap. Lawless is out checking the woods one more time, but he's not going to find anything because there's nothing there. It'll all be in my report, but unless you've got witnesses, and it doesn't sound like you do, you're going to have to figure it out some other way."

Virgil didn't want to hear that. He knew the value of forensic science and the role it played when it came to getting an arrest and conviction. Its value couldn't be overstated. He also knew it rarely solved the crime. The science was proof—

the modern age version of the smoking gun—but its benefit was only directive in nature if fingerprints or DNA were already on file. The bottom line was this: Without any witnesses, fingerprints, or DNA, they had virtually nothing to go on.

And it worried him. This didn't have the feel of a random attack. It felt like it had been planned out in advance. It was that very same feeling that caused the argument between Virgil and Delroy.

When Huma was released the following day, Virgil, Sandy, and Delroy were together at the hospital. Huma was in a wheelchair, a look of embarrassment on her face. Virgil knew the feeling well, as did anyone who's ever had to be wheeled out of a hospital building. The orderly pretended not to listen to the conversation as he wheeled the chair through the corridor, but the nature of the remarks made it all but impossible. It started when Huma looked up at Delroy and said, "It says that I'm not to be left alone for the first week. What do you think of that?" The tone and spirit of her voice made her remark sound as if she'd read it from a script for the first time, like an actor still learning their lines.

Sandy responded before Delroy had a chance to answer. "That won't be a problem. We'll get you straight home, and you're going to let me take care of you for a change. How does that sound?" They all quickly learned that Delroy had other plans.

Delroy looked at Sandy, then Virgil. "I need a week off, me. At least dat. Huma and I already talk about it. She's going to stay at my place for a while. I'll be over later to pick up some of her tings, me."

Virgil glanced at Sandy, then looked at Delroy. "Delroy, we don't have any idea what's happened or why. Don't you think she'd be safer with us?"

Delroy put his hand on the orderly's arm, an indication for him to stop. They were in the middle of the hallway that led to the lobby and people had to move to the side to get past the wheelchair and Huma's group of supporters. When Delroy turned and looked at Virgil, he tried to keep his voice calm. Later, he wouldn't be able to recall if he'd succeeded or not. "No disrespect, but you *do* know what happened, even though you say you don't. Someone tried to murder my woman and your place is where it happen."

"Delroy—"

"I don't want to hear it, me." His finger was in Virgil's face, something only a handful of people had ever pulled off in their lives. "Your father asked me to do someting I've been trying to do for years and I've failed at every attempt. I wake with regret every day of my life because you still working the street instead of da bar. The work you do bring nothing but misery and death to our door. Your father, Ed Donatti and his wife, Pam, are all gone." He looked at Sandy. "You almost lost this beautiful soul twice and both your boys. This time it Huma dat almost not make it. You say Delroy family? How about you start acting like it? Or who knows? Maybe you already are and I'm just now noticing. Either way, this family might be a little much for us right now." He nodded at the orderly. "Let's go."

Virgil got right in front of the chair and blocked the path. When the orderly tried to steer around him, Virgil grabbed the arm of the chair and jerked it to a halt. Huma's face began to color and a single tear escaped her eye. It ran down her cheek and she quickly wiped it away with the back of her wrist. No one seemed to notice.

Virgil gave the orderly a look, then he stood upright and faced Delroy. "Now wait a minute. Who do you think you're talking to? You work for me." He pointed at Huma. "She works for me. So make no mistake, I'm not asking you, I'm telling you—"

"*She?*" Delroy said, his face a mask of anger. "Don't you point to Huma and say 'she,' you. I won't allow you or anyone to disrespect my—"

"I'm not disrespecting anyone." Virgil was shouting now. "All I'm trying to do is protect the people I love. I'm trying to make sure everyone is safe and while I'm doing that, you've got the gall to try to tell me—"

Sandy placed her hand on her husband's arm. "Virgil? *Virgil?*"

Virgil spun and looked at her. "*What?*" That's when he saw the look on her face and for the first time noticed the crowd of onlookers who were staring at him. Some of the women had their hands covering either their throats or their mouths. An elderly patient using a walker was almost knocked to the ground as two hospital security personnel rounded the corner. Then things began to slow down and Virgil looked away and let Sandy pull him back from the chair.

When the orderly got Huma and Delroy to the hospital entrance, he locked the brake on the wheelchair and lifted the foot holders out of the way. Both men helped Huma to her feet, even though she told them it wasn't necessary.

Delroy turned and looked at the orderly. "Tank you. And I'm sorry, me."

The orderly nodded in a thoughtful way. "It's probably not my business, but I think your friend was only trying to help. It's stress. I see it every day."

"So do I," Delroy said, a register of sadness and regret in

his voice. When he looked back down the hallway he saw Virgil sitting on the floor, his back against the wall, his forearms resting on his knees, the security people standing on either side of him. Sandy was squatted down in front of him. Delroy started to walk back that way, but Huma touched him lightly on the arm. "Not now. What purpose would it serve?"

Delroy looked at her, searching for an answer that wouldn't come. The orderly placed his hand on Delroy's shoulder and said, "She's right. Go home. Take care of each other. Everything will look different tomorrow."

Huma looked down the hallway at Virgil and Sandy. "I hope so," she said.

The orderly was right. Things would look different the next day, just not the way they might have imagined.

GOOD SON THAT HE WAS, CARLOS IBARRA STAYED IN TOUCH with his mother as much as possible, always on a pre-paid burner as instructed. After the lottery scam, Lola Ibarra fled the country with the Pope twins, along with Wu, and his wife, Linda, where they now all lived a life of luxury on a large private estate in the hills of Jamaica, between the towns of Lucea and Negril. No charges were ever filed against Ibarra, or the Pope twins because the case could not be made against any of the people involved. But none of them wanted to tempt fate and return to the states. Besides, why would they? Life in Jamaica was perfect for them all.

Except for Lola Ibarra. She felt alone without her only child and begged her son to come and live with them, but he refused. He was registered and classified with the federal government under DACA as a Dreamer, and he intended to gain legal status by following the rules and doing the right things.

"Isn't that the way you raised me, *Mamá*?"

"I raised you to use your head. Nicky says he can get you papers that will pass any type of inspection. Passport, driver's license, and birth certificate. I do not understand why you wish to stay in the states. Especially now, given the political climate."

"Because unlike others, I wish to keep my name. Not to mention my honor. Besides, isn't his name Brian now?"

"Sí. Still, I forget sometimes."

"And this is how I am expected to live? Under a name that is not mine? Pretending to be someone I'm not? What does that make me? A false person? Two people? I cannot do it, *Mamá*."

Lola Ibarra didn't have the answers to her son's questions. "I am your *Madre*. I miss you more than you can imagine."

Carlos took the phone from his ear and held it to his chest for a moment. The sound of his mother's voice and the depths with which he missed her were sometimes too much to bear. He swallowed and rubbed the edge of his sleeve across his eyes before putting the phone back to his ear. "I miss you too, *Mamá*. But I am working my way through the system and following the rules. When I achieve legal status I will be free to come and go as I please, using my own name, the one that belonged to my *padre* and his *padre* before him. Even though you are my mother, I will not take a fake name just so the Pope twins can have their money."

"It is my money too, and with it we can do anything. We can be together again, my son."

Does she not care how I feel? Carlos thought. "One day we will be together again. I promise."

"And when will this day come? *Mañana*? Because even that would not be soon enough."

"No, *Mamá*. You know this. Not *mañana*. But soon. You will see."

Lola Ibarra sighed heavily into the phone. "Tell me of this work you are doing."

Carlos put a smile into his voice. "It is good and honest work, *Mamá*. I am a mechanic for a farming operation south of Indianapolis. It is what is called a Co-op. It is a place where many farmers work together and pool their resources. There are many mechanics and other people who work very hard here. We are *muy* busy this time of year. The crops are almost ready for harvest. It is my job to see that all the complex machinery is in proper working order."

"And these people? They treat you well?"

"Yes, *Mamá*. They are all good people who treat me with kindness and respect."

"I miss you so much, Carlos."

Carlos heard the beep of his pre-paid phone telling him he was almost out of minutes. "I miss you too, *Mamá*. But I must go. The phone, it is out of time. Plus, there is much work for me to do."

"I understand. *Adiós, mi amor.*"

"I will call you next week. *Adiós, Mamá.*"

Carlos Ibarra removed the SIM card from the burner phone and crushed it under his boot. He scooped the pieces from the pavement, then dropped them into the scrap metal bin in the workshop. He placed the phone in his pocket for disposal on his way home. Next week he'd purchase another and repeat the process all over.

Had he known the suffering they would soon endure, he'd have gladly taken the documents Nicky Pope offered and gone directly to Jamaica under any name at all.

CHAPTER NINE

Chris Dobson didn't like to be summoned. Who did? But it was beginning to bother him more and more that he found himself in a position where he was expected to drop everything and come running any time Ken Salter wanted to speak with him. Didn't he know he had a job to do? Not to mention his on-going side project...the payback for his broken arm and subsequent arrest and the personal and professional humiliation that went with it. As payback went, he was just getting started.

Another thing that bothered him: For reasons not explained, Salter didn't want to meet at his office this time. He wanted Dobson to come to his home—more specifically his father's home because the hotshot state senator still lived under daddy's roof. Although, to be fair, Dobson thought if his old man had a house like Salter's, he'd probably live there too. But his old man had been a prick of the highest order, so maybe not.

The Salter estate was set on eighty rolling acres in the heart of Shelby County. It was surrounded by woods on all four sides and virtually invisible from the roadway that led to the property. The driveway wound through a series of old-growth trees set close to the pavement that stretched almost a quarter-mile in length. The branches were perfectly manicured and hung over the drive forming an arch that blocked out the sun and left a visitor feeling as if they were driving through a tunnel. The branches that arched over the drive were so thick it looked as if you could walk across their tops. At the far end of the tunnel the grounds opened to a view of the mansion high up on top of a rolling hillside.

The house was impressive…three stories of fieldstone and timber, all collected from the building site itself. The steeply pitched green metal roof was spiked with ice breaks, and across the front part of the circular drive a portico made entirely of rough timber and bark-stripped, lacquered logs sparkled in the sunlight. A chandelier made of Elk and Buck antlers hung under the portico and was strung with clear, teardrop-shaped light bulbs. The double front doors were at least twelve feet tall and looked as though they could stop an armored vehicle.

Dobson parked under the portico and the front door was opened by one of Salter's security personnel before he was halfway up the steps. The guard wasn't an overly large man, but the look in his eyes left little doubt about the nature of his job description or the seriousness with which he conducted his affairs. He held a metal detection wand in his left hand. His right hand was empty, hanging loosely by his side.

"If you're armed sir, I suggest you leave your weapon in your vehicle. Either that, or I can secure it for you until your departure."

"I'm a federal agent with Immigrations and Customs Enforcement. Emphasis on *federal*. That means my weapon stays on my person, not in my car. It also means it doesn't get surrendered to you."

The security guard wasn't impressed. "Sir, if you'll look to your left and your right—and behind you, for that matter—you'll notice that I'm not the only one making the request."

Dobson turned and saw two more security personnel behind him on the far side of his car, and one at each corner of the house. The men at the corners had automatic weapons with folding wire stocks held casually at port arms. Every one of them looked ex-military. "Listen, I'm not sure what time the invasion starts, but I'm not part of it. Salter called me out here as an invited guest. How about you show some respect and stop making requests you know I can't accept?"

"It's been my personal experience that 'can't' usually means 'don't want to.'"

Before Dobson could respond another man appeared in the doorway and placed his hand on the security guard's shoulder. He was dressed in loose-fitting khaki trousers, a white dress shirt open at the collar with the sleeves turned up to his elbows, and a pair of black orthopedic shoes disguised as wingtips. His hair was shock white and looked freshly barbered. His black glasses were a stark contrast to his hair. When he spoke to the security guard, his voice was filled with authority, yet respectful. "Let's not make Agent Dobson do anything that might make him uncomfortable, John. I appreciate your diligence."

The security guard named John nodded, a single tip of his head and put the wand inside his jacket. When he did, Dobson saw the Mac-10 on a sling that hung from his shoulder. "Whatever you say, sir."

Ken Salter's father, Roger Salter extended his hand. "Nice to see you again, Chris. It's been a long time. It is okay if I call you Chris, isn't it? I don't want to disrespect your title. Come in, come in."

Dobson noticed that he'd not been given a chance to

answer. He also noticed despite the elder Salter's age, his handshake was firm, his eyes were clear, and he stood tall and erect. Not exactly the feeble old man his son, Ken had described. In fact, Ken had made it sound like his father had one foot in the grave. By the looks of him, Dobson thought the senior Salter might outlive them all.

The interior of the house looked like an upscale ski lodge that could have been transplanted straight out of Colorado or Idaho. The furnishings were rich and deep, the carpeting plush, the lighting balanced to perfection. Dobson followed the old man through the foyer, past a split staircase, and into a sitting room that opened up into a library with books shelved from floor to ceiling. A ladder with casters and rollers gave access to the highest shelves, and Dobson thought the chair in which he sat probably cost more than his annual salary.

"This is some place you've got here, Mr. Salter."

Salter ignored the compliment, as if he'd heard it so many times it didn't register with him anymore. "Would you care for some coffee or tea?"

"Whatever you're having is fine."

Salter still hadn't actually looked at Dobson. "It's still early. I think I'll have coffee, with a touch of cream, if you please."

Dobson rolled his tongue around the inside of his lower lip, then sucked on his cheeks. How to play this? Get the drinks and let the old man have his way, or show him he wasn't the type of guy who gets pushed around or messed with, no matter how wealthy he was. Dobson stood from his chair and was about to tell Salter to stick it where the sun didn't shine, when John, the security guard walked up behind him carrying two cups of coffee. He placed them on the table that fronted both men.

"Thank you, John," Salter said. "That will be all for now."

"Yes, Sir. I'll be right outside if you need anything else."

Dobson sat back down and made a show of stirring the cream in his coffee. He could feel the back of his neck turning red. Salter had purposely made him feel like a fool, and used his own social ineptness to do it. When he looked at the old man, he noticed a grin tugging at the corner of Salter's mouth.

"How long has it been, Chris?"

"Sir?"

"Call me Roger, please. Or Mr. Salter if you're not comfortable addressing your elders by their given name. Everyone calls me sir. I tire of it these days."

"Force of habit, sir…I mean, Mr. Salter. In my line of work, we're expected to address everyone as 'sir or ma'am.'"

"Even the, ah, how should I put it…the basket of deplorables you have to deal with on a daily basis?" He blew the steam from the top of his cup and took a small sip. "By God, I'll bet that makes your blood boil doesn't it?"

Salter had a way of asking questions he either didn't want the answers to, or didn't care what they might be. "A long time. Maybe twenty years?"

"What was that?"

"You asked how long it's been. I assumed you meant since we'd last seen each other."

"Yes, I did, didn't I? Twenty years you say? That must have been back when you boys were still in high school, up near the city. Well before all this." He lifted a hand and swept it around, indicating the expanse of the house.

"I was expecting to see Ken, Mr. Salter. He asked me to stop by."

"Did he now?"

"Yes, sir, he did."

Salter picked up his cup and looked at its contents, as if the words he were about to speak were in his hand instead of his head. Then he put the cup to his lips and finished it off in one long drink, seemingly unaffected by the temperature of the hot liquid. "Called you personally?"

"No, actually. It was his secretary. I don't remember her name."

"Of course you don't. Chris won't be joining us, I'm afraid. And it wasn't his secretary who called. It was one of my assistants. I wanted to see you."

"I don't understand."

"No, I don't suppose you would."

Dobson took a polite sip of his drink, then set the cup down on the table, perhaps a little harder than he intended to. Enough already. "Is there some reason you're condescending me, sir? Have I offended you in some way?"

Salter ignored the question. "I understand you've been assisting my son in matters that fall outside the scope of your professional responsibilities."

"I'm not sure I understand what you're getting at."

"Yes, you do. You speak of condescension yet you lie to me while sitting in my home and accepting my hospitality. There's very little that my son does that I'm not aware of. You haven't offended me…yet. But if you don't want to be condescended to, then I suggest you drop the deaf, dumb, and don't know routine. It's beneath you. Or is it? I guess I wouldn't know, would I?"

"We've helped each other out over the years, if that's what you mean."

Salter picked at a spot on his arm, his eyes never leaving Dobson. "By help, you mean he tells you to do something and you do it. All for a few dollars passed along in a plain white envelope, I imagine. Almost sounds like a bad movie, doesn't it?"

Salter's act was beginning to wear on Dobson. "Look, I'm friends with your son. If he needs something from me and I'm able to accommodate his request, I do. But because there is usually some amount of risk involved on my end, he compensates me for my time and trouble. If you have a point to make, Mr. Salter, I'd like to respectfully suggest you make it. Otherwise, I'll say adios." Dobson stood from his chair.

"Stop using words other than English. It takes a strong man to not be taken in by those with whom he spends most of his time. It seems like perhaps you're not up to the task. Sit down."

"I don't think so, Mr. Salter. In fact, I think we're done here." Dobson turned around and found himself face to face with John, the security guard. "Please sit down, sir."

"How about this?" Dobson pulled out his weapon and pointed it at John's forehead. "How about you kiss my ass, *amigo*. I'm leaving."

John reached up and grabbed Dobson's weapon and twisted it out of his hand. The move was almost without effort, as if he practiced it fifty times a day, like a boxer working a speed bag. He released the magazine and thumbed the bullets out one by one where they landed on the plush carpet without a sound. Then he inserted the magazine back into the gun and placed it in his pocket. "Sir, you're a guest in Mr. Salter's home. I won't ask you again. Please sit down. Would you care for another cup of coffee? Or a drink, perhaps?"

What the hell is this all about? Dobson thought. He tried to hold the security guard's stare, but felt his eyes slip away. He sat down without answering.

"Now, where were we?" Salter said. "Oh yes, the ass-kissing." He let out a cackle as if he actually thought it was funny. Then he leaned forward, his forearms resting on his thighs, his eyes sparkling with intensity. He leaned so far forward Dobson pressed himself deeper into his own chair to keep some distance between them. When Salter spoke again he said something Dobson didn't expect. "Tell me about the Jamaican."

CHAPTER TEN

Dobson was confused. Not by Salter's question, but how he knew about what had happened at the bar, and more to the point, why he wanted to know about the man who'd attacked him. "What about the Jamaican?"

"Delroy Rouche is his name, I believe. Do I have that correct? He broke your arm with a baseball bat. Snapped it clean in two as I understand it."

"Why are you asking me questions you clearly already know the answers to?"

Salter leaned back away from Dobson and looked at nothing for a beat. When he refocused his gaze back at Dobson he tipped his head slightly and raised his eyebrows.

Dobson took a sip of his coffee. The old man wanted to play games? Okay. He'd play. "What, exactly, are you looking for? Because you already seem to know the meat of it."

Salter shook his head. "I know what happened, but that's a little like saying I know there has been a plane crash, or an automobile accident, for example. What I want to know is why."

"Why what?"

"Good God, man, try to keep up, will you? This might be the worst job interview I've ever experienced. It's a wonder you're employed right now." He let out a little chuckle, then said, "Although, given the fact that you work for the federal government, I guess I shouldn't be too surprised."

Dobson blinked three times in rapid succession, his chin tucked into his chest like a boxer who was about to take a hard right hook. "A job interview?"

"I might be getting ahead of myself. In fact, I'm all but sure of it. Maybe you can change my mind though. The way to do that is to answer my original question."

"The Jamaican was a mistake," Dobson said. "I was supposed to take Agent Thorpe—a DHS agent—to some hilljack bar in the city so he could gather information about an undercover operation. Homeland had lost contact with one of their agents, along with a guy named Wheeler who was acting as a confidential informant, or undercover operative—I'm not exactly sure. Anyway, I tried to hurry things along and I sort of got carried away with the Jamaican. That got me hooked up by the state cops and when I tried to get away the Jamaican saw what was happening. He caught me by surprise and took a baseball bat to my arm."

"And it was my son who asked you to pick up Agent Thorpe?"

"Ask him."

"I have."

"Then why are you asking me?"

Salter ignored the question. "I understand you had a busy night last night."

I've been under surveillance, Dobson thought. He stood up again. "I don't know where or how you're getting your information, but this conversation is over."

Salter leaned to his left and looked past Dobson as if he'd not spoken. "John, would you be good enough to have one of your men bring me my laptop? I believe it's on my desk."

Dobson turned and saw John press a button on a wire that hung from an earbud and say something into a microphone attached to the wire. When he turned back to Salter, he saw him holding a cell phone to his ear. Dobson opened his mouth to say something, but Salter held up a finger. Then, into the phone: "Yes, it's me. And you'll have to forgive me, I need a moment if you don't mind. Yes, thank you." He put the phone to his chest. "Agent Dobson...Chris, please, sit. All the up and down on your part is distracting. It also demonstrates a lack of self-control. Relax for a few minutes, will you? I'm asking as a gentleman."

Dobson shook his head in an exasperated manner, then sat back down. Salter put the phone up to his ear. "The matter we discussed earlier? I'd like to proceed with that. Yes, immediately, if you would, please. Thank you. I'll send a little something your way later today. No, no, I insist. That's what friends are for. In fact, there'll be something for our union fellow as well. I trust you'll see that it makes its way to him? Wonderful." He pressed a button on the phone and placed it back on the table.

John walked over and handed the laptop to Salter. "Thank you, John."

"Of course, Mr. Salter." He turned and walked back to the door and stood at the entrance of the room.

Salter looked directly at Dobson. "The men I used before had something of a nickname for me. They didn't know that I was aware of it. They called me Gus, of all things. Something to do with a television program, I believe. I don't watch TV, so I never did quite understand it. In any event, it was fine with me. They had to call me something, after all, because they didn't know who I was, which is how I wanted it. You, on the other hand, do know who I am. That presents both a problem and an opportunity. Of course, the problem would go away should you decide to avail yourself of the opportunity. I should also tell you that if you decide not to take advantage of the opportunity, the problem won't be yours, it will be mine. Full disclosure and all that, you might say. So in the spirit of cooperation and a mutually beneficial arrangement, I do hope you'll find what I'm offering to be acceptable."

Dobson was genuinely confused. "Look, Mr. Salter, I don't want to be disrespectful, but I don't have any idea what you're doing or why."

Salter smiled at him, his teeth like tiny white tombstones. "I'm offering you a job, Chris. I thought I made that clear earlier."

"I already have a job."

"Do you?" Before Dobson could respond, his cell phone rang. "I'd take that call if I were you, Chris."

Dobson pulled out his phone and checked the screen. It was his supervisor. He pressed the answer button and put the phone to his ear. "Sorry boss, I'm in the middle of something. Let me call you right—"

The color began to drain from Dobson's face. He listened without interrupting then quietly slipped the phone back into his pocket.

Salter was working away at something on the laptop, his fingers gliding across the keyboard. When he was finished he pressed the enter key with his index finger and closed the lid. "You have no idea what sort of power and influence I have in this state, Chris. All across the country, actually. If there's something I want, I get it, no matter the cost or consequences. And there's something I want very badly."

"You got me fired?"

Salter turned his hands, palms up. "A word or two to the right people goes a long way these days. That's something no one seems to understand anymore. Although I will admit the money helps too. And to be clear, I didn't get you fired, I simply helped what appears to be an ongoing situation reach its natural conclusion. That little stunt you pulled last night with the Jamaican's girlfriend almost killed her. Was that your intent?"

Dobson turned in his chair and looked at the doorway. John, the security guard was still there.

"Don't worry about John. He knows his place. The conversation we're having right now doesn't affect him, hence, he's not even listening." Salter leaned to the side again and looked at John. "Isn't that right, John?"

"I'm sorry, Mr. Salter. Isn't what right?"

Salter looked back at Dobson. "See? All of this is only between you and me. So, where were we? Oh yes, the woman...Delroy's girlfriend. Did you intend to kill her?"

Dobson nodded without speaking.

Salter smiled at him. "Ah, you're worried about recording devices. You needn't worry." He paused for a beat. "I understand the feeling, the need for revenge. Unfortunately, you failed in your attempt. According to my sources, the woman—Huma Moon is her name, I believe —is alive and well. A little high, I imagine, but that's to be expected given what you did to her. Let's get back to problems and opportunities. Which would you like to discuss first? The opportunity for you or the problem for me?"

"What do you mean by unfortunately? Never mind. Look, Mr. Salter. I live paycheck to paycheck. Because of the suspension I've blown through my savings like a drunk on the Vegas strip. I'm behind on my rent and everything else for that matter. My credit is so far down in the toilet it's embarrassing for toilets."

Salter clapped his hands together and laughed. "A sense of humor, by God. I love it. I want you to work for me, Chris. And when I want something, I get it. That's the opportunity. Money won't be a problem any longer. Can you access your bank accounts from your cell phone?"

"Yes, I can. And it's account, by the way. As in singular."

"How much money do you have in your singular account, Chris?"

"About two hundred bucks."

"My goodness, things have been rather rough for you, haven't they? Are you sure about the amount? Perhaps now would be a good time to check your balance."

Dobson pulled out his phone and brought up his online banking app. When he checked his balance, he saw a deposit of ten thousand dollars had just been made. He glanced up and caught Salter's eyes. "How, exactly, do you have access to my bank account?"

Salter ignored the question. "That's simply for saying yes. I think an amount of three thousand a week to start sounds fair. Will that be sufficient?"

"And what will I be doing for ten grand out of the gate and three a week?"

A measure of politeness went out of Salter's voice. "Whatever I tell you to do." Then, just as quick, the politeness was back. "But with the hope you'd say yes, I've taken care of your past rent and the landlord has assured me your security deposit is on its way. Your apartment is being cleaned out as we speak. You'll be living in the guest house with John and the other fellows. It'll be quite a step up from your previous living situation. Your personal possessions should be arriving shortly. So, what'll it be? Take the opportunity I've presented, or create a problem for me?"

"I guess I don't have much of a choice, do I?"

"There are always choices, Chris. You know that as well as anybody. But I'll take that as a yes. That's all for now. John will get you set up and squared away. We'll be providing you with a cell phone. I strongly suggest you answer it when it rings." Salter opened his laptop and began working the keys again.

Dobson stood and turned to leave, then stopped. "What was the problem for you if I'd have said no?"

Salter looked up from the computer. "Oh Chris, don't distract yourself with things that are outside the scope of your understanding. Like the Jamaican for instance…or his girlfriend. Distractions aren't good for business. I understand you were wronged. I also understand the need for revenge. Let it go…for now. Who knows what the future holds?" He set the laptop aside, stood, and extended his hand. "Welcome aboard."

Dobson walked over and shook Salter's hand. "Still, out of curiosity, if I'd have said no…"

Salter nodded and gripped Dobson's hand tight. "As you wish. The problem for me Chris, would have been where to dispose of the body."

Dobson let a question form on his face, and even as he spoke the words, the feeling in his gut told him he already knew the answer. "The body? Whose body?"

Salter smiled, his tombstone teeth white and perfect, the lines at the corners of his eyes crinkling with pleasure, as if he hadn't a care in the world. "Why, your body, of course. In any event, as I said, welcome aboard. Would you mind waiting outside by your car for a moment? John will join you shortly."

Once Dobson was outside, Salter looked at John and said, "What do you think?"

"If you'll pardon the expression, Sir, I think we're shitting a little too close to where we eat."

Salter made a clicking noise with his tongue. "John, there's no need to be vulgar."

"My apologies, Sir."

"Dobson is a problem for us. A loose end, if you will. Even he admitted the Jamaican was a mistake."

"Yes, he did."

Salter looked at nothing, then said, "We live in a disposable society, wouldn't you agree?"

Fox understood. "How would you like it handled?"

"You have the information on the Jamaican?"

"Of course."

"Very well. Here's what I'd like you to do…"

CHAPTER ELEVEN

When Virgil turned his truck into his driveway that evening, he was surprised to see Murton's car there. He went inside and found Sandy making dinner for Jonas and Wyatt. He said hello to Jonas, and dodged a handful of baby food Wyatt was spreading around the tray of his highchair with glee. He sidestepped the goop, hugged Jonas, then snuck up behind the chair and kissed his other son on the top of his head before quickly backing away. He looked at Sandy and saw that her shirt was covered with green and orange blotches. "How's it going?"

She looked up at him. "Are you referring to the feeding or the redecorating of our kitchen?"

Virgil leaned down and kissed her, and when he did, Wyatt lobbed a handful of goop on top of Virgil's head. Virgil tried to wipe it away but only managed to smear it further into his hair. He had to laugh though. "Kid's going to have quite an arm. Might turn out to be a major league ballplayer."

"He's already major league."

"Want me to take over?"

Sandy stood from the chair and went to the sink and

rinsed her hands. "No, I've got it. You missed Delroy, though. He came for Huma's belongings."

Virgil shrugged...a defeated gesture. "He said he was going to."

Sandy wet a rag, told Virgil to hold still, and got most of the food out of his hair. "I'll tell you this, Virgil, he took almost everything. Definitely more than a week's worth." She dropped the rag in the sink and looked out the kitchen window that gave onto the backyard.

"I'll speak with him. Apologize. I was out of line."

When Sandy spoke again, it wasn't what he expected to hear. "You were out of line. But I do think we should give them a few days. Whatever happens next isn't up to us."

Virgil didn't want to hear that, even though he knew she was right. "What am I supposed to do?"

"I want you to go speak to your brother."

Virgil glanced out the kitchen window. "I saw his car in the drive. Speak to him about what?"

The look on Sandy's face was identical to the one Bell had given him, as if the answer was so obvious it didn't deserve a response.

Virgil puffed out his cheeks and walked out the back door.

Sadly, adults sometimes see their children through a flawed lens, one that holds the scars of their own parental blemishes, mistakes, and unaccomplished achievements. The emotional toll on the child is one not easily paid. Murton's father had beaten his wife and son with regularity, and had on more than one occasion threatened to kill them. He eventually succeeded with his wife. He failed twice with his son.

Murton was sitting in a lawn chair next to Mason's cross. He had a handful of pebbles and was tossing them into the pond one at a time. Virgil watched him for a few minutes before he walked over and joined him.

He pulled another chair close and sat down. "Why'd you walk out on me at the bar the other day?"

Murton tossed another rock into the pond. "Maybe because the conversation was over. Maybe because there are some things I like to keep to myself."

"Wasn't it you who once told me to get out of my own head? Something about being shaped by our past…the future being wide open and undefined? Any of that sound familiar to you, Murt? It should. They were your words. So how about you take your own advice? Forget about yesterday's score. The lights aren't coming back on and you're not going to replay the last inning."

Murton gave him a flat stare. "You get an F-minus for originality."

Virgil ignored the jab. "The power you think you lost? I've got news for you, Murt. You never did. Not for one second. That man had nothing for you when he was alive and he sure as hell doesn't get to define you now that he's gone. The war is over, brother."

"Is it?"

"Why wouldn't it be?"

Murton shook his head and threw another rock in the water. "Don't give me that bullshit. Any soldier will tell you that you don't fight the war until one side declares victory… you fight the war for the rest of your life. You of all people should know that. And now so does Small. All because of me. How do you think that makes me feel?"

"I don't know, Murt. I honestly don't. Why not tell me?

But before you do, you should know this: Sandy doesn't hold anything against you for what your father did."

"It makes me feel like I've failed. It makes me feel like I've put something on her that she'll carry for the rest of her life. It makes me feel like I've…assaulted her somehow."

"You've done nothing of the kind, Murt. You simply haven't. I know that for a fact."

"Maybe not. But I can't help how I feel. And it didn't start with Small taking out my old man. I'd think you'd know that better than anyone."

"I guess I do," Virgil said. "But it never hurts to talk about it."

Murton seemed to consider Virgil's statement before he spoke. "Then how about this: Thirty-five years ago your family, your father in particular, and in many ways you yourself have been protecting me, providing me with the kind of life I never would have had if things had gone differently."

"It was their way, Murt. I believe the night my dad brought you into our lives he already loved you as his own son."

Murton tossed the rest of the rocks into the water all at once. "You don't get it, do you?"

"Get what?"

"That a child never outgrows the need of a parent in their life. Small shot and killed the man who was my biological father, but you're my brother and Mason was my dad, just like he was yours."

"I know, Murt. That's what I've been trying to say ever since I came out here."

Murton looked out at the pond, his eyes shifting rapidly from side to side like that of a man who wasn't quite sure what to say next. That may have been the case, but he said it anyway. "Planting that shirt under the tree was my idea."

"I know that too, Murt."

"Ever since that night, in all ways, I was his son, wasn't I?"

"Of course you were."

When he turned back and faced Virgil, the pain and loss on his face were etched deep into his skin, every line, every crease like a topographical map of remorse. "Then why is it he only speaks to you?"

Virgil looked at his partner, his brother, his friend, and answered in the best way he could, his statement thoughtful, full of compassion, kindness, and what he hoped was a measure of wisdom. When he finished, Murton walked away without saying a word and Virgil felt as if his words might have been written on the wind.

AFTER MURTON LEFT, VIRGIL STAYED BY THE POND AND stared out across the water, his thoughts focused on his brother and friend. Murton was hurting in ways Virgil didn't fully understand. How could he? On a very fundamental level, Murton's feelings, and the question he'd asked were completely valid.

"Would you believe me if I told you it isn't up to me?" Mason said.

Virgil turned and looked at the cross. His father stood with one leg propped on the cross, his arms folded over his massive, bare chest. He was shirtless, and the scar left by the bullet wound that took his life was hidden behind his arms. Virgil stared at his father for a few moments before he answered. "Why wouldn't I?"

Mason uncrossed his arms and sat down in the grass, his back against the monument. "I can clearly remember the day

I taught you it was impolite to answer a question with a question."

Virgil looked down, a slight grin tugging at the corner of his mouth. "Me too."

"I never lied to you, Virg. Not once. I'm not about to start now."

"I don't understand it, Dad. I've never understood it."

Mason nodded, his expression thoughtful. "I don't believe you'll ever fully comprehend it…until you arrive. Sometimes certain things can't be explained." Mason paused for a moment, then added, "I heard what you said to Murt. I'm proud of you, Son."

"I don't think it helped much."

"Not everything happens at once, Virg. At least not over here on your side."

"What does that mean?"

Mason chuckled and shook his head. "We don't have that kind of time."

Virgil caught the double meaning and was about to say so, but decided to let it go. "I know you've never lied to me. But I've got to tell you, I'm sort of with Murt on this one. You raised him. You were his real father, not Ralph Wheeler. I know you loved him as much as you loved me because I'm living it right now, with Wyatt and Jonas. Wyatt has my blood, but Jonas is just as much my son as his little brother."

"Of course he is," Mason said.

"Then why can't you…" Virgil wasn't quite sure how to finish his thought.

"Appear to Murton?"

Virgil nodded.

Mason looked toward the pond and didn't answer for a long time. When he finally turned back, Virgil saw the frustration on his father's face. "Let me ask you something, Son. Ever made a mistake in your life?"

"You know I have."

"And you paid the price for those mistakes?"

"Sure, I guess. Most of them, anyway. What are you getting at?"

"What I'm getting at is something that will affect you. In other words, sometimes you have to do your job, and sometimes you have to do what's right. They aren't always the same thing. Remember that."

"Okay."

"The night I ran Ralph Wheeler out of town I was the sheriff."

"I know that."

"As sheriff, I should have made sure he stayed locked up. Instead, I beat him senseless and told him after he bonded out if he ever came back for Murton, I'd kill him."

"Why?"

"Because I knew if I simply arrested him, he'd bond out and Murton would be right back where he started."

"I know that. That's not what I meant. I meant why do you consider that a mistake? You told me yourself not that long ago that everything is exactly the way it should be. That Murton was meant to be with us."

"I didn't say that *I* consider it a mistake. But Murton has his doubts. He's carried them all his life and he doesn't even know it."

"He loves you with his whole heart, Dad."

"I know that, Virg. I know it as sure as I'm sitting here."

"Then why can't you—"

"What? Simply pop in and say hello?"

Virgil tilted his head, his mouth a tight line, the all too

familiar frustration beginning to show. He pointed his finger. "Yes. That. Exactly. Why the hell not?"

"I've already answered that question, Son. It isn't up to me. And the truth of it is, I have been talking to Murton. He just doesn't know it. I don't quite know how to explain this, but things are different here."

Virgil huffed. "How? Give me one concrete example. Help me understand. Please."

Mason considered his son's request. When he spoke, Virgil thought he sounded almost confused, as if any explanation he offered wouldn't be sufficient. "Time isn't real, Virg. People use it as a form of measurement, like an inch, or a mile. But what is an inch?" He held his thumb and forefinger about an inch apart. "It's a made-up thing, like a minute or an hour or even a lifetime. There is no before or after. There never was, and there never will be. There is only now. Everything that's ever happened, everything that will ever happen all takes place at once."

Virgil scratched the back of his head. "I can't begin to even process that."

"That's because you're not supposed to. At least not yet."

"So what am I supposed to do?"

"As difficult as it may be—for you and for him—my advice would be to let Murton find his own way. Besides, Murton isn't who you should be worried about right now."

Virgil thought for a moment. "If you're speaking of Huma, it looks like she's going to be okay. We're not exactly sure why it happened, but we're looking at everything we can."

Mason shook his head. "No, I don't mean Huma. You and Murt did a hell of a job saving her, but the reality is, she was only a warning shot. The opening salvo hasn't even begun. You say you're looking? You better look harder because they're right on your tail, Bud. Once they've got their hooks in you, they'll pull you all under."

"I have no idea what you're talking about."

"Then go talk to Delroy."

"*Delroy?*"

"He's about to be at the center of it."

"The center of what?"

"You thought Ralph Wheeler was bad? We're talking pure evil here, Virg."

CHAPTER TWELVE

Delroy wasn't a cop, but he'd spent enough time with them at the bar listening to their stories and their interrogation and interview techniques. Cops were like fishermen in that regard; they loved their stories. So he knew—on a very basic level—how they worked and the types of questions they asked. When he spoke with Huma about the attack, he had her tell him the story over and over until he was sure she hadn't left anything out. He took notes of everything she said, every detail, no matter how insignificant, and kept adding little things to the notebook every time they went over the incident. On the final run-through, she said something she hadn't mentioned before. She tossed it out there almost as an afterthought.

"What was dat you say?"

Huma frowned. "What?"

"At the end. You said right before he jabbed you in the neck you saw someting on his wrist."

Huma shook her head. "It wasn't only his wrist. It was also part of his forearm. He was wearing gloves. Thin leather ones...like driving gloves. They were short and barely reached the ends of his palms. Like I said, he had on long sleeves, but I'd pulled away as far as I could when I tried to get away. My door was open but in my panic I couldn't get the seatbelt unfastened. I was practically hanging out the driver's side door. He had to stretch when he reached for me, and when he stuck his arm out, his sleeve pulled back, like this." Huma stuck her arm out and her sleeve naturally pulled away from her wrist and exposed part of her own forearm.

Delroy did the same thing with both his arms, then nodded at her, an indication to continue.

"That's when I saw his skin." She stopped for a moment, thinking.

"What is it?"

"When I was a kid I broke my arm and I remember how the skin looked right after the cast came off. It looked sort of shriveled and…I don't know, deficient, I guess. His arm looked like that. But the coloring was wrong too. It wasn't only pale, it was, I don't know, blotchy. It looked like it was a bad tattoo or something that he might have tried to have removed at some point."

Delroy set the notebook down. "Do you tink you would recognize him if you saw him again, you?"

"No, I told you, he was wearing a mask."

"Dat not what I mean. Do you tink you would recognize his forearm?"

Huma thought for a moment. "Jeez, Delroy, I don't know. I mean, everything happened so fast and I was more scared than I've ever been in my life."

He took hold of Huma's hand. "Close your eyes."

"Why?"

"You trust Delroy?"

She put her other hand to his face. "You know I do."

"Den close your eyes, you."

Huma looked at him for a few seconds then closed her eyes. Delroy held on to her hand and spoke softly, his voice calm and relaxed.

"You left da bar late dat night. You were driving down the gravel road to Virgil's house. It was foggy and hard to see, so you were going slow. When you saw the lights of the other car you had to swerve out of the way and dat when you ran down into the ditch. When the door opened, you thought, *Virgil*, but when you saw the mask, you knew you were wrong. You tried to get away, but he reached out and grabbed you. Now, tink about dat. You saw his arm. You saw his skin. You know what it look like." He waited a few moments, then said, "Can you see it, you?"

Huma left her eyes closed for almost a full minute without speaking, and Delroy let her. He still held her hand, his fingers lightly brushing her wrist and he could feel her pulse quicken as she thought about what happened to her. When she opened her eyes she looked at him and said, "Yes. I know what it looks like. I'm sure of it. Let me see your notebook."

Delroy handed her the notebook and pen. She flipped to a blank page and spent a few minutes sketching her memory onto the pad. When she was finished she turned the notebook around and showed him the drawing. Delroy examined it, then set the pad aside.

"That's what it looks like, but so what?" Huma said. "What can we possibly do? Should we tell Virgil or Murton or one of the other guys?"

"Not yet, no. Delroy has an idea. I tink I know who it was that assault you, who almost kill you, Huma Moon. But we have to make sure."

"Have I ever told you how much I like the way you say my name?" Then before Delroy could answer, she added,

"And how are we going to make sure, Detective Rouche?" She held a playfulness in her voice that, no matter the situation, Delroy was relieved to hear. "First we go to bed and get some sleep. I know it's early, but it going to be a long night tonight."

Huma put her hands on his face. "I don't know what you've got planned, my beautiful Jamaican man, but that's not quite right. First we go to bed. *Then* we get some sleep."

When Delroy woke it was a little past two in the morning. He rose from the bed and dressed quietly, then went into the kitchen and pulled out a calendar. He had to check the dates to make sure he had them right. The first one was easy…the night Huma was attacked. The second took a little more thinking. He knew it was approximately three months ago, but couldn't remember the exact date. He thought through the entire day, from the time he got up, until he was home for the night, but nothing in particular popped out at him. He thought he'd have to figure it out another way, then he suddenly remembered it was the same day he'd stopped on his way to work to get the oil changed in his car. When he checked his bank statement for the charge, he had the date he needed. He wrote both dates down and put the slip of paper in his pocket. He made a pot of coffee and was pouring a cup when Huma walked into the kitchen. She was dressed in tight black stretch pants tucked into black boots, a long-sleeved black shirt, and had all of her white hair tucked inside a black scarf.

"It's the middle of the night so I thought I better dress the part. How do I look?"

Like a goddess, Delroy thought.

"What was that?" Huma said.

"You look beautiful, you." Delroy set his coffee down, walked over and kissed Huma long and hard. Then he stepped away and said, "I'll be right back."

"Where are you going?"

Delroy was dressed in tan slacks, loafers, and a white polo shirt. "You got the right idea, you. I have to change clothes. Maybe we make you da brains of the outfit."

Huma laughed. "You be the brains. I like being the beauty."

Thirty minutes later, after Delroy changed clothes and told her of his plan, they got in his car and drove away. Despite everything she'd been through, she couldn't remember the last time she'd been so excited…or scared.

THEY PARKED A BLOCK AWAY FROM THE BAR AND HAD TO wait about twenty minutes until the last of the customers and employees left the building. Once everyone was out, Delroy parked his car in the back lot and they went in through the kitchen. Running a bar, or being a nanny and a doula had prepared Delroy and Huma for their jobs and how they lived their lives, but it never taught them some of the things they could have used in the moment, like the acquired skills of counter-surveillance. And because of that, they never noticed the two men who'd been following them ever since they left Delroy's house. They had not, in fact, noticed that they'd been under constant surveillance ever since Delroy brought Huma home from the hospital.

The plan was simple enough. They would check the video feeds of two different dates from the bar's security system: One was the night Huma had been attacked—Delroy was skeptical about that one—Dobson had either been there or not, and the day from three months ago when Dobson had been in the bar and Delroy had broken his arm with the baseball bat.

They walked upstairs to the office and turned on the lights. Huma said she thought they should leave them off. "What if someone sees the lights and calls the cops?"

Delroy laughed. "What if day do? I own the place, remember? Part of it anyway." He sat down at Becky's desk and woke the computer.

Huma looked around the room. It was filled with an array of sophisticated electronic equipment, most of which she couldn't identify. "Do you know how to operate all this stuff?"

"No. But I do know how to get into the computer. Becky set up usernames and passwords for anyone who might need to access the video feeds, and dat's what we need." When the computer screen lit up, Delroy clicked on the proper icon and brought the video system up. When he clicked on the icon for the archived feeds, a box popped up and asked for a date. He typed in the date of the afternoon Dobson and Agent Thorpe had shown up at the bar and the screen split into eight separate boxes that covered the entirety of the bar, including the front and rear outside entrances.

Huma leaned in over Delroy's shoulder and looked at the monitor. "Now what?"

"Now we look for the rasshole named Dobson."

"You mean asshole?"

"In Jamaica, someone like this is called a rasshole. And,

look." He clicked on one of the boxes to enlarge it, then pointed at the screen. "There he is."

They both watched the video and saw Dobson push Delroy through the kitchen door and into the bar. They used the fast-forward to run the video up to the point where Delroy came out of the kitchen with the baseball bat. Huma gasped when she saw Delroy swing the bat and break Dobson's arm.

Delroy turned her way and shrugged his shoulders. "He was trying to get away."

"I see that. Unfortunately, he's wearing a suit. I can't see his arm, and until now, I've never seen his face. He looks like he's average size, but that doesn't tell us anything at all. Let's try the night of the attack."

Delroy typed in the other date and after a careful review, they finally found him, late in the evening, sitting alone. When the waitress brought him his drink he reached out to take it from her and Delroy paused the feed. The skin on his forearm matched—almost exactly—with the drawing Huma had made earlier in the night.

"That's him," Huma said. She practically shouted it. "That's the rasshole who tried to kill me." When she looked at Delroy the expression on his face was one she'd not seen before. "What is it?"

"Dat man try to kill you because of me…because of what I did to him. He tried to get to me through you."

"Delroy, it's not your fault."

"I tink it is. I'm sorry, me." He tried to hold her gaze, but felt his eyes slip away.

Huma lifted his face back to her own. "No more talk of fault, or apologies. He failed, Delroy. I'm fine, and so are you. What's done is done."

Delroy nodded at her. "Okay, but sometimes sorry doesn't go away dat easy…at least not for me." Then, "If what you say is true, we have a bigger problem, us. If he failed, he'll try again. I've had contact with dis man. I know what he capable of. So do you."

"What are you saying?"

"I'm saying we're not safe here. Delroy can feel it."

"What are we going to do?" Huma said.

Delroy shut the computer down and took Huma by the hand. "We're going to go where no one can get to you. Where no one can get to us."

"Where's that?"

Delroy thought for a moment. It was a valid question. As an ICE agent, Dobson had resources at his disposal that would make hiding their whereabouts extremely difficult, if not impossible. Where could they go? Virgil and Sandy's place was no good. That's where the attack happened in the first place, and Delroy wasn't about to put anyone else in danger because of him. That also eliminated Robert, Murton and Becky, and anyone else he could think of. "We need to get out of town for a while until all this is taken care of. We'll get someplace safe then let Virgil and Murton take care of Dobson."

"So where are we headed?" Huma asked.

"The safest place I know, me." Then Delroy smacked his forehead.

"What?"

"I still need the computer." He turned it back on and opened the web browser. Huma watched him work without saying anything until she figured out what he was up to. When she touched eyes with him her question couldn't have been simpler. "Really?"

"Really." He checked his watch. "And if we're going to make it, we have to go right now."

"But what about our stuff? We'll have to go back to your place and pack."

Delroy checked his watch again. "We don't have time. We'll buy whatever we need once we get there. Delroy can afford it."

CHAPTER THIRTEEN

John Fox, the senior security guard for Roger Salter waited until Delroy and Huma were in the bar. Then he looked at his partner and said, "Go. Quickly now, but let's be careful and quiet."

His partner, a small, wiry guy who looked like he could have been a jockey—he really was that small—dropped the tow truck in gear and they drove around to the rear of the building and he backed the truck up to Delroy's car. The jockey guy slid under the car with room to spare and hooked up the vehicle. The entire process took less than three minutes. They turned out of the lot with Delroy's vehicle in tow and headed over to the service garage where they'd borrowed the tow truck. A locksmith was waiting for them when they arrived, and he set about replacing the door lock and ignition switch. They'd used the tow truck before, so they had no worry there, but the smith—recommended by the service garage manager who had access to the tow truck—was new. And a little nervous.

"Nothing to worry about," Fox told him. "Simply replace

the lock and ignition, hand over the key, and go back home to your wife and kid."

The smith had already gained access to the interior of the vehicle by using a SlimJim and was in the process of installing the new exterior lock. He looked up at Fox and said, "How do you know about my family?"

Fox took out his phone and brought up the pictures of the locksmith's wife and child. He held the phone out and showed him the pictures. "We know everything."

"There's no need for any of that," the smith told him. "You can trust me."

Fox kept his voice calm and quiet. "We do trust you. If we didn't, you wouldn't be here. You're being paid an exorbitant fee tonight, and it's not for your services. It's for your discretion. This is nothing more than insurance in case you decide to get chatty."

The locksmith visibly swallowed. "That won't happen."

Fox nodded at him and said, "I know it won't. Now you do too. So, back to work, huh? We're on something of a schedule here."

An hour later he was done. Fox paid both men for their work, then reiterated the discretionary nature of the evening's activities. He told his partner where to take the original vehicle they'd arrived in. "I'll be ready as soon as you get my call. It's imperative you don't leave me waiting."

"I'll be there," his partner said. "I'll tell you something I don't quite understand." He nodded in the direction of the service garage. "Why involve those two?" He was speaking about the garage manager and the locksmith. "I know my way around cars. I could have hot-wired the Jamaican's car in about thirty seconds."

"Wouldn't have worked. We needed—" Then he stopped himself. It'd take too long to lay it all out for him. "I'll explain later." Then Fox thought of something. "Can you disable the airbags in this thing?"

"Sure. It's a piece of cake. Pop the hood." With the hood released, Fox's partner leaned into the engine compartment for a few seconds, then stood back and slammed the hood. "There you go. Nothing to it." Then with a lazy-eyed stare: "That's about how long it would have taken me to hot-wire it."

"Yeah, you told me. But we're doing this my way. Now, get back to the Jamaican's house, grab what we need, then get yourself in position. I've got to run over and see a guy."

"Who?"

"Like I said…later. Let's get to it." Fox got in Delroy's car without saying anything else and drove away.

Once both of Salter's men had left the service garage, the locksmith looked at the shop manager and said, "Who the hell are those guys? The little one sort of looked like a tall midget, or, I don't know, maybe a jockey. What was he…eighty pounds, tops?"

The shop manager gave him a blank stare. "I think the politically correct term is short person. But the important thing is this: There are only two types of people in this world…ones you don't mess with, and everyone else. Guess which group those guys belong to. The one that looks like a jockey? He spent ten years in federal lockup. They kept him in isolation the entire time. And it wasn't for his protection, it was for everyone else's. Utter a word of this to anyone and he'll visit you in the night and it won't be to tuck you in. He'll snap you like a twig, and do it with a smile on his face. You think I'm joking? That guy is absolutely batshit crazy. But if you do talk and by some miracle they don't come after you, I will. They've got pictures of my wife and kids too. I'm not fooling around here. Keep your mouth shut."

Fox made a call and when it was answered he said, "I'm almost there. What's it like?"

"It's almost three-thirty in the morning. What do you think it's like? It's dead. I'm the only one around."

"Good. I'm less than five minutes away. Get in position and wait for me."

"Sort of an unusual place to wait."

"Put your car in the lot and then walk out to the road. It's not that complicated."

"I didn't say it was complicated. I said it was unusual."

"Just be there." Fox killed the call.

Delroy shut the computer back down, killed the office lights and took Huma's hand. They went back through the kitchen where Delroy reset the security system before they stepped outside. When he closed the door and inserted his key to lock up, Huma, her voice calm, said, "Hey, Delroy?"

Delroy, who was jiggling the key in the lock—the damned thing was always sticking—answered her without turning around. "Yeah, mon?" When Huma didn't respond he turned and saw that his car was gone.

"Come on," Delroy said. "Back inside." He unlocked the door, pulled Huma in and deactivated the security system.

"How much time do we have?" Huma asked.

Delroy checked his watch and did the math. "Enough, but barely. I tink we have to hurry, us."

Huma took out her phone.

"What you do, you?"

"Calling the police. Your car has been stolen, Delroy. We have to report it."

"I don't care about that right now, me. Besides, we don't have that much time."

"What if it was Dobson who took your car?"

Delroy thought about it for a moment. "I don't tink so… not after what he tried to do to you. Stealing my car is too… minor."

"What about Virgil?"

"I don't want Virgil involved in this…at least until we're someplace where dat rasshole Dobson can't find us. Besides, once the police know my car has been stolen, they'll file a report and Dobson will have access to that information too."

Huma began working her phone anyway.

Delroy put his hand on her arm. "Please. We have to be smart."

"I am smart. And don't worry, I'm not calling Virgil or the police."

"Who den?"

"Someone who doesn't know or care who we are, will take us where we want to go, and won't ask any questions."

"Ha. Dat person don't exist."

Delroy watched as Huma worked her phone, pushing buttons and studying the screen. "Not only do they exist," she said, "they're right around the corner. They'll be here in less than a minute." She slid her phone back in her purse.

When they stepped back outside a car came around to the back of the building and pulled up right next to where they stood.

Delroy looked at the car, then at Huma. "Who you call, you?"

Before she could answer, the driver of the car buzzed his window down and said, "Uber for Miss Moon?"

"That's us," she said to the driver. Then to Delroy: "What? Best get-away service ever invented. Plus, I have a five-star rating with Uber. They never keep me waiting."

He didn't argue. "Yeah, mon. If you say so. Delroy don't know about da stars or da ratings. I'm just glad it worked. Let's go."

Fox pulled up to the intersection and saw the man waiting for him. He stood a block away with his back turned. Fox drove through the four-way stop to make a pass around the block. He wanted to make sure no one else was around. At the first turn he took out his phone, and punched in his partner's number. By the time he answered, he was making the second turn. He checked his rear-view mirror and said, "Come right now." When he made the third turn he killed the headlights of Delroy's car. When he turned the final corner and once again saw the man standing along the side of the road as instructed, he checked his mirrors one final time, then gripped the wheel with both hands and floored the accelerator.

The man who'd been waiting heard the car, but didn't see it. When he figured out the car was coming at him from the rear, he turned around. By the time he figured out the car wasn't going to stop—that the car was, in fact, speeding up, he tried to run. But the hesitation had cost him. In his panic, he did a little last-minute side-to-side juke that did him no good at all.

Fox hit him going nearly fifty miles per hour. The man flew up and cracked the windshield, and for a split second Fox thought he might actually come *through* the glass. He'd heard the horror stories of people hitting deer on the highway and how they'd smashed right through the glass, killing the driver. But that was mainly due to the weight of the animal and their antlers. This guy didn't have the weight. Or the antlers.

After cracking the glass, the man flew over the top of the vehicle and landed with a thud, the back of his head impacting the roadway. Fox slammed the brakes and got out of the car and walked over to look at the victim. Both his legs appeared to be broken, his face was covered in blood, and one of his shoes was missing.

But he was still alive.

The problem, Fox knew, was simple physics. He hadn't had enough speed when he hit him. The man was unconscious and blowing blood bubbles from his nostrils. Fox knew the man would die soon, except not soon enough. He didn't have time to wait. So he did what any reasonable killer would do in his situation. He got back in the car and ran him over…twice. Once in reverse, then once going forward. This time when he checked, the guy was definitely gone. His head looked like a watermelon that had slipped from someone's hands in the supermarket parking lot.

He caught a pair of headlights coming his way and the wiry partner pulled to a stop and tossed the bag to Fox. Fox removed the shoes from the bag, put them on and walked around the crime scene and through Dobson's blood. Then he removed the shoes, put them back in the bag and climbed in his partner's car. "Go."

They rode in silence for a few minutes, then the wiry guy laughed quietly.

"What's so funny?"

"I was thinking about what you said right before we left. You said you had to run over and see a guy, but what you really did was see a guy and run him over."

Fox sort of chuckled. "Yeah, I guess I did. Sort of threw you a syntax slider there, didn't I?"

"A what?"

"Never mind. Let's go. We'll get these shoes returned and, I don't know, you hungry?"

The wiry guy nodded. "Sure, I could eat."

The Uber driver made the turn and drifted into the lanes marked for departures. He glanced in his rear-view mirror and said, "Which airline, folks?"

"American, please," Huma said.

The driver pulled to the curb and for the first time noticed both his passengers were dressed in black and had no luggage. "What time's your flight?"

Delroy and Huma looked at each other, then the driver. Neither of them answered. When Huma reached for the door handle, the driver hit the lock button and that prevented her from opening the door. When he saw the looks on their faces he turned around and held out his hands...a peaceful gesture.

"No, no, it's alright. Miss Moon, please, put your phone away. I simply want to offer you some advice."

Huma looked at the driver for a moment, then slid her phone back into her purse. "Okay, what then?"

"Well, here's the thing. I run all over this city at night, and believe me when I tell you, I meet all kinds. Boy, the stuff I've seen. Anyway, you two are dressed like a couple of cat burglars, and with the exception of your purse, Miss Moon, you don't have any luggage. And while none of that is illegal, you're probably going to attract some attention from the fine folks at TSA. And even if you don't, you'll run into one of those 'see something, say something' do-gooders, who, upon seeing something, will, in all likelihood, say something. Then you'll be right back where you started…dealing with the TSA. Who needs that kind of grief?"

"So what are you suggesting?" Huma said.

"Hit the gift shops. Buy a couple of backpacks, and for Christ's sake, get a couple of T-shirts or something. Maybe some flip-flops and a couple of hats. The goofier the better. That shouldn't be a problem at an airport gift shop. Try to blend in a little."

Delroy looked at Huma. "He's right, him."

The driver shrugged. "Just trying to keep my star rating up."

Delroy nodded. "Okay. Good advice, you. Tanks." He tried to hand the driver a five-dollar bill.

The driver looked at Huma. "First timer, huh?"

She smiled and nodded. The driver politely declined the tip.

Delroy frowned and put his money away. "How about the doors now?"

The driver turned back toward the front and popped the locks. "Good luck. Hope I don't hear about you on the news."

"You won't," Huma said. "And really, thank you. Though it's not at all what it looks like."

"It never is," the driver said. "Besides, it doesn't look like anything to me, other than a nice couple going for a plane ride. Have a nice flight."

They got out of the car and the driver pulled away.

Delroy looked at Huma. "What all dis business about stars and ratings?"

Huma took his hand. "I'll explain on the plane. C'mon, let's go shopping and see if we can find some normal clothes."

THEIR OPTIONS WERE LIMITED, BUT THEY MANAGED TO convert themselves into somewhat normal-looking travelers. Delroy kept his black pants and shoes, and found a pale blue Indianapolis Zoo T-shirt that was one size too big. He also bought a Panama Jack hat that he wore jauntily to one side, the way Murton sometimes did. Huma bought a pair of neon green shorts and a yellow tank-top. She kept her boots and redid her hair so her dreads poked out the back of the scarf the way they normally did. They both bought backpacks and filled them with snacks, a couple of mystery novels, a few miscellaneous trinkets that could have passed as gifts for family members, and a host of toiletries.

At first they thought they looked ridiculous, but the more they looked around, the more normal they felt. They could have passed as middle-aged hipsters headed to the west coast.

Huma, who'd traveled the world before settling down with Virgil and Sandy had her passport in her purse at all times, simply out of habit. And Delroy, despite having dual citizenship in both the US and Jamaica, was a black man living in a large city. And even though he knew more cops than most because of his relationship with Virgil and Murton

—given the current political climate—he kept his passport with him at all times as well to prove his legal status. Bottom line, getting out of the country wouldn't be a problem.

And it wasn't. Six hours later—it would have been sooner but they had to change planes in Charlotte, North Carolina—they touched down in Montego Bay, Jamaica. The morning was hot and warm, the winds were gusting and the pilot had to work at it to get them on the ground. He crabbed the aircraft in sideways, then touched down hard before he lurched the aircraft straight and got it settled down.

As they were deplaning, the captain opened the cockpit door right as Delroy and Huma got to the front of the cabin. He looked at them both, a sheepish grin on his face, and said, "Sorry about that." He jerked his thumb behind him. "It was the co-pilot's landing. But in his defense, it is pretty gusty out there today. Anyhoo, welcome to Jamaica."

Delroy leaned past him and glanced at the co-pilot, who was standing behind the captain. He caught his eyes and said, "Two stars, mon."

CHAPTER FOURTEEN

THAT SAME MORNING VIRGIL TOLD SANDY WHAT HIS FATHER had said and despite her earlier statement about giving him time, agreed that Virgil should go over and speak with Delroy. When he arrived at Delroy's place he knocked on the door, but no one answered. No lights came from any of the windows. He took out his cell and tried to call and got the same result. No answer. He left a message and asked Delroy to call him back as soon as he could. Then he called right back and left another message, this one an apology for the things he said and the way he'd acted at the hospital. After that he made a quick run over to the bar to see if he might catch him there, but Robert simply shook his head.

"Not yet, mon, no. I tried to call earlier but he didn't answer, him."

"So did I," Virgil said. They stood there and stared at each other for a few seconds. "Well, if you speak with him, have him call me, will you? It's important."

"Yeah, mon. Everyting irie?"

Virgil put his hand on Robert's shoulder. "Have him call me."

Later in the morning Virgil still hadn't heard from Delroy and was beginning to worry. He'd already called Sandy, Murton, Becky, and Robert again and they all agreed they'd keep trying and let him know if and when they reached him or Huma. Delroy and Huma were definitely his priority, but Virgil had other commitments he couldn't ignore, especially this morning.

He drove down to Shelby County and maneuvered his truck out into the field and parked next to the site of the bomb blast. The blast occurred three months ago after a failed attempt by a group of hired criminals intent on ruining Virgil's land with a dirty bomb. And while the men who'd been hired were all dead, the person or persons who'd contracted the work were still unknown. There was more than a little speculation that the Russians were involved, but Virgil had a hard time believing that a foreign power—or at the very least, agents of a foreign power—would go to such extreme measures over what was, a relatively small amount of untapped natural resources.

But small was a relative term. Initial tests had shown millions of dollars worth of natural gas under the ground, the vast majority of it directly under Virgil's farmland. Potentially a life-changing amount of money for Virgil and his family. But enough to involve a foreign power? Virgil had his doubts. Regardless, someone with some juice had gone to extraordinary lengths to create a situation where Virgil would have no choice but to give up the land.

Another thought: After Virgil and Sandy had inherited the land—it came their way after they'd adopted their son, Jonas—Virgil had made it clear in a very public way that he would never frack the land to get the gas out. Pumping thousands of gallons of toxic chemicals into the ground to extract the gas went against everything Virgil believed in. He'd done interviews with all the major media outlets, and in a very carefully structured statement gave his word—both as a citizen and an officer of the state—that no poisoning of the land, and by extension, the Flatrock River would occur as long as his family owned the land. If that was the case, and it was, destroying the land itself with radioactive material might have forced his hand and made him sell, but once he did, they'd know exactly who was after the gas and more importantly, who was behind the bombing. The bottom line was this: None of it made sense, at least in a way that Virgil could comprehend.

With the exception of the dirt lane he'd followed into the field, and the crater left behind from the bomb blast, he was surrounded by a sea of green. It was late in the season and the corn was taller than he was. Virgil didn't know beans about farming, so he did none of the actual farming himself. That was all handled by the Shelby County Co-op, and more specifically, Carl Johnson, one of the Co-op members. The other two members of the Co-op, Basil Graves and Angus Mizner had already told Virgil that because of all the trouble over the last year or so, at the end of the season, Virgil and Johnson were out. It wouldn't have much of an impact on Johnson—he ran a smaller operation on his own prior to taking over the production side of things for Virgil & Company—but it was a real problem for Virgil. One he hoped to solve without making too much noise, or having the entire state, and more specifically Shelby County, come down on him for breaking his promise, which technically he wasn't. Sort of.

He heard the rumble of the truck bouncing down the lane as it approached. He glanced at his watch as he turned around and saw Rick Said and his niece, Patty Doyle pull to a stop next to his own truck.

He shook hands with Said, then turned his attention to Patty. He was both surprised and happy to see her. Virgil stuck out his hand but she walked up and wrapped her arms around him and pulled him close.

"When a man saves your life, a handshake doesn't cut it," Patty said. She kissed him on the cheek.

Virgil smiled through her embrace, his eyes meeting Said's, whose face was lit with compassion and delight. Then Virgil pulled back and held Patty at arm's length and took a good hard look at the young woman. This was the first time he'd seen her since he'd found her locked in a basement and left to die after being kidnapped. She looked good. Her hair had grown out and she'd dyed streaks of purple into it, her skin was clear, she'd gained her weight back, and her eyes, the color of violets, sparkled in the morning sunlight. She wore dusty jeans and a western-style snap-button shirt. "My God, Patty, you look wonderful. I wasn't expecting to see you here today. I thought you'd be off in some far-away land digging for artifacts."

She glanced quickly at her uncle then back at Virgil. "Me too." Then she jerked a thumb at Said. "Except someone made me an offer I couldn't refuse."

Virgil looked at Said and raised an eyebrow.

"I needed someone I could trust with our new venture," he told Virgil. "And I wanted it to be someone you could trust too."

"Must have been a hell of an offer," Virgil said to Patty.

She tipped her head in a non-committal way. "In many ways it was. In others, I think Uncle Rick here may have taken me over the hurdles."

"Hey."

She winked, though Virgil couldn't tell if it was directed at him, or Said.

"I'm simply stating fact," she said. "With what you guys are planning, I think I could be a real asset given my knowledge of geology, which is a big part of the study of archeology. Though I won't be using all the skills I learned in college, I will be using some. I think it's the 'some' part that enabled him to get me cheaper than I would have liked." She made little air quotes when she said the word 'some.'

Said shook his head. "I don't see it that way. It's still much more than you'd have made out in the field in some godforsaken place on the other side of the planet. And if the deal we have with Virgil pays off, you won't be complaining about the pay anymore. And I mean at all. This thing is going to be huge, Pickles."

"I thought we talked about that awful nickname."

Said opened then closed his mouth without saying anything.

Virgil watched the back and forth with a measure of fondness. It reminded him of the conversations he'd had with his father, Mason, when they were deciding on ownership and salaries before they bought the bar.

Patty turned her attention to Virgil. "It sort of feels like I'm being sold on penny stocks. There are a lot of ifs. If this happens, if that happens…if, if, if."

Virgil drew his mouth into a tight line before he spoke. "I won't kid you. There is some truth to that. Everything has to fall in line for this to work the way we want. But I think it will."

Everything amounted to this: Virgil had previously vowed never to frack the land. But hydraulic fracturing had a very specific and narrow definition. Water and other toxic chemicals went into the ground under extremely high pressure which allowed the natural gas trapped in the shale to be extracted. The problem was, the vast majority of the tainted water and chemicals that stayed in the ground ruined the land and left the water table contaminated for hundreds of years. Documentaries had been made that showed people living near fracking sites who could turn on their tap water and light it on fire.

The engineers at Said's company had invented a new way to extract the gas without pumping toxic waste into the ground. Instead of high-pressure water and toxic chemicals, they'd use a combination of computer-generated, modulated sonic waves to fracture the shale, and low-pressure vacuum pumps to bring the released gas to the surface. It was a completely new technology and Said's company owned the patent. Virgil's land would be the testbed for a new industry that not only had the potential to make them rich, it could chart a new course for the exploration and extraction of natural gas that was both cheaper and, more importantly, better for the environment.

"As long as it works," Patty said.

"There is that," Virgil agreed.

"It'll work," Said said. "Sound wave technology is amazing, and in my opinion, one of the most overlooked technologies of our time. It can shatter glass, levitate small objects, and even incapacitate people. But the basic technology has been ignored when it comes to something like this." He looked at both Virgil and Patty. "You guys have seen the test results from the lab. So, like I said, it'll work."

"It better," Virgil said. "If it doesn't, next spring I'm

going to be in real trouble. We've been booted from the Co-op and I can't find anyone to farm the land."

"It'll all work out," Patty said.

"Yeah well, if it doesn't, remember, it was your idea from the jump."

Patty punched him in the shoulder. Virgil frowned at her, then said, "Have you ever met my researcher, Becky Taylor?"

"Who?"

Virgil rubbed his shoulder. "Never mind." He looked at Said. "When does the equipment get here?"

Said looked over Virgil's shoulder and tipped his head in that direction. "Turn around."

Virgil turned and saw two large semi-tractors pulling flatbed trailers. One of the trailers held a boring machine and the other carried a large crane. The drivers of the rigs pulled up close to where Virgil, Rick Said, and Patty Doyle stood. The hiss of the semi's air brakes startled Patty and she jumped. Virgil laughed quietly, but Patty caught it and moved in for another punch. Virgil high-stepped it away and held his palms out. "Okay, okay. Sorry."

CHAPTER FIFTEEN

THE SEMI-DRIVERS BEGAN TO RELEASE THE CHAINS THAT HELD the equipment in place on the trailers. Virgil looked at Said, a question on his face. "Where's the rest of it?"

Patty answered for him. "This is all we need for now," she said. "The crane will be used to put the boring unit in place and move it around so we can get all the various core samples we need."

Said nodded. "Once that's complete, we'll take the boring samples back to the lab and get them analyzed so we'll know exactly where we want to set up."

Virgil was a little confused. "How many samples? And I thought we already knew where to set up. The geological survey that Lipkins ordered last year showed—"

Said was already shaking his head. He held up a wait-a-minute finger to Virgil. "Patty, grab the iPad out of the truck, will you?"

"You bet." She turned and looked at Virgil before walking away. "Probably about fifty samples if we want a proper reading of what's underneath us."

Virgil puffed out his cheeks. A lot of samples. Patty ran

over to the truck and grabbed the iPad. When she bent over and reached inside, both Virgil and Said caught one of the semi drivers giving her figure a hard look, his hand adjusting the outside of his jeans, his tongue rolling across the outer edge of his bottom teeth. Said stuck two fingers in his mouth and whistled, a nasty screeching sound that got the driver's attention. When he saw the look on Said's face he turned around and went back to work.

Said looked at Virgil. "He doesn't know it yet, but that just got him fired."

"That's a little much, don't you think?" It was Said's business and the remark came out casually. When Said didn't reply, Virgil continued. "She's a beautiful young woman, Rick. She's going to turn a head or two every once in a while. I don't think he meant anything. You've never watched a beautiful young woman walk by?"

Said wasn't having it. He turned and faced Virgil, the anger in his voice evident. "Of course I have. But I've never grabbed my dick while doing it. Did you see the look on his face? You better than anyone know I almost lost her a few months ago. I'll forever be in your debt, Jonesy, so don't take it personally when I tell you to butt out. She's still in therapy over what happened. Why do you think I gave her this job? I want to keep her close and protect her any way I can. There are exactly two men I trust when it comes to Patty. I'm one. You're the other."

"Hold on too tight and you'll lose her anyway." Virgil's own remark made him think of Delroy and Huma and the confrontation at the hospital, how easily and quickly it had gone wrong and escalated into something that never should have occurred, all of it his fault.

"I almost lost her once. It won't happen again." When

Virgil didn't respond, Said gave him an elbow. "Hey, you with me, Jonesy?"

"Yeah, sorry. I was thinking I need to take my own advice."

"About what?"

Virgil shook his head. "It doesn't matter." He looked over Said's shoulder, lowered his voice, and said, "Let's drop it. Here she comes."

Patty walked up with the iPad in her hand. She looked at both men for a moment then said, "You know what I've noticed ever since Virgil here rescued me?"

Virgil and Said looked at each other, then back at Patty. Neither answered her question.

"I've noticed that when I walk up to a group of two or more people who know what I've been through the conversation suddenly stops. It's starting to fry my wires a little." She glanced in the direction of the semi-driver. "I knew he was checking me out. It's no big deal, Uncle Rick."

Said was shaking his head. "It is a big deal, Patty. He had his hand on his crotch and he was licking his teeth like a back-alley dog."

She shook her head and handed the iPad to her uncle. "Please don't make me part of the 'Me Too' movement. I've got enough to deal with as it is."

Said took the device and brought up a map of Virgil's land, his fingers stabbing at the screen much harder than necessary.

"Are you going to bring up the geo survey?" Patty said. "Or are you trying to demonstrate the ruggedness of Apple's equipment?" She held out her hand. "Here, let me."

Said handed her the device. She pulled up a Google Earth image of Virgil's land, then overlaid it with the geological survey, which looked much like a topographical map. She looked at the screen, then turned in a full circle, taking in her surroundings. "I hate to tell you this, Jonesy, but you're going to lose some crops in the process."

Virgil frowned at her. "I already have. I'd hate to lose any more. I thought you could take the samples from right here. This area's been destroyed anyway."

Said, who'd managed to calm down, looked at the screen and turned in a full circle as his niece had. "She's right, Jonesy. Can't do it here. When that bomb went off, it disturbed not only the topsoil, but the ground underneath... and that's the important part."

Virgil had his hands on his hips. "So where are you thinking?"

Said used his thumb and forefinger to adjust the screen. He zoomed the image in and out a few times and checked the scale reference at the bottom corner of the screen. "I'd say about a half-mile south by southeast. Right...here." He pointed at the screen.

"Over how big of an area?"

Said looked at Patty for the answer. "Five acres ought to do it," she said. "That'll give us ten samples per acre."

Virgil scratched the side of his head with his fingers. "I don't have an access road into that area. That means I'm not only going to lose the five acres, I'm going to lose the half-mile swath to get the equipment in there."

Said gave him a shrug. "Can't be helped. We need virgin samples."

They spent a few minutes looking at the maps and other possibilities but in the end it made little difference. Virgil was going to lose some corn. He didn't like it. They were all so caught up in the discussion they failed to notice Carl Johnson's arrival. He walked over and Virgil made the introductions.

"So what's going on?" Johnson asked.

Johnson knew about the plan…Virgil had told him to expect the equipment and manpower. But like Virgil, he'd expected the process would take place in the part of the field that was already ruined. When it was explained to him where they needed to take the equipment he looked at Virgil. "Gonna lose some corn."

Virgil was already nodding. "I know, I know. Can't be helped though. If this works out, it won't matter. I don't exactly like it, but it's a short-term loss for what I hope is going to be a long-term gain. Sometimes you gotta let it go."

Later Virgil would realize his statement was a portent of what was to come, except it would be in ways that he never would have believed.

CARL JOHNSON LEFT TO GO GET A DOZER TO CLEAR THE acreage and a path for the semi rigs to get through. Rick Said told the semi drivers to hold off on the unloading process and explained why, his directions short and clipped. The drivers, Jim and Joe Davis were brothers, and it was Jim who'd eyed Patty and grabbed his crotch. But both men knew the boss wasn't happy about it. Joe tried to help his brother get back on the boss's good side. It took him twenty minutes to work up the nerve, but eventually he walked over and said, "I've got an idea."

Said pointed a finger at him. "I've had enough ideas from you two for one day."

"Hey, I didn't do nothing," Joe said.

Patty touched her uncle lightly on the side of his arm. Then she looked at Joe and said, "What is it?"

He looked at Patty with an expression that was both

grateful and apologetic at the same time. Patty caught the look and nodded at him. "Go ahead. Joe isn't it?"

Davis nodded at her. "I'm sorry about what my brother did back there. He ain't quite right in the head ever since he got back from the 'Stan. Anyway, it ain't going to help with the five acres and all…doesn't seem like there's much to be done about that. But Jim and me talked about it and figured if we unload the drill unit and the crane right here, we could hoist the drill up and walk it back to the site with the crane. We measured it and it looks like the wheels will fit right between the rows of corn." He looked at Virgil. "You'll still lose some corn, but not nearly as much."

Patty's face reddened and Joe caught it. "What?"

Said, who was still upset about the gawking incident shook his head in disgust and walked away. Patty followed him. Joe looked at Virgil, his face a puzzle.

Virgil, who knew Joe was only trying to help his brother's situation put it to him as gently as possible. "Don't think that crane is big enough to lift a dozer."

Joe's face reddened just as Patty's had. He hadn't thought of that. He looked down at his boots, then over at Rick Said and Patty Doyle. When he finally turned in Virgil's direction, his words were heavy with regret. "I guess he screwed the pooch on this one, huh?" He was speaking of his brother, Jim.

"Not for me to say. As a casual observer, he probably would have gotten away with a simple look. Grabbing his dick was over the top though."

"I don't think he meant nothing by it."

Virgil put some cop in his voice. "Then he shouldn't have done it. Period. Take it up with Said." He turned to walk away.

"You're not staying?"

Virgil heard the rumble of the bulldozer headed their way.

"And watch the carnage? No thanks." He was speaking of the loss of five acres of crops and the swath they'd have to cut to get there, but Joe Davis thought he was talking about his brother, Jim. He looked like he'd been punched in the gut.

JOHNSON BROUGHT THE DOZER RIGHT UP NEXT TO WHERE Virgil stood with Said and Patty. He shut the big diesel engine down and climbed from the machine. "Want to give it a go?" he asked Virgil. "It's not that difficult once you get the hang of it."

Virgil shook his head. "No thanks. I'm outta here."

Rick Said asked Virgil for a ride back to Indy. "Patty will pick me up when she's done here. I've got a meeting with an investor I really can't miss. You mind?"

Virgil shook his head. "Not at all. I'm ready when you are." He said goodbye to Patty and she told him they'd be in touch with the core results. As Virgil and Said were walking away they heard Patty say to Johnson, "I'd like to give it a try. You'll have to show me how though." Both men stopped and turned to watch.

Johnson glanced at Said, who narrowed his eyes but eventually gave him a nod. "C'mon, climb on up and take the seat. I'll show you how to do it."

Patty grabbed one of the rungs, climbed on the track and sat in the operator's seat. She looked around at all the levers and dials. "Jeez, are you sure about this?"

Johnson waved her question away. "You bet. There's really nothing to it. Here, let me show you." He flipped a few switches and the big diesel roared to life. They let it idle for a few minutes as Johnson demonstrated the operation of all the levers and knobs. Then they brought the engine up to speed and Patty spun the dozer on its tracks before plunging through the rows of corn. She lowered the blade and though Virgil couldn't hear her, he saw her tip her head back and laugh like a kid on the playground as they disappeared into the field. Said turned and looked at Virgil. "You okay with this?" He was speaking of Patty and Johnson.

"Carl Johnson's about as honest and decent as they come anymore, Rick."

"He better be."

Said watched as his niece and Carl Johnson drove off in the dozer, but Virgil couldn't do it. They were literally grinding his profit into the dirt, the dozer's tracks zippering the ground, the blade snapping the stalks at their base, destroying the crops. As he walked away he thought about the remark he'd made earlier…about letting things go. He was literally betting the farm on Said and his new technology. But what choice did he have?

Once Said joined him in his truck, they drove down the lane that would take them out of the field. Virgil's phone buzzed at him and when he checked the display, the screen read, Cora: WORK.

He glanced at Said. "Looks like you're not the only one with a meeting you can't miss." He punched the answer button. "Hey Cora, I'm about an hour away. What's up?"

"My office in an hour, then," Cora said. "Don't be late."

"You got it," Virgil said. When he glanced over at Said, he noticed the smirk on his face. "What?"

"An hour? In a Raptor with lights and siren?"

Virgil shook his head. "Believe it or not, Rick, there are rules. I can't flip the switches and go screaming down the highway whenever I want. There has to be a reason."

Said held up his hands. "Okay, okay, I'm just saying, is all." He turned his head and looked out the side window.

Virgil thought he heard him say, 'pussy' under his breath. "What was that?"

"I didn't say anything," Said said, though the look on his face suggested otherwise.

"You know," Virgil said, "my boss is the governor's chief of staff. And she did say not to be late, which technically could be interpreted as—"

Said was already shaking his head. "Hey, you can justify it any way you'd like." He crossed his arms and let his chin rest against his chest. "Wake me when we get there." Then he cracked his left eye open and added, "If we ever do, that is."

Virgil hit the switches on the center console and increased his speed. "How's this?"

Said raised his head. "My grandmother drives faster than this on her way to church."

"Oh yeah? How'd she die?"

"Who said she did? She's ninety-eight and still going strong." Then Said turned and looked out the back window. "In fact, I think that's her behind us. Looks like she's catching up too."

"Yeah, yeah," Virgil said. Fucking businessmen.

CHAPTER SIXTEEN

VIRGIL AND MURTON WORKED FOR THE STATE'S MAJOR Crimes Unit, which was run by Ron Miles. The MCU had been Governor Hewitt (Mac) McConnell's idea as a way to solve major crimes in the state, and assist county law enforcement as needed. When the unit was formed, the governor hired Cora to run it and they chose Virgil as the unit's lead detective. But Virgil, who'd managed to get himself severely beaten and almost killed, ended up with an addiction to prescription pain meds and it cost him his job. When the governor's former chief of staff, Bradley Pearson was killed, Cora stepped into his position, and Miles was moved up to take over for Cora. Virgil eventually beat back the drugs—no small task—and was later rehired by the governor himself. Murton Wheeler, a former federal agent, was brought on as well.

Virgil and Murton covered the center part of the state and officially reported to Miles. But unofficially, they worked directly for the governor on cases that were highly sensitive, and often political in nature. They both reported directly to Cora, something that Virgil and Miles were still learning to navigate. Miles was the boss, but Virgil and Murton essentially ran their own show and Miles didn't like it. There'd been some rough sailing recently, but things were beginning to calm down and the two men—while not yet back in smooth waters—were finding their way past the breakers.

When Virgil walked into Cora's office he found her at her desk, with the governor leaning over one shoulder, and Miles the other. They were examining a small stack of papers spread across the desk. Everyone looked up when he entered.

"Jonesy," Cora said. "Get the door, will you?"

Virgil closed the door behind him and when Cora pointed with her eyes to one of the two chairs that fronted her desk, he sat down. "Hello, Mac. Cora." He nodded to Miles, who nodded back. "What's up?"

The governor stood erect, straightened his vest by tugging it from the bottom, and said, "Jonesy. How's Huma?"

He hesitated and they both caught it. Cora glanced at the governor, then right back to Virgil. "Jones-man?"

Virgil sucked on a cheek before he spoke. "She's fine." He paused for a beat, then added, "As far as I know."

"What do you mean, as far as you know?" Miles said. "She lives with and works for you, unless something's changed that I'm not aware of."

He had a whiff of authority in his voice that Virgil didn't care for, but he was in a room with the three people who essentially ran his professional life. Though he didn't like the way the conversation was going already, he knew this wasn't the time to make waves.

He looked at Miles and nodded rapidly. "Nothing's changed in that regard." Then he rubbed the top of his forehead with his fingertips and revised his own statement. "The truth of it is, when she checked out of the hospital after the attack she went to stay with Delroy for a while. I think the fact that the assault on her person happened at my place scared her more than I realized."

The governor looked out the window when he spoke. "That's understandable, I would think." Virgil wasn't quite sure if the governor's remark was about his own miscalculation of Huma's fear, or Huma herself. He let it go. When the governor turned back he opened his mouth to say something else, then looked at Cora as if he wasn't quite sure how to continue.

When Cora looked at Virgil, the compassion in her eyes was evident and on a fundamental level, it gave him pause. When she spoke, it downright scared him. "Jonesy, we have to talk to you about Delroy. He's…" She stopped, as if the proper words were lost to her. She glanced at Miles.

"When was the last time you spoke with Delroy?" Miles said, his question direct, his voice neutral.

Virgil leaned forward slightly in his chair. "What's this about?"

"When, exactly, Detective?" Cora said.

Virgil looked at the governor, then Cora. The use of his formal title in a private setting wasn't lost on him. He fought his urge to ask more questions, which, for Virgil, was not something easily accomplished. "At the hospital when Huma was being released. Why?" He winced internally at his own lack of self-control when he tagged a question onto the end of his statement.

"Tell us about that," the governor said.

"We…Delroy and I, got into something of a minor disagreement regarding Huma's rehabilitative accommodations. Sandy and I naturally thought she would be staying with us. Delroy had ideas of his own."

Miles made a rude noise with his lips. "Rehabilitative

accommodations? That sounds like something out of a brochure."

Virgil gave him a look. "What's the issue here, Ron?"

"The issue? You called it a minor disagreement," Miles said. "The hospital administrator filed a report regarding the incident."

"Ron," Cora said. She had an elemental warning in her tone. "Let's let that go."

Virgil wanted to keep his cool, especially in front of the governor, whom he greatly admired and respected. Virgil and Miles had known each other for a long time, and in fact had always been friendly with each other until Miles took Virgil's job after the governor let him go. But regardless of their past differences, he really was trying to have a better working relationship with Miles. He knew the words he was about to speak wouldn't help that cause, but they crossed his lips anyway. "So what?" He stood up and began moving around the room. When he spoke again, the worry and frustration in his voice were evident. "Things got a little out of hand. I was upset. Hell, everyone was upset. What happened at the hospital wasn't that big of a deal. And quite frankly—no disrespect to anyone in this room—it's nobody's goddamned business. It's personal and it's between me and Delroy. We'll work it out."

The governor turned and looked away, and Virgil, who was hot now, looked at Cora, then pointed at Miles. "Why is he here?"

Then Miles did something that completely surprised Virgil. He moved from behind Cora's desk and stood next to him by the chairs. He put his arm on Virgil's shoulder and said, "Because I run the MCU, and we take care of our own." He'd taken the cop out of his voice and suddenly Virgil was worried.

"We've got something to tell you," the governor said. Virgil caught the unhappiness in his voice. "I'm afraid it's not going to be easy to hear."

"Would someone please tell me what's going on?"

Cora pointed to the chair and Virgil sat back down. He took a deep breath and waited.

Cora picked up a piece of paper from her desk. "At approximately four-thirty this morning a body was found along the side of West Maryland Street, east of Victory Field."

"That's the minor league ball club park," Virgil said.

Cora nodded somberly. "That's right. One of the city cruisers caught it while on patrol. Victim was a middle-aged male. Cause of death appears to be hit and run."

Virgil felt himself swallow. They'd been asking about Delroy ever since he walked into the office. And not only asking. They'd been dancing around it, as if they didn't quite know how to break the news. When he spoke, the words caught in his throat and he had to choke them out. "Dear God. Not Delroy?" He stood from his chair again, placed his hands on Cora's desk, and let his head hang until his chin met his chest. When he spoke again, he didn't look up. "Please tell me it's not Delroy."

CHAPTER SEVENTEEN

DELROY AND HUMA CAUGHT A CAB FROM THE MONTEGO BAY airport to Lucea, and had the driver drop them in the center of town. Delroy paid the driver, then took Huma's hand and led her past the tourist shops and storefronts, the sights and sounds of his native land and hometown like medicine to his heart and soul. He tipped his head back and inhaled deeply. When he looked at Huma, her eyes were rimmed with moisture.

"What is it, you?"

"I've never seen you like this before. You look different."

"Different how?" Delroy said.

Huma studied him for a moment. "I'm not quite sure how to describe it. Despite everything that's happened, you look as peaceful as I've ever seen. You look…free."

They were standing in front of a street cafe and the reggae music that played inside spilled out into the street. Delroy took her in his arms and they began to dance. He looked into her eyes and said, "Delroy tell you a story."

Huma shook her head. "In a minute. Let's just dance for now."

Delroy laughed his big Jamaican laugh as Huma buried her face in his chest. "Anyting you want, Huma Moon. Anyting at all, you."

Inside the cafe, near the front window, a young couple was finishing their lunch when the woman looked at her companion and said, "I don't believe this."

"Believe what?" The young man said.

"Look who's dancing in the street."

The man looked out the window and said, "So what? Looks like a couple of tourists having a romantic moment. It's sort of sweet. I'll bet they just arrived. Either that or they're on their way out."

The woman thought for a second, then let out a small chuckle. "That's right. I forgot. You never met him."

"Met who?"

She tipped her head outside. "The dancing man."

"Who is he?"

The woman reached into her purse and pulled out her phone. "Linda, it's me. Tell Wu to run a full sweep of the estate. And get the equipment set up. I'm headed your way right now."

"What's going on?" Linda asked.

Nichole Pope looked out the window of the cafe. Delroy and the woman were still dancing. "I'm not sure. But we're going to find out. See you in thirty."

After she killed the call, Nicky Pope looked at his sister. "Well?"

"Remember our cop friend from Indy?"

"I'd hardly call him a friend. He killed our father, in case you've forgotten."

Nichole's eyes went dark. "I haven't forgotten. But that man out there dancing in the street? That's his partner at the bar they own. His name is Delroy Rouche. And we need to find out why he's here. I'm going out the back. I can't let him see me. But since he's never seen you, I want you to follow them wherever they go. Think you can handle that?"

"Yeah, but have Wu join me when he's finished with the sweep. It'll be easier to stay out of sight that way."

Nichole said she would, then stood and left through the back. Nicky Pope, who publicly went by the name of Brian Addison paid the tab, then sat back and watched Delroy and the woman as they danced in the street.

When a natural break in the music occurred, Delroy led Huma inside the cafe. They took the only open table, one by the window right next to a young man who was sitting alone. Delroy did a quick double-take on the young man. He looked…familiar somehow. The young man caught it and smiled at him. "You looked like you were about to say something to me, Sir."

Delroy shook his head. "No. Respect, mon, respect."

The young man held his smile until Delroy turned away and sat down. "Do you know that man?" Huma asked him.

"No. But he looks very familiar. I can't quite figure it out, me."

"Then don't. You said you wanted to tell me a story?"

Delroy pulled his eyes off the back of the young man's head and looked at Huma. "Before Robert and I opened our own place we used to work at a resort in Negril. Every day the buses would come and drop off the arriving guests and the first ting everyone was told was 'Welcome home.' It didn't matter if they'd ever been there before or not. We always greet them dat way. Day loved it."

Huma tipped her head. "I'm sure they did, but why do I feel like that's not the whole story?"

Delroy looked at the back of the man's head, then at Huma. "Probably because it's not. When the resort was bought out, Robert and me were let go. We'd saved some money—not much—but it was enough to open our own stand. We'd barely gotten started when we met Virgil." Then he waved his hand in the air as if he were batting a fly away. "You know the rest of the story."

"Based on the look on your face right now, I'm not sure I do," Huma said. She reached across the table and took his hand. "This is one of those moments, Delroy."

"What moment is dat?"

"One of those moments where we decide we're not going to keep anything from each other. Ever. I've had enough betrayal to last me a lifetime."

"Interesting choice of words, you."

"So tell me."

"When Virgil and Mason open da bar, they didn't know what they were doing. Not really. And me and Robert were barely making it here. Virgil fixed it for us to come to the states and work for them. I tell you this, me, it was perfect for all of us. Dat Mason Jones, he was a beautiful man, him, inside his heart. You tink Virgil and I are close? Mason was like a brother to me. Like me and Robert, or Virgil and Murton. None of us related by blood, but brothers just the same. One day, not long before he die, Mason come to me and ask me someting. No dat not quite right. He beg me someting, him. He beg me to help him get Virgil off da streets."

"That doesn't sound like something someone would put on a friend."

"I don't know how to explain it, but I tink Mason had a feeling he was near his own end. I don't hold it against him, me. But I haven't been able to do it…to get Virgil to come run da bar and leave all the misery behind. I tink it like a drug to him. And I've seen how Virgil handle drugs. They kill him in the end."

Huma looked out the window as she spoke. "How does that relate to welcome home?"

"It relate like this: I've been away too long. This my home. This where I long to be. Not living in da city trying to convince one of the best friends I ever had, me, dat he making da same mistake over and over. Why do you tink we fought so hard at the hospital? When it finally touch the woman I love, I have to do someting about it."

Huma turned away from the window and looked at Delroy. "Say that again, would you please? I want to be looking at you when I hear it."

"I love you, Huma Moon. True and true."

HUMA STOOD FROM THE TABLE AND MOVED OVER NEXT TO Delroy and took his hands in her own. "I think a lot of people reach a certain age in life and wonder if they'll ever hear those words. And even if they do, they wonder if they'll come from the right person. I've waited my entire adult life for you, Delroy Rouche. I love you, too. With my whole heart, I love you."

Delroy reached up and gently wiped a tear from Huma's cheek. "Den why you cry, you?"

"Because half of me wants to forget about everything and stay here forever."

"What the other half want?"

"You already know the answer to that."

This time it was Delroy who turned his gaze out the window of the cafe. "I guess I do, me. Virgil and Sandy, the boys, Murton and Becky, Robert, day all part of our family. We can't leave them, can we?"

"No, we can't. And the truth is, I don't want to, Delroy. Neither of us ever had a real family until we met Virgil and Sandy. They need us, and we need them. Maybe now more than ever."

"We can't go back until we know it's safe."

"I know," Huma said. "But they must be worried sick by now. Don't you think we should let them know where we are and that we're okay?"

Delroy nodded. "You right, you. But I'm afraid that if we tell them where we are, somehow the people who tried to hurt you might find out." Then, "What, you think I'm being paranoid?"

"No, but it's only a phone call."

"When it come to your safety, I'm not taking any chances, me. I almost lost you and I'm not going to let dat happen again."

Huma was torn, caught between her love for Delroy and her responsibilities to Virgil, Sandy, and the boys. Delroy saw it in her eyes.

"Let's find a place to stay and get settled in," he said. "I don't tink we'll be going back right away. At least not until they figure out who tried to hurt you."

Huma smiled at him. "I hope you're right. I could use a week or two here."

"Yeah, mon. Delroy could use a month." He took her

hand and they stood from the table. "C'mon, I know a great place to stay. It right around da corner from here. As far as contacting Virgil, we'll figure that out soon enough. They're already worried. I don't think another day or two will matter all dat much, me."

THEY LEFT WITHOUT ORDERING, AND NEITHER OF THEM noticed the young man as he followed them to the hotel. Once they were inside, Nicky Pope waited until he was sure they were checked in and staying put, then he turned and walked back toward the cafe. He called his sister to find out if Wu was on his way.

"Not yet. He's still doing the sweep. He's almost finished."

"Good. Keep him there. I'll be back in a few." He hopped on his scooter and headed through the busy streets of Lucea before disappearing up into the hills. When he arrived back at the estate, Wu was putting his equipment away. He'd finished the sweep.

"Wu all through. We're as clean as the day we moved in."

"Perfect," Nicky said. "Let's get the computers set up. There are a few things I want to look into."

"Wu can do. What else?"

"Do you know when Lola last spoke with Carlos?"

Wu thought for a moment. "Wu not sure. Will ask."

"Do that," Nicky said. Then he told Wu where Delroy and Huma were staying. "Can you get into their system, get their room number, phones, all that?"

Wu let his eyelids droop. "You going to insult me now?" Both Wu and Nicky were master coders and hackers.

Both men laughed. "It's something to do. Where's my sister?"

"She in the kitchen with Linda. Lola on the back deck."

"Okay. Never mind about Carlos. I'll speak with Lola about that. Just get us set up."

"Wu already be done setting up if you quit talking."

"Yeah, yeah, everything is my fault. C'mon, Wu, chop-chop."

Wu picked up a banana from a tray of fresh fruit and lobbed it at him. "You know how much Wu hate the chop-chop."

Nicky caught the banana, did a quick peel, and took a bite. "Uh-huh." One of Nicky's favorite hobbies was getting Wu riled up. "You throw like a girl, Wu."

Wu picked up an apple this time. "Yeah, and with a little practice you can too." He made like he was going to chuck the apple at him, but Nicky turned and ran out of the room before he had the chance. Wu didn't throw like a girl. He threw like a major league pitcher. The apple could do some serious damage.

CHAPTER EIGHTEEN

"Jonesy, Delroy wasn't the victim," Cora said.

Virgil closed his eyes, rubbed the back of his neck and rolled his head. Though he tried to stop it, he felt his jaw quiver as a feeling of relief swept through his entire body. He took a couple of deep breaths to try to get his heart rate down. It didn't help much. "Say that again, please."

"I said Delroy was not the victim."

"Then who was?"

"I'll get to that in a second," Cora said. "Right now, I'm more interested in the vehicle and who it belongs to. You should be too."

"Why?"

"Because the car that was used in the hit and run belongs to your partner and bar manager, Delroy Rouche."

Virgil shook his head. He didn't believe what he was hearing, and at the moment, he didn't really care. If Delroy was okay, that was all that mattered to him. Bell, or maybe someone else—in the moment Virgil couldn't remember who —had once told him that anger was nothing more than fear. When he finally spoke, his words came out a little more hostile than he would have liked. "You're saying Delroy was involved in an accident and left the scene? That's bullshit. It's completely out of character for him. He simply wouldn't do that."

This time it was Cora who shook her head. "Sometimes people do things that no one…not even their closest friends think them capable of. And this doesn't appear to be an accident. The victim was not only hit, the medical examiner says he was run over, twice mind you, after the initial impact."

"*What?*"

"You asked me who the victim was. Remember that ICE agent by the name of Chris Dobson? His body—no pun intended—is on ice at the county morgue as we speak. Isn't he the one Delroy attacked at the bar a few months ago?"

The look on Cora's face suggested her question was rhetorical in nature, so instead of answering, Virgil's thoughts went immediately to Delroy and Huma, and more specifically, the attack on Huma's person only days ago. It was easy to follow Cora's logic and conclude that Dobson had gone after Huma as revenge for what happened in the bar when Delroy broke Dobson's arm with the baseball bat.

But that also presented a problem for Virgil, and even more so for Delroy. If he was correct—if it had been Dobson who attacked Huma—and if Delroy's car had been used to kill Dobson, as one of Virgil's closest friends, Delroy would be the prime suspect in Dobson's murder. The fact that both Delroy and Huma were nowhere to be found, at least not yet, was also a major concern. If they were running, it didn't look good for either of them. In short, they had to be found as quickly as possible because Virgil knew in his gut that Delroy simply didn't have it in him to commit murder. But if that was the case, why would he run? And who would kill Dobson and why? He took out his phone and began to punch in Murton's number. He'd been so caught up in his thought process that he momentarily forgot where he was, and who was in the room with him.

"What are you doing?" Cora asked. "Jonesy?"

"I'm calling Murt."

"No, you're not," Cora said.

Virgil all but ignored her. When Murton came on the line, he said, "What's up, Jones-man?"

Virgil glanced at Cora. "Too late."

Murton thought he was speaking to him. "Too late for what?"

Cora nodded to Miles, who took the phone from Virgil before he realized what had happened. When Virgil stood from his chair to take back his phone, the governor said, "Detective." The tone in his voice was clear.

Miles put the phone up to his ear. "Murton? It's Ron. We'll get back to you." He ended the call without waiting for a response.

Virgil glared at Miles then looked at Cora. "Say it."

"I'm surprised I have to," she said. "We've been down this road before. Admittedly, the circumstances are different, but there's no getting around this one Jonesy. Delroy works for you. He's your partner at the bar. What do you think the optics on this would be like if we let you—or Murton, for that matter—investigate a homicide of a federal agent where the prime suspect is one of your business associates and a close friend? A friend, I might add who appears to be on the run."

"I don't give two genuine shits about optics. My main concern right now…my only concern, is the well-being of Delroy and Huma."

"And that is exactly why you can't and won't be working this investigation, Detective," Miles said. "As an officer of the state, your main concern should be finding out why your friend and business partner killed a federal agent."

Virgil snatched his phone from Ron's hand and stuck it in his pocket. "You don't know that. All you know is his car was used in a hit and run. You know as well as I do that it was probably stolen."

"That's certainly one possibility," Miles said. "Another would be that it was borrowed."

"Oh, bullshit. Borrowed by whom?"

"Huma and Delroy are dating, is that right?"

"Yes. So what? It's not a secret."

Miles raised his eyebrows at Virgil.

"Oh, okay. So let me see if I've got this straight, *Detective*," Virgil said. "You believe that the woman dating Delroy, the woman who was viciously attacked a few days ago outside my house, the woman who lives in my home with me and my wife and cares for our children took Delroy's car. Then, as part of her master plan, she somehow managed to track down a federal agent in the middle of the night and run him over and kill him? No, no, wait, I'm not finished. She did all of this with no proof whatsoever that Dobson was the one who attacked her, and don't forget, she's never seen his face because her attacker wore a mask. Explain the logic there for me, Ron, because I don't see it. And while you're at it, what happened to 'We're the MCU, and we take care of our own?' It sounds more to me like 'We're from the MCU and we care more about how things look than solving a crime.'"

"You're out of line, Jones," Miles said.

"And you're out of your mind," Virgil said. "As a matter of fact, I'm beginning to think you're not cut out for the job you currently have."

"Then what do you make of this?" Ron reached down and plopped an evidence bag on Cora's desk. The bag was made of clear plastic and it contained a pair of shoes, the soles covered in blood. "I wasn't talking about Huma. I was talking about Delroy. We searched his home and there's a nice trail of bloody footprints at his place, footprints that match the crime scene perfectly. What do have to say for yourself now, Jones?"

Cora stood from behind her desk. "That's enough. Both of you." She looked at Ron. "Back to work. Now. Get Rosie and Ross out in the field and Mimi and Lawless on the car. I want this figured out, and I want it figured out fast."

Miles gave Virgil a look, grabbed the evidence bag and headed for the door. Virgil spun and looked at Cora. She held up a wait-a-minute finger before he could say anything. The governor was leaning with one shoulder against the wall, his hands in his pockets, his ankles crossed, something of a bemused look on his face. Miles walked out and closed the door behind him.

THE GOVERNOR PUSHED HIMSELF OFF THE WALL AND loosened his tie. He looked at Virgil. "My goodness, that was worth the price of admission for the entertainment value alone."

Virgil wasn't up for it. "Well, Jesus Christ, Mac, I'm glad you found it so amusing." He snapped it at him.

The governor opened his mouth to say something, then left it open, his eyes narrowing slightly. He moved his jaw side to side like he might have been trying to get his ears to pop. When he finally spoke, he said, "I'll be in my office, Cora." He was looking at Virgil when he said it.

Once they were alone, Virgil looked at Cora and simply waited. He didn't have to wait very long. "I'm going to tell you something, Jonesy, and I want you to hear it all before you say anything. Understood?"

Virgil ran his tongue across one of his molars, his jaw extended. He nodded at her, his blood pumping, his temper right on the edge of control.

"Whether you like it or not, optics *do* matter. We're doing you a favor here. The MCU is going to handle this by the book and every single thing they discover will come straight through this office." She stepped out from behind her desk and sat next to Virgil. "I want you to know that I don't believe Delroy and Huma are capable of committing this crime any more than you do. Neither does Mac, for that matter. But since you and Murton have both a personal and professional relationship outside of the work you do for the state, you can't officially be a part of the investigation. As such, effective immediately, I'm placing you and Murton on paid administrative leave. Since we don't have any pressing administrative needs at the moment, you'll both be free to do what you want." She pointed a finger at him. "But you better do it quietly, or we'll all be in deep shit, especially the governor. Do you understand what I'm saying? The man who runs the state is personally going out on a limb for you and your friends. Any idea how many times he's done that before, for anybody? Here's the answer: Exactly never."

Virgil nodded at her. He waited a moment before he spoke. "Cora, I'm sorry. I thought—"

"Yeah, yeah, you thought," she said, her voice at once sarcastic, yet compassionate. "Go figure this thing out, because it's deeper than a stolen car and a hit and run. It has to be."

"We will."

"One more thing."

"What's that?"

"You know who wanted to tell you all this? It was Mac. He was here because he knew you'd be upset. He wanted you to know that like me, he's got your back no matter what. He told me personally and I believe him. After everything that happened with Pearson and what you and Murt did on his behalf, he considers you a friend. And believe it or not, despite his affable personality and his charm and all that happy horse shit, he doesn't have many friends. He has plenty of people who want something from him, but as for the people he trusts, admires, and can turn to when he needs an ear, you're on that list. And it's a very short list, Jonesy. I think you sort of took the wind out of his sails a moment ago. An apology might be in order."

Virgil knew she was right. He stood and glanced at the connecting door between Cora's office and the governor's. "He alone in there?"

Cora stood and leaned over her desk and checked her computer. "Yeah, for the next twenty minutes or so. Then he's got a meeting with a state legislator. Guy named Salter."

"Why does that name sound familiar?"

"Because as a caring and well-informed citizen and officer of the state you stay up to date on elected officials?"

Virgil gave her a smirk. "Hardly...other than Mac, of course."

"Of course. Maybe he sounds familiar because his father is a former United States senator. As I understand it, he lives down in your neck of the woods, and by woods, I mean farmland."

"Shelby County?"

"That's the one."

"You said former. What's he do now?" Virgil asked.

"Good question. Maybe you should look into that. Quietly. Very quietly, Jonesy."

Virgil said, "Huh." Then he said, "What's the meeting about?"

"Same answer."

"Okay. You'll keep us up?"

"Count on it, Jones-man. Despite your differences, what Ron said is true. We take care of our own. I have a feeling Delroy and Huma are in over their heads and they don't even know it."

"I hope you're wrong about that."

"So do I," she said. Then she pointed at the connecting door with her eyes. Virgil walked over to the door and gave it a rap with a knuckle. He heard a couple of muffled thumps, like shoes being dropped on the carpet. A few seconds later he heard the governor holler 'come in.' Virgil turned the knob and walked through the door.

CHAPTER NINETEEN

THE GOVERNOR HAD HIS SHOES OFF, HIS SOCKED FEET crossed at the ankles and resting over the corner of his massive desk. He was tipped back in his chair and held a copy of the Indy Star, his elbows propped on his thighs, the open newspaper obscuring his face.

"Hey, Mac." When the governor didn't respond, Virgil closed the door and stepped close to the desk. "Cora briefed me on the, uh, situational landscape, I guess is the best way to put it. I'd like you to know that I regret the way I spoke to you out there."

The governor slowly turned the page of the newspaper without saying anything or revealing his face.

"What I'm trying to say here, Mac, is that I value not only our working relationship, but our friendship as well. In fact, our friendship is one of the main reasons I keep doing this job. That means I don't do it only for the paycheck, I do it for you. I have a tremendous amount of respect for you, not only for the work you do on behalf of the people of our state, but as a person and especially as a friend. I was out of line and I'm really very sorry."

The governor folded the paper back and exposed his face, his expression fixed and blank. When he spoke, his tone was as neutral as the look on his face. "Anything else?"

Virgil glanced down at his boots for a second or two. When he looked up he had to suck on his cheeks in an attempt not to smile. "Well, uh, I don't know if I should mention this or not, but as a casual observation, I couldn't help but notice that you're holding your newspaper upside down."

Despite everything that was happening and the gravity of the situation, they ended up laughing like a couple of kids. The governor tossed the paper aside and waved Virgil out of his office with the back of his hand.

He was still laughing when Virgil closed the door. It reminded him of what his father had told him the last time they spoke. *There's only now.*

When Murton answered the phone, he said, "Jonesy's Rastabarian. Warm beer and lousy food served daily."

Virgil frowned into his phone. "You know, when Delroy says it, you can tell that our slogan is an obvious play on words. You make it sound like we really do have warm beer and lousy food."

"That's because right now we do. Something's wrong with the refrigeration unit in the beer cooler. The service guy is in there right now sweating and swearing like a drunken sailor on shore leave. And if that isn't enough, Robert is so upset about what's happening with Delroy and Huma that he took the day off to go look for them."

Shit.

"I'll be there in about fifteen minutes, give or take. Is Becky there?"

"Yeah. What's up?"

"I want her to look into someone for us. You ever hear of a guy named Salter?"

"Ken, the legislator from Shelby County, or his old man, Roger, the former US senator and businessman?"

"What are you, practicing to be on Jeopardy or something?"

"You asked. I answered. By the way, I understand that you and I are on indefinite leave. Mind telling me what you've done now?"

Virgil frowned into his phone. "I didn't do anything. And I was going to tell you as soon as I got to the bar. How'd you hear about it?"

"I just got off the phone with Cora. She called, told me you'd explain the situation, then she hung up on me. I'm not sure, but I think she enjoys doing that, for some reason. Apparently Miles does too. Anyway, she sounded…mmm…worried."

She should be, Virgil thought.

"What was that?"

"I said at least it's paid leave. It'll all work out."

"You're the optimist now?"

"Yeah. When have I ever been anything else?"

Murton laughed, and Virgil was glad to hear it. "See you in a few. And Murt?"

"What?"

Virgil wanted to tell him of the things his father had said…how Mason had been speaking to him even though he couldn't hear him or see him the way Virgil could. He wanted to tell him that Mason's love for his adopted son was everything Murton had ever wanted, and more. But something stopped him from saying those things, though he didn't know what it was, or why. *Now isn't the time,* Virgil thought. Based on the statement his father had made, the irony of his own thought process wasn't lost on him. "Never mind. We'll talk about it later."

Except they never did.

JOHNSON LET PATTY DRIVE THE DOZER ALL THE WAY TO THE center of the cut. The dozer's blade wasn't wide enough that a single pass would be sufficient for the semis to get through, so Johnson asked if she wanted to make another pass back with him.

Patty pulled the iPad out of her backpack and checked their location. She tipped the screen so Johnson could get a better look. "Tell you what, I'll take us back to here." She pointed to a spot with her finger. "That will be our first corner marker, right where we came in. Then I'll hop off and let you cut the rest of the road in while I mark off the boundary rows."

Johnson nodded as he looked at the screen. "Sounds fine to me. I'll have to make a few more passes. And listen, you don't have to mark every stalk along the parallel runs. Just mark the corners. But on the cross-cut, if you could mark every ten rows or so, I'll be able to keep a nice straight line at the front and back borders. Once the borders are cut, the rest is a piece of cake. Follow?"

"Sure," Patty said. "It's like one big rectangle."

"Yeah, but you gotta remember I need room for the overburden. Those will be some pretty hefty piles, depending on how deep you want the cut in here."

Patty hadn't thought of that. "Man, Virgil isn't going to like that."

Johnson gave her a what-can-you-do? shrug. "So, how deep?"

"Well, we definitely want the crops out of the way, and then if you could sort of level the cut—that's really all we need. Certainly no more than a foot of topsoil, I'd say. Ready?"

"You're the boss, young lady."

With that, Patty spun the dozer around while Johnson gave her minor hand signals as she cleared their way to the front left corner of the cut where the access road would join up with the five-acre area to be cleared. She put the iPad back in her pack, hopped down, and when she did Johnson tipped the bill of his John Deere hat at her, the way a pro golfer would after sinking a birdie putt. Then he waited until Patty was clear before he repositioned the dozer and started back for another half-mile run. He figured three more passes would be enough to get the semis through. That would also give Patty plenty of time to get the boundaries marked.

PATTY WATCHED JOHNSON DRIVE OFF IN THE DOZER UNTIL HE was out of sight, then got to work. She marked the first corner boundary by tying a bright orange ribbon as high as she could around one of the stalks of corn. Then, with the iPad map, she simply walked down one of the rows until the map told her she was in the proper spot. She reached behind her, pulled another ribbon from her pack and tied the marker to the stalk, then turned ninety-degrees to her right and started crossing the rows. She tied an orange ribbon to one of the stalks every ten rows. It was a little more difficult than she thought...

crossing the rows of corn and staying in a straight line. The corn was packed tight and the leaves on the stalks were razor sharp. She had to go slow to keep from cutting her face and hands. And she had to constantly correct her course. According to the map, she had a tendency to drift to the left.

She made it all the way to the next corner, stopping every ten rows to tie a ribbon. When she got to the far corner, she made another ninety-degree turn that would parallel the row she'd started on. It'd be an easy path back to the front of the cut, then she'd have to cross between the rows again, marking every tenth one. She took her time walking along the main row. The sun was out and hot, and the bugs in the field swirled around her head. At one point it got so bad she pulled a bandana out of her pack and tied it across her face. The tiny bugs kept trying to get inside her nostrils.

Something else: The corn scared her. She wasn't actually afraid of the corn itself, but she didn't like the way it felt to be out in the field alone, the tops of the stalks above her line of sight. She felt...trapped and isolated. Boxed in. It reminded her of when she'd been kidnapped and left to die in the basement of a farmhouse that—according to her map—was less than three miles from where she stood.

Get a hold of yourself, girl, she thought. She made it to the end of the row, tied another corner ribbon and plunged back across the rows where she would eventually pop out right where she started.

The entire process took about an hour. Johnson already had the access road cut in and was making a pass down along the markers, getting the first part of the clearing ready. The semis were parked next to each other at the front corner of the cut, the Davis brothers unloading the crane and the huge drill unit. By the time Johnson came back up the row, widening the area, the equipment was offloaded and ready to go. They repositioned the crane and once the drill rig was reattached to the crane's boom, Jim Davis made a twirling motion with his arm. Joe brought the crane's power up, but when he tried to lift the rig, nothing happened. Then a huge puff of smoke billowed out from under the crane's engine housing and the air was filled with a foul odor.

Joe killed the engine and jumped down from the cab right as Johnson pulled up in the dozer.

"What happened?" Johnson asked.

"Not sure," Joe said. "I think we blew a hydraulic line. I've got power, but nothing to the boom."

Johnson got down in the dirt and looked under the crane, stuck his finger in the fluid then brought it up to his nose and gave it a sniff. "Yup. Hydraulic fluid, all right."

Patty walked over. "What's going on?"

"Blew a line on the crane," Johnson said.

"Can you fix it?" She asked no one in particular. The Davis brothers shook their heads. Johnson looked at her and said, "I can get one of our mechanics out here to take a look. Somebody'll have to cover the expense though. Time and material and the like."

Patty nodded at him. "Do it. We'll cover any costs."

Johnson made the call and twenty minutes later Carlos Ibarra showed up in a maintenance vehicle and got to work. Johnson told Patty he was going to go work the back of the cut—mainly so he'd be out of the way—then climbed on the dozer and headed off.

The Davis brothers and Patty naturally walked over and watched Carlos work. "How long to get it fixed?" Patty asked him.

Carlos pulled his head out of the engine compartment and said, "Mmm, probably about ninety minutes if everything goes okay."

The Davis brothers looked at each other, then they both turned to Patty. "Want to go get some lunch?" Joe asked her. "I'm about to starve."

You don't know anything about starvation. "No, I'd better not. I think I'll stay here and keep an eye on things. But thanks anyway."

Joe looked at his brother. "You coming?"

Jim shook his head. "Naw. Just bring me something back. You know what I like." He was looking at Patty when he said it. She turned away and pretended not to notice.

"Suit yourself," Joe said. "See you in a while."

CHAPTER TWENTY

Patty left Carlos to his work and wandered away from Jim Davis, studying the map on her iPad. She could feel Davis's eyes on her, but it didn't really bother her. She was standing right at the first marker ribbon she'd tied earlier and noticed that Johnson hadn't been kidding when he said there'd be overburden to deal with. He'd bulldozed at least ten rows past the marker ribbons on his initial cross-cut. Patty thought she'd better get a count for Virgil, so she put her iPad back in her pack and pushed through the mounds of dirt and destroyed corn.

It was impossible to get an accurate count simply by looking at the piles, so she had to backtrack toward the road that had been cut in. Once there, she lined up with the original marker row and began her count. She was ten rows in and still counting when she sensed something wasn't quite right. Patty had learned the hard way about listening to her gut, and she wasn't going to make the same mistake twice. She froze in place and listened. She could hear Johnson on the dozer, working the back of the clearing, the sound muffled by the corn and mounds of dirt. She listened for a full two minutes without moving, but she didn't hear anything else over the noise of the machine. The feeling didn't go away though.

The stalks of corn were packed so tight every time Patty crossed a row she had to turn her body sideways and sort of slither between the stalks. She'd duck her head and push through to the next row, and then be out in the open between the rows. Because of the feeling she had, she looked to her left and right every time she entered another row. This time when she lifted her head and looked to her right, she saw him. No more than a flash of one leg disappearing into the next row. Someone was out here with her, shadowing her.

She dropped low to the ground and tried to see between the stalks, but it was almost impossible, the corn thick and tall and strong. When she heard him begin to move her way, she turned and ran toward the clearing, the stalks and leaves tearing at her skin, slicing her face and arms.

She fell twice and may have gotten turned around. She was disoriented and didn't know which way to run. Then, out of nowhere, he was right in front of her, less than ten feet away in the same row. He looked like he was close to her own age, maybe five years older, if that. His hair was jet black and parted down the center of his head, tied back in a single long braid, his skin dark, his chest bare. He wore dusty jeans tucked into worn boots. A dull and dark turquoise belt was cinched tight around his waist, a leather scabbard hooked to one side, the knife sheathed to its hilt. A bow was slung across one shoulder, a quiver cross-strapped over the other, the feathers of the arrows plainly visible.

He slowly brought one hand up, palm out. Patty thought, *this is where he says, 'How.'* If she hadn't been so startled she would have laughed at the absurdity of her own thought. She opened her mouth to speak but before she could say anything, the Indian placed his index finger to his lips. An indication for Patty to not make any noise. Then he pointed to the next row over and ducked through the stalks. Patty did the same.

They repeated the process over ten rows, until Patty knew where she was, no longer lost or disoriented in the corn. She was only one row away from the clearing. She could, in fact, see it between the stalks of corn. The Indian pointed again, but this time he didn't move. Patty never took her eyes from him as she slid through the final row. Once back out in the opening, she spun and took a few steps backward to get some distance between herself and the Indian. But he never came through the final row of corn and into the clearing.

Patty waited almost a full minute, then stuck her head back through the row from which she'd just emerged.

The Indian was gone. She looked in both directions, and even pushed back through a few rows, but he was nowhere to be found. Had she imagined the entire incident? She pushed back through another row and looked at the ground. She could clearly see her own footprints in the dirt. When she moved to the area where the Indian had been she saw a feather lying in the dirt. It looked exactly like the kind that stuck out of the Indian's quiver. She picked up the feather and pushed her way out into the clearing.

And ran right into Jim Davis.

DAVIS GRABBED HER BY HER ARMS AND HELD ON TIGHT. "Hey, slow down there, gorgeous."

"Let go of me."

Davis pulled her close. "What's the matter? I'm only trying to help." He pulled her closer still and thrust his hips into her. "Why not have a little fun while we're out here. No one will know. What do you say?"

Patty began pounding his chest with her fists, but she couldn't get any power into her punches because Davis had her pulled in so tight. When she tried to knee him in the groin he turned his body sideways, blocking the blows. But this was Patty Doyle, who never gave up. The same Patty Doyle who survived being kidnapped and chained in a basement and left to die. The same Patty Doyle who broke her own thumb to free her hand from the shackle that held her. She yanked one arm free and clawed at his eyes with her nails. Davis howled in pain, but managed to hold on tight.

She made a fist and meant to strike again, except Davis was a little quicker than she thought. He head-butted her and then everything went dark as she fell face-first into the dirt.

That's more like it, Davis thought.

He carried her over to the back of the lowboy semi-trailer and laid her down face-first. He unbuckled her jeans and yanked them down past her knees, then ripped her underwear off. He began to pull his own pants down, his brain running in overdrive now, the lust and power and hate running through him like wildfire when he heard the noise behind him. Someone shouted "Hey!"

He turned in time to see the mechanic swing the giant wrench at him.

Carlos held a large torque wrench that was over two feet long. He swung the wrench, aiming for Davis's side, but Davis—who'd stood up after dropping his pants—got his feet tangled up and began to fall. Carlos was already in the middle of his swing and didn't have time to stop or adjust his trajectory. The business end of the wrench caught Davis right above his ear with a sickening crack and caved in the side of his head. He was dead before he hit the ground.

Carlos dropped the wrench in the dirt and picked up Patty and carried her to the front of the semi. He sat her down on the ground, then removed his shirt to cover her private area. He held her hand in his own and gently patted her wrist and the side of her face until she came around.

When she opened her eyes, she blinked rapidly and looked at Carlos. When she glanced over his shoulder she saw Carl Johnson running toward them. She also saw the Indian as he ducked back into the corn. Johnson—who hadn't seen what happened, but did see a half-naked Patty Doyle on the ground next to a shirtless mechanic who hovered over her —threw his arm around Carlos's neck and yanked him away.

Patty screamed at him. "Mr. Johnson, no! Wait!" Johnson spun around as Carlos got to his feet. "It wasn't him. It was the semi-driver. The Davis guy...Jim Davis. He tried...he tried to..." Then for the first time, Patty realized her bare ass was sitting in the dirt. "I'm okay...I think." She looked at Johnson. "Carlos saved me. Would you both please look away for a moment?"

Johnson looked at Carlos. "What the hell is going on, Ibarra?"

"Please," Patty said. "I'd like to get my pants up." Both men turned away while Patty stood and wiggled back into her jeans. Her head was pounding from the blow Davis had given her, but she thought herself lucky that was the worst of it. "Okay. You can turn around now." She walked up to Carlos and hugged him. "Thank you. Are you hurt?"

Carlos visibly swallowed. "No. I am fine." He looked at Johnson. "I would never—"

"Ah, I know it," Johnson said. "I'm sorry, Carlos. I thought…well, never mind what I thought. I'm sorry."

"It is okay," Carlos said. He ran his hands through his hair and wiped his face on his sleeve. "But now I have a problem."

"What problem?" Johnson asked.

Carlos led them to the back of the trailer where Davis was lying in the dirt. The side of his head was completely caved in. It looked like a pumpkin that had been left on the porch to rot after Halloween. When Patty saw Davis's head she turned and vomited in the dirt.

CHAPTER TWENTY-ONE

Virgil drove to the bar and walked in through the back as usual. He was immediately surrounded by the kitchen staff. Everyone wanted to know where Chef was and when he'd be back. Virgil told them he wasn't sure and to do the best they could until Robert returned. "Cut the menu down if you have to. Simplify as much as necessary. You guys are all good at what you do or you wouldn't be here. Just do your jobs and everything will be fine."

When he entered the bar, he saw Murton and one of the fill-in bartenders taking care of business in Delroy's absence. Murton tipped his head up toward the office. "Becky's upstairs waiting for you. I'll be up in a minute."

"Everything okay?"

Murton lowered his eyelids. "Yeah. We're running like clockwork."

Virgil knew better than to respond, so he headed up the steps to the office. When he opened the door, he couldn't quite believe what he saw. The office was a mess and Becky had at least half the electronic equipment disassembled on the floor. "Watch where you step," she said. "In fact, it'd probably be best if you didn't move, at least for a minute."

"What the hell is going on in here, Becks?"

"I screwed up, is what's going on."

Becky wasn't given to an abundance of errors in her job, and it got Virgil's attention. "Tell me."

"That thumb drive? You know, the one you plugged into your computer and started messing around with?"

Virgil sighed. "Do we have to go over that again? I learned my lesson."

"Congratulations. That makes one of us."

"What happened?"

"Remember how I said I was going to go to your place and make sure your system was clean?"

"Yeah."

"Well, if you think back on it, I never did."

"You're saying our system has been compromised?"

"Something like that. I'm not sure how bad the damage is, but I'm not taking any chances. I'm replacing all the hard drives and other vital components and when I'm finished with all that I'll have to do a full recovery of our data from the cloud. In the meantime, I've called Sandy and told her to take all your home equipment off-line."

Virgil had to force himself not to yawn.

"Why are you doing that with your mouth?" Becky asked him.

"Doing what?"

"You look like you're trying not to yawn."

Virgil turned his head and brought his hand up and scratched the side of his neck. The fold of his arm gave him almost enough cover.

"I saw that."

"I'm a little tired, is all. Listen, I know you've got your

hands full, but I need you to get me some background on a guy named Salter."

"The legislator, Ken, from Shelby County, or his old man, Roger, the former senator and big shot businessman?"

Virgil frowned at her. "How is it that everyone knows who these guys are except me?"

"I'm not sure. Want me to research that, too?"

Virgil let the reins loose on his sarcasm. "No, I don't think that will be necessary."

"Probably wouldn't be very productive either," Becky added.

"Your cop humor is coming along nicely."

"You can thank your brother for that."

Virgil really *was* tired. "Can I at least sit down?"

"Sure, but watch your step. No, no, don't go that way. Take the long way around to the other side."

Virgil frowned and bent over to move some things out of the way.

"Jonesy, please don't touch anything. It'll mess me up. Go the other way."

"Okay, okay. Jesus, you're as bad as Murt sometimes. Anybody ever tell you that? Everything has to be a certain way or it's the end of the world."

"Murt? Are you even listening to yourself?"

Apparently not as often as I should, Virgil thought.

"What was that?"

Virgil walked along the side wall of the office and sat down on the sofa. "I didn't say anything."

"You said something."

Virgil took a deep breath. "Anyway, the Salters. I think I might be more interested in the son, Ken, so you might as well start there. But do the old man as well."

"You got it, Jonesy." Then, after a moment, "Hey, Jonesman, you with me?"

Virgil looked up. "What? Yeah. Sorry. I was thinking about something else."

"Delroy and Huma." It wasn't a question.

He nodded at her. "We might be losing them."

"What are you talking about? Didn't Murt tell you?"

"He told me he'd be right up. What's going on?"

Becky gave him a satisfied grin. "I've got something you're going to want to look at. Come over here and sit down in front of the main monitor. Watch where you step though."

Virgil did as Becky asked. She powered up the monitor and turned it so they both could see it clearly. "Security feeds from last night. Actually, very early this morning." She hit the play button and Virgil watched Delroy and Huma enter through the kitchen and make their way up to the office.

Virgil looked at the view of the office on the security feed, then turned and looked behind him. "Man, you did a lot of damage in a short amount of time. How long did it take to make this mess?"

"Had to be done. Now, start asking me the right questions."

"Okay, why are Delroy and Huma on the computer at a little past three in the morning, and how did you know about it?"

"Great questions, both, Sherlock. I've got a program that notifies me if the system has been accessed by anyone other than myself since the last time I used it. And it had. I'll tell you more about that in a minute, because it matters. Anyway, I pulled the system logs and discovered Delroy accessed two archived files. The problem is, I can't tell which files until I'm done rebuilding and cleaning the system."

Virgil was a little confused. "Then how is it you're able to show me this?" He pointed at the monitor.

"Because I'm cleaning and rebuilding as I go. I've started with the easy stuff…like our security system. That's the other thing I wanted to talk about. Delroy and Huma aren't the only ones who accessed our system."

Virgil thought for a few seconds. "If it came from the thumb drive…"

Becky was nodding. "That's right, big boy. The Pope twins are up to something…again."

Murton was leaning against the door jamb. "I thought I was Big Boy."

"You are," Becky said, batting her eyelashes at him.

"Could the Pope twins be involved in Agent Dobson's death? Why would they be?" Virgil was speaking to himself.

Murton and Becky stared at him. "Dobson is dead?" Murton asked.

Virgil turned and looked at him. "Yeah. Killed by a hit and run."

Murton said, "Huh." Then he added, "I hate to admit it, but after everything he did to Delroy, and possibly Huma, federal agent or not, I say good riddance."

Virgil rubbed his face with both hands. "I'd agree with you, except Delroy's car was used to do it, and Miles found a pair of bloody shoes at Delroy's house that match up perfectly. Both he and Huma are being sought for questioning, and nobody can find them." He looked at Murton, then glanced at Becky. "It's going to be on us to clear Delroy and Huma and figure out what's behind it all."

"What about Miles and the rest of the crew?"

"I'm surprised you have to ask," Virgil said. "As usual, Ron is playing it by the book and I think Delroy and Huma are his primary suspects. Guilty until proven innocent."

"Maybe you should cut the guy a little slack," Murton said.

"I have been," Virgil said. "I don't think he's noticed. In fact, I don't think anyone else has either."

"I have," Becky said.

Virgil and Murton both looked at her without saying anything. "What? I have. I'm serious."

Virgil tipped his head. "Thank you." Then to Murton, "Are you ready to do some detecting?"

Murton nodded. "Yup. Been waiting on you."

"Listen," Virgil said to Becky. "I do want to know about these Salter guys. Both of them. But Delroy and Huma are the priority, okay? After that you can do a deep dive on the Salters. I'd like to know how the old man made his money, how much he's got, where it came from, etcetera."

Becky shrugged. "Okay. Shouldn't be too difficult. Have to get my system in order first though."

"Do that." He stood and looked at Murt. "You ready?"

"You asked me that question less than thirty seconds ago." He shook his head, turned and walked down the stairs.

Virgil watched him go, then looked at Becky. "He doing okay?"

Becky chewed on her lower lip. "He's getting there. He needs you, I can tell you that."

"How do you mean?"

"Just be you, Jonesy. Be present for him."

Virgil promised her he would. When he turned around to leave he wasn't watching where he stepped and heard something crunch under his boot. He froze. "Uh, was that something important?"

Becky leaned to the side and looked at the floor. "Yup. Expensive, too."

CHAPTER TWENTY-TWO

They got in Virgil's truck. "Where are we headed?" Murton asked.

Virgil looked at his watch. "I'd like to get a look at Delroy's car, but I'm sure Mimi and Lawless have it back at the MCU lab by now."

"So let's go take a look."

"Can't. Cora wants us to keep a low profile. We're unofficially on official administrative leave, remember?"

Murton rolled his eyes in an overly dramatic fashion, then took out his phone. When it was answered on the other end he said, "Has anyone ever told you your voice could melt the polar ice caps?"

Virgil looked at Murton. "Is that Mimi?"

"Hold on," Murton said into the phone. Then he gave Virgil a deadpan stare. "No, it's Chip Lawless. I've reached a point in my life where I've decided to explore my sexuality."

"You must be with Jonesy, huh?" Mimi said.

"Who else?"

Mimi laughed. "So, what's up, handsome?"

"Is Miles around there?"

"No. I think he's still out at the scene where the vehicle was recovered. They're looking for witnesses and security footage from all the surrounding buildings. Last I heard they didn't have anything."

"Would it do us any good to come look at the car?" Murton asked.

"Well, it'd do me some good to see you, but other than that, no."

Murton smiled into the phone. "Becky has my heart, Mimi. Not only that, she'd rip your limbs off if she knew how you're always hitting on me."

"All in good fun. And though she has your heart, does she have my voice?"

"She has been practicing," Murton said.

"Making any progress?"

"No, but if you tell her I said so, I'll deny it."

Virgil put his face in his hands.

"Okay, time to get serious. Dudley Do-Right over here is about to pass out or have a conniption or something. Did you guys get anything off Delroy's car?" Murton put her on speaker so Virgil could listen.

"Nothing definitive, but we did discover some interesting anomalies."

"What?" Virgil asked.

"Hey Jonesy," Mimi said. "How are you?"

"I'm well," Virgil said, trying to keep the impatience out of his voice. "What anomalies?"

Mimi was silent. Virgil finally got it. "And how are you today, Mimi?"

"Atta boy. I'm doing great. Thanks for asking. The car was definitely used to kill the victim. No question there whatsoever. Blood spatter, impact impressions, blood type, and all the usual stuff we look at matches up. Plus, because the victim appears to have been run over—twice, is the information we have—the undercarriage is covered in pieces of clothing, not to mention...well, you get the picture. So, like I said, no question there at all. But Lawless noticed something that, quite frankly, would have gotten past me."

"What's that?" Virgil said, his voice clipped and tight.

"Hey, what's with the 'tude, Dude?"

Virgil took a breath. "I'm sorry, Mimi. I'm just worried. Delroy and Huma are like family to me."

Mimi was silent for a beat. "Okay, I get it. Chip noticed that the exterior door lock on the driver's side door looked newer than the other locks on the vehicle. Like, brand new, out-of-the-box new."

"So?"

"The keys weren't with the car. We got a locksmith out here and he made a key to fit the lock. It works the driver's side door and the ignition, but that's all. It didn't work the passenger side door, the glove box, or the trunk. He made another key from the passenger side door lock and that key works everything except the driver's door and the ignition. When you compare the two keys, they aren't even close."

"That is odd," Murton said.

"Right?" Mimi said. "And we can't think of a good reason for it. I mean, what, you lose your keys, you get another set made. But that key should work everything and it doesn't."

"Maybe he broke the key in the lock at some point and had to have it replaced, or the lock was bad or something like that."

"That could be," Mimi said. "But the locksmith said the lock could be pinned to match the others, so that doesn't make much sense. When we pulled the ignition, we ran the part numbers and as it turns out, the ignition switch in the car

—even though it fits—is a generic aftermarket version that wasn't specific to that make or model. You could tell a couple of the wires were crossed to make it work, so, it's…weird."

Murton looked at Virgil. "Delroy ever say anything about losing his keys or anything like that?"

Virgil shook his head. "Not to me."

"Me either."

"Okay, thanks, Mimi," Virgil said.

"You're welcome, but I'm not done. Delroy's prints are all over the vehicle, as you'd expect since it's his car and all. Except the steering wheel, the shifter, the seatbelt mechanism, and the driver's side door handle don't have one single usable print. Lots of smudges, but nothing definitive."

"So it's almost certain that his car was stolen."

"Or someone tried to make it look like it'd been stolen," Mimi said.

"I don't think Delroy has that kind of thought process," Virgil said. "I think it's more likely that someone wanted the car to look like it *hadn't* been stolen. That's why the lock and ignition got swapped out. But they couldn't leave any prints behind so they wore gloves. That's where your smudges are coming from."

"Either way," Mimi said. "Not my area of expertise, but this is: That car took some pretty heavy damage to the front end. Enough to deploy the airbags? Maybe, maybe not. But when we looked under the hood, we noticed the fuse that controls the airbags had been removed. Yes, we're that thorough. We got a partial print from the fusebox cover and it matches a partial on the hood."

"That doesn't sync up with the glove theory very well," Virgil said.

"Unless you had more than one person involved," Mimi said. "And there must have been, right? Unless of course, you're talking about a mechanic or a locksmith as your suspect or suspects."

Virgil and Murton looked at each other again. Murton said it for everyone. "I'll tell you guys something, Delroy doesn't know that much about cars. I had to give him a jump start once last winter. He'd left his headlights on and when I was hooking up the cables to the batteries he asked me why one cable was red and the other was black. It was a serious question. He really didn't know."

"He'd never driven—legally anyway—until he and Robert got to the states," Virgil added. "This isn't Delroy, and it damned sure isn't Huma. Someone stole his car and used it to try and frame him for Dobson's murder. If you were going to purposely use a car to run someone over, you wouldn't want the airbags to deploy on you, that's for sure."

"It's a pretty good theory," Mimi said.

"How much of this does Ron know?" Virgil asked.

"Exactly none of it. Not yet anyway. The locksmith left half an hour ago and we're still examining the rest of the car. I don't think he's interested in a partial report. He came down and took a quick peek at the car, then asked me to write everything up when we were finished."

"So do that," Virgil said. "But Mimi?"

"Yeah?"

"How about you leave the prints out of your report and send them to Becky instead?"

"You guys operating again?"

"Something like that." The silence on the other end of the line made him think he'd lost the connection. "Mimi?"

"Technically, if I left that out of the report, I'd be breaking the law. Chip and I could lose our jobs."

"So put it in the report," Murton said. "Bury the stuff about the lock and switch inside the painfully dry lexical analysis that constitutes the vast majority of the verbiage you guys always use."

"Painfully dry lexical analysis?" Mimi said. "And you wonder why I'm hot for you."

Murton frowned at the phone. "Who says I wonder? Anyway, get the prints to Becky as fast as you can—like right now—then give them to Ron once you've finished the full workup on the car. That's exactly what he asked you to do anyway, so you'd be following his orders to the letter."

"You're a bad boy, Murton Wheeler."

"You don't know the half of it."

Mimi put a little extra huskiness in her voice. "Maybe you could fill me in some time."

Virgil took the phone from Murton, said goodbye to Mimi, killed the connection, then tossed the phone back to his partner.

"What?" Murton said. "She digs me."

Virgil didn't respond, and when Murton spoke, it was as much to himself as it was to his brother. "Delroy busts up Dobson's arm at the bar. He figures out that Delroy and Huma are dating. She gets attacked—in all likelihood by Dobson—and then Dobson is conveniently murdered by someone driving Delroy's car. Delroy and Huma are missing, presumably on the run—that'd be the best-case scenario right now—and we have no idea who killed Dobson or why. In the meantime, the Pope twins are circling overhead, again for reasons unknown, and other than a couple of partial prints, we have no tangible, exploitable evidence to work with."

"That about says it," Virgil said. "What's your point?"

Murton simply stared at him.

"What? Oh…sorry. I was sort of spitballing out loud there. My point is that I'm willing to entertain suggestions on what to do next. It's either that, or go back inside and tend bar."

"The prints will be a start."

"Becky said it was going to take a while to get the system back up before she can even begin to work out a match."

Virgil was a little frustrated. "Yeah, yeah, I heard her."

"When was the last time you had your blood pressure checked?"

"My blood pressure is fine."

Murton gave him a look.

"I'm serious," Virgil said. "Bell did a full workup. I'm as healthy as a horse."

"If you say so."

"I'm not saying so. Bell is."

Murton was quiet for a moment. "What's our interest in these Salter guys?"

"That might be the question of the day. It also might be nothing. But Cora pointed me at them and said to keep it quiet. Like she wanted us to look, but she didn't want it to come back on her…or Mac."

"How is Mac-daddy these days? I haven't seen him lately."

"Would you please stop calling him that?"

"Would you please answer the question?"

"He's fine…as far as I know."

Murton shook his head and Virgil caught it. "What?"

"This whole thing. I know I give Cora a hard time, and she gives it right back to me. I enjoy it. I think she does too."

"I might be missing your point," Virgil said.

"I'd hate to see her turn into Pearson. He really was a

snake, and if he was still alive, he'd tell you every single thing he did was for Mac's protection."

Virgil looked out the window of his truck. He didn't respond. What was there to say? Cora would either stay inside the lines or she wouldn't. The real question was this: Did she expect others to go outside the lines on her behalf?

"So…what exactly are we going to do?" Murton finally asked.

Virgil was about to say he didn't know. Then his phone rang and when he saw who was calling, his mood improved, if only a little. Patty.

Virgil liked her. She was like a kid sister to him—all grown up now and starting a life of her own. She was a breath of fresh air, full of energy and enthusiasm. Not only that, she and her uncle were very likely to keep Virgil & Co. financially afloat until he could figure out what to do with his land. But when he heard the sound of her voice on the other end of the phone, the way her words ran together and how she blurted everything out in one long sentence, he knew right away that something was very wrong.

"Hey, Patty. What's up? Everything on schedule down—"

"Virgil I can't get a hold of my Uncle Rick. His cell is off because he's in a meeting or something and when I called the office where the meeting is being held they wouldn't put him on the phone and when I tried to explain what was going on they hung up on me like I was some sort of crazy woman or something and I need you to get down here like right now because I don't know what's happening and I sure as hell don't know what to do next."

"Hey, hey, hey, slow down, okay? Take a breath and tell me what's wrong."

Patty laughed into the phone, but it sounded joyless. Her voice was almost hysterical, and completely out of character. "What's wrong? *What's wrong?*" She took a deep breath and managed to get herself under control. "Okay, where to start? Shelby County's finest are here, led by Sheriff Bolden or what-the-hell-ever his name is, along with the rest of his remaining deputies. They've got me and Mr. Johnson sitting in the dirt in handcuffs, and your mechanic, Carlos, has been shot in the leg. I'm not sure how bad his injury is."

"*What*? Say that again."

"That's not all. You know the semi driver who was eyeing me?"

"Yeah." Virgil closed his eyes. He knew whatever Patty was about to say wouldn't be good.

"He's dead. He tried to rape me, and his brother, Joe, the, uh, nice one, I guess? He's being airlifted out of here with an arrow lodged in the center of his chest. I heard one of the paramedics say something about a nicked aorta and a sucking chest wound, whatever that means. They don't think he's going to survive. Two of the deputies are hurt very badly as well. One got knocked unconscious—I think he's going to be okay—but it doesn't look like the other one is going to make it. Joe Davis shot him in the neck right before the arrow got him. If Joe hadn't shot the deputy, I think the Indian would have left him alone."

And Virgil thought, *The Indian?*

HE KNEW ON SOME INSTINCTUAL LEVEL THAT, GIVEN HER condition, he wouldn't get any more useful information out of

Patty. She was clearly in shock. He could hear it in her voice, her shortness of breath, the way her words ran together. Virgil wanted to ask her some very basic questions, but he knew the best way to get the answers he wanted was to get back to Shelby County as quickly as he could. He did ask her one question though. "What's the contact number for your Uncle?"

She gave Virgil the number and he pinched the phone between his cheek and shoulder as he wrote it down on his hand. Then he told Patty to get with one of the paramedics and stay with them until they got there.

"I can't. I'm handcuffed, remember?"

"I'll take care of that. Is the sheriff nearby?"

"When you say nearby if you mean standing right next to me and listening to every word I say, then yes. He's holding the phone for me because my hands are cuffed behind my back."

"Put him on." Virgil said it through his teeth.

When Sheriff Holden came on the line he didn't bother trying to hide the anger in his voice. "Jones, if you're not down here in the next hour, I'm putting everyone in jail, and then I'm going to speak to the county prosecutor about issuing an injunction to keep you out of my county."

"On what grounds?"

"Anything I can think of. Disturbing the peace comes to mind."

"Save it, Holden. We're on our way. And lose the attitude. I've had enough of your huckleberry bullshit."

"*You've* had enough? If I wasn't standing next to a puddle of my own deputy's blood, I'd actually be laughing right now. You've had enough. You've been nothing but trouble ever since you showed up in my county acting like some sort of pontificating asshole, throwing your weight around as if you're better than us. If anything—"

Virgil was tired of it. "Shut up. That young lady you've got cuffed and sitting in the dirt? She's the victim, you idiot. I want you—you, personally—to release her this instant. Then you're going to walk her over to the paramedics and stay right by her side until we get there. If I show up and find you more than five feet away, I'll arrest you, and it won't be for disturbing the peace. It will be for interfering with an ongoing state investigation. You think I'm joking? Go ahead and walk away." He ended the call and punched in the number Patty had given him.

"Boy, you and that Holden guy really don't get along, do you?" Murton said. "What's going on?"

Virgil pulled the phone away from his ear for a moment. "I'm not sure you'd believe me. Get Cool on the phone and tell him we're on our way."

Murton made the call and when Virgil put the phone back up to his ear, he realized it had already been answered. What he heard gave him pause. "Salter Enterprises. How may I direct your call?"

CHAPTER TWENTY-THREE

MURTON HAD COOL ON THE PHONE AND WAS ABOUT TO END the call when Virgil got his attention and held up a finger. Murton tipped his chin up as an acknowledgment, and told Cool to hang on.

"Are you still at the same location where I dropped you?" Virgil asked Said.

Said had finally come on the line after Virgil threatened the Salter Enterprises' receptionist with legal action if she didn't get him on the phone immediately. She made a little huff noise the way a teenaged girl might and dropped the receiver on her desk. The noise was so loud Virgil had to pull the phone away from his ear for a moment. A few moments later he had Said. "Yes. In fact, I was getting ready to give you a call. What's up? The receptionist looked a little pissed when she told me you were on the phone."

"I'll explain when we get there. Can you get a car?"

Said was quiet for a few seconds, then asked, "Jonesy, what's going on? Is Patty okay?"

Virgil heard the apprehension edging into Said's voice and knew he had to tell him something. "She's fine, Rick, I promise you, but we've got to get back to the site right now. I'll explain when we meet. Hold on for a second." He put the phone to his chest and told Murton to ask Cool if he could meet them at Eagle Creek airport, which was closer for everyone.

Murton brought his phone up. "You hear that, Cool?"

"Yep. I can be there in less than ten minutes," Cool said.

"Do it," Murton said, nodding at Virgil.

Virgil put his phone back to his ear and said, "Get a car and get to the Eagle Creek airport. Cool's going to be there with the chopper. You know where that is? Eagle Creek?"

"No, but that won't be a problem. I've already got an Uber coming. Now how about you tell me what's going on."

"See you there. Don't linger." Virgil killed the connection before Said could ask him any more questions. Then he dropped the truck in gear, turned on his flashers, and burped his siren as they pulled out of the lot.

"Tell me," Murton said.

Virgil glanced at him. "You ever think about walking away…maybe just run the bar? The money's not that bad, you know."

"Not really. Only once or twice a day, is all. But then some sort of interesting shit starts to go down and I understand why we're called the Major Crimes Unit and how much I enjoy the rush." Then, "Watch it, watch it…on the right."

"I see him." Virgil burped the siren again and a pedestrian who'd stepped into the street jumped back on the curb. He shouted something and flipped them off as they went flying past.

"Like that," Murton said. "He didn't even look before he stepped out on the street. His head was buried in his phone, and had it been anyone else besides us, he'd be dead right now, but everybody hates the cops. I'm tired of it." He paused for a second, then said, "Okay, end of rant. You going to tell me what's happening, or not?"

Virgil told him everything Patty had said on the phone. When he was finished, Murton looked at him and said, "Maybe you should try to lighten up on Holden. He's old and out of his element. And he's just trying to do his job. I don't think we make it very easy for him." Then, "An Indian, huh?"

When they arrived at the Eagle Creek airport they found Cool and Said waiting by the helicopter. Virgil dumped the truck in the lot and he and Murton badged the security guard and ran out onto the tarmac. Cool had the engine running by the time they were on board and once everyone was strapped in he increased the power, pulled on the collective, hovered in place for a moment, then spun them around and headed south. Said pressed the microphone of his headset close to his lips and looked at Virgil. "What the hell is going on down there?"

Virgil and Said were sitting across from each other in the rear of the chopper. Virgil leaned forward, put his hand on Said's knee and said, "Rick, I want to emphasize that Patty is okay."

"The more you emphasize that particular point, the more worried I get. Would you please come out with it already?"

Virgil told him everything he knew. When he was finished, Said turned and stared out the window without saying a word. Virgil wanted to ask him about the meeting at Salter Enterprises, but the look on Said's face before he turned away told him it could wait.

It happened like this: Carlos Ibarra, who had his head buried inside the engine compartment of the crane, was running a grinding wheel across the housing of the pump where the new line would go in. He thought maybe he could do a simple cut and splice—a quick field fix—but when he saw the condition of the line, he decided to do it right. That meant the removal of the entire damaged line. To do that, the couplings that connected the line to the pump housing had to come off as well. When he got everything removed, the gasket didn't want to completely let go of the housing, thus the grinder.

The grinder made a hell of a racket, but it only took a few minutes to get the surface area clear. With that done, he headed to the maintenance truck to fabricate a new gasket. He traced an outline of the coupling around its edges, cut the gasket material to size, then grabbed a long-handled torque wrench to bolt everything back together. The wrench he'd used during the removal process was a little small and he needed more leverage to get everything nice and tight. Plus, the bolts that attached the couplings had to be torqued to a specific value or everything would leak, new gasket or not. That's when he heard…something. It sounded like a yelp. Like someone might be hurt and in pain.

He jogged over to the other side of his own truck—he still had the big torque wrench in his hand—and looked at the semi-trailers. That's when he saw one of the drivers behind Patty, his pants and underwear down around his ankles.

He ran that way, his thought process now powered by pure instinct. When he shouted 'Hey!' he was already winding up to swing the giant wrench. The semi-driver turned at the sound of Carlos's voice and saw the wrench coming at his side. He was already tightening up, pulling his arms in to try to save his ribs, but with his pants down around his ankles his feet got tangled when he turned, and he began to fall.

Carlos saw the man start to go down and tried to stop his swing, or at the very least take some of the velocity out of it, but with the weight of the wrench and the amount of adrenaline running through his system it was much too late. The driver went down and when the wrench made contact, it hit him square in the side of his head with a sound not unlike that of a major league batter who'd managed to connect with a hanging slider. When Davis hit the ground his eyes were locked wide and unblinking, his jaw extended, one arm sticking straight up in the air as if he were pointing at something in the sky. His wires had been cut and Carlos knew without a doubt he had killed the man without meaning to.

He dropped the wrench in the dirt, and took off his work shirt, then picked Patty up and carried her to the front of his maintenance truck. He sat her down, then used his work shirt to cover her private area. He held her hand in his own and gently patted her wrist and the side of her face until she came around.

JOHNSON CALLED 9-1-1 AND THE FIRST DEPUTY TO ARRIVE was a rookie by the name of Brian Cooper. He saw Davis off in the distance, lying in the dirt, and instead of requesting an explanation, or checking on Davis, he made the mistake of asking a quick question. He looked at the three people in front of him and said, "Who did this?"

Carlos glanced down at the ground, then looked up at Deputy Cooper. "I did. He was—"

That was as far as he got.

"I should have known," Cooper said. He drew his weapon and pointed it at Carlos. "On the ground, asshole. Right now. Don't make me say it twice."

Johnson stepped forward and made a mistake of his own. He placed his hand on Cooper's arm and tried to get him to lower his weapon. "Say, hold on there, young man. This isn't what it looks like."

Cooper, who'd graduated from the police academy only two months ago still had the voice of his tactical instructor ringing in his head. *Never let them get on top of you. Never let them put their hands on your person. Control the situation at all costs. Use force if necessary, for your safety and the safety of those around you.* He jumped back and pointed his gun at Johnson. "Don't touch me. You never put your hands on a police officer."

Patty, who'd been silent so far, noticed that Deputy Cooper's gun hand was shaking. She was certain that if she didn't do or say something, someone was going to get shot, probably by accident. "Deputy, please. Listen to us. That man…"

But Cooper wasn't listening. Cooper was all alone in the middle of a cornfield with no help, and three people he considered adversarial in nature. He swung his gun from person to person, and when he spoke his voice was full of fear and much louder than necessary. "That's it. Everybody on the ground, right now. C'mon, down on the ground, face first. Put your hands behind your backs and cross your ankles. Do it now."

Carlos, Johnson, and Patty all looked at each other. Patty took the lead and got down in the dirt. Carlos and Johnson did the same. The deputy reached for the microphone clipped to his epaulet and called for backup. Then he cuffed everyone and finally ran over to check the victim. When he saw the side of Davis's head, he vomited just like Patty had.

It didn't take Sheriff Holden and another deputy long to arrive. They pulled up in a two-tone brown and tan County SUV, bouncing along the dirt path Johnson had bulldozed out only a couple of hours ago. Cooper ran over and explained what he knew to the sheriff and the other deputy, Mike Lowe, which by all accounts, wasn't much.

"You haven't questioned the suspects yet?" Holden asked Cooper.

"No Sir. I thought maybe I'd better wait for you to get here. The woman said it wasn't what it looked like, but that's what they all say, ain't it?"

Holden gave him a quick tip of the head. "Yup." *But sometimes it's true.* "Well, let's take a look at the victim first. You've got everyone restrained?"

Cooper hitched up his gun belt, a bit of confidence coming back to him now. "Yes, Sir. They ain't going nowhere."

"Go keep an eye on them just the same."

"You had lunch yet?" Cooper asked them.

They both looked at him but didn't respond.

"I, uh, may have contaminated the crime scene a little."

Holden nodded. "It happens. They been Mirandized yet?"

Cooper looked down at the dirt. "I was about to do that."

"Now might be a good time," Holden said. "We'll be right back."

Cooper walked back over to the three people sitting in the dirt, their hands cuffed behind their backs. Patty gave it another try, even though she was pretty sure it wouldn't work.

"Look, officer...?"

"It's Deputy," he corrected her. "Deputy Cooper."

Patty nodded, trying to be cooperative. "Yes, of course.

I'm sorry. Deputy Cooper, if I could simply explain what happened—"

Cooper held his hand up, palm first. "Yeah, yeah, I've heard it all before." He put a mocking tone in his voice. "*If I could simply explain.*" Except Cooper hadn't heard it all before. As a rookie, he'd heard almost nothing except bad excuses from people trying to talk their way out of a speeding ticket, or explain that they simply hadn't seen the stop sign. If they had, they would have stopped. He reached into his breast pocket and took out a card. "Before you say anything, I got to tell you your rights. Then you might think twice before you say anything because it can and will be held against you in a court of law."

Patty shook her head and gave up. The three of them listened as Deputy Cooper read them their rights. When he got to the part about an attorney he mispronounced the word appointed—he said anointed—and Johnson laughed out loud.

Cooper got right in his face. "You think this is funny?"

"No, no. It just sort of slipped out when you said anointed."

"That's not what I said."

"Yeah," Patty said. "You sorta did."

They were still debating it when Sheriff Holden and the other deputy, Mike Lowe, returned.

Holden looked at Johnson. "Carl. How'd you get mixed up in this?"

"I'm not sure I should answer before my attorney has been anointed," Johnson said.

Cooper stepped forward. "Oh, that's real fucking funny."

Holden reached out and pulled Cooper back. "How about it on the language, Coop?"

"They were making fun of me for no good reason."

Before anyone could say anything else, Carlos spoke up.

"That man was trying to rape this woman." He tipped his head toward Patty. "I was trying to protect her. I think I may have killed him, but I did not mean to do so."

Holden turned to Deputy Lowe and said, "Mike, you'd better go wait over by the victim. He shouldn't be left lying there all alone. Get his ID if you can find it, call for the paramedics and the coroner, then get the tarp and cover him up."

Lowe walked back to where Davis was and Holden once again looked at Johnson. "How about it, Carl? You done being cute? There's a dead man over there in the dirt."

But Patty had had enough. "This is ridiculous." She pointed at Carlos with her chin. "Didn't you hear what he said? That man lying back there? The one you and your deputy keep referring to as the victim? He knocked me unconscious and tried to rape me."

Holden turned and looked at her. "I'm asking Mr. Johnson to corroborate what the Mexican said, Missy, because I know him. I don't know you, and I don't know the Mexican, so how about you hold your water for a minute? I'll get to you when I'm ready."

"*Missy?* Say that again."

It may have been the look in her eyes, or the tone of her voice, but either way, Holden didn't respond. He looked at Johnson yet again, who was about to confirm what Carlos had said when they all heard the rumble of the semi-tractor coming down the dirt path and then the hiss of air brakes as it skidded to a stop.

Joe Davis was back from lunch.

CHAPTER TWENTY-FOUR

IN HIS HEAD HE ALWAYS THOUGHT OF HIMSELF BY HIS PROPER name, which was Anthony Stronghill, though others not of his kind invariably called him Tony Hill. He allowed it, and often even encouraged it, depending on the situation. African Americans thought they had it rough? Try being Native American living alone, off the Rez, surrounded by people who thought their Christian upbringing gave them power and authority over those who were here long before history had been rewritten by the victors.

His parents had taught him his ancestral history, proud of the fact that they were all direct descendants of Chief Little Turtle of the Miami Native Indian tribe of the Ohio and Indiana territories. During the battle of the Wabash in 1791, Chief Little Turtle led one thousand warriors in a fight against more than fourteen hundred federal troops. When it was over, Little Turtle and his Braves had beat back the Americans and handed the US Army its worst defeat of the time against the Native Indians. But Little Turtle's own subsequent defeats over the next four years forced him to cede much of Ohio and Indiana to the United States government.

Most of the Indians migrated west, but a few remained, scattered around the Ohio Valley and South-Central Indiana, trying to live off the land they once called their own. Generations came and went and over two hundred years later, one of Little Turtle's descendants, Anthony Stronghill kept his people's memories and spirits a part of his life, both in his heart and his actions. He hunted the land, ate what he killed, and lived a solitary life of both the quick and the dead.

He also—as Tony Hill—had a social security card and driver's license. He worked part-time as a landscaper and gardener for a wealthy family who lived on a country estate so lush and full of excess it proved the rich and powerful had no limits of their own and were able to write the rulebook, one with few boundaries. But a job was a job and he was glad to have it, especially this one. He worked hard and well, paid his taxes, and kept his head down and his mouth shut. When he walked through town or was at work, his long braids remained tucked under his hat. But when he was home at his trailer outside of town, he often went shirtless—even in the winter—and was never without his bow, or the long-handled blade he kept sheathed and strapped to his turquoise belt.

His employer allowed him one day off a week—his wages low enough that he sometimes struggled to curb his hunger—so that meant it was time to hunt. But Indian or not, bow hunting this particular time of the year was illegal. Never mind that it was on someone else's land, land that had been stolen from his ancestors. Didn't that make it his, at least on some fundamental level?

This day he was in search of a nice fat Cottontail for dinner. A three-pounder, after gutting and skinning, would net him a pound of meat—enough protein for two big meals, or three small ones, and the fur was useful in ways that were almost too numerous to count. And since the Cottontails loved corn, Stronghill was out in the fields.

When he saw the young woman in the field he knew she was frightened by him. The thought of it almost made him laugh out loud. If she'd somehow been able to see him at work, she'd walk right by without giving him a second thought. Or maybe she'd glance at his shirt, the one with 'Tony' sewn above the breast pocket, before commenting on how beautiful the grounds looked, or how wonderful the flower garden smelled when the wind was just right. But out here in the field, on this day, he was a predator, and he sensed the recognition on her part.

Perhaps that's why she ran. When he caught up to her— which wasn't very hard at all—they both stopped and stared at each other. He knew others were nearby and he didn't want her to scream or cry out, so he put his finger to his lips and held out his hand, palm forward. A peaceful gesture.

He hoped.

She turned her head and looked around, and Stronghill knew she had become disoriented in the field. He wanted to help, just like he would have helped her in any other situation. And something about him must have intrigued the young woman, because she let him guide her back to the area where they were working the land. He had no idea why they were destroying the corn, and in truth, he didn't care. He simply didn't want to get caught hunting where he wasn't allowed.

When she ducked through the final row and back into the clearing, Stronghill turned and went the other way, his footsteps light, his body moving with the rhythm of the land, the way his ancestors had taught him, not against it like the ways of the white man. Job and taxes aside, Anthony Stronghill considered himself a true Native American.

Still, he had to be careful.

The men and machinery and their activities were a source of curiosity though. Once the woman was back in the clearing, he should have left—gone back to his trailer and made a grilled cheese or heated up a can of Dinty Moore's in a pot over the Sterno. But he decided to stay and see what the Whites were up to. He pushed his way through the rows of corn and sat on his haunches and waited.

After she was in the clearing, the woman stuck her head back through, looking for him. She even pushed through a few rows before she gave up and turned back. When she popped out into the clearing, Stronghill moved forward and that's when he saw the man grab her by the shoulders. He watched her fight for herself, gouging the man's eye with her fingers. She was a fighter…a warrior, and the feral look in her eyes intrigued him. He thought she could take the man, but when he smashed his forehead against hers, it knocked her unconscious. Then when he bent her over the end of the trailer and yanked her pants down, Stronghill had seen enough. He pulled his knife from its sheath, the blade razor-sharp and glinting in the sun as he ran toward the man who was assaulting the young woman.

He pushed through the corn, without making a sound, flipped the knife in his hand and was less than a half-second from letting it fly when the Mexican came running from behind the other truck. When he swung the wrench, Stronghill stepped back, flipped the knife again and slipped it back into its sheath before disappearing in the corn.

He wasn't exactly sure what was about to happen, but he wanted to be ready. He reached across his shoulder and pulled an arrow, nocked it with the bow, then settled in again to wait and watch. The Mexican never saw him.

When Joe saw the County SUV and the other squad car he accelerated down the path. When he saw his brother lying in the dirt at the back of the lowboy trailer, he skidded to a stop right next to him. If he'd have parked anywhere else, things may have unfolded differently and he might have lived. But his rig blocked the line of sight between where his dead brother was, and the three people sitting handcuffed in the dirt.

He jumped down from the cab and ran over to his brother. Deputy Lowe had a folded tarp in his hands—he'd not yet covered the dead man—and tried to stop him, but Joe pushed past, got down on the ground, grabbed his brother's body and pulled him close. When he saw the side of his brother's head, his stomach rolled. "Who did this to my brother?" he asked the deputy. His voice was tight and low, almost a whisper.

Deputy Lowe dropped the tarp and put a hand on Davis's shoulder. "Sir, I'm terribly sorry about this. We arrived only a few minutes ago. We've got the suspects detained. It'd be best if you, uh, left your brother's body undisturbed until the medical examiner gets here. Sir, please."

Davis gently laid his brother aside then stood and looked at the deputy. "He wasn't right in the head." Then he realized the cruelty of his own thought process and the words he produced. "That's a hell of a thing to say about someone who's had their head smashed in, ain't it?"

"Sir, I really am sorry. But like I said, we've got the suspects detained. May I see some identification, Sir?"

"What for?"

"It's simply protocol. I'll need it for the report."

Davis ignored the request and subsequent explanation. "Who done it?"

Lowe knew he shouldn't answer, but the pain and grief on the face of the man who stood before him was too much to bear. Lowe had lost a brother of his own to violence years ago, and it was the reason he was now an officer of the law. When he responded, it was against his better judgment, but he knew how the man felt and wanted to help alleviate some of his grief, even if it was only fractional and in the moment. "I heard the Mexican confess. Heard it with my own ears. He'll pay for it, sir, believe you me."

"The Mexican, huh?"

"Yes, sir. We have him and the others detained. You can't see him from here. Your rig is blocking the view, but they're right over there by the other equipment." He turned and pointed past the semi's cab and when he did, Joe reached down in the dirt and grabbed the wrench the Mexican had used to kill his brother.

He hit Lowe on the back of his head, right at the base of his skull. It wasn't a killing blow, but it knocked Lowe out. Davis reached down and pulled Lowe's service revolver from its holster, then peeked around the front end of the semi. He saw two county cops. One was young and looked like he wasn't quite sure what to do with his hands. The other was much older and when he walked, his legs wobbled like his knees were about to give out. And he was headed his way.

The cop with the bad knees didn't see Davis. He was looking at the ground as he moved, like he had to watch his step. Davis saw the three people sitting in the dirt, their hands behind their backs.

The Mexican was on the end.

Davis pulled his head back, then ducked low and snuck behind the trailer and into the corn. He went three rows in then started moving toward the others.

Sheriff Holden didn't carry a weapon on his person. He was old, his knees were bad, and the weight of the damned thing always bumping against his leg drove him crazy. When his secretary, an older, fiery redhead named Betty reminded him to take his gun before he left, he told her that when he wore the damned thing, it left a bruise on the side of his thigh that was roughly the size and shape of an unripened Chiquita banana. "Who needs that sort of misery?"

"If you don't wear it, one of these days you're going to need it and you won't have it," she said. "Then you'll get shot and killed. How do you think your leg will feel then?"

Sheriff Holden put his hand over his chest. "Like a great weight has been lifted from my soul. Can I go now? I'm not going to get shot, but Cooper's got almost enough experience to get himself killed."

"You hired him, not me."

"Who put a bee in your bonnet today?"

Betty waved him out the door and when he left, it was without his weapon. He left it in his desk drawer where it belonged. Besides, Cooper and Lowe were armed. One more gun wouldn't make that much difference. Cooper called in for backup regarding a scuffle of some sort. Out in Jones's field no less. Big surprise.

Holden wanted to go speak with the driver of the semi and check on Lowe. He started that way, watching the ground as he walked. He didn't get far.

"Hey Sheriff," Johnson said. "What Patty said is true."

Holden stopped and turned. "Who's Patty?"

I am, you moron. The one you called Missy. "That would be me. Do you see any other females around here? Have any of them tried to tell you what happened? Do they have a swollen face and a cut on their forehead like I do because they were head-butted and almost raped?"

He took off his hat and wiped his forehead with a neckerchief he kept tucked inside his breast pocket. "Givin' me lip is only going to prolong the process, *Miss*. Do you have any identification on you?"

"Of course I do. If you'll release me, I'd be happy to—" That's when she saw Joe Davis push through the row of corn, Deputy Lowe's gun held in a two-handed grip. He was moving fast, crabbing to the side, and it looked like he was trying to get a bead on Carlos. "Sheriff, look out! Behind you!" Patty rolled and threw herself into Carlos, knocking them both flat. Her timing was barely fast enough. She felt the bullet buzz through her hair, missing her scalp by inches.

Deputy Cooper and Sheriff Holden both turned at the sound of the gunfire. Cooper suddenly felt like everything was moving in slow motion. He thought he heard the sheriff say, "Oh, Betty." Betty was the departmental secretary. Why would he say her name? And where was Lowe? Then he saw Sheriff Holden do something he didn't think was possible. He saw him start to run. He ran straight at the man with the gun. Cooper slid sideways to keep the sheriff out of his line of fire, and brought his weapon up. But the man who'd popped out of the corn was still trying to get to the Mexican—still crabbing sideways, and Cooper was too afraid of hitting the sheriff to fire his own gun.

Patty, who was still not fully recovered from the kidnapping incident went into full flight mode. She rolled over and over, trying to reach the cover of Carlos's truck. The rolling saved her life. Davis fired again, and this time he connected with his target, hitting Carlos high in the back of his right leg, right below his ass. Carlos screamed in pain and when Sheriff Holden looked back over his shoulder to see who'd been hit, he tripped and went down.

Cooper suddenly had a clear line of fire. But rookie that he was, he made the mistake of talking instead of shooting. He shouted, "Freeze," at the man with the gun, surprised that his voice was an octave higher than normal. "Drop the gun and get down on the ground."

Davis wasn't listening. In fact, Davis couldn't even hear after firing twice in a row. All he heard was a high-pitched whine. He saw the older cop on the ground, his hands wrapped around one of his knees, and thought he'd hit him by mistake. Somewhere in the deepest part of his brain he thought, 'oh no.' He looked at the younger cop, saw the look in his eyes, the weapon pointed at his head. His thoughts were of his dead brother, the only family he had left, the ways he'd tried to help him and protect him all these years since the death of their parents. But it was all slipping away and like everything else over the course of his life, it was happening in ways he couldn't control. When he pulled the trigger again, Cooper went down, blood spurting from the side of his neck.

Davis, now completely out of control, swung the gun, looking for other targets when he felt a terrible bolt of pain shoot through his chest. The pain was so intense it was impossible to breathe. He dropped the gun and fell to his knees, and for an instant he thought he might be having a heart attack. When he looked down the last thing he saw before he passed out was the multi-colored feathers on the shaft of the arrow that had buried itself in his chest.

Sheriff Holden grabbed the microphone clipped to his shoulder and pressed the button. "Shots fired. Officer down. Multiple casualties. Repeat, shots fired."

Betty, who was filing paperwork back at the office heard the call over the scanner. She picked up the microphone and said, "Sheriff? Ben, are you there? What's happening? Where are you?"

"We're in the Jones field, Betty, off the access road, south of the Co-op. Get EMS out here and send everyone we've got. Send them all right now."

CHAPTER TWENTY-FIVE

COOL HAD THE HELICOPTER DOWN TO ONE THOUSAND FEET BY the time they reached the Co-op. He continued his descent as he followed the access road, and by the time they reached the site they were down to five hundred feet above the ground. He made a sweeping pass around the five-acre perimeter of the clearing, looking for the best place to land, one that wouldn't blow debris everywhere. He determined the best spot would be at the back of the clearing in the area Johnson had already bulldozed. They could walk in from there.

The other reason to steer clear of the main crime scene was obvious...at least from above. The area was filled with all different types of vehicles. There were five county squad cars, the coroner's van, two fire rescue vehicles, an EMS unit, and the Shelby County Crime Scene Investigation van. All of that was in addition to the semi-tractors, their lowboy trailers, the bulldozer, crane, drill rig, the Co-op maintenance truck and the vehicle Patty and Rick Said had arrived in earlier.

"Looks like 465 on a Friday afternoon in the middle of a cornfield," Murton said.

When Virgil looked down and scanned the area he saw

Patty sitting on the back bumper of the EMS unit, one wrist cuffed to a vertical handhold on the outside of the vehicle. He was instantly hot. He leaned forward, tapped Cool on the shoulder and said, "Put me right in the middle of it."

Cool tipped his head to the side and held it there. "Not a good idea, Jonesy. The crime scene people will have a fit. We'll blow any evidence right out of the area."

Virgil wasn't having it. "Fuck 'em. Right in the middle, Cool."

"You're the boss." Then to no one in particular: "This ought to be good."

When Virgil glanced at Murton he noticed he was sucking on his cheeks. They were at the back of the clearing and Cool came in low, right over the top of the corn stalks. He crabbed slightly to his left to avoid the large crane then put them down in the dirt, right in the middle of all the vehicles. Everyone on the ground scattered out of the way and turned their backs against all the debris that was being kicked up by the rotor wash. Two of the crime scene technicians had to use both their hands and feet to hold down the tarp that covered Jim Davis's body. Sheriff Holden stood right next to where the helicopter landed, no more than ten feet away, his back turned, his face buried in the crook of his arm.

Virgil had the door open and he and Said were out of the chopper the moment it landed. Cool began shutting everything down as quickly as he could. He knew Virgil was mad, and he could see the people on the ground were not happy either. The fact that he was in his State Police uniform probably saved what was going to be a tense situation from becoming much worse.

Four deputies were at the scene in addition to the sheriff. Said ran straight toward Patty and was cut off by one of Holden's men. When he tried to shove him out of the way, the deputy wrapped him up and took him to the ground. Murton saw what was happening and started to run that way, while Virgil went straight toward Holden.

He grabbed him by the arm and spun him around. "What the hell is going on here, Holden? Why is the victim in all of this mess handcuffed to the ambulance instead of being treated? Look at her face."

Cool jumped from the helicopter and ran toward Virgil. Holden's remaining three deputies were closing in fast, their weapons drawn, their movements designed to flank Virgil and his people.

Murton yanked the deputy off Said, spun him down face-first, then put a knee in his back and cuffed him before helping Said to his feet. Said shook him off and went to Patty.

"You've got some nerve," Holden said, "dropping out of the sky and blowing our crime scene all across hell and gone."

"And I told you that Patty Doyle was the victim. Why is she still restrained?"

"Because she's under arrest for trying to help the Mexican get away."

Patty, who was only about ten yards away heard the exchange. "That's bullshit, Jonesy. When everyone started shooting I threw myself into Carlos to get him on the ground. Then I rolled away to get out of the line of fire. He was already shot by then and he wasn't going anywhere. I wasn't about to be next. They've already transported him to the hospital."

Virgil looked back at Holden for a response, but Cool interrupted their exchange. "Jonesy, we're about to have a problem here." He had his sidearm drawn, holding it against his leg, pointed at the ground. When Virgil looked around, he saw Holden's deputies had them surrounded and were inching their way forward.

Virgil still had the sheriff by the arm. "Tell your men to stand down, Holden."

"I'm doing no such thing," Holden said. "I got word that one of my men has died and the other has a fractured vertebrae at the base of his skull."

"And how much of that is her fault?" Virgil said, pointing at Patty. "She was assaulted, almost raped, and by the looks of things around here, the only reason you've got her cuffed to the back of the EMS truck is because you and your men are either incompetent or deliberately trying to piss me off."

"Don't flatter yourself, Jones. And get your hands off of me right now, or we're going to have a problem."

Cool knew the situation was spiraling out of control and put his hand on Virgil's shoulder. He leaned in close and whispered in his ear. "Time to take the high road, Jonesman." Then, without waiting for a response, he holstered his weapon and made sure the deputies saw him do it. Then he put one hand on Virgil's wrist and the other on Holden's arm and very gently pulled the two men apart. Virgil let him.

He looked at the deputies and said, "I'm Richard Cool, Indiana State Police. Under orders of the governor, we're taking control of this crime scene, effective immediately. Secure your weapons and stand down. It's not a request. It's an order from the governor himself."

None of the deputies did what he asked. Cool turned his back on them and looked at the Sheriff. When he spoke, his voice was calm, his manner relaxed, and his eyes had a sleepy glaze. "Tell your men to stand down, Sheriff, and do it right now. That's option number one. Option number two is this: I personally handcuff you, put you in the back of that helicopter and transport you directly to Indianapolis. Once there, you'll be perp-walked into the Marion County jail on charges of obstruction and threatening the lives of officers of the state. You think you've got problems with Virgil, here? You ain't seen nothing yet, partner." He inched forward as he spoke and by the time he was finished he stood so close to Holden that the bill of his hat was bouncing off the center of the sheriff's forehead. He said it all so calmly, so matter of fact that Holden believed him.

Holden stepped into his deputies' line of sight. "Do as he says, boys. No sense in letting things get out of hand. We're all on the same side here."

The deputies didn't like it, but they did as they were told. Murton walked over and released the handcuffs that held Patty to the EMS unit, while one of Holden's men released the cuffs from the deputy Murton had taken down. Said put his arm around Patty and helped her inside the back of the unit where one of the paramedics began to address the cut on her forehead and the swelling on her face.

Once the deputy was released, he stood up and headed for the ambulance. He walked up behind Murton and said, "Hey, asshole."

Murton knew what was coming. He moved as close to the EMS vehicle as he could before he turned around. When the deputy threw the punch, Murton sidestepped it with ease and the deputy's fist connected solidly with the flat panel on the back of the van. There was an audible crack and the deputy's face went white as he grabbed his wrist and dropped to his knees. Murton looked down at him and said, "Hurts, doesn't it? Next time, if you're going to do it, do it. Don't talk about it." Then he stuck his head into the back of the van and made eye contact with the medic who was examining Patty. "When you've got a minute there's another victim out here. No rush." Then he walked over to Cool and said, "Nice job. Best line of bullshit I've heard in a while, and you gotta remember, I work part-time in a cop bar."

Virgil asked, as politely as possible, for the sheriff to join him. They walked over to one of the lowboy trailers—the one that hadn't been used as a platform during Patty's assault—and Virgil sat down. He looked up at Holden. "You going to play nice?"

Holden sat down next to him. He didn't speak for a long time, and when he did, he sounded tired and sad. "It's good to get some weight off my knee."

"Tell me everything," Virgil said. "Start at the beginning."

"I heard what Patty said to you on the phone. It was a little mixed up—she may have been in shock—but she hit the highlights. What she didn't tell you was this: When the paramedics were treating the Mexican—"

"Carlos."

Holden waved the interruption away. "Whatever. Never met the man. Anyway, when the paramedics were treating him—he'd been shot in the leg and was bleeding pretty badly—one of my men handcuffed him to the side rail of the gurney. He was the one who killed the Davis fellow, so it was standard procedure, right out of the book, and you know it."

"You're right, Ben, it was. But I have to ask myself this: Why make a bad situation worse? As I understand it, he killed Davis in defense of another. I'm speaking of Patty. He'd knocked her out and was trying to rape her."

"I know that," Holden said, his words tight and clipped. "But when we got here, the whole situation went bad right from the get-go. I've got a dead rookie—Cooper is his name in case you're interested—and the other Davis fellow knocked Lowe, another one of my boys on the back of his neck, right below the base of his skull. He's got a broken neck and will have to wear a halo for six months at least. Don't know if he'll ever be able to go back to active duty. And now, Williams over there, probably has a busted wrist. I heard the crack."

Virgil nodded in sympathy, and it was genuine. "I did too. But he shouldn't have swung on Murton. In fact, if I'm being honest with you, Ben, none of what happened when we arrived would have taken place if you'd simply treated Patty as the victim."

"That's what I'm trying to tell you. She ain't all victim."

"Meaning what, exactly?" Virgil asked.

"Meaning after the shooting had stopped and the backup arrived, we had everything under control." Holden shook his head and let out a sad chuckle. "Listen to me…under control. I had two cops down and two civilians dead—one with an arrow in his chest for Christ's sake—and a bleedin' Mexican to boot. But we'd already taken the cuffs off Johnson and the Doyle woman. They were getting ready to treat her head injury. She'll have a nasty bruise tomorrow, that's for sure. Anyway, Williams, the one with the busted wrist? When he cuffed that Mexican fellow to the gurney, Patty sort of lost her wits or something and started screaming at him…at Williams. She tried to stop him from doing his job by taking a swing at him. But Williams was only doing what he was told. Defense of others or not, the Mexican killed a man."

"I can't help but notice that you keep referring to Carlos as 'the Mexican.'"

Holden shot him a look. "You sayin' I'm racist, now?"

It sure sounds like it. Virgil ignored the question, and Holden let him. "I'm simply wondering if there might have been a better way to handle it. Patty is still in shock over what happened to her a few months ago. Carlos saved her from something that she might never have recovered from, emotionally speaking." They sat with that for a few minutes before Virgil asked Holden another question. "You have a daughter?"

The sheriff looked at him. "Yup. Why?"

"You know why, Ben."

"You're sayin' if it'd been my daughter I would have done it different?"

"You're saying you wouldn't have?"

This time it was Holden who ignored the question. "She tried to punch an officer of the law. He simply needed her out of the equation for a minute."

"You going to charge her?" Virgil asked.

"Like I need that kind of grief." He rubbed at his knee again.

"You hurt?"

"I'm old, is what I am. I've also lost almost half my patrol force to either death or serious injury." He stood and looked around and seemed to notice for the first time that a large section of corn had been bulldozed away. "What the hell are you guys up to out here, anyway?"

Virgil was going to give him the full explanation, but he had other things to discuss with the sheriff. "Trying to save my ass without destroying the Flatrock River, and the water table."

"The gas. It always comes back to money, doesn't it?"

Virgil wasn't quite sure how to respond, but the sheriff's question made him think about something else. "How well do you know the Salters?"

"The old man, or his son, the state legislator?"

"Both."

"Don't know the son much at all. In fact, don't think I'd know him if I passed him on the street."

"And his father?"

Holden closed his eyes in thought. "He's an odd one. Served two terms in the US Senate years ago. I'm sure you know that. That was back when he lived up in the city. When he built his estate down here in my county I didn't give it much thought. He keeps to himself. I haven't seen him in… well, I don't know how long."

"You said he was an odd one. What's odd about him?"

"You asking as a cop or a friend?"

Virgil laughed. "You saying we're friends now?"

Holden chuckled a little to himself. "Maybe I been a little too hard on you. The truth of it is, I admire you, Jones. You fight for what you believe in, you stand on principle, and you don't take no truck from anyone."

Virgil was surprised by Holden's statement. "What, I left you speechless or something?"

"Thank you," Virgil said. He wondered if Holden was being genuine, or trying to evade the question. Only one way to find out. "So, Salter. What makes him odd?"

"Maybe odd ain't quite the right word, but it's the only one my old and tired brain can think of right now. For starters, he's polite."

"That hardly makes him odd."

"I'll give you that. But it's like he goes out of his way to be polite. But it comes off as an act. You can see it in his eyes. He'll thank you for holding the door or passing the silverware or whatnot. But the look in his eyes when he does it makes you think he's politely asked for the silverware so he can stick the knife in your throat. He made his money in natural gas exploration, you know."

"Huh. I didn't know that."

"Why are you asking?"

"I'm not entirely sure," Virgil said. "His name came up, is all."

"Well, for what it's worth, he was tight with Cal Lipkins."

"Is that right?"

"Yup. Back when everyone started thinking they were going to make a mint by fracking their own farmland; it was Lipkins who ordered the geological survey."

"I know that, Ben. So what?"

"Ain't you listening to me? That's what Salter's company does. They aren't drillers, or refiners, or anything like that. They're explorers. They find the gas, and take a piece of the pie for doing so. Lots of profit and very little overhead, as I understand it."

Holden's comment made Virgil remember his phone call to Said less than two hours ago. He was at a meeting at Salter Enterprises in the city.

Virgil thought, *Son of a bitch.*

Holden stood and looked at Virgil. "I gotta get back to work. We've got a hell of a mess to tackle here."

Virgil stood with him, pleased with the way the conversation had gone. He'd been expecting another confrontation. "Look, Ben, I know we got off to a rough start a few months back."

Holden waved him away. "How about we both agree it was all your fault and move on?" He stuck out his hand.

Virgil laughed and shook hands with him. "I'm going to exercise my right to remain silent on that. Let me ask you one more thing, though."

"What's that?"

"What's the story with the Indian?"

"I don't have any idea," Holden said. "My best guess is he was hunting in your field and stumbled across everything that happened."

"Do you have anyone looking?"

"Nope. Not yet. Tell you the truth, I'm not sure how much time we'll put into it."

The statement surprised Virgil. "Why's that?"

"Because he killed the man responsible for killing one of my men and quite possibly crippling the other. For all I know, he saved my life."

Virgil wanted to be careful here, but still, it had to be said. "And how is that any different from what Carlos did to save Patty?"

Holden's response surprised him. "Not much, I guess. The problem for your *mechanic* is this: The computer spit out some information on him. He's part of the DACA program. I don't know what your politics are, and quite frankly, I don't want to know. But I do know the law. Once he's recovered from his gunshot wound—they said he's going to need surgery—he'll be deported. ICE will see to that, and hero to Patty Doyle or not, there's nothing that can be done to stop it."

"You might be right about that," Virgil said. "In fact, you probably are. But they also take mitigating circumstances into account. The way it was described to me, the Indian may have been a witness—the only witness—to what actually happened. Patty was out cold, and the man who attacked her is dead. If the Indian, whomever he is, saw what happened, it could have a profound impact on what happens to Carlos."

Holden thought about that for a moment. "We do have our fair share of Native Americans around here. But they're scattered here and about. Don't think it'll be easy to find him. It's probably too late, but maybe you could get your pilot to fly a quick search pattern. We might get lucky."

"I'll ask him right now," Virgil said.

"Isn't he the one everybody calls 'that Cool motherfucker?'" Then, "Don't look at me like that. It's been one of those days."

CHAPTER TWENTY-SIX

Virgil asked Cool to run a pattern. "I don't know how much good it'll do, but it's worth a shot."

Cool said he'd give it a look, and took Murton to help him spot. Once they were on their way, Virgil spent some time going over the sequence of events with Patty and Carl Johnson. Everything they told him matched up with what he already knew. Said sat quietly and listened, his face red, his body language tight, restless.

Virgil thanked Johnson and told him he could take off. Once he was gone they all sat down on the same trailer where Virgil and Sheriff Holden sat earlier and discussed everything that had happened in the field. "It's all my fault," Said said. "If I'd have stayed, none of this would have taken place."

"Maybe not, Rick," Virgil said. "But you can't blame yourself for every single thing that goes wrong. For all you know, if you'd have stayed, you'd be dead right now."

"That may or may not be true. But I can tell you this, when we start back up out here, I'm going to have security in place for the duration."

"Not a bad idea," Virgil agreed. "I can recommend someone if you need—"

"That won't be necessary." Said snapped it at him.

"You okay, Rick?"

"He doesn't do well when he's mad at himself," Patty said. Then she touched Virgil on the arm and said, "Speaking of being mad at one's self, am I in any trouble for what happened with the deputy or the sheriff?"

Virgil shook his head. "It's taken care of."

She smiled at him. "Thank you. Should I go apologize?"

Virgil thought about it. "I wouldn't. He was only doing his job. On many levels it's expected. It's a weird thing with cops, but many of them don't take apologies well, especially if they've played a part in what went wrong."

"If you say so. And listen, if it's all the same to you, I think I've had enough for one day. I've already given my statement, and since we don't have anyone out here who knows how to run the equipment, I'll start fresh with the core samples and a new crew tomorrow, if you don't mind."

"Of course I don't mind. In fact, if you tried to suggest otherwise, I'd have to throw you off my land. Go home. Get some rest. And call me before you come back. Tomorrow may be too soon."

"You worry as much as this one," Patty said, jerking a thumb at her uncle.

"You're probably right," Virgil said, some heaviness creeping into his voice. "Except that's not exactly what I meant. It might not be too soon for you, but three people died out here today, Patty, and others were seriously injured. And one of the killers—who also happens to be a material witness—is still on the loose. This entire area is probably going to be considered a crime scene for at least another day. Maybe longer."

"Okay. I hadn't thought of that. But Virgil, that Indian? He probably saved everyone who was still alive after Davis shot Deputy Cooper. That has to count for something."

"Justice isn't as blind as everyone likes to think it is, Patty. But the Indian, whomever he is, may come out of this okay…if we can find him. We'll have to wait and see. Right now he's considered a fugitive in a murder investigation. But it's a little complicated because he's also a witness to what Carlos did to save you, and the one who stopped Davis from killing anyone else. If we can find him and get him to talk, it may work out fine. A good lawyer could get the charges dropped by saying he did what he had to do in defense of another. It's the whole 'stand your ground law' scenario."

"Does Indiana have that law?" Patty asked.

"The short answer is yes, we do."

"Then why does the sound of your voice suggest the long answer isn't what we want to hear?" Said asked.

"Because the law is very clear cut when you're talking about certain situations, like inside your own home."

"What if you're not in your home?" Patty asked.

Virgil held up his hands. "Look, I'm not a lawyer…"

"But your job is to enforce the law," Patty said. "So you must have a reasonable understanding of what we're talking about."

Virgil nodded. "I do…mostly." He thought for a moment. "There's an old adage among cops: If you get into an altercation with someone on your front porch and you shoot and kill them, the best thing you could do is drag them inside before you dial 9-1-1. But dragging them inside after the fact would be a crime in itself. People have done it though. There are other considerations as well. You have to understand that the justification of using the stand your ground law can be limited if the defendant was engaged in illegal activities. As I understand it—if that's the case—then the defendant is not entitled to benefit from any provisions of the law."

"Who says he was doing anything illegal?"

Virgil didn't want to come across as dogmatic, but the question deserved an answer. "If nothing else, he was trespassing." He looked directly at Patty. "You said he had a bow and arrow. This is the Midwest, not the Wild West, so that means he was probably hunting. I doubt he had a hunting license, but even if we give him the benefit of the doubt and he did have a license, it isn't bow hunting season right now. So there are two, maybe three things against him, right there. And the prosecutor could—if he wanted to—use those things to rule against the use of that particular defense."

"So what you're saying is even though he saved me and Sheriff Holden and everyone else, he could be convicted of murder because he was *trespassing*?"

"That may be an oversimplification of the interpretation of the law and how it applies in this particular case. I'll say it again…I'm not a lawyer." Virgil wanted to get them off the subject, mostly because it was one of those situations where no matter what he thought or how he felt, it wouldn't change anything. The courts would have to decide. "Can you describe him? The Indian?"

Patty gave him a look. "Yeah. Close your eyes."

Virgil tipped his head. "Patty, c'mon."

"No, I'm serious. Close your eyes."

Virgil closed his eyes. "Okay, now what?"

"Picture a regular male Native American Indian. Not someone with war paint or a big feathered headdress or anything like that. Not a TV Indian, but a young man. He was shirtless, brown-skinned, wore jeans tucked into his boots, and had a turquoise belt. He had long, black, braided hair. He was maybe my age or a little older, but not by much. Can you picture him?"

Virgil opened his eyes and stuck his tongue in his cheek. "I guess."

"So…that's what he looked like."

"Would you recognize him if you saw him again?"

"Of course. He saved me from something I can barely stand to think about. But listen, let me ask you this: What about Carlos?"

"That's a little more complicated. He's here under the DACA program. Unless we can find the Indian, it's quite likely he'll be deported."

"Because he stopped a man from raping me?"

"Because he killed him."

"It was an accident," Patty said. "He didn't mean to hit him in the head. He was aiming for his side. Except when he fell, the wrench hit him in the head."

"And you know this how? You were unconscious."

"Carlos told me."

"And that's the problem. No witnesses. It's why we need to find the Indian," Virgil said. When they heard the sound of the helicopter's rotor blades, they all stood and watched Cool land at the far end of the clearing. Virgil turned and looked at Said. "There's something I'd like to speak with you about." He glanced at Patty as he spoke, an indication that he wanted some privacy.

Patty got the message and started to walk away. She only made it two small steps before she wobbled and started to go down. Virgil and Said both grabbed her before she fell.

"Sorry, I think I stood up a little too fast."

"No way, Patty," her uncle said. "We're getting you to the doctor for an examination. A head injury is nothing to screw around with."

"I'm fine, Uncle Rick."

Said looked at Virgil. "Can it wait?"

"Of course," Virgil said. "I'll call you. Let me know what the doctor says."

Said told him he would. He helped Patty into their vehicle and Virgil watched them drive away.

Once they were gone, he walked over to the helicopter to speak with Murton and Cool. "Anything?" Virgil asked.

Cool shook his head. "Waste of fuel. The corn is tall and thick and he could have gone in any direction. Even on foot he had a hell of a head start. Using the clearing here as a starting point and the distance he could have traveled on foot over a given period of time, when you apply the formula of Pi times the radius squared, we're talking about a search area—"

Virgil waved him off. "Yeah, yeah, I get it. A needle in a haystack."

Cool frowned at him. "Actually…no. It's not like that at all. Boy, you must have ducked out on your math classes back in the day. Anyhow, search area aside, we could have been right on top of him and not known it. If I fly low to get a better view it severely limits the search speed, and if I fly high enough to make it worthwhile—formulationally speaking—we couldn't see well enough into the corn. So, waste of time."

"I may have cut out on some math classes, but I can tell you this: 'formulationally' isn't a word."

Cool scratched at the back of his head. "Are you sure? It seems like it would be." He looked at Murton. "Is he right?"

Murton nodded, and Virgil said, "See?" A smug look on his face.

Cool shrugged his shoulders. "Whatever, Dude. Your smoking hot wife still has my blood running through her veins." He let his eyes fall to half-mast and put a little breath into his voice. "Sometimes at night, when I'm alone, I can feel her thinking about me. It's like we've got this unbreakable connection now…like two bodies with one soul, bound together by blood. Get me?"

"You need to spend more time working on your cop humor," Virgil said. "I saw that one coming from a mile away." Before Cool could get another jab in, Virgil's phone buzzed at him. Cora.

When he answered, she said, "The governor would like to respectfully request the use of his helicopter and pilot. He has a meeting this evening and wants to avoid the traffic. By the way, what happened to keeping a low profile?" Before Virgil could answer, she added, "Is Murton there?"

"Yeah, why?"

"Give him the phone, would you please?"

"Hold on." Virgil handed the phone to Murton. "It's Cora."

"What's she want?"

"I don't know, Murt. Why don't you ask her?"

Murton shook his head. "Nope. Tell her I'm busy."

Virgil thrust the phone at him. "Murt, this is the governor's chief of staff. She isn't someone you can ignore."

Murton sighed heavily, then took the phone. "Hello?"

Cora waited a half-second, then hung up. Murton thought he heard her laughing right before the line went dead.

Murton handed the phone back.

"What was that all about?"

"Cop humor…from more than a mile away." Then he looked at Cool. "She's a master."

ONCE THEY WERE READY TO GO, MURTON AND COOL climbed on board the helicopter. Virgil told them he'd be right there. He wanted to touch base with Sheriff Holden before they left. He also—no matter what he'd told Patty—wanted to apologize. "It was completely unprofessional of me, Ben…the way I had Cool land right in the middle of your crime scene. If I'm being honest with you, I'm not only embarrassed, I'm ashamed of myself." When Holden didn't respond, Virgil said, "This is the part where you say something like, 'Aw shucks, Jonesy, it don't matter none.'"

"Well, it does matter," Holden said, still annoyed by what Virgil had done, regardless of their earlier conversation. "And quit making fun of the way I talk. I'll spend some time thinking about accepting your apology, though."

"Fair enough," Virgil said. Then he added, "You really should start wearing your gun. You could have been killed."

Holden thought about it for a moment. "Or it could have been the very thing that saved my life…not having my gun on me. That Davis fellow—you weren't here, so you don't know—but I saw the look in his eyes. He was going to keep shooting until he was either out of bullets or out of targets. If I'd have had a weapon pointed at him, I probably wouldn't be standing here right now, I'd be lying next to Cooper at the morgue."

"Yeah…I've seen that look, so I know what you mean. Still."

Holden held his hands up. "Okay, okay, I'll think about it,

Betty. And I'll let you know when you can have your field back. Won't be tomorrow, but probably the day after."

"Good enough," Virgil said. Holden turned and walked away and Virgil walked over and climbed aboard the helicopter. Then he thought, *Betty?*

CHAPTER TWENTY-SEVEN

Virgil knew that Sandy was a little worn down with Huma gone, so once he was home later that evening he offered to make dinner for everyone. Wyatt was the easiest. He simply twisted the lid on a jar of Gerber's and dumped it in a plastic bowl. He'd put on some protective clothing and spoon it to him later, when they all sat down to eat. After that, things got a little more complicated. He was tending to the salad, chopping vegetables at the kitchen island, his hands busy with one task, his mind elsewhere when Jonas walked up and tugged at his sleeve.

"Not now, buddy. I've got a sharp knife in my hand."

Jonas shrugged and walked away. Two minutes later, when he glanced out the back window, Virgil saw the smoke billowing from his new gas grill. He threw the knife in the sink, ran outside, spun the gas knobs to the off position and tossed open the lid, but it was too late. The chicken was burnt well past the point of what any reasonable person would define as culinary edibility. He removed the charred meat and dumped it in the trash container by the back door.

Jonas was standing there, an appropriate childlike smirk on his face. "I tried to tell you."

Sandy took over and ended up ordering delivery pizza for dinner to compliment the salad. After everyone had eaten and had a good laugh about Virgil's grilling skills—though Virgil didn't find it all that amusing—they tackled the baths and bedtime stories, which included Wyatt's crying fits, and Jonas's multiple out-of-bed excursions. They decided Jonas was testing them. They also decided they'd failed the test, their self-imposed grade based on the simple fact that they had to resort to bribery to keep him in his room…a new video game if he stayed put. Failed grade or not, it worked.

When things finally quieted down and they had some time to themselves, Sandy went into the bedroom to change her clothes. Feeding Wyatt was like being a referee in a food fight. Her outfit was a mess. Virgil made a mental note to grab some Tyvek suits from the crime scene supply closet.

He went out on the back deck and lit a small fire in the deck's built-in fire pit. Even in summer, the nights were often cool, especially when the sky was clear and cloudless, as it was this evening.

"You know," Sandy said once she'd joined him outside, "I'm sure we could get you some grilling lessons. There must be a cooking class around here somewhere that could teach you how to, mmm, better manage your meat."

Virgil ran his tongue across his bottom teeth. "I manage my meat, just fine, thank you very much." Then he added, "I think one of the burners isn't firing properly. Or maybe the regulator isn't functioning quite right. I'll have someone come out and take a look at it."

"Yeah, that ought to do it," Sandy said, a hint of sarcasm sneaking into her voice. "So how was your day?" She'd changed into a long, white, almost see-through nightgown with thin shoulder straps and a low cut front. She sat with her feet in Virgil's lap.

"Oh, you know, the usual," Virgil said as he rubbed her feet. He didn't want to talk about work…the death and misery and destruction out in the cornfield. He changed the subject by saying, "You're beautiful."

"Thank you." She dug her toes into Virgil's thigh. "But really, tell me about your day."

"I'd rather talk about something else. Tell me about you and the boys. I've missed you. All of you."

"I've missed you too, boyfriend. Why do you think I want to talk about something other than my day? I can't get the theme song of Barney the dinosaur out of my head."

Virgil chuckled. "That's not good."

"No, it isn't," she said, her voice taking on a monosyllabic tone. "It just keeps going and going. It's about to drive me nuts."

"When that happens to me, I usually think of a different song, then sing that to myself. It helps. Sometimes."

"You know what else I can't get out of my head?"

"Tell me."

She paused for a few seconds, then said, "It's cool."

The problem was, Virgil *had* been thinking about his day —not actively, but the thoughts were simmering in the back of his mind—along with everything that was happening… how all the disparate parts of the investigation were somehow connected, yet the connections weren't clear to him, at least not in any meaningful way. The sky was clear and full of stars, and the temperature had dropped a few degrees. He could feel the difference in the short time they'd been outside. So when Sandy said, 'its cool,' he didn't see it coming… though he should have. "You want me to get you a blanket?"

Sandy looked away and stared at nothing as she spoke.

"No, I don't want a blanket. I don't think you understand. I'm not cold. In fact, I'm kind of hot. I'm speaking about Cool, as in Richard Cool. I love you, Virgil, and I always will. I know you know that. Except, well, I don't quite know how to explain this because I don't want to hurt you, but ever since he saved me with that blood transfusion, it's like we have this unbreakable connection…like we're two bodies sharing one soul. It's like we're bound together by blood. When I think about him—and I know this is going to sound crazy—I can feel him thinking about me." She tipped her head back and closed her eyes. "God, he's so damned cool." She opened one eye and peeked at her husband. "Get me?"

Virgil had not only taken the bait, he'd practically swallowed the entire tackle box. "Very funny. That's, like, the most hilarious thing I've heard all day."

Sandy started to laugh. "I knew you'd appreciate it."

"Uh-huh. When did he call?"

She was laughing so hard she had trouble getting the words out. "When you were…when you were out…trying to…"

"Trying to what?"

"Trying to weld the chickens together. He said to tell you, and I quote, 'A mile away, my ass.'"

"Maybe it's time to change our phone number," Virgil said. Then he stood, bent over and picked up his wife and tossed her over his shoulder. He slapped her on the ass for good measure.

Sandy howled with delight. "Virgil, put me down. You're going to wake the boys."

"You're the one making all the noise."

"What are you doing?"

"I'm taking you inside."

"Oh yeah? What for?"

"To prove that I know how to manage my meat."
"Is it going to be hot?"
"It won't be Cool, that's for sure."
"Says you. I'll still be thinking about him, you know."
"We'll see about that. Prepare to brace yourself, Betty."
"*Betty*? Who's Betty?"
"I have no idea," Virgil said. "I really don't."

Afterwards, Virgil took a shower and even though the hour was late, the encounter with Sandy…her joy, enthusiasm and playfulness, not to mention the shower, all left him wide awake. He toweled off and when he went into the bedroom he found his wife sound asleep. He kissed her cheek, covered her with the sheets, then dressed and went back outside and walked out to the pond and laid down in the grass next to his father's cross, his hands behind his head, thoughts of the day's events swirling through his mind.

He knew if he went back inside he would eventually fall asleep. Going to sleep wasn't the problem though. It was the thoughts that took control of his brain when he woke that he wanted to avoid. But what was he supposed to do? Stay awake for days on end?

"That won't work," Mason said.

Virgil sat partway up, leaned on an elbow and looked at his father's cross. Mason sat Indian-style in the grass, next to the cross, facing his son.

"Exactly how much of my mind can you read?"

"None of it," Mason said. "Why would you ask me that?"

"Because of these thoughts I have when I wake up in the morning. Bell called it a disassociated state. I was thinking that if I didn't go to sleep, I wouldn't have them anymore."

"That won't work."

"I know. You already said that. That's what I thought you were talking about."

"Nope. I was talking about what Sandy said."

"What?"

"You know, about maybe taking some grilling lessons. Most people have a multitude of particular skill sets, Virg. Grilling doesn't seem to be among yours."

"So I've been told. Plenty of times, by the way."

"Okay. I wasn't being critical. It was simply an observation." They were both quiet for a beat. Then Mason said, "Have you heard from Delroy or Huma yet?"

Virgil shook his head. "No, not yet. I'm surprised you have to ask. I thought spying on me was sort of your hobby or something."

"I don't spy on you, Son. That'd be more of a sublunary sort of activity. I do notice things, though."

"Do you know where he is?"

Mason seemed to consider the question. "Not exactly. It's more of a sense. But as a point of fact, I think you do."

"I hate to tell you this—your astute observations about my skill sets aside—but I have no idea where they are."

"I think you do. No, no, hear me out on this. Remember when Jonas asked if he could talk to his father and what Sandy told him? That he had to listen with his heart?"

"Yeah."

"So if you're wondering where Delroy and Huma are, stop thinking with your head and use your heart, Son."

Virgil thought about it for a few minutes but didn't get anywhere. "I don't want to come across like a dunce, but I'm stumped."

Mason pointed at his heart, his finger very close to the scar left by the bullet that ended his life. "They're in love,

Virg. And Delroy is doing everything he can to protect the woman he loves from harm. If you were Delroy, where would you take her? In other words, where is the one place he knows better than anywhere else?"

"You're saying they're in Jamaica?"

"It seems likely, don't you think?"

"I guess it does." Virgil shook his head.

"What is it?" Mason asked.

"I wish he'd call. I need to speak to him. The threat doesn't exist anymore."

"Doesn't it?"

"No. The man who attacked and tried to kill Huma is dead."

"Is he?"

Virgil felt the all too familiar frustration begin to scramble across his brain. It was an actual physical sensation, like ants crawling across his dura mater. "Yes, Dad, he is. His body is at the county morgue."

"Remind me again, will you?"

"Remind you of what?"

"What the 'M' stands for in MCU. It's the opposite of minor, if I'm not mistaken."

"Forget the grilling class. Maybe I should take one on cryptology instead."

"Huma may or may not be safe, Virgil. I'd go as far to say that she probably is. The fact that the man who tried to hurt her is dead has little to do with it."

"Want to explain that?"

"You know as much as I do."

"I find that hard to believe. But I do know this: The longer Delroy and Huma stay missing, the harder it's going to be to persuade Miles, not to mention the prosecutor, that they had nothing to do with Dobson's death. They disappeared after his car was used to kill the man who we suspect was responsible for Huma's attack."

"Let me ask you something," Mason said. "Did you enjoy our family dinners when you were a kid?"

Virgil sat upright. His arm was starting to ache. "I may need grilling lessons, but your segue skills could use a little spit and polish. In any event, to answer your question, yes, of course I did. They were the best part of my day."

"Mine too," Mason said, something of a melancholy look on his face. "I always sort of wondered if you and Murt found the lessons of our conversations boring, or maybe…"

"Dad, we loved them. The debates, forcing us to look at something from different points of view; we were fascinated with the process and what it taught us. I think in many ways it helped shape us into who we are today. Except maybe you should have included showing me how to use the grill."

"Using a grill is simple, Virg. It requires only one thing. You simply have to pay attention. And that, Son, is one of the things you are good at. Very good. Usually."

"What do you mean, usually?"

"I mean you usually get it. But sometimes you don't. In fact, if you'd been paying proper attention, you'd know that something is happening right now. It's been happening during our entire conversation. Except you haven't noticed."

Virgil looked at his father. "What? What haven't I noticed?"

"Virgil, come to bed."

When Virgil turned he saw Sandy on the deck, her hands resting on the railing, her nightgown billowing softly in the evening breeze, the outline of her bare body backlit by the interior lights of the house. He stood from the grass, and when he spoke, he still had his back to the cross. "I think I'm going to go inside now, Dad."

Mason laughed, and the sound brought a measure of joy to Virgil's heart.

"With good reason, I'd say," Mason replied.

Virgil still had his eyes on Sandy, her blonde hair, her unassuming seductive pose. "But before I do, tell me this one thing, will you? What was it I missed during our conversation?"

When Mason didn't answer, Virgil peeled his eyes away from Sandy and glanced back across his shoulder.

His father was gone.

CHAPTER TWENTY-EIGHT

WHEN MORNING CAME, VIRGIL WOKE FROM A DISTURBING dream. He couldn't remember all of it. In fact, the only part he could remember was the falling at the very end of the dream. Except falling wasn't quite right. He wasn't in a classic free-fall dream, his arms and legs flailing away as the ground rose up to meet him. It was more of a slide off a steep hillside, or perhaps even an actual slide, much like the kind found in an amusement park where you sat on a piece of cloth made from burlap and barreled down a giant slope before coming safely to a stop at the end. But in the dream Virgil was going down the slide feet first, on his stomach, his hands seeking purchase of anything that might stop his descent. He could actually feel his body against the structure, whatever it was. As he slid downward, he noticed that the slide or hill or whatever surface area on which he rode was covered—painted—with giant words and phrases. The problem was, he was moving with such velocity that he couldn't make out what any of the words or phrases were. It was all a giant blur as he went whizzing downward, faster and faster.

He sat on the side of the bed and closed his eyes, willing

himself to remember, to somehow replay the dream in slow motion so he could see the words and perhaps discover what meaning they held, if any.

But it didn't work. Everything was a blur and the harder he thought about the dream, the faster it all faded away. He finally gave up and got out of bed and dressed in his running gear. His thoughts were a mess, partly because of the dream, and partly because of the way his mornings now unfolded…a new normal of jumbled mental imagery that filled his head and made no sense to him whatsoever. The picture in his mind was similar to that of an old fashioned reeled projector, one where the film sockets had slipped the gears and the scenes—meant to be crisp and clear—now flickered diagonally, the broken pictures half out of frame, leaving a giant white space on the screen of his memory.

Sandy was still asleep, and despite how he felt, he had enough mental acuity to check on the boys who were also—thank God—still sleeping. He stretched for a moment, getting his body loose, mostly unaware of what he was doing. He walked outside, then he made his way down the drive and out toward the road.

It was just past six-thirty.

He was only halfway out to the road, his body operating mainly on autopilot when the limousine turned into his drive and stopped at the entrance. For a moment, Virgil wondered if it was real, or if it was part of his disassociated state. He'd stopped walking when the car turned in, but as it sat there at the end of the drive, Virgil found himself moving forward, almost against his will, as if he were being drawn to the car by an unseen force. Somewhere in the recesses of his functional brain, where his thought process was clear and unabated he thought, *I should have my gun.*

The limo wasn't a stretch version. It was a black town car,

its windows tinted as dark as the vehicle's paint. The sun shone bright and reflected off the front windshield, obscuring the interior view and the driver of the car. But when Virgil got closer, the angle of the windshield walked the sun's glare off the glass and a portion of the interior became visible. He noticed the blue flasher mounted on the backside of the rearview mirror. He saw the driver, dressed in a business suit, a pin with the state seal of Indiana attached to his lapel, identifying him to those in the know as a state trooper. A uniformed trooper would draw too much attention to the vehicle and its passenger. The trooper nodded at him, a single, slow, almost imperceptible tip of his head.

When Virgil reached the back door of the vehicle the window lowered quietly and with such speed it seemed to just disappear. But Virgil knew because his mind was still not fully engaged, it wasn't trickery...it was simply quality vehicular engineering.

"Good morning, Sunshine," the governor said, his eyes bright, his expression open and warm. He popped the door and stepped out. "It looks like I've interrupted your morning run."

Virgil stepped back to make room for the governor to exit the vehicle. "I was, uh, just getting started, actually."

The governor closed the door, then gave Virgil the once-over. "You okay, there, Jonesy? You look a little pallid. Whey-faced, as my mother used to say, God bless her." Without waiting for an answer, he rapped a knuckle on the driver's side glass. When the driver lowered the window, the governor said, "We won't be too long." He never took his eyes off Virgil.

The trooper said, "Yes, Sir," then looked at Virgil. "Detective."

The governor appeared to have a new detail driver, one

Virgil had not yet met, so he simply tipped his head at him before turning his attention back to the governor. He raised an eyebrow at him.

"I'm not dressed for a workout and, as a point of fact, I was done with mine by five. Early-bird, the worm, and all that. You up for a walk, maybe a little conversation, sleepyhead?"

"Sure," Virgil said. He wondered if the governor heard the uncertainty in his voice. If he did, he didn't say so.

Virgil and the governor weren't the only ones getting an early start to their day. In fact, Wu and Nicky Pope had been up all night, working their system, checking their facts, and digging into every database they had access to. As for the ones they didn't, it was only a matter of time.

"You're rusty, Wu," Nicky said to his partner. "I could have been in hours ago."

"You can have it fast, or you can have it right. Wu want right. That way, we can avoid the traps and they won't know where to find us."

Lola Ibarra walked into the systems room—a converted extra bedroom on the main level of the mansion.

Wu looked at her and said. "Nicky is doing it again," he told her.

"Doing what?" She carried a tray that contained a pot of coffee, two cups, and a very large bowl of sugar.

"He give Wu the chop-chop."

She set the tray down and looked at Nicky. "You know how much he hates the chop-chop, Nicholas."

"I think he secretly likes it," Nicky said.

"You are mistaken," Wu said.

"Wu are too," Nicky said back to him.

Lola knew they were the best of friends, but she wasn't in the mood for their banter. She looked at the giant monitors on the wall. They were currently blank. Nicky and Wu were using their desktop monitors. "Enough of this." She snapped it at them, which was completely out of character for her. "Tell me. You have found more information on my Carlos?"

Nicky pushed his wheeled chair away from the workstation and slid across the marble floor before using his feet as brakes to stop next to the table with the coffee. "Not yet, Lola. But we're close. Maybe a few more hours."

Lola looked around the room and waved her hands in the air. "I do not understand all this." The anxiety and stress in her voice was almost electric. The bags around her eyes had grown heavier by the hour, ever since they'd heard the news of Carlos's injury and subsequent arrest. She'd gotten no sleep and Nicky was genuinely concerned that if she didn't get some rest, or some good news, she might have a nervous breakdown. She looked and sounded that bad. At one point in the evening—maybe six hours ago or so—he even tried to get her to smoke some weed to calm her down.

"I am not good with the Chess," she'd said.

They'd heard about what happened to Carlos not through some sophisticated system of code and backdoor entries into any federal, state or municipal law enforcement database. They heard about it the old-fashioned way, through Google Alerts. Nicky had set one up shortly after they arrived in Jamaica, and if the name Carlos Ibarra ever popped up anywhere online, Google would let them know. They had false positives to deal with—even Google wasn't perfect—but yesterday the alerts had been genuine, and they were popping up all over the net in a very big way.

The first ping came in from a local Indiana newspaper in

Shelbyville. The actual story didn't make the paper—it'd been too late in the day—but their website had the incident up as their lead, above the fold. It was picked up by the AP, then the Star got it, and before long they had so many alerts coming at them that Nicky wanted to delete the whole thing. Wu talked him out of it.

"Let's ignore them for now. We'll get what we can once we're in the hospital's database."

"Most hospitals have hardened their firewalls ever since they've become targets of ransomware," Nicky said. "And it appears they've done a pretty good job of it."

Wu clapped his hands together. "But not good enough. Look at this," he said, pointing at his monitor. "I found our way in." Then with a bit of satisfaction: "Couple of hours, Wu's ass."

"Show me," Nicky said as he slid his chair back into place at the worktable.

Lola walked to the table and leaned over their shoulders. "I would like to see as well."

Wu punched a few keys and mirrored his monitor to one of the large screens on the wall. "Up there," he said, tipping his head toward the monitor without taking his eyes off the screen.

Lola spent a few minutes watching the code scroll across the giant monitor. She turned and looked back at Nicky and Wu, their fingers flying across the keys. When she turned her attention back to the monitor on the wall, all she saw were layers of code, some of it in red, most of it in green or white. To her, it was a jumble of letters and numbers and symbols that meant nothing. "I do not understand," she said, pointing at the screen. "This is all, mmm, what is the word? Gibbery?"

"Gibberish," Nicky said. "But it is exactly what we were looking for."

"It is not what I was looking for," Lola said. "I want to actually *see* Carlos."

"Now that we're in their system we should be able to do that," Nicky said. "Wu?"

"Wu can do. One moment, please." He tapped out a few more keystrokes, then pointed at the other giant monitor on the wall. "There. That is Carlos, no?"

Lola let out a gasp, then walked over and got close to the monitor. Wu had tapped into the hospital's video security system and once they had Carlos's room number, he simply entered that information into his search query. With that, the security camera in the ceiling showed Carlos as he laid in the hospital bed, his injured leg heavily bandaged, an IV line taped to the back of his hand. The other hand was cuffed to the side rail of the bed. "Yes, that is my boy," Lola said. "He is restrained like a common *el prisionero*."

Nicky turned in his chair and took Lola's hand. "That's because he is a prisoner, Lola. We talked about this, remember? The police arrested him for murder."

She pulled her hand away. "I do not believe the *policía*. They are liars. Carlos would never do such a thing. He is kind and caring and doesn't have a mean bone in his body. He works hard, he is honest, and he is as gentle and quiet as a holy rodent."

Nicky knew Lola was upset, and he didn't want to seem insensitive. He choked on his coffee trying not to laugh. When he finally got control of his breathing he said, "Sorry. Went down the wrong tube, there. Lola, let us see what we can find out, okay? It won't be long now. We'll figure something out, I promise."

Lola Ibarra looked at the image of her son handcuffed to the hospital bed. Then she turned and looked at Nicky. "Say this again to me."

"I've never let you down before, Lola. I'm not going to start now. You always told me I was like a son to you." He pointed at the big screen on the wall. "That makes Carlos my…" Nicky had been working on his Spanish, picking up little bits here and there, mostly for Lola's sake. "That makes him *mi hermano*…my brother. We'll figure something out. I promise."

Lola gave the monitor a hard stare. Nicky thought if he didn't do or say something, she'd stare at the screen until she went blind. "Say, Lola, why not take Linda and Nichole to the market and get us all something to eat? You guys could use the distraction and we could use the privacy."

Lola knew Nicky was right on both counts. She understood little of what they did with their computers, but she did know that it took a great deal of concentration. She didn't like the idea of being away, even if only for a short while. On the other hand, if it helped Nicky and Wu accomplish their tasks, she'd do it.

"Very well. We will go to the market and gather what we need for breakfast."

"Try not to worry, Lola. We're doing everything we can." Lola thanked them, then walked out of the room. Once she was gone Wu looked at Nicky. "Holy rodent?"

"Church mouse," Nicky said.

CHAPTER TWENTY-NINE

Virgil and the governor walked up the drive and around to the backyard. They eventually found themselves next to Mason's cross. The governor looked across the water at the tree line on the far side of the pond, then glanced back at Virgil's house. Neither of them had said a word during their walk and Virgil had the impression that the governor was waiting for a prompt. Or maybe not. Either way, Virgil said, "Mac?"

The governor looked down at the cross, then ran his hand across its smooth surface, his fingers gliding over the outline of Mason's name, the lettering carved into the cross by Virgil after he'd been forced to cut the tree when a small tornado snapped it in half. "The very first time I was ever here, at your home, was at that party you and Sandy hosted. It was both the best backyard party I'd ever been to and one of the worst days of my life."

"Mine too," Virgil said. Then he added, "Ed." It was almost a whisper.

The governor nodded. "Yes, Edward. But before all that, even in the wake of Bradley's death, I sat down here by the pond with Cora." He tipped his head at the cross. "This was still a tree. And though Cora and I were talking shop, working out the optics and the politics of it all, I was having a good time. That female trooper dancing with Delroy…"

"Mac?"

The governor looked at Virgil for a long time before he spoke. "You'll forgive the question, but people talk, you know?"

"What question is that, Mac?"

The governor ran his hand over the cross again. "They say he speaks to you. That you have actual conversations."

Virgil didn't answer right away. He turned and looked out across the water. "I guess you could say I'm a progressionist in the strictest form of its interpretation."

"I'll tell you something, Jonesy: I admire the way you pull out your vocabulary every once in a while. It's just enough to let people know you have a full and complete grasp of the English language. It's as if you're as comfortable talking to someone on the street as you would be in a lecture hall."

"Thank you."

The corners of the governor's eyes crinkled a bit and he said, "I understand you could bone up on your math skills though."

When Virgil looked at him, the governor kept his elbows close and raised his hands, palms up. "What can I say? Cool said you tried to compare the calculation for determining the area of a circle against, what was it? Hay bales or something?"

Virgil pointed a finger at him. "Now you're messing with me. We were discussing search areas and I compared what he said to a needle in a haystack. I was simply trying to move the conversation along, but he thought I didn't know the formula."

"Yes, well, who cares what other people think? Am I right?"

"I guess so," Virgil said, unsure if the governor was speaking of mathematical equations, or the conversations he had with his dead father. What he said next, though, was unmistakable.

"Cora doesn't know I'm out here, Jonesy."

Virgil thought about the implications of the governor's statement. "And you'd like it to remain that way." It wasn't a question.

The governor nodded at him. "For now, if it's not too much to ask."

"So far neither of us has said anything that seems worthy of mentioning." Then, with a touch of sarcasm: "To anyone."

The governor chuckled. "You certainly know how to tee it up, don't you? Listen, this isn't the reason I came out here this morning, but before I forget, I'd like to invite you and Sandy to the mansion for dinner Sunday evening. Would that be all right with you?"

Both men still faced the pond, their backs to the house. When Sandy walked up behind them with two mugs of coffee, it startled them both. "Thought you guys might like a cup of Jamaica's finest."

They both spun around at the sound of her voice. She was still dressed in the same nightgown she'd worn to bed the previous evening, along with a pair of Virgil's Timberland's, the laces untied and flopping in the grass.

"My goodness," the governor said, his hand on his chest. "You do know how to get someone's heart rate going."

Virgil wasn't sure if the governor was referring to the way Sandy was dressed, or the fact that she'd surprised them. He suspected the former because he found the contrariety between the nightgown and the boots oddly alluring.

Sandy smiled at the governor then looked at Virgil. "So I've been told." She handed the mugs to both men. "Am I interrupting?"

"Not at all," the governor said. He took a sip of his coffee, then glanced up quickly. "My God, this might be the best cup of coffee I've ever tasted. It's absolutely fantastic."

"Straight from the Blue Mountains of Jamaica," Sandy said. "I'm surprised you've never had it before."

"I'll have some ordered before the day is out, I assure you." He took another sip, this one much longer.

"Don't bother," Virgil said. "We get regular shipments at the bar. I'll have some sent over."

The governor didn't respond, as if having Virgil send the coffee had been his intention all along.

Virgil looked at Sandy. "The governor would like us to join him for dinner at his place Sunday evening."

Sandy tipped her head and ran her fingers through her hair at the top of her scalp, the way women do. "Really? Some sort of formal affair?"

The governor shook his head. "No, no. Nothing like that. Very informal, as a matter of fact. Blue jeans and T-shirts… you know, the way Virgil here is always dressed."

"Why does everyone always pick on my clothing? I like to be comfortable."

The governor looked at Sandy. "He's very sensitive in the morning." Before anyone could respond: "So? Sunday evening then?"

"Well, we don't have anything scheduled," Sandy said. Then a look of disappointment drifted across her face and the governor caught it.

"What is it?"

"I guess you probably know this, but our nanny, Huma, is, um, unavailable at the moment. We've come to rely on her so heavily that we don't have anyone to watch the kids. I could ask Becky, but I know she's got her hands full. I'm sorry."

The governor waved her off. "So bring the boys along. I love kids. Plus, I've got a houseful of staff who are always running around trying to look busy, even though half of them don't have anything to do."

"Are you sure?" Virgil asked.

"If I wasn't sure, Jonesy, I wouldn't have said anything. Now that I know, I insist you bring them."

"You can't deny the insist," Virgil said.

"No, you can't," Sandy said dryly.

"Sounds like an inside joke," the governor said. "Anyway, we'll throw some burgers on the grill, have a few drinks and a nice little chat. The kids will be fine. In fact, I've got a game room that's so full of fun stuff you'll have Jonas begging to spend the night. Besides, none of it ever gets used. What do you say?" He swallowed the rest of his coffee and set the mug on top of the cross. Sandy stepped forward quickly and removed it. The governor didn't seem to notice.

Virgil and Sandy looked at each other. They both shrugged and that was all the governor needed. He turned on his thousand-watt smile and said, "Wonderful. How's six o'clock sound?"

"That'll be fine," Sandy said. "But don't let Virgil near the grill."

The governor raised his eyebrows. "Really? Why's that?"

Virgil gave Sandy a dry look.

"Trust me," she said.

The light never left the governor's eyes, but the tone of his voice changed, and the flavor of his words were official and serious. He looked directly at Sandy when he spoke. "I do. Completely. In ways you couldn't imagine."

SANDY WAS GOING TO ASK FOR AN EXPLANATION OF THE governor's statement, but she sensed the energy of the conversation had changed, so she let it go, excusing herself to go take care of the boys. "Wyatt will be up any minute," she said.

The governor told her goodbye and spent a few seconds watching her walk away. Then he tossed his arm around Virgil's shoulder and directed him back toward the front drive. Virgil let himself be steered along, and eventually said, "Mac? You mentioned there was something else."

"Hmm. I did, didn't I?"

"What was it?"

Virgil waited for his response as they walked. They made it all the way out to the town car before the governor spoke. He opened the door, climbed in and made the window disappear again. "It'll keep. We'll discuss it over dinner. I'm looking forward to it, Detective." The window reappeared, the trooper gave Virgil another nod, and the town car backed out of the driveway and made its way down the gravel road. Virgil stood and watched until the car was out of sight. Mac rarely addressed him by his formal title when they were alone. He knew something was up, but he didn't know what.

DELROY HELD HUMA'S HAND AS THEY WALKED ALONG THE main drag of Lucea, taking in the sounds and aromas of his native land. They stopped in various shops, overpaid for items they needed and others they did not. When they exited one of the shops, they turned to their right and walked past a fruit stand.

"What the heck is that?" Huma said, pointing to an unusual-looking piece of fruit displayed front and center on the vendor's table.

Delroy grinned at her. The piece of fruit Huma had pointed to had what most anyone would describe as a very unsightly appearance. It was oddly shaped…lumpy, like a giant egg with tumors, its coloring a garish green and yellow, its rind rough and wrinkled. Delroy pulled two dollars out of his pocket and paid the vendor before selecting two from the basket. He looked at Huma and said, "Grab some napkins, there. We're going to need them."

Huma looked at the fruit and said, "Oh, Delroy, I'm not really very hungry. I was simply wondering what they were."

Delroy sat down at the table next to the vendor's stand and began pulling away the outer skin. "It called Jamaican Ugly fruit. Easy to see why, huh?"

"What does it taste like? Because if it's anything like it looks, then I really don't want any."

"Uh-huh." Delroy had peeled the rind away and pulled off a chunk of fruit. The juice ran across his fingers and down his wrist. He held it up to Huma and said, "Try this, you."

Huma took a bite of the fruit and when the taste hit her tongue she opened her eyes wide, the orange pulpy citrus unlike anything she'd ever experienced. "Oh my God, that's delicious. What is it?"

"Delroy already say. Jamaican Ugly fruit."

"No, no, I mean what *kind* of fruit?"

Delroy laughed. "Ugly. But tasty too, no?"

Huma gave him a look and he smiled at her. "It's a

hybrid, native to the island. A combination of grapefruit, orange, and tangerine."

Huma grabbed the other one and began to peel.

"Thought you weren't hungry, you?"

"It seems I've suddenly got my appetite back. Grab some more napkins, will you?"

"Sure." Delroy turned in his chair to grab a few more napkins and that's when he saw her. Her hair was different... she'd colored it brown with streaks of varying shades of dark blond and red, but he knew who the woman was. Then, as was often the case when someone is staring at another without their knowledge, a little psychic connection was made. The woman turned her head and locked eyes with Delroy.

Neither of them could pretend they hadn't recognized each other, so she walked over and played the only hand she had. Huma was so busy enjoying her fruit, she failed to notice the woman's approach until she stood right next to them at the table. Delroy, being the gentleman he was, stood as she approached.

"Hello handsome," Nichole Pope said. "Fancy meeting you here." She looked at Huma and said, "Who might this be?"

"I never imagined I'd see you again," Delroy said. Then he remembered his manners. "This is Huma Moon. Huma, this is—"

"An old friend," Nichole said quickly. "I'm sure Delroy here will give you all the details. I hope when you hear them you'll take it all with a grain of salt, so to speak." She turned her attention back to Delroy. "Virgil with you?"

Delroy shook his head. "He back in da states. Huma and I on someting of an adventure."

Nichole laughed. "That's one way of looking at it. From what I hear, you're on the run."

"What else you hear, you?"

Nichole ignored the question. "I wish things hadn't turned out the way they did. Virgil...well, he thinks I'm the devil reincarnate, doesn't he?"

"I don't know what it is he tink, me."

Nichole raised her eyebrows. "Trouble in paradise?"

Huma stood and placed her hand in the crook of Delroy's arm. "I'm sorry, I didn't catch your name?"

"No, you didn't, did you?" She looked at Delroy. "I liked you from the moment we met, Delroy. Tell Virgil I said hello, would you? Huma, a pleasure, I'm sure."

She turned and walked away. She was around the corner and gone before Delroy could decide what he should do, if anything.

"Who was that?" Huma asked.

"I'm not sure. I don't tink she even know. Her name was Nichole Pope."

"Was?"

They sat back down and Delroy told her the story.

Huma thought for a long time before she spoke. "Is she a threat to us while we're here?"

Delroy shook his head. "I don't tink so, me. But it hard to tell with dat woman. There's more than one person living inside her skin."

"What about Virgil or Sandy and the kids? Would they be in any danger?"

"Not while she's here. We should probably change hotels, though, us."

"Or maybe we should go home," Huma said.

"Not yet. Maybe see if we can find someting out before

we do. Delroy have people he could ask, but it wouldn't do much good without a picture."

Huma picked up her phone from the table and handed it to Delroy. She'd captured a perfect picture of Nichole. "Will this work?"

CHAPTER THIRTY

VIRGIL DECIDED TO SKIP HIS RUN AND INSTEAD HELP SANDY with the boys before showering and leaving for work. As he was getting ready to go, Sandy said, "What do you think that was all about?"

"I honestly don't know. Yesterday in Cora's office Ron and I got into it over Delroy and Huma's whereabouts and the evidentiary value he was placing on Delroy's car and the shoes. You know how Ron is…A plus B, equals C. Anyway, Mac was there and after Ron left he made a comment…something about the argument being worth the price of admission. I wasn't thinking and sort of jumped down his throat."

"And that got us a dinner invite at the Governor's mansion?"

"Not exactly. After Mac left, Cora told me something I didn't know. She said no matter what Ron thinks, she and Mac both believe that Delroy wasn't involved in Dobson's death, and that they both are willing to back me up on that, based on nothing more than pure friendship."

"What about the evidence?"

"The evidence will come together, eventually. It always

does. Mimi is already halfway there. Anyway, Cora and Mac simply wanted me to know that I had their support. Mac in particular. And not only as my boss, but more importantly as his friend."

"So what happened?"

"I apologized to Mac, he accepted, and that was it. Then he showed up here this morning and asked us to dinner. But…"

"But what?"

"There was something else. Something he wasn't saying. I think he was about to tell me right before you came out with the coffee. When I asked him about it, he said it could wait until we met for dinner. He told me Cora didn't know he was out here and he didn't want her to know."

"Why would that be?"

"I don't know."

"Maybe it wasn't anything too important."

Virgil shook his head. "I doubt it. Cora said something to me when she was telling me to go and apologize to Mac. She said something to the effect of, 'this thing is bigger than a hit and run.' She also made a vague reference to a guy named Salter. Ever heard of him?"

"The legislator or his father, the former US senator?"

Virgil rolled his eyes.

"Please don't do that." Sandy said.

"Okay, okay. So…you've heard of them." When Sandy nodded he continued. "The elder Salter…Roger, owns a company called Salter Enterprises. His son, Ken is a part of it as well. They're a geological surveying company, and they happen to be the same company Cal Lipkins called when the Co-op members started thinking about fracking instead of farming."

Sandy thought about that for a moment. "It could be coincidental."

"Yeah, it could. And maybe it is. Except when everything went to shit out there—"

"*Virgil.*" Sandy tilted her head toward Jonas, who was sitting at the kitchen table, eating a bowl of cereal.

Jonas said, "Swear jar." He never even looked up from the bowl.

Virgil said, "Sorry buddy." He reached into his pocket for a dollar...that was the deal. A buck a swear. Two bucks if it was the F-bomb. Virgil didn't have any cash on him. "I'll have to owe it."

Jonas got up from the table and got a piece of paper and a pencil from the junk drawer. He wrote an amount on the paper, folded it in half, then gave it to Virgil to put in the jar because he couldn't reach it without standing on a chair, and even then it was a stretch. Virgil took the note and glanced at it before he put it in the jar. When he saw the amount, he said, "Hey, what's this? It's supposed to be a buck a swear. That's the rule."

"That's right," Jonas said.

"Then why does this say two dollars?"

"Gotta pay the vig, Dad."

"Vig?"

"Yeah. As in vigorish."

"Who taught you that?"

"Uncle Murt. Who else? You've got until the end of the week. Then it's four. Week after that it's eight. Week after that it's—"

"Okay, okay, I get it. Jesus Christ, I'm gonna go broke."

Jonas shook his head, like maybe he was dealing with the slow student, got up from his chair and took another piece of paper from the drawer. Sandy had her hand over her mouth, her shoulders shaking. Eventually she said, "Maybe we should finish this in the other room before you wind up bankrupting us or getting kneecapped or something."

They went into the family room. "You were saying?"

"I don't remember," Virgil said. "I got interrupted by the swear fuzz."

"You were telling me about Salter Enterprises."

Virgil nodded rapidly. "Yeah, yeah." He lowered his voice to almost a whisper. "Okay, so when everything went to shit out in the field…" Virgil heard the chair scrape on the kitchen floor and flapped his arms. He hollered into the kitchen. "It doesn't count if you're eavesdropping."

"I don't make the rules," Jonas said. "I just live with them."

Virgil looked down at the floor for a moment, and when he spoke, he chose his words with care. "When everything went *bad* in the field, I needed to find Said. He was in a meeting in the city. Patty gave me the number and when I called I discovered his meeting was at Salter Enterprises. Said is using the same company Lipkins used for the survey."

Sandy thought about it for a few seconds. "How many of these types of companies are there in Indy?"

"Geo survey companies that specialize in natural gas discovery? I don't know. I'm going to have Becky check before I talk to Said about it." Virgil was getting wound up, his voice a little louder. "I'll tell you this: It's either one hell of a big coincidence, or Said has some explaining to do."

Virgil heard the chair scrape, then a few seconds later Jonas said, "Mom, we're almost out of paper."

"See?" Sandy said.

"See what?"

"This is why you should tell me about your day when I ask."

Virgil kissed his wife. "That's it. I'm outta here."

"Where are you going?"

"Right now? I'm going to have a talk with Uncle Murt. I don't mind the swear jar. In fact, I think it's a good idea. But the whole vig thing is utter bullshit."

From the kitchen: "Mom, where's the pencil sharpener?"

Virgil ran.

HE GOT THE CALL AS HE WAS TURNING INTO THE BAR'S parking lot. He threw his truck into park and hit a button on the steering wheel that placed him on the Raptor's speaker system.

"You can have your field back, Virgil," Sheriff Holden said.

The statement came as a surprise. "Really? Your crime scene people are done already? That seems a little…fast."

"Maybe the word you were looking for was 'efficient.' Or maybe you're saying we don't know what we're doing."

Virgil sighed. "No, Ben, I'm not saying that at all. It simply strikes me as odd that after everything that happened out there yesterday they'd be finished by now."

Holden ran through it for him. "We know exactly how both the Davis brothers were killed. We know exactly how one of my deputies was incapacitated. We know exactly how the other was killed. We know how the Mex—how Mr. Ibarra was shot. Everyone left alive has given their statements. All weapons used have been recovered, along with anything else of evidentiary value. Everything was photographed and videoed, properly labeled and secured in the evidence locker should any of it ever be needed for trial, a Grand Jury indictment, or depositions in a criminal or civil lawsuit. Have I left anything out?"

Virgil thought there might have been some verbal italicization on the word 'civil.' He let it go. "What about the Indian?"

"What about him?"

"Are you looking for him?"

"Maybe you didn't hear me yesterday when I said that I'd lost about half my force. In case you didn't, now you have. I don't have the manpower to run that kind of search. If he turns up, he'll be arrested. My injured deputies are going to be fine. Except Lowe, the one who got himself knocked on the head. He's going to be out for six to nine months. Thanks for asking."

"I was going to ask, Ben. We were talking about the case, is all."

"Uh-huh. The other, the one who tried to sucker punch your man, Wheeler…he's got a spiral fracture in one of his wrist bones—I don't remember the name of it, the bone—and he'll be on the desk for almost as long as Lowe. So that's what I've got. You want your field back or not?"

"Yes, of course. Thank you."

"You want to thank me, get me some people down here to find that Injun."

"I'll be getting that process started today. We really do need to speak to him."

"Uh-huh." Virgil thought the sheriff sounded like he didn't care whether they found the Indian or not.

"So we're clear," Holden said. "The crime scene is back under your control."

"Is there something you're not telling me, Sheriff?"

Some of the rancor went out of Holden's voice. "You really think you can pull the gas out of the ground without causing any harm to the Flatrock or the water table around here?"

"That's what we're hoping for. I can promise you this, Ben, if that turns out not to be the case, I'll shut it down. I've given my word on that and I intend to keep it."

"How well do you know your partner, this Said fellow?"

"Why do you ask?"

"Because I've got four armed men out in my parking lot as we speak. I'm standing at the window looking at them right now. They left my office about three minutes ago. They said their visit was a courtesy, that they're security for the operation out in your field and wanted to know when the crime scene was going to be considered cleared."

Virgil pinched the bridge of his nose with his thumb and forefinger. "Ah, I'm sorry about that. After what happened with Patty and everything, Said told me he was going to have security out there. I should have mentioned it to you."

"Yup, I reckon that would have been a good idea. But that's neither here nor there, Virgil."

"I'm not entirely sure what you mean by that, Ben."

"Why do you think I asked you about Said? Those boys out in the lot? They're not from Pinkerton's. They've all got that ex-military look about them, all sunglasses and buzz cuts, black outfits, the works. They look like they just stepped off a movie set or something."

"You asked me how well I know Said. I know him well enough to know this: He doesn't screw around, especially when it comes to his niece. I'm not surprised he's hired security, and it doesn't surprise me that they're probably ex-military. But I'm sure it's nothing to worry about. Patty indicated it'd only take a day or two to get all the samples. Once that's done, they'll be gone."

"No, they won't."

"What does that mean?"

"It means I've seen these boys before, Virgil. And I'm not talking about a type. I mean I've seen these actual men. They're a part of Roger Salter's security detail at his estate. Said is using Salter's men to guard his niece, your land, and the operation you all have started out there."

That got Virgil's attention. It wasn't exactly good news. "Well, it's your county, Sheriff. If you think there's something illegal going on, you have every right to intervene."

"Boy oh boy, you don't get it, do you? I made this call because I wanted you to be informed. I've done that, so now I'm done."

"What's got you so upset about this, Ben?"

"Mostly my own damned incompetence. Do you know who Deputy Cooper was?"

"Other than one of your men, no."

"He was probably one of the worst deputies I've ever hired."

"Then why did you hire him?"

"Because I didn't have a choice, that's why. Who do you think financed my campaign, Jones? C'mon, I'll give you three guesses. The man is a former United States senator for Christ's sake. Do you know how much power and influence he has? I don't want to stick my nose where it doesn't belong, but you might want to have a talk with Said about all this."

"Why?"

"Because Cooper was Roger Salter's nephew," Holden said. "That's why." Then he hung up.

Virgil tried to call Said and got his voice mail. He left a message and asked him to call back as soon as possible. He thought about what Holden had told him, how Deputy Cooper fit into the equation, and how it was Salter's men who'd be providing security for the drilling exploration process. If taken at face value, it might not mean anything at all. Except it couldn't be taken at face value due to all the extenuating circumstances.

Ever since the death of Charlie Esser—the previous owner of Virgil & Co.'s land—the number of people killed or injured because of the natural resources under the ground was almost too difficult to calculate. Had the Salters been behind everything all along? Cora had indicated that Mac was in meetings with Ken Salter, the state legislator, over land management issues. What issues, specifically, was she referring to? He should have asked the governor earlier, but hadn't thought of it at the time. Said was working—in some unknown capacity—with Ken's father, Roger, who owned and operated a geological surveying company that specialized in the discovery of natural gas resources. Deputy Cooper had been shot and killed by one of Said's employees, and the one name that now kept popping up over and over?

Salter.

Virgil dialed the phone again—this time to call Patty. She answered immediately. Virgil could hear the traffic noise in the background. "Where are you headed?"

"Out to the field, where else? Didn't you hear? The crime scene has been cleared."

"I did hear," Virgil said. "A few minutes ago. That's why I was calling. Who told you?"

"Uncle Rick. I spoke with him before you called. He said we'd be good to go."

"We?"

"Yeah, me, and the drill and crane operators."

Virgil suddenly felt very protective. "And you know these guys?"

"Never met them. But I'm sure they're okay, Jonesy. They work for the geological survey company. Plus, Uncle Rick said he'd have security in place by the time we got there."

"And the survey company...ah, jeez, I can't remember their name." Virgil felt like an ass, deceiving Patty.

"Salter Engineering or something like that. Or is it Slater? I don't know. Uncle Rick has been handling all that. My job is to get the samples. Anyway...Slater, Salter...I don't remember. Why? What's with the twenty questions routine?"

Virgil was relieved that Patty couldn't quite remember the name of Salter's company. It indicated her lack of culpability in any nefarious activities regarding the drilling operation...if in fact, any existed. Virgil wasn't entirely sure. At least not yet.

"Just keeping an eye on things, is all," Virgil said. "And speaking of eyes, keep an eye out for that Indian. I doubt he'll be back after everything that's happened, but maintain your situational awareness anyway, will you?"

"Of course. But listen, and I know I've said this already, but that Indian, whomever he is, saved us all, Jonesy. I'm absolutely certain of it."

"I don't doubt you, Patty. Not for one second. But from a legal standpoint, he's committed a very serious crime. Until and unless we find him or he turns himself in, he's considered an armed and dangerous fugitive. I'm going to have men down there today looking for him. They may come out to the field. They're my guys and they are very good. Tom Rosencrantz and Andrew Ross. And you know Murton. He may be out there as well."

"Okay, I'll look for them. What have you heard about your mechanic, Carlos? Is he doing all right? I don't know if you watch the news or not, but that's all they're talking about. The left is calling him a hero and the right is using him as the poster child for funding the wall."

"I try to stay away from the news as much as possible. I do like to check the weather in the morning sometimes. But no, I haven't seen any of the coverage. I need to speak with Carlos and I'll be doing that today. I'll let you know how he is after I see him. I'm going over there shortly."

"Okay, thanks. Listen, I'm turning into the clearing now. I'll keep you updated with our progress."

"Patty?"

"Yes?"

"Be careful."

She laughed. "I will, Uncle Virgil. Promise." Then she was gone.

CHAPTER THIRTY-ONE

VIRGIL WENT UP TO THE OFFICE AND CHECKED IN WITH BECKY and Murton. Murton was helping her rebuild the system and when he asked how long before they'd be finished, Becky told him it'd be another day, at the earliest.

"We really need that print from Delroy's car, Becks. And I'd like the background information on the Salters as well. We need to find Delroy and Huma, and I also need you to find out how many geological survey companies there are in the state that specialize in natural gas exploration and discovery."

Becky looked at him like he was out of his mind. "Anything else? Maybe I should research how many people I need to get all that done, because if you keep adding to the list, I'm going to need an assistant."

"That's why I'm here," Murton said. "Sometimes I think my critical contributions to fighting crime are severely undervalued."

They both ignored him. "How much longer until your system is back up?" Virgil asked.

"It's getting longer by the minute, due largely in part to this conversation. Also, it'd go much faster if you took my helper along with you." She made air quotes when she said the word 'helper.' "As a matter of fact, there's no maybe about it."

Murton was lying on the sofa, his hands behind his head. He gave Virgil a fake yawn. "What are you talking about? You said you need an assistant. And, even though I'm not one to normally pat myself on the back, as a simple matter of fact, we wouldn't be half as far along as we are now if it weren't for my advice, assistance, and expert tutelage."

Becky looked at Virgil. "Please?"

"I really could use your help, Murt," Virgil said.

Murton sat up and stretched. "What's going on?"

"I was hoping you'd go down to Shelby County with Ross and Rosie and look for an Indian."

"Dot or feather?"

Becky made a clicking noise with her tongue. "That's racist."

"It's inquisitive," Murton said. Then to Virgil: "The one from your field?"

"Yeah. He's gotta be living down there somewhere and Holden doesn't have the manpower. There are other complications for him as well."

"The Indian, or Holden?"

Virgil didn't get a chance to answer.

"If you already knew what Indian he was talking about," Becky said, "then it was racist. I'm dating a racist."

"I was simply making sure the investigation hadn't taken on an additional international element. We're already dealing with Jamaicans and Mexicans. It's a perfectly normal question that any decent investigator would ask given the volatile nature of this case, not to mention the current political climate under which we live in today's society."

"Please," Becky said to Virgil again. "I'm begging you. I promise I'll have everything back up and running by this time tomorrow, maybe even sooner if you'll take him with you."

Virgil looked at Murton. "Murt?"

"Sure," Murton said as he stood from the sofa. He winked at Virgil. "I know when I'm wanted, and when I'm not." He turned to Becky. "I can't believe it's come to this. I divorce thee."

"I get half of everything," Becky said. "Now go."

When they arrived at the Statehouse, Murton turned to Virgil and said, "What are we doing here?"

Virgil had filled Murton in on everything he'd learned on the ride over. "I already told you. We, as in you and me, are going to convince Cora to assign Rosie and Ross to look for the Indian."

Murton frowned at him. "No, that's not what you said. You said you wanted me to go down there and help them."

Virgil nodded. "Right. So we're on the same page then."

"You implied that it was already a done deal. I didn't know we were going to have to sell it to Cora."

"I don't think it's worth splitting hairs over. We're not selling anything. I simply want to make sure everyone is on the same page regarding investigative assignments and whatnot."

"Uh-huh. You don't want Miles crawling up your butt about allocation of resources regarding a case that we're not supposed to be working."

"Yeah, I just said that. C'mon, let's go."

When Virgil outlined what he needed, he expected all kinds of resistance from Cora. What she said surprised him. "That's fine." She barely looked up from her laptop when she spoke.

Virgil and Murton looked at each other. They were expecting a battle and when they didn't get one, it left them a little off balance.

Cora finally looked up. "I said it's fine. Miles is down with the flu, anyway. He called in earlier this morning. Sound's like he's going to be out for a while. Rosie and Ross are yours. They're wandering around looking for something to do anyway. But let me remind you both, you're not supposed to be working this case. What you're supposed to be doing is keeping a low profile." Then, as if she needed to hammer home her point, she added, "Hovering into the middle of a crime scene in the state's helicopter isn't exactly what I had in mind when I asked you to keep things quiet."

Murton grinned. "Atta girl. That's more like it."

Cora pointed a finger at him and was about to say something when the governor popped his head into her office. "Ah, I thought I heard you two out here. Any new developments?"

Virgil spoke without thinking. "Not since this morning, no."

Murton looked at the governor, then Virgil. "What happened this morning?"

The governor looked at Virgil, his eyes much wider than normal. Virgil had forgotten—though he didn't yet know why

—Mac didn't want Cora to know he'd been out to see him at his house.

"Nothing," Virgil said, much too quickly. "I mean, uh—"

The governor saved him. "I spoke with Jonesy this morning regarding a personal matter. It was nothing really. In addition, I've invited him and Sandy and the boys over for dinner Sunday evening. Just a casual get-together."

Virgil nodded rapidly. "That's it. Exactly. Dinner with friends. That sort of thing. Happens all the time."

"Yes, well, I better get back to it then," the governor said by way of an escape. "Jonesy, see you Sunday." He nodded a goodbye to Murton. "Murt."

Murton looked at the governor. "Dinner with friends, huh? Okay. I get it."

The governor opened the door a little wider. "No, no, Murt, it's nothing like that…"

"It's alright. I know when I'm not wanted." He opened the outer door to Cora's office, glanced back at the governor and said, "I divorce thee."

Cora looked at Virgil and said, "Someone's feeling better."

The security men, led by John Fox, all introduced themselves to Patty, as did the equipment operators. Fox assured Patty that he, along with the other men would stay out of their way. Patty thanked him, and tried very hard not to stare at the weapons and other gear the men had with them. They didn't look like they were providing security for a drilling operation in south-central Indiana. They looked like they were ready for urban warfare somewhere in the Middle East.

Fox put one man at each corner of the five-acre clearing and he covered the access road that Johnson had bulldozed when they opened up the field. Patty showed the equipment operators the grid pattern she'd worked out on her iPad, the survey marked with little red x's that showed the areas where she wanted to pull the samples. She had a handful of marker flags and told them that she'd place the flags in the proper spots, and they could simply drill down everywhere they saw a flag.

"How many are there?" The drill operator asked.

"Fifty. We've got a five-acre clearing here, and I want to get ten samples per acre."

"And how deep?"

Patty consulted her geological records for a few minutes. "I think thirty to forty feet should do it."

The drill operator laughed, but in a kind way. "Oh, okay."

"Is that too deep?"

"Are you kidding? I was expecting you to say two or three hundred."

Patty laughed right back at him. "Oh, God no. We only need to determine the stability of the ground above the shale. According to the survey, being this close to the river, it's not that deep. Will you be able to tell when you hit it? The shale?"

"Absolutely," the driller said. "Once I get the parameters entered into the system, as soon as the drill hits the shale it will shut down automatically."

Patty was impressed. "Okay. Sounds kind of neat."

"It is, until about the second hole. Then it's all cigarettes and coffee and daydreaming. You taking the samples back to a lab, or are you doing a field study?"

"Both. Why?"

"Because if you're transporting, I'll use heavier core

casings to protect the contents during transport. Going all the way back to Kentucky?"

"No, up to Indy, actually."

"Well, that's not much of a difference, distance-wise. Anyway, if you could let me know which areas are going to be looked at out here, I can use casings that'll be easier to move around."

"It doesn't really matter which ones, as long as we have a representative sample per acre. So, one in ten."

The driller nodded at her. "Fine by me. Makes my job a lot easier. You get your flags set and we'll be done by the end of the day."

That surprised Patty. "Really? It'll go that fast?"

"Should. As a matter of fact, it'll take longer to position the rig than it will to get the samples."

"Jeez, that's great. I'll get started right now." She looked at her map again, then asked, "Would it be better to start at the front or the back of the clearing?"

"It might not matter, but I'd say the back."

"Why's that?"

"You said it yourself. We're fairly close to the river. The water table isn't very low around here. Hope you brought your boots. It's gonna get muddy."

After everything Patty had been through—both in the last three months, and the last day or two—a little mud was nothing. "I think I can handle it. Let's go."

It took Patty an hour or so to set the flags, then she stood back and watched the crane and drill operators do their work. The driller had been right...it took much longer to move, set, then level the drill unit than it did to get the actual core samples. At the end of the first acre, on the tenth sample, she watched with great interest, as this would be one of the cores she'd break open out in the field and examine herself. It wasn't ancient Egypt, but she found herself excited by the prospect of putting her talents and education to good use.

She cracked the first field casing open and began to measure the different layers of soil and strata, making notes as she went along. At first, the security men had shown some interest in what she was doing, especially the one named Fox, but after a few hours she saw the boredom start to set in, like they were hoping for another shooting spree, which obviously wasn't going to happen. She felt sorry for them, standing around, doing nothing but staring at the endless rows of corn. She was about to suggest that they go ahead and take a lunch break when she noticed something in the stratum. Something that shouldn't have been there.

She went back to her truck, grabbed her field bag and took out the tools she needed. First she photographed the core, then measured the depth. She then laid a measuring tape next to the core and took another picture. Once she had everything on film, she put on a pair of latex gloves and gently removed the object from the core sample.

She brushed it off, then took a bottle of water and rinsed it clean. When she was sure of what she was looking at, she took out her phone and called the Co-op and asked for Carl Johnson. She had to wait almost ten minutes before he came on the line.

"Sorry," he said by way of a greeting. They didn't know where to find me. I was—"

Patty didn't care. She interrupted him. "Mr. Johnson, do you have an excavator or backhoe you could bring out to the clearing?"

"You sound a little out of breath. Everything okay out there?"

Good question. "Yes, everything is fine. So, do you?"

"How deep do you need to go?"

Patty checked her measurements one more time before answering. "I can't say for sure, but at least seven feet."

"That's no problem. I'll bring the tractor with a backhoe attachment. Easier to drive out there than the excavator. What's going on?"

"How long before you can get here?"

"Twenty minutes or so. Patty, what's going on?"

"I'm not sure. That's why I need the backhoe."

"I'm on my way, little darling. Sit tight."

She told him she would. After she was done with Johnson, she started to dial Virgil's number, then stopped. No sense in getting everyone all riled up if it turned out to be nothing.

Patty held the object in her hand and thought, *But this was hardly nothing. This is definitely something.* She pulled a towel from her bag and wrapped the object to protect it, then set it in the dirt, right next to the area where she'd pulled it from the open casing.

She consulted her map and set three more flags in a triangular pattern spaced ten yards away from the hole where the field sample was pulled from the ground. Then she went and talked to the drill operator.

"So you want field samples from those areas next?"

"Yes," Patty said, trying to keep the anxiety out of her voice.

"Same depth?"

"No. Only ten feet each."

He smiled at her. "Find something good?"

Patty gave him a serious look. "Right away, if you could please."

Then she walked to the front of the field and spoke with the security supervisor. "Mr. Fox, in a few minutes one of the Co-op people is bringing another piece of equipment out here. His name is Carl Johnson. He'll be on a tractor with a backhoe. Please allow him through when he arrives."

"You got it," Fox said.

CHAPTER THIRTY-TWO

DESPITE THE FACT THEY WEREN'T SUPPOSED TO BE WORKING the case, both Virgil and Murton ended up at the MCU facility to meet with Rosencrantz and Ross. They were after all, on administrative leave…not banned from the building. And the leave was in place to help them, not as a punishment or in advance of punitive action. But they *did* have to be careful. What was it the governor had said to him? People talk. So Virgil didn't want to spend too much time in the building. Not that he ever did anyway.

They found them in Rosencrantz's office. Ross had his sniper rifle out of the case, broken down in pieces on a table. He was getting ready to demonstrate the assembly process to Rosencrantz. In addition to being a regular MCU detective, Ross was their designated sniper, hired on Virgil's recommendation, and the most junior investigator on the unit. He'd not yet had to snipe anybody since joining the MCU…at least not with his weapon. Although Virgil and a few other people had witnessed a verbal sniping against Miles a few months ago, one that remained legendary to everyone, Miles being the possible exception.

"I once saw him drop all six shells from a speed loader at the range during his annual re-qualification," Murton said to Ross. He was speaking of Rosencrantz.

"It was the first stage, and I was a little nervous," Rosencrantz said. "Plus, they wanted me to use this piece of shit six-shooter I'd never seen before."

"Piece of shit? It was a brand new Smith .357, right out of the box. You had this look on your face like…"

Ross interrupted and spoke in a rapid, monotonous tone, his eyes fixed on a spot between Murton and Rosencrantz, never once looking at the rifle during the reassembly process. His hands moved with the dexterity of an accomplished pianist, one who might every now and again look away from the sheet music and turn his eyes toward the audience before him. "First Stage - 3-yard line - twelve rounds - six rounds fired one-handed with the strong hand and six rounds fired one-handed with the support hand. On command, load and holster. Shooters may load with six or twelve rounds depending on the weapon. On command, fire two shot strings. Six with your strong hand only and six with your support hand only. Once the weapon clears the holster all firing is completed before weapon is re-holstered. A ten-second delay between strong hand firing and support hand firing will allow shooters a reloading period if necessary." By the time he finished his little speech, he had his rifle assembled and back in the case.

Virgil, Murton and Rosencrantz all looked at each other, then at Ross. No one said anything. Finally Rosencrantz looked at Virgil and said, "Jesus Christ, Jonesy, you not only hired some sort of savant, you've made him my partner?"

"What?" Ross said. "I know the police academy re-qual rules. So what?"

Virgil was smiling. "I can pick 'em, can't I?" Then he got

serious. "I spoke with Cora. She wants you guys to head down to Shelby County and find an Indian."

"*She* does?" Murton said, letting his head take a large, lazy roll in Virgil's direction.

"Dot or feather?" Rosencrantz asked.

"That's racist," Murton said, his head rolling back the other way. It looked like he might be watching a slow-motion tennis match.

"No it isn't," Rosencrantz said.

"Take it up with Becky, dude."

"Guys," Virgil said.

"He meant Hindu or Native American," Ross said.

Rosencrantz looked at Ross. "I can speak for myself, *Rain Man*." Then he looked at Virgil. "I meant Hindu or Native American."

"Native American. Murt is going with you." He gave them the rundown on everything that had happened out in the field, including his thoughts on Salter's involvement with Rick Said, and the fact that Salter was providing security for the test drilling.

"Sounds like we should be talking with Salter," Ross said.

Rosencrantz held his palm out to Ross. "As the junior member of the squad, I know you're still learning how things work around here, getting the lay of the land and all that. I also recognize that in your own sincere—albeit somewhat clumsy way—that you're only trying to help. But please, let me handle this so you don't embarrass yourself." He looked at Virgil and said, "Sounds like we should be talking with Salter."

"I'm going to, as soon as Becky gets me the information I need." He turned his attention to Murton. "Pack a bag. I want you guys down there until you find this Indian. Don't come back without him. I'm serious."

Murton spoke for the group. "Jonesy, we'll find your Indian at some point, I'm sure. Unless of course he's headed off for points unknown out west. But I've been down there and you know it. Where are we supposed to stay? It's nothing except narrow roads and cornfields. The closest town to your land is Flat Rock. They don't have any hotels. You want us to bivouac in one of your fields?"

"That's probably where you'll find the Indian."

"Which still doesn't answer my question."

Virgil thought about it for a few minutes. Then his face lit up. He reached into his pocket, pulled a set of keys off his ring and tossed them to Murton.

"What's this?"

"Keys to the Esser house. Except it's my house now. Fully furnished and ready to go. I haven't done anything with it yet." Nobody said anything in response and Virgil said, "What?"

"You want us to stay in the house where Charlie Esser killed his wife?" Murton said.

Virgil rubbed his forehead with his fingertips. "That's not entirely accurate, Murt. He only *tried* to kill her there. She died at the hospital. It's just a house. I was in there not long ago. The place is perfect." He began to slowly back out of the office. "It's clean as a whistle. I'll admit, there's a lot of rooster wallpaper in the kitchen, and you'll want to air the place out a little, but other than that, it really is perfect."

"I've seen the wallpaper," Rosencrantz said. "I didn't like it at first, but it does sort of grow on you."

Ross, who really hadn't sniped anyone lately, took his shot. "Enjoy being surrounded by cocks, do you?"

Rosencrantz looked at Virgil, who said, "What? You walked right into that one. Besides, tell me Donatti wouldn't have said almost exactly the same thing."

"He would have," Murton agreed. "I was thinking it, but Ross beat me to it, is all."

"You can't hesitate," Ross said, matter of fact. "You line up the shot and squeeze…ever so gently."

Rosencrantz was staring at the carpet, but Virgil could see the corners of his mouth turned up. Ross was fitting in nicely, and the fact that Rosencrantz was giving him grief told Virgil that the two men were going to make great partners.

He'd almost made it to the door before Murton said, "What are you going to do?"

"I'm going to the hospital to have a chat with Carlos."

"Which one is he, again?" Rosencrantz asked.

"He's one of the mechanics from the Co-op. When the crane blew a line, he came out to fix it. He's the one who saved Patty and took a round to the leg for his trouble. His situation is sort of complicated. He's part of the DACA program and Holden says ICE is already looking to deport him."

"Yeah, I got all that," Rosencrantz said. "I meant what is his last name?"

"Ibarra. Carlos Ibarra."

Rosencrantz looked up at the ceiling in thought, and said, "Huh."

"Huh, what?" Virgil said.

"I don't know. Maybe nothing. It's a pretty common last name, except earlier, you referred to him only by his first name and his position. This is the first time I've heard his full name."

"So what?"

"Well, back when you were, mmm, on sabbatical and recovering from your own leg injury…right at the beginning of the Pope case, when everyone thought Nicholas Pope had been killed, one of the first people we interviewed was a woman named Lola Ibarra. In fact, she's the one who called the fuzz to begin with. She's also the one who ended up collecting the lottery money. It was all in Ron's report."

"Jesus, that's right," Virgil said. "I'd forgotten about that. Think there's a connection there?"

"Could be," Rosencrantz said. "When you talk to him, you should ask him who his *Madre* is."

"*Madre* is Spanish for mother," Ross said to no one. None of them took the bait, not that any was readily visible, but with Ross, you never knew, his ghillie suit always at the ready.

"You know what else?" Murton said to Virgil.

Virgil pointed a finger at him. "The thumb drive."

Murton nodded. "Yep."

"What thumb drive?" Rosencrantz said.

"The Pope twins were tight with Lola Ibarra. Nichole Pope gave me a thumb drive after the investigation was over. She said it contained everything they'd ever put together on Bradley Pearson and his misdeeds. I never did anything with it until I plugged it into my computer one day a few months ago. We think the Pope twins are involved in all of this somehow because that thumb drive compromised Becky's entire system. Murt will fill you in on the rest of it. Now I *really* need to speak with Carlos."

"You sure there's no place else to stay down there?" Murton said. Virgil had been inching closer to the door and now stood right at the opening.

"Not that I know of. Oh, and listen, I almost forgot, be careful with the toilet flushing and all that. I think the septic system is full. It's about to back up. Who needs that kind of grief?"

He pulled the door closed behind him and took off.

THE BULLET WOUND IN CARLOS'S LEG HAD BEEN BAD ENOUGH that the surgeons in Shelbyville didn't want to attempt the surgery. The bullet passed through his leg, but a piece of bone had been nicked, and the fragment had shattered, and the shattering had done a fair amount of arterial and nerve damage. In total, it'd take an Ortho guy for the bone, a Vascular specialist to repair the blood vessels, and a Neurologist to make sure as many nerves as possible were properly fixed. So the Shelbyville surgeon stabilized him and got him patched up well enough for transport and he was sent to Indianapolis via air ambulance for the proper level of care and recovery.

When Virgil left the MCU he went to the hospital where Carlos now was—which happened to be the same one where he and Murton had taken Huma after her attack—and found Carlos's room, but no Carlos. The bed was empty. A few seconds later, a nurse came in pushing an array of monitoring devices attached to a wheeled equipment rack. Virgil identified himself and when he asked about Carlos, she told him he was in surgery.

"That's what all this equipment is for. After he's out, we'll get him all hooked up. Pretty standard stuff."

"Well, shoot. I waited to come and speak with him because I thought he'd be out of surgery by now," he said, which wasn't a total lie. "If I'd have known they weren't going to do the surgery right away, I would have spoken to him beforehand."

The nurse spoke as she got all the equipment in order. "As a cop, you probably know this, but there is always some risk of infection from a gunshot wound. His Sed rates were up already."

"I know about infection and Sed rates," Virgil said. The sound of his voice told her he wasn't kidding.

"Been through it, have you?"

Virgil nodded. "Had the PICC line and the whole works."

"Gunshot?"

He shook his head. "Naw, I got the snot beat out of me a few years ago. My leg needed a few pins and it was the surgery itself that almost got me. It really was sort of touch and go there for a while."

The nurse spoke in a nonchalant way. "It happens. They tell you there's always a risk of infection from surgery, and it's true. But the numbers are small. One or two percent usually."

"I can tell you this: The numbers are only small if you're one of the lucky ninety-eight or ninety-nine percent."

"That's true. Anyway, with a gunshot, little bits of clothing and debris and all kinds of things can follow the bullet in. That's generally what causes the infection. The Shelbyville docs did a pretty good job of cleaning him out, but they might have missed something. The docs wanted to pump him full of antibiotics before they went in. Get a little head start, so to speak. And they wanted to wait to let the antibiotics take hold, but they didn't want to wait too long because of the vascular damage. That creates its own risks as well. Wait too long and it can cause the tissue to start to break down. Once that starts to happen, there can be a cascade effect that's hard to stop. It'd be a different story if he'd been shot in the foot or something, because you could just take the foot. But the wound was so high up on the leg that wouldn't be an option. He wouldn't lose his leg. He'd probably lose his life."

"Any idea when I'll be able to speak with him?"

"You know, I really shouldn't be speaking to you about any of this, with HIPPA, and all that."

"I understand," Virgil said. "But Mr. Ibarra is being detained as a suspect in the death of another, and probable deportation. As an officer of the state, believe it or not, I'm trying to prevent that."

The nurse put her hands on her hips and shot him a nasty look. "Why? So you can throw him in prison here? The way I understand it, he saved a woman's life."

Virgil held up his hands. "No, no. I'm only trying to help. The woman he saved is a friend of mine—"

"Wait a second," the nurse said, a little excitement in her voice. "I recognize you. You're the cop who saved that IU student who'd been kidnapped, right?"

"Yeah. Her name is Patty Doyle."

"I knew it. Saw you on the news."

She was loosening up and Virgil noticed. He didn't want to push his luck though. "Can you at least tell me when I can talk to him?"

The nurse gave him a thoughtful look, then turned around and began clicking the mouse connected to a computer on the equipment rack she'd wheeled in. "It looks like the surgery is scheduled for eight hours. They've got three docs working on him, but they have to sort of take turns. The ortho guy should be the quickest. He'll pin him then let the vascular and neurologist people do their thing. That takes some time. Especially the nerve stuff. You wouldn't believe the amount of sensors they have to attach to check every nerve. That part alone can take two or three hours and they only started two hours ago, so you've got at least eight more to go."

"I thought you said it would be eight hours total."

"No, I said it was scheduled for eight hours. But I've seen dozens of these types of surgeries. The last one went fourteen hours and that wasn't even the record for the longest amount of time. He's essentially having three surgeries at once." When Virgil didn't say anything she said, "Hold on."

She clicked a few more times and a different screen popped up, though Virgil couldn't read what it said because the monitor had one of those privacy covers on it. Unless you were directly in front of the screen, you couldn't see anything. "They just put him on the sniffer, so that means they're really only now getting started."

"The sniffer?"

"Sorry. Hospital jargon. They just put him under."

Virgil checked his watch. "So eight hours at least, then."

She shook her head. "No, more like thirty-six at the earliest. He'll be in recovery for a few hours at least, then the ICU after that. You wouldn't be allowed in there, even if he was the Unabomber and you were the director of the FBI. So unless you want to come back in the middle of the night tomorrow, try two days from now."

When Virgil spoke, he was really thinking out loud. "Huh. Gonna be a hell of a bill, and all of it on the state's tab."

The nurse's eyes got wide and Virgil noticed.

"What is it?"

"Look, I know I'm not supposed to tell you this, and if you tell anyone I did, I'll deny it till the day I die, okay?"

"Tell me what?"

"Well, people talk, you know?"

Do I ever. "Yeah?" Virgil vocally drew the word out. "What are they talking about?"

"The bill you mentioned. By the time it's all said and done, with the surgical fee, the ICU stay, the doctor's fees, the labs, the meds, the MRIs, CAT scans, the private room…

it all adds up. We're talking hundreds of thousands of dollars."

"I know," Virgil said.

"You're missing my point."

"And that point would be…"

"The state isn't paying for anything. It's already been paid for. The entire bill was worked out in advance and the hospital got a wire transfer almost immediately. Anything left over is supposed to be considered an anonymous donation. And believe me, from what I've heard, there'll be some left over."

And Virgil thought, *Bingo.* The Pope twins.

CHAPTER THIRTY-THREE

Wu, his wife, Linda, the Popes, and Lola Ibarra were all in the systems room discussing their next move. They were trying to work out a plan to get Carlos out of the country and down to Jamaica with them. Carlos was in surgery and one of the giant monitors on the wall showed his room, the empty bed a constant source of worry for Lola. Nicky had offered to pull up the surgical suite's camera, but Lola refused.

"I do not think I could stand to watch them open my boy up. Besides, if I was there, they would not let me in to watch. I am religious, not superstitious, but I think watching would be bad, mmm, what is the word? Moho?"

"Mojo," Wu said. "Bad mojo. Moho is short word for Mohorovičić discontinuity, the boundary surface between the earth's crust and mantle. It is about ten or twelve kilometers under the ocean floor and about forty to fifty kilometers under the continents."

They all slowly turned their heads and looked at him. "He watches the Science Channel," Linda said. "A lot. It helps him fall asleep at night."

"Wu knew things," he said.

Linda patted her husband on the thigh. "It's 'knows' things, sweetheart. Wu *knows* things."

"We shall need a plan," Lola said. "Nichole, you are the planner. What do we do?"

"I'm working on it. I've already got most of it in motion."

Nicky suddenly stood up and pointed at the screen. "Hey, look at that."

They all turned and watched as Virgil entered Carlos's hospital room. Wu tapped the volume button on the keyboard and brought the sound up as a nurse followed him in.

They caught the whole conversation.

When Johnson came bouncing down the path on the tractor with the backhoe attachment, Fox waved him through. The tractor was a bright orange Kubota M62 with stabilizing arms and a bucket with a thumb that could reach a depth of fourteen feet. He parked the tractor away from all the other equipment and walked over toward Patty, who was directing the second drilling of the three triangular placements she'd marked earlier. He stood back out of the way and watched as the driller pulled the casing out of the ground. The crane operator grabbed the tube—it wiggled around like a stiff snake—and manhandled it out of the way before unhooking it from the drill. Its diameter wasn't very big, but it was heavy because it was packed full of earth material. It was also slippery. They got the casing on the ground and unhooked, then set about hooking the crane up to the drill to move it to its next position.

The drill and crane both made a hell of a racket, so Patty hadn't heard Johnson walk up, but she felt his presence…

something she'd noticed about herself ever since the kidnapping. When she turned, he jerked his thumb at the tractor. "That should do it, whatever 'it' is," he said. "I can go down as low as fourteen feet. Want me to bring it over?"

"Not yet," Patty said. "We've got one more hole to go, then we'll start."

Johnson took off his hat and scratched his scalp. "What are we starting?"

"Maybe something, then again, maybe nothing." They both watched the crane operator move the drill unit to the final point of the triangle. Once she was sure they had it set in the proper place, she tugged at Johnson's sleeve and said, "Come take a look at something."

She walked him over to the first casing she'd cracked, then picked up the cloth that held the object she'd found. She carefully unwrapped it. "I'm going to hold it and I don't want you to touch it, okay?"

Johnson let out a nervous little laugh. "Sure. Whatcha got in there, a gold nugget or something?"

"Not exactly, but it could be worth just as much, to the right people, anyway." She finished unwrapping the cloth and when Johnson looked at what she held in her hands, Patty could see the confusion—and maybe a hint of disappointment on his face.

"What the heck is that? For a second there, I really did think you were going to show me a gold nugget. That thing looks like an old arrowhead."

"Yeah, it sort of does, doesn't it? Except that's not what it is." Patty didn't have her gloves on, so she manipulated the cloth until the object rolled over. "It's called a Sacrum."

"Patty, I'm a farmer, and I ain't all that bright. I'm not educated like you. I did get myself a GED, though. But I've been a farmer ever since I was old enough to carry a bucket of feed. That's no joke. My old man had me slinging pig flop and…oh never mind. What's a Sacrum?"

Patty frowned at him. "Don't do that."

"Do what?"

"Disrespect yourself, or your job, for that matter. I have a tremendous amount of respect for farmers, and you, in particular because we know each other. You know things others don't…not the least of which is how to keep us all fed. You might have a piece of paper that says you have a general education, but as far as I'm concerned, you've got a Ph.D. when it comes to farming."

Johnson's face turned red. "Well, I know a thing or two about growing beans and corn and such. And I do run my own business. Take care of the books and everything."

"There you go. You could start telling me something about farming and I'd have no idea what you're talking about. Sort of like that Einstein quote about the fish and the tree."

Johnson didn't know the quote, and said so. Patty told it to him. "Einstein said: 'Everybody is a genius. But if you judge a fish by its ability to climb a tree, it will live its whole life believing that it is stupid.'"

"So you're saying because I don't know what a Sacrum is, that doesn't make me stupid."

Patty tipped a finger at him. "Exactly. Anyway, a Sacrum is a human triangular-shaped bone in the lower back formed from fused vertebrae and situated between the two hipbones of the pelvis."

"You're saying you found human bones."

"Yes. This one appears to be female."

"How do you know that?" Johnson asked.

"The female sacrum is shorter and wider than a male one. The curvature would be different as well if it was a male. I'm not one hundred percent sure, but I'm close. Also, I'd say it is from an adult female." She pointed to a specific area with her pinky finger. "See how this area right here is fused together?"

He gave her a counterfeit nod. He really didn't see it, but he didn't want her to know after she'd just praised his intelligence. The fact that the intelligence of a fish was used in the praising didn't matter to Johnson.

"The fusion process that takes place in the Sacrum isn't complete until about age eighteen or so. That's not definitive, mind you, but the bottom line is this: We're looking at a bone that belonged to a female, at least old enough to be in her late teens."

"Holy cow," Johnson said. "We'd better call Virgil."

Patty nodded. "We're going to, but I want you to do a little digging for me first."

Johnson shook his head and waved his hands in front of himself. "I'm sorry, Patty, but I don't think I can do that. Virgil would have my head on a pike for messing with a crime scene, especially on his own land."

Patty turned her back, not in anger or frustration. She didn't want Johnson to see her trying to hide her smile. She pointed and said, "Look. They've got the last casing out." When she turned back she had her smile under control. "Carl, this Sacrum bone isn't recent. It's at least one hundred years old. This isn't a crime scene. The state of Indiana got its name from the word Indian."

"Believe it or not, that much I did know."

"Then it's quite possible we may have uncovered an ancient Indian burial ground."

JOHNSON KNEW PATTY WAS SMART, AND HE WAS SMART enough to know when he was out of his element. He didn't want to be truculent, but he didn't want to go to jail, either. So instead, he asked a simple question. "Are you sure?"

"Yes. Look, Carl, this is what I went to school for. I know bones, and I know how they look after spending varying amounts of time buried in the earth. If you put your foot down and say no, I'll honor your wishes because I like and respect you. But in the end, you'll simply be delaying the inevitable because this area is going to get dug up either way. Plus, if I'm wrong, I'll take all the blame, plead ignorance, and ask for forgiveness after the fact."

"Ignorance is hardly a word anyone would use if they were to describe you, and I imagine the forgiveness would be a foregone conclusion."

"So you'll do it?"

Johnson sighed heavily. "Where do you want to start?"

"Right here, first. Then we'll check out the other spots I've triangulated." She pointed to the other three casings. Then she had a thought. "Tell you what…let's crack those other three casings before we do any digging at all. See what we see."

"What if we find a skull or something?"

I hope we do. "Well, we won't find one in the casings, at least not one that's intact. The diameter of the tubes is too narrow. Plus the drill would chew right through the bone. That's why I wanted the backhoe. You think you could be gentle enough with that thing to get us down close to where we need to be?"

"I've been running equipment like that all my life, darling. I could butter your biscuits with that backhoe without knocking the plate off the dinner table if that's what you wanted."

"Perfect," Patty said. She had Johnson hooked. "Let's go find the dough."

They cracked open the remaining three casings and Patty found more bones in all three. Not only that, all the bones were very close to the same depth as they were in the first casing. Patty looked at Johnson. "Better bring your butter knife over, Carl."

Johnson fired up the Kubota and positioned it so he'd have room to dump the excavated material as far from the trench as possible. Patty wanted a long narrow swath cut, no deeper than a foot above the level of the bones. When Johnson was finished with the first trenched area, he asked her if he should start on the next one or wait for her.

"I'd like you to wait. I'm sort of a stickler for details." She glanced at the Kubota and saw the shovel attached to a side mount. "Borrow that shovel?"

Johnson pried the shovel from the clamps and handed it to her. "Want some help?"

"I better take it from here. I believe you about buttering the biscuits and all, but this is pretty delicate work."

"Suit yourself." Johnson had dug the trench according to Patty's specifications. It was nearly forty feet long with a gentle slope on one end. The slope would allow entry into the swath. Patty walked over to the end and began walking down to the deep part. Johnson sat on the front tire of the tractor as she dug. He couldn't actually see her...only the tip of the shovel as she tossed the dirt out of the trench. After a while the amount of dirt getting tossed became smaller and smaller. Eventually, it stopped altogether. Patty had been down in the trench for over an hour. A few minutes later, she called out to him.

"Hey Carl, you still out there?"

Johnson was, but he was on the far side of the tractor,

with one hand on the cab, the other holding little Johnson as he relieved himself in the dirt.

"Carl?"

Johnson finished his business, gave little J a shake, zipped up, then walked around to the other side of the tractor and headed toward the trench. "Yup. Right here. What'd you find?"

"You better come see for yourself."

Johnson walked up to the edge of the trench and looked down. At first he said nothing, his eyes fixed on the ground where Patty stood, almost seven feet below. When he finally looked directly at Patty, he noticed she was covered in dirt. It was on her clothes, her hands and face, and even in her hair. She was a mess. But her teeth were white and seemed to sparkle as she looked up at him, her violet eyes crinkling with delight at her discovery.

When Johnson finally spoke, the words he used summed it all up. "Holy mother of God."

Fox, the security team leader, had been watching the activity from his post at the entrance to the clearing. After a while, mostly out of boredom—and maybe a pinch of curiosity—he walked over and looked down in the trench. He walked away without saying anything, but when he made it back to his post, he took out his phone and made a call.

Patty had to step carefully to avoid the bones as she made her way back out of the trench. Hundreds, perhaps thousands of bones were at the bottom of the trenched area, and this was only the first area they'd excavated. When she made it to the top she looked at Johnson and said, "I think it's time to call Virgil."

CHAPTER THIRTY-FOUR

Virgil had just thought, *bingo,* when his phone buzzed. He thanked the nurse and stepped out of the room before putting the phone to his ear. "Hey, Patty. How's the test drilling going?" Virgil's mind was still on Carlos and what the nurse had told him.

"We had to stop again."

"Another problem?" He was speaking of mechanical breakdowns. He'd seen the equipment Said had sent out to the site, and if he was being honest with himself, he wasn't all that impressed. It looked old and tired, like something that'd been dragged out of the back corner of a farm equipment dealer's implement junkyard, hosed down, then loaded on the trailers.

"I guess it depends on your perspective. I hate to ask, but do you think you could get down here, like, right away? I don't want to continue with the test drilling until you see something."

"Ah, jeez, Patty, I don't know. You're digging test holes. What is there to see? I'm trying to track a few things down up here. I'm at the hospital now. I was going to speak with

Carlos and get his version of events, but they've got him in surgery so that'll have to wait. Plus, you and your uncle are the experts on this sonic drilling stuff. I don't know anything about it. What good would I be?"

Patty ignored the excuses. "So you've got time."

The truth was, Virgil did have time. He simply didn't want to make the drive unless it was absolutely necessary. "Maybe. What's going on?"

When Patty explained what she'd discovered, Virgil told her he'd be there in less than an hour. "Keep an eye out for my guys. They're on their way as well." Virgil checked his watch. "In fact, they should be there any time now."

"You got it."

"Listen, Patty, I don't want to insult your intelligence, but how sure are you that this isn't a crime scene? Some sort of mass grave."

"Jonesy, I know what I'm looking at here. This isn't one or two bodies, or even ten for that matter. We're talking hundreds, and that's only from one site. There are not only bones, we've found genuine Indian artifacts as well, the kinds of things you'd find at a burial site."

"You're sure? As in sure, sure?"

Patty's voice was a mixture of excitement and exasperation. "Look, the Native Americans of this region, back in the day, had what were—by today's standards—very elaborate procedures for their deceased. After they were buried, they dug up their corpses, cleaned the bones and saved the skeletons of their dead for a mass burial that included furs and ornaments for the dead spirits' use in the afterlife. I've found exactly that. Bones that appear to have been cleaned, no tissue, lots of pieces of jewelry, crude ax heads, rotted wood that may or may not have been hatchet handles, beads, rotted furs, everything. This isn't a crime scene, Jonesy, and as the landowner, I need you down here. With one phone call, this entire area will be flooded with anthropologists and archaeologists from universities and private organizations all across the Midwest. Probably the entire country. You're going to have to manage all that."

Virgil let his head drop until his chin met his chest. All he wanted was one good year of crops so he wouldn't go broke, and a little time to see if they could get the gas out of the ground. Somewhere in the back of his brain he had the thought if someone, anyone at all, walked up to him right now and offered to take the land off his hands for free, he'd sign the papers and run.

"I'm on my way. And Patty?"

"Yeah?"

"That phone call you spoke of?"

"What about it?"

"Don't make it until I get there, okay?"

"It's your land, Jonesy. That means it's your call."

Virgil didn't know how to respond to that. Patty was dear to him, but he didn't feel all that bad when he hung up on her.

They left the island on a chartered Bombardier Global 8000 aircraft, one of the most well-equipped and fastest luxury business jets in the world. It had a top speed that put it close to Mach 1, a cabin that could be configured for business or pleasure, and best of all—at least for Nicky and Wu—access to high-speed internet, which they'd be using during most of the flights.

Wu configured a VPN—a virtual private network—and connected via TOR—The Onion Router—to help eliminate any sort of electronic trail. They bounced their internet connections all across the globe before reaching both the plane on one end, and the hospital in Indy on the other. Any signal intercepts would be impossible to trace, let alone determine an exact location.

The aircraft had been chartered through a shell company set up by Nichole, and relief pilots were standing by at various locations to avoid any crew duty restrictions. Nichole had also arranged for medical care from a surgical nurse practitioner—the closest thing to a doctor they could get—out of Montreal, and told the charter company that they needed the aircraft configured and equipped for medical patient transport.

Something of a minor disagreement ensued between Lola and the others about the nurse. She wanted an actual doctor, and they had to talk her out of it.

"Doctors don't know how to keep their mouths shut," Nichole had told her. "Plus, most of them don't need the money, and the ones who do, we wouldn't want. Believe me, a nurse practitioner is the way to go."

"And if something goes wrong?"

"Nothing is going to go wrong, Lola. I promise."

"You should not make promises you cannot keep."

Linda sat down next to Lola and took her hand. "Lola, Nicky and my husband are the best at what they do. They'll be monitoring Carlos's condition at the hospital every step of the way. They're monitoring him right now. We won't take him unless it's absolutely safe."

Lola shook her head. "I know all this, yet still, I do not like it."

It took some doing, but they eventually brought her around, and Nicky was the one who got the job done. "Remember what I told you, Lola. Carlos is like my brother. I will not let anything happen to him. I give you my word. If something isn't right with his health, we'll call it off and figure out another way."

"There is no other way," Lola admitted. It was something they all knew. Once Carlos was ready for transport only two options remained: He'd go with them, or he'd be deported, and wind up in a Mexican jail. In the end, Lola agreed to the nurse, but the capitulation weighed on her.

A Medevac helicopter was set up in Indianapolis and they had a backup chopper waiting, just in case, at the Lawrenceville-Vincennes airport, which was located right across the Wabash River in Illinois. Their plan wasn't elaborate, at least not by their own standards, but there were critical timing elements that could not be ignored. Chief among them was the basis of Lola's argument for an actual doctor: When could Carlos be safely transported?

The first leg of their flight was non-stop from Montego Bay to Montreal. Clearing customs would not be a problem for any of them, as they all had multiple IDs that were good enough to pass both human and machine scrutiny. Montreal was chosen through Nicky and Wu's connections on the dark web. It was not only where they'd found the nurse practitioner, who, for a very hefty sum, would keep her mouth shut, it also helped them fly under the radar, so to speak. They didn't want to go straight from Jamaica to Indianapolis. That in itself wouldn't cause any alarm bells to ring, especially with their alternate IDs, but medical supplies—the nurse assured them she'd have no trouble procuring what they needed—were much easier to come by in Canada. In addition, if anyone started asking the wrong sorts of questions, a flight from Montreal to Indianapolis was another broken link in what they hoped would be an untraceable chain of events.

The entire plan wasn't nearly as muddled as it appeared. With the money they all had from the lottery gig, much of what they needed was accomplished with a series of calls made with international burners, also untraceable. The shell company Nichole had in place to charter the aircraft was one of many. The company would be used for this purpose only and never again. They'd let it sit afterward for a few months, maybe even a year, then transfer any remaining funds to another, for future use if need be. The same was true for the medevac transportation, the nurse practitioner, and all their accommodations along the way.

They left while Carlos was still in surgery. He'd been under for close to six hours already. The flight to Montreal was a tad over nineteen hundred miles. The Bombardier would get them there in less than four hours, give or take, depending on the winds aloft. Nicky and Wu monitored Carlos's surgical progress the entire flight and by the time they landed and cleared customs, his surgery was not yet half over. The nurse practitioner was waiting when they arrived and after she completed the outbound security checks, the pilots helped her load all the supplies on board the aircraft. An hour later they were back in the air. Less than an hour after that, they touched down at Indianapolis Executive Airport, about twenty miles north of the city and the hospital.

With the Medevac helicopter waiting, twenty miles wouldn't be a problem. They gave the pilots—both the fixed-wing, and helicopter—their contact information and told them to get some rest. They also advised them that they'd need them ready to go on a moment's notice. The pilots didn't mind. They were used to it. All part of the job.

They rented two cars and drove to a nearby hotel. The Wu's checked in first, while Lola and the Pope twins waited at a coffee shop around the corner. Lola went in fifteen minutes later, then the Popes ten minutes after that.

Nicky and Wu set up their gear in Wu's room. After that,

they settled in to wait. Carlos was still in surgery, and the progress reports from the hospital's logs showed they were almost finished. The ICU wait was the outlier. No way of predicting how long that would be. Carlos was young, healthy, and fit, so they were hoping for the best.

Of course, they would have hoped for the best even if he was old, fat, and incontinent, so they simply waited, and monitored.

Lola prayed. The rest of them, not having a single religious bone in their collective bodies, simply hoped for the best.

Murton, Rosencrantz, and Ross arrived in Shelby County, deciding on the way down they first wanted to get a look at the clearing where the Indian had been sighted, and let Patty know they were there. It took them a little longer than it should have to find the clearing…they got turned around on one of the back roads and went the wrong direction for a few miles.

"I thought you said you knew where you were going," Rosencrantz said.

"I do," Murton said. "But with all the corn around here, everything sort of looks the same. Plus, we flew in last time. I've never actually made the drive."

"Should have flown in this time," Ross said. He was in the back seat of Murton's car. Rosencrantz turned and looked at him.

"If you're about to say what I think you're about to say, please don't," Ross said.

Rosencrantz turned back around and looked at Murton. "Do you know where we are now?"

"Yeah. I missed the turn, is all."

"We should have flown in," Rosencrantz said.

"Wouldn't have had a way to get around," Murton said.

"Take it up with Ross. It was his idea."

"You agreed with me," Ross said.

Rosencrantz lifted his chin. "No, I didn't. Had you been paying attention to my tone, you'd have realized my remark was mordant… a critical bon mot, if you will."

"Uh-huh," Ross said. He slipped his phone from his pocket and pulled up Google.

Rosencrantz said, "Put your phone away. It means I was trying to be funny."

"Yeah, well, you better tone it down. You're so funny I'm about to piss myself back here. Besides, I know what your fancy words mean. I was looking at Google maps."

"I believe you," Rosencrantz said. "I really do."

Ross couldn't tell if Rosencrantz was being truthful or not. Murton had been trying to tune them out, but it was impossible. He missed the turn again.

HE FINALLY FOUND THE RIGHT SPOT, TURNED ONTO THE access road, then drove down the bulldozed path. When they got to the opening of the clearing they were met by Fox, who had his hand resting on the butt of his holstered weapon. His rifle had a folding wire stock and hung from a sling that wrapped around his shoulders. When Murton stopped, Fox walked up to the passenger side of the vehicle. Rosencrantz buzzed the window down, gave Fox a lazy look and said, "We're from the government and we're here to help."

"John Fox. Head of security."

Murton spotted the other members of the security detail,

taking note of their combat gear, their weapons, and overall military appearance. He saw Rosie looking at them as well.

"Have we missed the start of the war or are we early?" Rosencrantz said.

"I don't know, sir. To which war are you referring?"

"There's so many it's hard to keep track these days," Rosencrantz said. "The war on drugs, the war on poverty, the war on science, the war on terror, the war on cancer…the list goes on. There's even a war on Christmas now, or so I've heard. Sometimes I wonder what the world is coming to. You guys, on the other hand look like you're not wondering whatsoever, being locked and loaded and all squared away. High and tight, isn't it? Can I hold one of your RPGs?"

Fox gave him a blank stare. "We do like to be prepared for whatever comes our way. And believe me, sir, we are. We did manage to show some restraint and leave the rocket-propelled grenade launchers behind. This time, anyway."

Rosencrantz shuddered. "Spooky."

Fox ignored the jab. "We're here at the behest of Mr. Roger Salter, former United States senator and owner of Salter Enterprises, who, for reasons unbeknownst to me, has charged us with security and oversight of the people who are working this clearing."

Rosencrantz turned to Murton and said, "Behest. Unbeknownst. I like this guy already."

Murton leaned over and said. "Have you or your men seen an Indian since you've been here?"

"No sir. But we were instructed to keep an eye out. Would you mind very much having your associate in the back seat put his weapon away?"

Rosencrantz turned and looked at Ross, who had his handgun out. It rested on his lap, his grip relaxed, the barrel pointed in the general direction of Fox. He turned his attention back to Fox. "Yes, I would mind. It's a great comfort to him. Like a pacifier. It helps keep him calm. And believe me, you want him calm."

"Perhaps he should suck on it."

Ross pulled the hammer back. Rosencrantz saw Fox's fingers twitch slightly, but his weapon remained holstered.

"Anyway, the Indian?" Rosencrantz said. "What were you supposed to do with him? Shoot to kill, that sort of thing?"

"No, sir. We were to detain him, then call the proper authorities."

"And yet the proper authorities are here."

"Are they, sir?"

Rosencrantz put his hand over his heart. "That stings. And right at the beginning of what I thought might turn out to be a beautiful friendship. Now I don't think I'll be able to sleep tonight."

"I could certainly help you with that. I take it you're here to speak with Miss Doyle?"

"No, I already told you, we're here to find the Indian."

"He's not here."

"Miss Doyle it is, then," Rosencrantz said, his fake smile big and bright.

"You'll find her on the other side of the clearing past the drill and crane units. As officers of the law, I take it our presence here is no longer required?"

"You can take it any way you like, as long as you leave," Rosencrantz said.

"Happy hunting, gentlemen."

Murton put the car in gear and pulled away. He looked at Rosencrantz. "Why do you do that? Get everyone wound up like that?"

"Quickest way to tell which side of the fence they're on."

"He was lying about the Indian," Ross said as he put his gun back in his shoulder rig.

Rosencrantz turned in his seat. "How do you know?"

"You mentioned it twice. He looked away both times. The rest of the time, his eyes never left your face, even when Murt spoke and when I set the hammer. I'd bet you a week's pay we could find that Indian by the end of the day. All we need to do is follow that Fox guy when he leaves."

"Can't be done," Murton said. "Not out here. He'd see us a mile away."

"We could arrest him," Ross said.

"What the hell for?" Murton said.

"You heard what he said. He clearly threatened Rosie when he said he could help him to sleep."

"I don't think that was a threat."

"It sure sounded like one to me," Ross said.

Murton glanced at Rosencrantz and smiled. "I think he was hitting on him."

Rosencrantz looked at Murton and laughed. "I've missed you, man."

CHAPTER THIRTY-FIVE

MURTON PARKED HIS CAR AND THEY ALL WALKED OVER TO where Patty and Johnson stood near one of the trenches. Johnson had already buttered the remaining biscuits, and Patty, though not yet finished scraping off the final layer of the second trench, came up to say hello. After everyone was either introduced or re-introduced, Murton looked at Johnson and said, "Those boys giving you any trouble?" He was referring to Salter's men.

Johnson pushed out his bottom lip. "Not a lick," he said. "They showed some curiosity, which didn't strike me as particularly out of character, but they kept to their station. The one in charge come over and after he saw the bones I noticed he made a call. Don't know to who, of course, but it doesn't take a rocket doctor to figure it must have been the boss."

"Roger Salter?"

"Pretty sure it wasn't his missus."

Murton smiled. He liked Johnson. His direct, open and honest mannerisms made it easy to see why Virgil had placed his trust in the man. "Haven't seen any Indians lurking around, have you?"

Johnson shook his head. "Nope. Didn't even see the one from before, during all the excitement."

"Any idea where we might look?" Rosencrantz asked.

Johnson considered the question for a few moments. He removed his hat and scratched at the top of his head. It was purely out of habit, but it looked like he was trying to stimulate his brain cells. "Well, there's always a few here and there around the town of Flat Rock, and I know one in particular that does some landscaping work over at the Salter estate. Don't know his name, just seen him there to nod at on occasion. He tends to the flowers and gardening and what have you."

"What occasion did you have to be at the Salter estate?" Ross wanted to know.

"Meaning what's a fellow like me doing at a place like that?" Johnson said, a pinch of rancor in his voice.

Ross could be direct—they all knew it and had witnessed it before. But this wasn't one of those times. The question was valid. He held out his hands in a peaceful gesture. "No, Sir. I didn't mean to give offense. In our line of work, one question generally leads to another. You'd be surprised how often the things that don't matter lead to the things that do."

Nice recovery, Murton thought.

"Such as?" Johnson said, the rancor now mostly a soupçon of its former self.

"It depends on the answer, really," Ross said. "I meant no disrespect, Mr. Johnson, really. So if you could answer the question…"

"Alright. I guess I'm a little wound up with the shooting and the Indian bones and artifacts and whatnot." Then his face softened and even took on a look of satisfaction. "Anyways, I grow about forty acres of organic sweetcorn each year. Been doing it for well over a decade now. Best in the county. Maybe even the state, though I wouldn't have any way of actually knowing that particular fact. Bottom line? It's damned good. Been doing it long before everyone started saying Monsanto was the devil in disguise. I'll tell you this, with the way the pesticides are working these days, and by that I mean not working, if it weren't for Monsanto and the like—corn byproducts being in almost all processed food— we wouldn't be able to afford to eat."

"And Salter buys your sweetcorn?" Murton said.

"Yup. He throws a big barbecue every year and takes as much as I can give him. I'm taking a load over later today. His annual party is tomorrow night. Well, that ain't quite right. The party starts in the middle of the afternoon, but it runs well into the evening."

"How much is that?" Ross asked.

"How much is what?"

"How much corn are you taking him for his barbecue?"

"Oh." Johnson took off his hat again and stimulated his calculator. "He usually asks for ten bushels. I try to keep that much aside for him. It ain't always easy. Organic corn is hard to come by, especially fresh on the cob."

All the cops were city boys, their exposure to bushels mostly coming from the grocery store when they walked through the vegetable section looking for meat and booze. "How much is that? Ten bushels?"

"You talking cost, or amount of corn?"

"Amount."

Johnson scratched at his calculator some more. Murton thought if he kept at it, his hair might catch fire.

"Well, let's see. An average bushel holds about fifty ears, give or take. That'd be about five hundred ears or so, total."

Ross was starting to get interested. "Must be a hell of a shindig."

"Oh it is," Johnson said. "He invites the entire town of Flat Rock. He says it's his way of giving back to his former constituents, but I think he's really showing everyone that he's better than them. Or at least better off. He likes to be surrounded by the common folk. There's always a smattering of important types as well. You can tell who they are because their jeans are creased like they might have come back from the dry cleaners earlier the same day. Usually their boots don't fit quite right either and if you haven't spotted them right away, you'll know them by the end of the night... limping around with blisters on their heels."

Ross looked around the clearing where they currently stood. "How big is this area right here?"

"Five acres, if little miss pretty's map is accurate."

"It is," Patty said.

Johnson nudged her with his elbow. "I know, darling. Just ribbing you." She nudged him right back.

He looked at the others. "Been doing this so long I can look at a plot of land and tell you within half an acre how big it is. This one is right at five."

"So you grow organic corn in a field that's eight times this size?" Ross asked.

"Yes, eight times the size of this clearing."

"And how many bushels in an acre?"

"Well, it sort of depends."

"On what?"

"Oh, you know, the usual variables. Weather conditions during the growing season, pests and the like. It averages out to around two hundred bushels per acre, give or take."

"So if you've got forty acres at an average of two hundred

bushels per, that'd be…what? Eight thousand bushels? Is that right?"

"Yup," Johnson said, his tone matter of fact.

"And at fifty ears per bushel, you're talking…" He looked at Johnson.

Scratch, scratch, scratch. "About four hundred thousand ears."

"Jesus Christ," Rosencrantz said. "That's a lot of corn." Suddenly the amount Salter was taking didn't seem like that much. "What do you do with the rest?"

"Well, I keep some for myself for eating because it's the best corn I've ever had, and some for the next planting. Corn begets corn, like everything else that comes out of the ground. I sell the rest to organic food markets, like Trader Joe's, Whole Foods, and so on. It's a big deal these days. At first I thought maybe it was going to be a fad, but it really took off. Sort of funny if you think about it."

"In what way?" Murton asked.

"The old way of growing the things we eat is now the new and expensive way. Things have gone so well the past few years I'm going to start packaging the kernels and selling them online, through Amazon and other outfits. Got the packaging equipment coming any day now, and I received my USDA Organic Certification last month. I'll be able to sell a package of organic seeds for twice the price of one ear, and that's after taxes, fees, shipping and everything." He glanced at Patty. "Trees and fish, huh?"

Patty smiled. She was impressed.

Ross shook his head. "I don't know what trees and fish have to do with anything, but I'm starting to think that maybe I should have been a farmer."

"Might want to have a conversation with Virgil about that," Johnson said to Ross. "It's not nearly as simple as it sounds. Anyway, now that we've figured out all things organic, mind telling me how all your questions are going to help you find that Indian you're looking for?"

"Sure," Murton said. "You want some help delivering that corn to Mr. Salter?"

Johnson shook his head. "Naw. I got someone to take care of that."

"You're not talking about that orange-headed smart ass, are you?" Murton said.

"He ain't all that bad," Johnson said, though his eyes drifted away as he made the statement.

"Why not give him the rest of the day off? We'll deliver the corn for you."

"Guess that'd be alright. Gonna have a look-see, are you?"

"Something like that. And you said he invites everyone from around here?"

"That's right."

"So it's an open party."

"Yup," Johnson said. "Free food, free booze, a band, dance floor under a big white tent, the works. There'll be two or three hundred people coming and going all day and night."

Murton looked at Ross and Rosencrantz. "Looks like we'll be going to a party, boys."

"What about all this?" Ross said, waving his arms around at the trenches and bones.

Rosencrantz looked at Murton. "I apologize. I thought we'd be further along in his training by now."

"What the heck does that mean," Ross said.

"It means it's Jonesy's land. That makes it Jonesy's problem."

They heard Virgil's truck as it came down the path and

into the field. Ross turned to Rosencrantz. "I'll be sure to tell him you said so."

"The hell you will," Rosencrantz said, his face suddenly full of worry.

Murton laughed. "Looks like the training is complete, if you ask me, Rosie."

"I'm not," Rosencrantz said.

Virgil got out of his truck and walked over to the group, a dour expression on his face that seemed to precede him by about six paces. He offered no greeting of any kind. "You find that Indian yet?" he said to no one in particular.

Murton answered for the group. "Not exactly. But at least we know where his relatives are." He pointed to the trenches, then said, "Say, you want to go to a party tomorrow? You look like you need to relax a little."

CHAPTER THIRTY-SIX

KEN SALTER SAT WITH HIS FATHER ON THE VERANDA THAT overlooked the acreage of their backyard. Both men watched with mild interest as the various vendors came and went, setting up for the annual summer party. They attended to their particular tasks with little instruction from the staff. They knew their jobs.

"I really don't understand why you keep having this gathering," Ken said to his father.

Roger Salter looked at his son and wondered where he'd gone wrong. Was it the way he'd raised him, giving the boy almost anything he'd wished for since he was old enough to ask? Maybe it was the lack of attention during his younger years...after his mother had passed. *Well, passed was a little disingenuous wasn't it?*

No matter. Gone was gone. And it was all so long ago. In many ways Roger Salter had convinced himself he'd had nothing whatsoever to do with her death. Plus, it wasn't as if the boy hadn't had a female influence during his formative years. Yes, yes, it might have been better if there'd been some consistency regarding the nannies and tutors and so forth, but the point was this: there *had* been women in his life, and while none of them were his actual biological mother, he'd had, on balance, what Roger Salter felt was a decent measure of influential feminine support and guidance. Ruling that out of the equation, it left only his fathering, or lack thereof, as the root cause of his son's lack of…what? Foresight? Clarity of thought? Vision? Drive? How about all of the above?

Roger Salter turned to his son. "We have the party to let the people know that we're on their side. That we understand their struggles. It sends a message that we're one of them. Nobody likes to be on the outside looking in, Son. They want to be on the inside looking out. Quite a difference, wouldn't you agree?"

"Of course, father. It's just that since you're no longer in a position of—"

"Of what? Power and influence? That's what you were going to say, wasn't it?"

"I meant no disrespect. The point I'm trying to make is you're no longer in office…nor are you running for office, yet we still have these extravagant parties every year. I thought this year, especially after the very recent loss of Brian, you might postpone, or even cancel for that matter."

"Brian Cooper was my nephew. But now he's dead, and nothing we do will change that. The men who killed him are dead as well. Based on what I've been told, had Tony not acted as quickly as he did, others might have died as well, including Sheriff Holden. Is it sad? Of course. Will the world stop turning because of it? No. What would you have me do? Sulk about and dab at the corners of my eyes with a handkerchief like a woman? Life is for the living, and the living will be showing up tomorrow. Speaking of showing up, I assume you've received the governor's assurance regarding his attendance?"

"He said he'd be here."

"Wonderful. I'll have some prepared remarks regarding Brian's courageous exit. I think it will play well. There are going to be some very influential people this year, as always. There are a few in particular that I'd like you to pay special attention to. The governor is one, of course, and I've emailed you a list of the others. Don't be their lapdog, you understand, but make sure they feel, mmm, tended to. Be present for them. You can do that for me, can't you, Son?"

"Of course. And what of Tony?"

"Yes…what of him?"

"I heard he was hunting in the field when everything happened. He could be in some trouble."

Roger Salter chuckled. "I can take care of that with one phone call. The sheriff does what he's told. No one will be bothering Tony."

"The sheriff isn't the problem, father. My sources tell me the state is involved and they are actively seeking his whereabouts. It's not the sort of attention we need right now."

"Then Tony will be taken care of accordingly. I'll have the backdated paperwork that shows he was fired some time ago, his whereabouts unknown. Mr. Fox will see to his disposal. Is that a problem for you?"

"I don't even know the man. Why would it be a problem for me?"

They sat quietly for a few moments before Roger spoke again. "I've been meaning to address the situation regarding your friend, Agent Dobson."

"Chris? What about him?"

"Well, if nothing else, to offer my condolences to you. I know you two had a long-standing relationship."

"We don't have any kind of relationship now, thanks to your Mr. Fox and his handiwork."

Roger Salter looked across the grounds. The giant tent was being raised, the men setting the enormous center poles, then tying the ropes to the large spikes they'd hammered into the ground. Watching the tent go up was something the elder Salter always enjoyed. It brought a sense of festiveness to the property that, no matter its natural beauty, somehow always seemed lacking.

"I'm sorry about that, Son. But you must understand that Agent Dobson brought about his own demise. His actions regarding the Jamaican remained a distraction we could no longer tolerate."

"I could have brought him around."

"You had three months to bring him around. I suspect you thought you'd accomplished that, am I right?"

"He told me he was going to let it all go."

Roger nodded in a thoughtful way. "Being misled by a friend is a difficult thing to accept once you've learned of the deception. I've experienced it myself over the years. Don't be upset with John. He was only doing as he was instructed. Had we not kept an eye on Agent Dobson, who knows what might have happened?"

"Surely there must have been another way."

"So you'll stand on the moral high ground for Dobson, but Tony has to go. Do I have that right?" He didn't wait for an answer. "I don't want to be harsh with you, but look at the damage you've created. Dobson was simply the first. Ironically, to protect our interests, you'll get your wish. The Jamaican will be among those tended to as well. He's in hiding now, but he'll turn up eventually. It's unfortunate because had you not involved Dobson in the first place, none of it would be necessary. You never involve your friends in your business affairs. How many times have I told you that?"

Plenty. "But isn't that what you're doing? Isn't that what you do every year with this grand party of yours?"

Roger Salter shook his head. "No, it isn't. I don't *have* any friends, Son. I have acquaintances, business partners, trusted employees, and you. If I did have friends, I wouldn't involve them with something of such import, the way you did with Agent Dobson. Had you come to me for assistance, things may have turned out differently for Chris, and the others."

"You asked me to find out what was going on regarding the Jones property. I used Chris because I'd used him before and I knew I could trust him."

"You're attempting to redirect everything back on me. It's not only embarrassing, it's beneath you. Further, it won't work. I asked you for information. That's all. You decided, with no forethought whatsoever that involving your friend, Chris, was a wise choice. And that's where your thinking went off the rails, so to speak. Your friend, as you call him, was unstable. You've known that over the course of your entire friendship with him. That should have been enough to stop you right there. But it wasn't. He proved his instability by attacking an innocent man, then when he got his comeuppance, he sought revenge. I don't necessarily fault him for that, but if we hadn't intervened, how long do you think it would have been before Agent Dobson started speaking with his superiors—superiors, I might add, who work for the federal government—and dragged us through the muck with him?"

Ken knew his father was right. Father was always right.

"Are you with me, Kenneth?"

"Yes. You know I am. Here's what I don't understand: I know you want the land and I know you want the gas under the ground. After all the trouble, after all the manipulation, the failed plans, the deception—not to mention the deaths—why not simply buy it from the man? Based on what I've heard he's willing to sell. He's not only willing, he's actively been seeking out buyers. It's listed on the open market, for Christ's sake."

"Language, Son, please." Roger Salter spent a few moments in thought, still trying to process his son's ineptness. He sighed heavily. "Of course he's willing to sell. In fact, if my sources are correct, and they always are if they want to remain on the payroll, he's all but ready to give the land away just to be free of it. He's lowered his asking price twice since putting it on the market. He clearly wants to be out from under all the death and destruction that has been brought into his life as a result of mere ownership…most of that my doing, I'll grant you. But what he's not willing to do, what he has publicly vowed never to do, is sell the mineral rights with the land. I'm a lot of things, my boy, some good, most of them not. That's a long-winded way of saying unlike you, I know my limitations. I'm not a farmer and I don't want to be one. I'm also of the age that I neither want nor have time for a long legal battle that would take from what little reserves we have left instead of adding to them."

"Then why not let the whole thing go?"

"It's statements of that sort that make me ask myself where I've failed you. It's not about the money. It's never been about the money. It's about power. It's about making sure I'm never on the outside looking in. Money has nothing to do with that. There will be people at this party who have much more money than we do, but still, they feel as if they're looking through the fence from the wrong side, otherwise they wouldn't attend. Only power puts you on the right side of the barriers. My God, boy, don't you get it? Haven't I taught you better than that?"

Salter's phone rang and when he pulled it out of his pocket he stared at it for a few seconds, as if deciding whether or not to answer. He put the phone to his ear without speaking and simply listened. The only words he said to the caller were 'thank you,' before he put the phone back in his pocket.

He looked at his son and when he spoke, his voice was at once sharp and tainted with sorrow. "See to that list I've provided. And the next time you see Mr. Fox, instead of pouting like a teenaged girl, you might want to thank him. If it weren't for him, you'd already be on the inside looking out."

"Isn't that the goal you referred to earlier?" Ken said, his tone bitter.

"What a disappointment you've turned out to be. I'm not speaking metaphorically. I'm talking about a jail cell, Son."

Ken Salter laughed at his father, something that was almost unheard of, then stood and swept his arm across the wide expanse of the property. "What do you call all this? There's more than one type of cell, father. Your hunger for power and control has tainted your own vision. You're in a cell of your own making."

WHILE THE SALTER MEN WERE HAVING THEIR DISCUSSION, Anthony Stronghill was right around the corner from the veranda where they were seated. He'd been tending to the flowering bushes, trimming off the dead stems and yanking the occasional weed. It hadn't been his intention to listen in on the conversation, but he heard every word, all the same. When their conversation ended, he snuck away and made his way past the vendor and servants, none of whom gave him any attention. When he entered the bunkhouse he was alone. He sat on the edge of his bed.

He knew he'd done the right thing by killing the man who'd murdered Mr. Salter's nephew, but now they meant to kill him? He pulled his phone from his back pocket and listened to the recording he'd made as the men spoke. He hadn't caught all of it, but he had enough to do some serious damage.

If I live long enough, that is.

Because of his position, he had no means of mechanical transportation, and very little money. He'd have to stay and fight, knowing full well he'd be fighting for his life. One mistake along the way and he'd be finished. So would the Jamaican, whoever he was. They wouldn't kill him right away, not with the party so close and all the attention it brought. So he had some time. At least two days.

He hoped.

He listened to the recording once more and thought of his people's history, their struggles, how they'd been exiled from their land. He thought of Little Turtle and wondered what he would do if faced with the same decision.

And that thought alone made the choice clear, as if Little Turtle himself was speaking to him from the grave.

CHAPTER THIRTY-SEVEN

Murton told Virgil everything that'd happened since he and Rosencrantz and Ross had arrived, all while they inspected the trenches Johnson had dug with the backhoe. Virgil tried to concentrate, doing his best to keep his emotions in check, but he was only able to half-listen, his mind going back to the night when they discovered that the land was now theirs, and how happy they'd all been. When he saw the bones and heard Patty describe how she'd found them, happiness regarding the land was so far away he couldn't imagine ever getting it back.

He turned to Murton. "Have you guys been to the Esser place yet?"

"Not yet. I already told you that. We wanted to check in here first."

"And you're going to deliver the corn to Salter's for Carl?"

"Yes," Murton said, drawing the word out. "I told you that too. Johnson said an Indian works the grounds there. It's someplace to start. Besides, with the way that guy's name keeps popping up…"

"Yeah, yeah, I hear you."

"Do you?"

"What's that supposed to mean?"

"I'm wondering if you're okay, Jones-man."

"Never better."

"Great. We're lying to each other now." When Virgil didn't respond, Murton said, "You coming or not?"

Virgil did want to go. He not only wanted to go, he wanted to run from the field, the corn, the equipment, the bones, the artifacts, Patty, Said and his new technology, all of it. *Oh, Delroy, where are you?*

"What was that?" Murton said.

"I can't," Virgil said. "I have to address this, this…"

"Archeological treasure, Jonesy," Patty said with enthusiasm. "That's exactly what it is."

The excitement in her voice was lost on Virgil. "Is it?"

"Yes. That's exactly what it is. I know this changes everything, and I know how disappointing and discouraging it must seem right now, but this is an amazing find. We can't simply fill the holes back up and forget about it."

"Why not?" He said it through his teeth. "Why the hell not? It's my land. Who am I…who are we to decide that it's our place to disturb this…" The words he searched for eluded him, and instead of simply letting it go, he said, "This mess you've found."

Virgil saw the look on her face before she turned and walked away. He reached out to stop her, but felt Murton's arm on his own.

Way to go, Jonesy, he thought.

"Time to pull it together, Jones-man," Murton said, his voice quiet and kind.

"Let go of my arm."

Murton let go and they both turned at the sound of

another vehicle approaching. Rick Said had arrived. Patty walked up and said something to her uncle, then put her arms around him. Her shoulders shook as Said held her, his eyes locked on Virgil the entire time.

Virgil asked Murton to carry on…to take the corn to the Salter estate, check out the Indian if they saw him, then maybe look around town if they thought it would do any good. He'd meet up with them at the Esser house later.

"You sure you're all right?"

"Why do you keep asking me the same questions over and over?" Then, as if he wasn't aware of the statement he'd just made, he asked, "When did you say that party was?"

CARLOS WAS OUT OF SURGERY AND IN THE INTENSIVE CARE Unit. Nicky and Wu had the video feed up for Lola. She was relieved that her son was no longer handcuffed to the bed, but they all knew the only reason he remained unrestrained was because he wasn't conscious. Plus, he had so many IV tubes attached to his arms there simply wasn't any logical way to restrain him without interfering with the flow of liquids that were getting pumped into his body. A restraint on his good leg was an option, but it was also one the ICE agents guarding him ultimately decided against…a little help from the nursing staff helped them with the convincing process. Carlos, the nurses assured the agents, wasn't going anywhere soon.

"What do the reports say?" Lola asked.

Nicky scanned the real-time reports and read the results to Lola. "His condition is listed as stable. They had to put two pins in his upper femur to stabilize the leg. The initial reports indicated the bone had been nicked, but it appears from the surgical reports that there'd been a full fracture as well, so the pins were a necessity. The bullet passed completely through his leg, so they had to manage some muscle damage, but according to this, it looks as though that won't be a long-term problem. The vascular doc reported, mmm, just a moment, I have to change screens, here." Nicky tapped at the keyboard and after a few moments continued his report to Lola. "The vascular doc reports that the femoral artery remained intact, which is very good news, though a significant amount of damage to a number of secondary circulatory vessels occurred. But they were all successfully repaired, and the blood work shows that his Sed rate is down. He remains on antibiotics, which means the chance of infection is almost non-existent. That's all very good news, Lola."

Maybe it was the sound of his voice, or the way he tried to editorialize the reports to make everything sound better than it actually was. Whatever the case, Lola caught the hesitation between the words and the counterfeit enthusiasm of his tone.

"What aren't you telling me?"

He looked up at Lola from his chair and discovered he wasn't able to hold her eyes with his own. He had to look back at the screen before he could continue, even though he knew what the report said. "I'm afraid the neurologist's report isn't quite as...definitive. It's not exactly bad news, but apparently the wound caused some minor damage to his sciatic nerve. The bone fragment clipped the nerve. They're cautiously optimistic regarding the repair they did—a very delicate grafting process was involved—but they won't know for sure until he wakes up and tells them exactly what he feels."

Lola shook her head and waved her hands in front of

herself. "What is this nerve, this, this…sky attic nerve? I have never heard of such a thing. What does it do?"

"Sciatic. It is the main nerve for his entire leg. If it is damaged, there could be some sensory problems. Maybe some difficulties with mobility as well."

"You are saying he may be paralyzed?"

"No. I'm only telling you what the report says. It doesn't speak of paralyzation. It's not mentioned anywhere. It simply says they won't know more until he's able to communicate with them and tell them exactly what it feels like." But Nicky needed to hedge his bets, not wanting to leave Lola with false hope. "In a worst-case scenario, it would only be in the one leg, Lola."

Lola tossed her hands in the air and let them flop down against her thighs. "Oh well, only the one leg, you say? This is great news then, is it not? When he hops around on his good leg I don't think he'll even notice that he's dragging his other leg behind him, leaving a trail in the dirt. Perhaps he will use this trail to find his way home, should he ever get lost. Yes, this is wonderful news."

"Lola, let's not get ahead of ourselves. The report says they repaired the nerve. We'll simply have to wait and see."

"No," Lola said, her anger bordering on the edge of hysteria. "That is not what I mean. We will wait, yes. This we must do because there is no other choice. But we will do something else as well while we wait. We will find out how and why this happened. We will find out who is responsible."

"Why?" Nicky asked. "What is it you want to do?"

"This I do not yet know. But I will when the time comes." She wagged her finger at the computers. "Press your buttons and get me the information I want."

"Wu will do."

"Thank you, Wu." Then Lola looked back at Nicky. "I am

going to speak with Nichole about this. Do not try to change my mind, or worse, deceive me regarding the information I seek, Nicholas. You must promise me."

Lola Ibarra was the closest thing to a real mother Nicky Pope had, his own mother now long gone. He'd do whatever she wanted. "I promise, Lola. We'll figure it all out."

Murton, Rosencrantz, and Ross left with Johnson to load up the corn for delivery to the Salter estate. Said spent a few more minutes with Patty before approaching Virgil. He walked over and said, "I think you owe Patty an apology."

Virgil looked over where Patty sat on the tailgate of Said's truck. "I do. I'll speak with her in a minute, but I need to share something with you first." He needed to let Said know that he'd have to find another way to field test his new technology. When he told him as much, the reaction he got wasn't what he expected.

"Don't worry about it, Jonesy. Your plate is full. And it's about to become even more so."

"If I'm being honest with you, Rick, I thought you'd be more upset."

Said made a noise that landed somewhere between a chuckle and an outright sardonic snicker. "Virgil, after what you did for Patty, I'll always hold you in the highest regard. That's why I wanted to use your field as our testbed. I thought I was doing you a favor. The truth of it is, I've got landowners lined up and waiting. Most of them are offering to pay me to use their land. But I wanted to use yours as a way of saying thank you for saving Patty's life. This new technology, the patents, the gas…none of it would have mattered to me had I lost that young lady."

"I believe you." They stood quietly for a beat. Virgil had calmed down, remembering his father's advice. *There's only now.* "So what are you going to do?"

"I'm going to do what any good businessman in my shoes would do. I'm going to speak with the other landowners—the calls have been coming in from all across the country, by the way—and let them do what they've been wanting to do for three months: I'm going to open the process up for bidding. I'll probably recover the sum total of all my research and development costs in one afternoon. Hell, might even make a little money to boot…and that's just to see if the damned thing will work."

"Ah, it'll work, and you know it."

Said nodded. "Yeah, you're right about that. But here's the question: What are you going to do?"

"About the bones and all that?"

Said nodded.

"I don't know," Virgil said. "I really don't."

"I think you do or we wouldn't be having this conversation. Let me ask you something, if I may."

"Fire at will," Virgil said, his voice lifeless and dull.

"Do you enjoy what you do? Being a cop?"

The question took him by surprise. "You know something, Rick, I really do. I enjoy helping people, the excitement, the hunt, the danger, the sense of satisfaction that comes from knowing that if I do my job, there's one less bad guy out there every once in a while to worry about."

"And how do you know you're doing it well? Beyond the statistics, I mean."

Virgil laughed without humor. "Sometimes it's easy, like with Patty. That was a win, pure and simple. Other times, I wonder, Rick. I really do."

"I'm asking a serious question."

"I know you are."

"Then how about answering."

Virgil shrugged. "I guess it's my gut. I've learned how to listen to it over the years. Learned the hard way, let me tell you."

"I can't even imagine." Said looked down in the trench. "What's your gut tell you about all this?"

Virgil looked over at Patty and stared at her for a long time before he answered. "I'm way out of my element here, Rick. I'd need the kind of help that only Patty—or someone like her—could provide. Unfortunately, she's the only one I know of. Anyone else would be a shot in the dark."

Said made sure he had Virgil's eyes before he spoke, his tone emphatic. "Thus, the apology."

"It's not that simple."

"Of course it is. People have a way of making things harder or more complicated than they need to be. The ones who don't are the good ones…the successful ones. I've seen it time and time again."

"I don't doubt it, but there are things I can't control. I'm tempted to fill in the holes and walk away. But even if I don't, I can't afford to hire her, Rick. I'm barely squeaking by as it is."

"Ah, the money will work itself out, Jonesy. It always does. For starters, I'll cover her salary and we'll see how it goes from there. Patty gets to do what she's always wanted to do, and it'll be close to home. And that makes me very happy."

"You know, when you say the money will work itself out, it sort of pisses me off."

"Why's that?"

"Because that's the way rich people think. It's easy to not worry about money when you already have it. It's like walking up to an indigent person and saying something like, 'if you're so hungry, why not cook yourself some dinner?'"

Said waved his statement away like a bothersome mosquito, then pointed at the trenches. "Do you have any idea how much money gets thrown at these types of things? Don't get me wrong, it's not natural gas level money, but it leans in that direction if you know what I mean."

Virgil found that hard to believe, but the statement caught his interest. "Really?"

"Oh yeah. Go the way I'm suggesting and you'll have offers on this land coming from around the globe. And it won't be at market value based on yield, either. It'll be based on many other factors, not the least of which will be based on want…on ego. With some people, there's no limit to that sort of thing. It's like a drug to them. That's not an exaggeration."

Virgil was warming to the idea. "I won't let the mineral rights go. Not because of the value, but to protect the environment."

"I wouldn't expect you to."

"I also wouldn't want Patty to feel manipulated in any way."

"I don't see that happening, Jonesy. The only way I was able to hire her in the first place was because you agreed to let me use your land. She's not here because of some new patent I have and the amount of money it will generate. She's here for you. She's here because of you. She feels she owes you that."

"She doesn't owe me a damned thing, Rick."

"Well, we could spend all day debating that point and it wouldn't matter one single bit."

"Why not?"

"Because it's how she *feels*, Virgil. Go talk to her. Let her do her thing out here. My gut tells me it's the right thing to do. The question is: what say your gut?"

Virgil looked down in the trench, then over at Patty. A few seconds later he walked over and sat down next to her on the tailgate. They talked about archeology for almost a half-hour and the more they talked, Virgil knew what he needed to do. When they finished, she hugged him, and when Virgil looked at Said, he thought the smile on his face could probably be seen from outer space.

CHAPTER THIRTY-EIGHT

Patty took out her phone and began to make the calls on Virgil's behalf. She stood near the trenches, one hand holding the phone to her ear, the other hand speaking its own language as she waved it about during her conversations. Virgil sat by himself on the tailgate of Said's truck for a few minutes and watched, knowing in his gut he'd made the right decision. When Said approached, Virgil wanted to do nothing more than shake his hand and say thank you. But suddenly he had a thought.

"Hey, Rick, do you have that iPad with the geological survey handy?"

"Yes. It's in the cab. Why?"

"May I see it?"

Said walked around to the passenger side of the truck, grabbed the iPad and brought it over. He pulled up the survey on the screen and handed it to him.

"How did you do that before…overlay the survey and the Google Earth images?"

Said took the iPad back and tapped a few times, then gave it back. "You mean like this?"

"Yeah." Virgil used his thumb and forefinger to manipulate the imagery and zoomed out as wide as he could.

"What are you doing?" Said asked.

Virgil didn't answer directly, mainly because he didn't want to get ahead of himself. "That bidding process you spoke of?"

"What about it?"

"How urgent is it?"

Said considered the question. "In what context?"

"You said you had people willing to pay to use their land to test your technology."

"That's right."

"But you were willing to forego that to use my land."

"Yes."

"And were you serious when you said the bids would be enough that you could recoup your research and development costs?"

Said put a wicked smile on his face, the type Virgil'd not seen from him before. "I may have been trying to steer you a little there. Truth is, I don't want those costs covered."

Virgil found that hard to believe. "Why not?"

"There are some federal tax dollars available for R and D on a project like this. Plus, there are tax credits on the other end if everything pans out. Taking money for the use of land while still in the R and D stage—which is where I am right now—would abrogate the access to the federal money…at both ends of the spectrum. Why do you ask?"

"Three reasons. One, I'd still like to help you. Two, I'd like to offer some friendly payback to someone who's done his level best to keep me afloat—"

"Carl Johnson."

"That's right. If it hadn't been for him, I'd already be sunk."

"And the third reason? You said there were three."

"A little more friendly payback…of a different sort," Virgil said, a wicked smile of his own painted across his face.

"Carl Johnson's land is too far away from where we need to be."

"I know that. We don't need Johnson's land."

"Tell me what you've got up your sleeve."

Virgil took fifteen minutes and laid it all out for Said, who during Virgil's presentation didn't say a word. When he was finished, Said looked at him and said, "Now I know where the term poetic justice comes from." Then, "Glad we're on the same side."

Virgil gave him an odd look, and Said caught it. "What?"

"There's something else I need to speak with you about," Virgil said. "Tell me about Roger Salter."

Murton, with Rosencrantz and Ross in tow, followed Johnson back to Sunnydale Farms to load the corn for delivery to the Salter estate. They made Ross do all the loading. "You know what we need?" he said to Murton and Rosencrantz.

They both looked at him, their expressions dull and uninterested.

"A new guy on the squad."

"We have a new guy," Murton said. "It's you."

"I know. Know how I know? I'm the one doing all the heavy lifting."

"I've got a bad back," Rosencrantz said.

"I don't want to get my clothes dirty," Murton added. "Besides, it's only ten bushels."

"Not only that," Rosencrantz said, "if we tried to divide it up equally among the three of us, there'd be one left over and then you'd bitch about having to do the extra work, which you'd have to do, because you're the new guy. So since we knew you were going to bitch about the inequity regarding the division of labor, we figured it didn't make much sense for us to load any of it." He tapped the side of his head with his index finger. "That's my superior intelligence at work, right there."

"I suppose you want me to drive the truck too?" They were using one of Johnson's flatbeds.

"No, you look a little tired. I'll drive."

"Shotgun," Murton said.

Ross tossed the final bushel on the truck and shook his head. "Whatever."

"Did he just whatever us?" Murton said to Rosencrantz.

"Kids these days."

Johnson, who'd been standing there the entire time finally said, "Is it always like this with you guys?"

Murton pulled his head back and tucked his chin. "Like what?"

"Never mind." He handed Murton a slip of paper that had Salter's address on it, along with an invoice. "Make sure you get the payment before you unload. I made the mistake of sending a bill once. Ever try to get a rich person to pay a bill on time, or at all, for that matter?"

Murton looked at the invoice. "Holy smokes. Maybe he couldn't afford it."

"Like I said, it's good corn."

The three men crammed into the cab of the truck, Rosencrantz behind the wheel. The truck was an old Ford, with a manual transmission, the shifter on the steering column. Rosencrantz wasn't paying attention and assumed it was an automatic. When he turned the key to fire it up, the truck lurched forward then stopped. Ross banged his head on the back window. "It's a manual transmission," he said, rubbing the back of his head.

"I see that now," Rosencrantz said, his face a little red. He pushed the clutch to the floor, then grabbed the shifter, pulled it toward the wheel and pushed up.

"I don't think—"

"Shut up kid, I've got this."

Rosencrantz gave it some gas, then let the clutch out. Fortunately they weren't going all that fast when they backed into the tree.

"First gear is toward you and down," Ross said. "Second is up and away. Third is down and away." Then he tapped the side of his head and said, "That's my superior intelligence, right there."

They got out and looked at the back bumper. There didn't seem to be much damage…to the tree. The bumper, however, had a large dent right in the center. Johnson walked over, looked at Rosencrantz and said, "You mad at my tree?"

"I think the clutch slips a little, is all."

"I guess that'd explain it." He pointed down the drive. "The Salter estate is that way."

They got back in the truck, Rosencrantz found first gear and they lurched their way down the drive. Johnson had wondered if they'd be able to collect the money for the corn. Now he was beginning to wonder if he'd ever see his truck again…let alone the money. He went inside and got on the computer. He'd need a new back bumper for the truck.

"WHAT ABOUT HIM?" SAID ASKED.

"How deep into him are you?"

"Would you mind telling me why you want to know?"

Virgil needed to be careful here. He trusted Said, but he couldn't let his trust determine the direction of the conversation, nor the investigation, for that matter. "His name came up, is all. Our researcher is doing a little background workup on the man." He tipped his finger at Said. "That's confidential, by the way."

"I hear you."

"When I found out that he's involved with your new technology, it got my attention. He is involved…I have that right?"

Said shrugged his shoulders—an innocent gesture. "It's strictly business."

"That's pretty vague, Rick. I was hoping you could be a little more specific."

Said tipped his head back in thought. When he spoke, he sounded at ease. "You've heard the expression, Jonesy…it's usually something along the lines of, 'He built the company with his own blood, sweat, and tears.'"

"Yes. So what?"

"That's the way I've built every business I've ever had a hand in, with one minor difference. It's always been my blood, my sweat, and my tears…but it's also always—and I mean every single time—someone else's money. You never risk your own money on a new venture. You let someone else risk theirs."

"Why?"

"Never took any business courses in college, huh?"

"I didn't go to college, Rick. I went to the war, courtesy of the United States Army."

"Is this the part where I thank you for your service?"

Virgil was watching Said closely, looking for any sign of deception. "No. It's the part where you answer the question."

Said shrugged again. "It's the way these things work. Any new venture is expensive. Some more than others. This one was…is, very expensive. Not only that, we're talking about proprietary information and technology that will change the way natural gas is extracted from the earth. It will make some people extremely wealthy. It will also shutter many others, or at the very least, force them to change their operational methods. If they do decide to change, they'll have to pay me to do it. And we're not talking about mom and pop operations here, Jonesy. We're talking about corporations that help make up the Fortune Five Hundred. As the owner of a geological survey company that specializes in the discovery of natural gas deposits, Salter was a good choice. As a former United States senator with power, influence, and clout with the CEOs of those same companies—not to mention his relationships in Washington—his involvement makes him a great choice. The amount of pushback that's headed my way is something I don't care to think about. Salter is the type of guy who can make it all go away, or at the very least shelter me from the worst of it."

"Does he have anything on you?"

Said didn't hesitate. "Not a thing. Know why? There's nothing to be had. I'm sure he'd like something. In fact, I'd be surprised, maybe even mildly offended if he wasn't trying to find something. But he won't because there's nothing to find. You know that, Jonesy."

Virgil nodded. "I do. What if he tried to create something?"

"I know how to watch my back."

"Could you do it without him?"

"Why?"

"I'm trying to protect you, here, Rick."

"I understand. And I'm grateful, I truly am." Said thought for a moment. "The short answer is both yes and no."

"What's the longer short answer?"

"Have you ever driven a Tesla?"

"No."

"I own one. It's a fantastic car, brought about by exactly three things: A man with a vision, new technology that made it all possible, and the desire of people who want reliable transportation without destroying the planet. The really fascinating part of the whole thing is the fact that electric cars have been around since the eighteen hundreds. But nobody wanted them. Know why?"

"No, I don't," Virgil admitted.

"Because the oil and gas industry, even way back then, knew how to manipulate the market. And if you can manipulate the market, you can control the people who are the market."

"The consumers," Virgil said.

Said tipped a finger at him. "Exactly. My new sonic drilling technology is the exact same thing, and this is the eighteen hundreds, all over again. Different industry of course, but the outcome would be the same. Could I do it without Salter's money? Yes, but why would I when his is readily available?"

"So how deep is he in? Salter."

"Deep enough that I'm not looking forward to the conversation regarding what's happening out here, with the bones and all that."

"You're talking about the delay…finding another test bed and all that?"

Said nodded.

"Do you have to tell him right away?"

"I don't have to tell him at all. He already knows. Those

were his men out here today. He called and wants me at his place to talk about it. Figure out the next steps and all that."

Virgil thought about that for a moment. "Did he sound upset?"

Said shook his head. "No. He never sounds upset. He's shrewd and smart and all that, but he keeps his manners. I don't think I've ever heard him raise his voice."

Virgil thought about what his father had told him. *We're talking pure evil, here, Virg.* "So you're not worried?"

"About what?" Said asked. He was genuinely confused.

Virgil waved his hands in the air. "Ah, I don't know."

"It's just business, Jonesy. Besides, the delay will amount to no more than a day or two. I wasn't kidding when I said I had landowners lined up and waiting. One phone call and everything will be ready to go. After that, it's simply a matter of getting the equipment in place, like we did out here. Listen, I've got to run. I'm late for a meeting."

"Watch your back, Rick."

Said tipped a finger at him. "Watch your own back, hotshot. I'm good."

CHAPTER THIRTY-NINE

They arrived at the estate, purposely parking away from all the other vendors, giving them an excuse to walk around and get a good look at the grounds. "I can see why you've got a bad back," Ross said to Rosencrantz. "Mine is killing me."

"Very funny," Rosencrantz said. "Believe it or not, I've never driven a stick shift before."

"I believe you," Ross said. "No further convincing required."

"I think I did okay…once I got the hang of it."

"When, exactly, was that? I must have passed out when it happened. Probably from when I hit my head."

"Why put the shifter on the column, anyway? Jesus Christ, it's like trying to fly the space shuttle or something."

Ross looked at the truck before he turned and spoke to Rosencrantz. "Ground Control to Major Tom."

Tom Rosencrantz, who could give as good as he got, thought he might have finally met his match. He refused to look at Ross, instead focusing his attention on Murton.

"That's hilarious. Maybe he should try his material at an open mic night sometime. What do you think?"

"I don't think he was trying to be funny," Murton said, a tinge of urgency in his voice.

Rosencrantz turned to Ross and jerked his thumb at Murton. "This one says you weren't trying to be funny. So what was it you were trying to do?"

"Get your attention. More specifically, I was wondering if you set the parking brake on the truck." He pointed past Rosencrantz's shoulder. "It looks like the lunar lander is about to break orbit."

Rosencrantz turned and looked back at the truck. They'd parked on a shallow incline and the truck was beginning to roll backward. It was headed straight for the giant tent.

"Oh fuck me," Rosencrantz said. Then he started to run.

The truck didn't get far, thanks to what any weekend golfer would happily describe as a country club bounce. The left front wheel hit a natural depression in the grass and it was just enough to steer the vehicle away from the tent. Rosencrantz, who didn't actually have a bad back made a running leap and dove through the driver's side window and hit the brake pedal with his left hand. Once the truck was stopped, he set the parking brake with his other hand and pushed himself up on the seat. When he wiggled back out the window, he got a round of applause from a group of workers setting up tables and chairs under the big tent.

He gave them a sweeping bow, then walked back over to Murton and Ross.

"Well done, Major," Ross said.

Rosencrantz pointed a finger at him. "You knew about the parking brake, didn't you?"

"You made it clear you didn't want my help. I was only following your instructions." He held his hands up and finished with, "Planet earth is blue, and there's nothing I can do."

"Enough with the Bowie, already," Rosencrantz said. Then he looked at Murton. "Pretty nice save, huh?"

"Yeah, as saves go, it was pretty good. I'll be sure to make note of it in my report." He turned to Ross, "You've actually got a pretty nice singing voice."

"Thank you."

"Whatever," Rosencrantz said. "Clearly I'm the only one here who cared enough to do anything about it. Hey, look at that." He pointed to a long, narrow, one-story building.

When they looked, they saw a man exiting the building. He carried a shovel, rake, and an electric hedge trimmer. He had dark brown skin and his denim work shirt was tucked into his jeans. The turquoise belt was cinched tight around his waist, like maybe his pants were one size too big. When he set his tools down and removed his hat to wipe his brow, his long, jet-black hair fell to his shoulders. He reached up and gathered it together before tucking it back under his hat. He retrieved his tools and began walking toward the side of the main house.

"Johnson said an Indian does landscape work here," Rosencrantz said.

Murton nodded. "When Jonesy told me what Patty said, I got the description of the Indian. That could very well be him."

"Want me to take him?" Ross asked.

"No," Murton said. "It doesn't look like he's going anywhere. Besides, we can't arrest someone without a positive ID. What we need is a picture to show Patty. If it's him, we'll come back with a warrant and pick him up."

Ross shrugged. "I can get a picture, no problem. You guys handle the corn."

"You're giving the orders now?" Rosencrantz said.

"No. I'm simply saying I can get a picture."

"Twenty bucks says you don't."

Ross looked at his partner. "Twenty, plus the unloading of the corn."

"Deal." Rosencrantz said.

"And I get to drive back," Ross said.

"I was going to let you anyway, so…"

"Let me?" Ross took out his phone and headed for the main house. Murton and Rosencrantz headed for the tent to find out where to off-load the five hundred ears of corn.

Ross had his phone out and was walking around the area where the main party would be held. He took pictures of the tent, the landscaping, a particularly large old-growth tree that really was picture-worthy, and anything else that made him look like someone who enjoyed taking pictures for pleasure. Everyone was so busy with their individual tasks no one seemed to pay him any sort of attention. He gradually worked his way toward the side of the main house, close to where the Indian was working. When he was close enough, he stopped by a section of roses and took a few shots. He'd positioned himself in such a way that if the Indian looked at him, all he had to do was hit the button and he'd have him.

Tony Hill turned and looked at the man taking photographs. "What are you doing?" He removed his hat to wipe the sweat from his forehead before tucking his hair back inside.

Ross turned, never taking his finger from the button. "Oh, I'm sorry. I hope I'm not disturbing you. I was getting some shots of these roses, here. They're beautiful. I take the pictures, then use them as a guide for my painting. I'm not very good. With the painting, I mean. It's a hobby…one I should probably give up."

"I don't think Mr. Salter would like you doing that… taking the pictures."

Ross put the phone in his pocket and held out his hands in a peaceful gesture. "They're just flowers. But I'm sure you're right. Wouldn't be the first time I've gotten in hot water with someone for snapping a few pics without their permission. Maybe we could keep it our little secret?"

"Why are you really here?"

Ross didn't skip a beat. "Delivering the sweetcorn from Sunnydale farms on behalf of Mr. Carl Johnson." He pointed to Murton and Rosencrantz. They'd just finished unloading the corn. "I let my underlings do the grunt work."

"It looks like they are finished. I would not linger, if I were you."

Ross nodded. "I hear you. Rich folks, huh?"

The Indian simply stared at him.

"Anyway, nice talking to you." He took a last look at the flowers. "You do good work." He stuck out his hand and said, "My name is Andrew."

The Indian didn't offer to shake Ross's hand or respond in any way, so Ross shrugged and headed for the truck. He wanted to check his phone to make sure he'd gotten the shot, but he could feel the Indian's eyes on his back, so he left the phone in his pocket and kept walking.

By the time they got the corn unloaded, Ross was back and they all piled into the truck.

"Get the shot?" Murton asked.

"Get the check?"

Murton tapped his breast pocket. "Right here. Now how about the shot?"

"We'll know in a minute," Ross said as he dropped the truck in gear and pulled away. "I'd like to get off the property before we all start looking at pictures I wasn't supposed to be taking in the first place. Besides, distracted driving is the leading cause of death in traffic accidents." He drove the truck from the tent area and onto the driveway. They passed under the arched branches and wound their way out to the road. Once clear of the property, Ross pulled over and took his phone from his pocket. When he looked at the photos, he smiled and glanced at Rosencrantz. "You owe me twenty bucks."

Rosencrantz took the phone and looked at the pictures of the Indian. "They're a little blurry, but if we're lucky, maybe one of them will be good enough that Patty can make a positive ID."

Murton leaned over and looked at the phone's screen. "A little blurry? These are perfect. It looks like something you'd see on the cover of Modern Indian magazine. Give the kid some credit, why don't you?"

"Is that a thing? Modern Indian magazine?" Ross asked Murton.

"That's why," Rosencrantz said to Murton. Then he looked at Ross. "No. It's not a thing. Drive already, will you? And watch the clutch. It tends to slip."

Ross put the truck in gear and drove them away from the

Salter estate and back to Johnson's. The ride was smooth, Ross working the shifter like a pro, which kept Rosencrantz quiet for the rest of the ride. By the time they returned the truck, gave Johnson the check and retrieved Murton's car, the hour was late, and dusk had settled in on the day. Johnson told them everyone had already left the field, so they went straight to the Esser house to meet up with Virgil.

CHAPTER FORTY

Carlos had regained consciousness, but it wasn't without its difficulties. He'd been under for so long the medical team began to worry when he didn't wake up as scheduled. Even though his vital signs were well within normal parameters, the doctors finally decided it was time to wake him up. And that's when things went a little sideways.

Without a full medical history—which they didn't have—the doctors had no way of knowing that Carlos was allergic to the medicine they used to bring him around. They'd no sooner pushed the meds through the IV line when he began to have a Grand Mal seizure. It rarely happened, but because it had been known to happen, they were ready. They administered a different medication to stop the seizure, and it worked. Except there were two problems: Carlos still didn't wake up, and the medicine used to stop the seizure also stopped his heart.

A crash cart was wheeled over and they had to shock him twice to get his heart started again. Once all that was under control, they drew blood for testing, and decided to use a different medicine to wake him. This time, it worked.

Wu and Nicky Pope sat with their faces glued to the monitors, watching the entire process unfold. When everything finally settled down, they sat back, both of them drenched in sweat having witnessed Carlos's near-death experience.

"I know what I said to Lola…about not deceiving her," Nicky said. "But I think this is something we should keep to ourselves."

"Wu do too."

They backed the video feed up—the entire thing was hooked into a digital video recorder—and deleted the few minutes where the medical staff almost lost Carlos. Then they spliced the segments together. After looking at it a few times, they decided it'd take an expert eye to notice the splice. Lola didn't have an expert eye. Lola had cataracts and trifocals.

"I think we're okay," Nicky said.

"It not us Wu worry about. Carlos had a heart attack only minutes ago. What if he has another?"

"He's strong, Wu. He'll be okay."

"It will delay our plans. We have pilots and aircraft waiting."

"Then they'll have to wait longer. For the amount of money we're paying them, they'll wait as long as we need."

Lola walked into the room and Wu and Nicky both looked at her. "What is it? I can see it on your faces. What is wrong?"

"Nothing, Lola," Nicky said with a forced smile. "Carlos is beginning to wake up."

Lola crossed herself, then said, "Thank God. Let me see."

Wu turned his monitor so Lola could have a better look.

"Why are there so many people at his bedside?"

Wu visibly swallowed but didn't say anything.

"It's because he just woke up," Nicky said. "I'm sure

there are lots of tests to be administered. But it's all very good news."

Lola looked at them both. "You are finding the information I requested?"

Nicky nodded rapidly at her. "This is everything we could get." He handed her a thin stack of papers.

"Nichole and I will be determining our next steps. How long before Carlos can be moved? Have they said?"

"It may be longer than we anticipated."

"Good."

Her response surprised Nicky and Wu. "Why good?" Wu said.

"Because we are not leaving until the people responsible for this have been made to pay."

Nicole and Lola sat together on the sofa and looked at the information Nicky had provided. Linda stood and stared out the window, listening. She didn't need to see the information Nicky and her husband had gathered. She simply wanted to be present for her friend, Lola. Nichole was their leader, and if Lola pushed too hard, Nichole would push back. It rarely happened, but Linda had seen it before. Nichole could sometimes be a little…harsh.

On the face of it, there didn't seem to be that much information, but it was enough to connect certain dots, and Nicky, as usual, had connected them. What they did with the dots would be up to Nichole, if they did anything at all.

"Getting him out of the hospital and out of the country is our primary goal, Lola. Our plans are already in place."

"This I know. But if there is an opportunity for some sort of, mmm, justice, then I would like to explore it."

Nichole thought about it for a few minutes. "It may have to wait."

"And you say this why?"

"For two reasons. I've already stated the first. Carlos. We cannot let emotions get in the way of his rescue. The other reason is we do not want to do anything that would jeopardize our own futures, and that includes Carlos. If we move too quickly, the police would know who was responsible. Maybe not right away, but they would figure it out."

"I see," Lola said, her anger evident. "So they will simply get away with almost killing my son. That is what you are saying, is it not?"

"No, Lola, that is not what I am saying. I'm saying that if we wait, and plan, your day will come…Carlos's day will come. Nicky and I waited decades to take down the men responsible for our father's death."

"Yet the man who actually killed him still walks the streets, working as a police officer."

"He does. But I don't really blame him for my father's death. He acted honorably and he did so for the protection of himself and others."

"Yet the man he protected was Bradley Pearson, one of the men you and your brother blame for your father's death."

"That's true. But in the end, the man I blamed was killed and that was good enough for Nicky and me. Blaming Virgil Jones for my father's death would be like blaming the bullet that was fired from his gun. What good would that do? And we never had any intentions of actually killing Pearson, or Pate. We never intended to kill anyone for that matter. We're not murderers, Lola. Things went a certain direction and people died…but they did it to themselves. That's why we are still free today. All we wanted was for them to go to jail."

"And this is what I want for the man who almost killed my Carlos."

"The man who almost killed Carlos is dead, Lola."

"This I know. But the men responsible…the men who operated behind the scenes…they must go to jail. You were after Bradley Pearson, but Mr. Pate was the one who pulled his strings. I will have my Mr. Pate."

"Your Mr. Pate, as you call him, is a man named Roger Salter. He's a former United States senator and a very powerful and influential person. People like that don't get to where they are by wearing blinders."

"I do not know what you mean," Lola said.

"I mean he'd see us coming from a mile away. But if we wait and plan very carefully, we may be able to either put him in jail, or take his money. Maybe both. So the question is, do we wait and do it right, or do we try to throw something together in a rush, maybe putting Carlos's freedom at risk?"

Lola was so worked up and emotional that her hands shook as she spoke. "Then we will wait. But you must promise me something. Should an opportunity arise, something unexpected that we perhaps cannot see at this moment…if it is safe, we will make our move."

"I promise, Lola. But only if it is safe."

"Sí. Only if it is safe."

Lola stood to go check the video feed again.

"And Lola?"

She stopped and turned to face Nichole. "I decide if it is safe. Agreed?"

"*Sí, Sí.*" She walked out of the room and Nichole looked at Linda.

"What do you think?"

"I think we'll have to watch her," Linda said. "She wants them to pay."

Nichole nodded. She knew Linda was right. Lola was dear to them all. If she wasn't, they wouldn't be risking their freedom to rescue her son. "At some point, a line might have to be drawn."

"Let me know when that is," Linda said. "I don't want to be around to see it."

Lola Ibarra did her best to keep her emotions in check when she heard the name Roger Salter, the man who'd abused her for so long, all those years ago. Now she was faced with a decision. Did she simply focus her efforts on freeing her son, or did she take her revenge against the man who'd held them both captive, the man who'd repeatedly raped her and kept her passport locked away in his safe?

She would not risk Carlos's safety. Of that she was sure. But if she could find a way to get to Roger Salter and do something, she would do it. The other question: What did *something* look like? What could she, Lola Ibarra, do to a man like him? His wealth and power were of such proportions, Lola couldn't imagine a scenario where anything she did would be of consequence to the man. Yes, she had money. In fact, her own wealth was formidable, yet she lacked the critical thinking and necessary skill sets it took to bring a man like Roger Salter to his knees. In the end, she decided she had only two choices: Choice one, do nothing. That meant she would live the rest of her life knowing the man who'd damaged her physically and emotionally, the man who degraded her and humiliated her was living his life unhampered, free from fear that the actions of his past might one day bring about his own demise in ways he could never anticipate. Or, choice two—take some sort of action, an action that could only be done with the help of the ones she loved, perhaps placing them all in grave danger.

The first choice was the obvious one. Lola knew this. The second choice would be much harder, harder in ways Lola didn't want to think about. She would have to tell the others what had happened to her. She would have to relive the humiliation and degradation all over again. She would have to expose herself to the others in ways she rarely thought about herself. How else were they to understand? And even if she put herself through all that, the question remained. What would they do?

Only one way to find out.

She went back and checked on Carlos again. Nicky and Wu told her there'd been little change.

"I see. Would you both come with me?"

Wu and Nicky looked at each other, then at Lola. "Sure," Nicky said. "What's up?"

"What is up is what we shall discuss."

They went into Nichole's room then had to wait for Linda, who was making a pizza run for dinner. Lola paced around the room while they waited, the others watching her move nervously about. When Linda finally returned, Lola asked everyone to listen very carefully to what she was about to say. She also asked for their forgiveness in advance if she struggled while divulging her tale.

She spent almost a full hour telling her friends of her ordeal all those years ago when she arrived in the states. She spoke of finding work with the Salter family, the disappearance of Salter's wife, the dismissal of any actual investigation by the authorities, the way she was held prisoner, and most importantly, how Roger Salter had repeatedly raped and abused her all throughout Carlos's childhood. She cried often as she told her story, and when she finished she began to sob so hard it became difficult for her to breathe. It was so bad that for a moment, they thought she might be in need of medical attention.

Nichole ushered everyone out of the room and sat on the sofa, her arms wrapped around Lola's shuddering body. They sat for a long time without any words, and when Lola finally regained her composure, Nichole looked her in the eye and told her she was drawing a line. But it wasn't the line she and Linda had spoken of earlier. This was a different line altogether.

Salter would pay.

Virgil called Sandy to check in and let her know he'd be spending the night at the Esser house. He brought her up to speed regarding the findings in the field and Salter's connection to Said's operation.

Sandy was excited by the archeological aspect of the discovery. The stress she and Virgil had been under regarding the land remained untenable. Something had to be done, and they were at the point where it almost didn't matter what that something was. Anything would be a relief. "And Rick thinks Patty can pull it all together?"

"He says so. I spoke with her about it as well. She knows her stuff. I'll tell you something else, she also knows what she doesn't know. Not only that, she freely admits it. That's the sort of thing that tells me she's the one for the job."

"Will we be able to get out from under the land in time?"

"According to Patty, once word gets out, the offers will start coming in. She said it might come down to an auction. An actual bidding war."

"Yes, but how long will that take?"

"I'm not entirely sure. But there's time. We've got this year's harvest to keep us going, and I've got some other ideas. Nothing I want to talk about on the phone, though. The boys doing okay?"

It was a lot of information for Sandy to digest. "They're fine, Virgil. How are you?"

"Tired. That's how I am."

"Get a good night's rest."

"I will."

They were about to hang up when Sandy said, "Don't forget."

"Forget what?"

"To watch the toilet flushing and all that. The septic is about to back up, remember?"

CHAPTER FORTY-ONE

HE'D JUST FINISHED WITH SANDY WHEN HIS PHONE RANG. Becky.

"Hey, boss-man. Do you want the good news, the really good news, or the great news?"

Virgil was instantly skeptical. "Why do I feel like I'm being set up?"

"Because you spend too much time with Rosencrantz?"

Virgil laughed. "You're probably right. Tell you what, I'll take the news in any order you care to dish it out…so dish away."

"Fair enough," Becky said. "The good news is the system is clean and back in order."

"That is good news. I'll take some more, please."

"Got your laptop handy?"

Virgil did. "Yeah. Give me a second to fire it up."

Becky said she would. When she heard Virgil set his phone down, she hung up on him.

He pulled his laptop from its bag and fired it up. Once he had it ready, he picked the phone up and said, "Okay, let me have it. Hello? Becky?" He pulled the phone away from his ear and checked the screen. He'd lost her. He was about to call her back when his laptop chimed at him. Becky was Face-timing him. He sighed and hit the connect key.

"Don't look at me like that."

"Becks, you know I don't like to Face time."

"Yeah, but I do. Anyway, I've got them."

Virgil suddenly perked up. "Delroy and Huma?"

"No, Jonas and Wyatt. Try to keep up, will you? Yes, Delroy and Huma. Remember when I said I pulled the system logs and discovered Delroy accessed two archived files?"

"Yeah."

"And the problem was I couldn't tell which files they'd accessed until I was done rebuilding and cleaning the system?"

"Boy, you really know how to lead into something."

Becky ignored him. "I accessed the files they looked at. I'll play them whenever you're ready."

"What do I have to do?" Virgil asked.

"Nothing. I've already done it. That's why you've got me, and why we need to talk about a pay raise."

"Becky…"

"Alright, alright. I'm just messing with ya. Watch the screen on your computer, sharp stuff." Becky punched in a series of keystrokes and Virgil watched as the screen split in two. One side showed Delroy and Huma entering the bar, while the other showed a tow truck maneuver into position as two men hooked up Delroy's car before towing it away. "Watch the timestamps on the videos."

Virgil watched the video's timestamps at the top of the screen. They matched perfectly.

Virgil pumped a fist and said, "Yes! That clears him right there."

Becky smiled at him from a tiny box in the upper right-hand side of Virgil's computer screen. "And if that doesn't, all this should." She held a few sheets of paper in front of the computer.

"What's that?"

"More good news. Open your email."

Virgil did. After a few moments he said, "Okay, I've got it. What am I looking at here?"

"The first page is a system's log that shows Delroy accessed the internet from this station and bought two tickets from Indy to Montego Bay, with a connection in Charlotte, North Carolina."

Virgil scrolled to the next page. "And the next?"

"That was much harder to get. I had to bounce a packet through Ukraine, of all places. They had a backdoor that opened a secure socket layer—"

"Becky?"

"What?"

"How about you give me the English version? I don't know what the hell any of that means."

"Gotcha. It's a system log from Uber that shows one of their drivers picking up Delroy and Huma and taking them to the airport. Now watch the video. It should be right there on the screen."

Virgil watched as Delroy and Huma got into a dark-colored sedan and left the bar. "And the next?" Virgil asked again as he continued his scroll.

"That one should have been the hardest to get a hold of, but it was actually the easiest. It's the flight manifests for the American Airlines flights. Both the one from Indy to Charlotte, and the one from Charlotte to Montego Bay. Delroy and Huma are in Jamaica, Jonesy, and the timing of it all is irrefutable proof that neither of them was involved in Dobson's death."

"When was the last time I told you I love you?"

She batted her eyelashes at him. "It's been so long I can't remember."

"Well I do…love you. You're the best, Becks."

Rosencrantz, Ross and Murton came in the Esser house and found Virgil in the kitchen talking to his computer. Murton caught the last part of Virgil's statement, and said, "If you're putting the moves on my woman, you could at least have the decency to do it when I'm not around."

"I didn't hear you come in," Virgil said.

"That's because he was expressing his love for me," Becky said over the computer. "Besides, you divorced me, remember?"

Virgil looked at Murton. "Becky is getting a raise," he said. "A big one."

"Excellent," Becky said.

Murton tossed his car keys on the table, then leaned over Virgil's shoulder and looked at Becky on the screen. "I may have acted harshly about the divorce. I'm willing to work things out."

Virgil scrolled through the final pages Becky had emailed to him. No explanation on her part was necessary. They were screen grabs of the men who stole Delroy's car, and the license plate of the tow truck used to do it.

"I know you don't like me to run plates without asking first," Becky said. She held a final piece of paper in her hand and wiggled it in front of the computer's camera. "But, I've got the address of the towing company. I'm texting it to you now."

Virgil's phone dinged when the text came through. "Thank you. Listen, Delroy and Huma will be staying someplace in or very close to a town in Jamaica called Lucea. It's pronounced 'Lucy,' but spelled L-u-c-e-a. Can you run their cards and figure it out?"

"I already have. I've got the hotel where they're staying and everything they've purchased since they arrived. Looks like they left without packing."

"As would anyone who thinks they're under attack."

Virgil looked at Ross. "I'm volunteering you to drive back up to Indy. Tonight."

Ross liked to be near the action. He sensed the trip would take him away from it. "Why me?"

Virgil ignored the question. "Get with Becky and take hard copies of everything, wrap it up into a report and get it to the district attorney's office first thing in the morning. We'll need a warrant for the towing company and I want the identities of the men on these video clips before the ink is dry."

Becky wasn't finished. "Hey, Jonesy?"

Virgil looked at the computer. "What is it, Becks?"

"You didn't let me get to the really great news."

All four men were now huddled around the computer, looking at Becky on the screen. "I got the print back...the one you had Mimi send over. It comes back to a guy that spent a large percentage of his life in federal custody, all of it in solitary confinement. He's smaller than me, but apparently meaner than a barn mule. I looked at the prison psychologist's notes on this guy. We're talking full-blown sociopath."

Virgil looked at Rosie. "You're going too."

Rosencrantz nodded. Things were getting serious now.

Becky continued: "The arrest record and booking photo of the barn mule—his name is Dale Jakes, by the way—matches the video." She clicked a few keystrokes and a photo of Jakes popped up on the screen. "Here's a screen-grab of him from the video."

"Never seen him before," Virgil said. He looked at the others and they all shook their heads. "What about the other guy in the video? The driver. I know he never got out of the tow truck, but did you get a good shot of him?"

Becky hit a few more keys and sent the photo. "It's not nearly as good. I cleaned it up the best I could. I also ran a credit report on Jakes to find out his employment history since he's been out of prison. He works for a company called—"

The photo came through and Becky didn't get a chance to finish because Rosencrantz interrupted her when he said, "Jesus Christ." He looked at Murton and Ross. They were both nodding their heads in agreement.

"What?" Virgil said.

"They were already gone by the time you got there," Murton said to Virgil.

"Got where?"

"Out to your field...at the clearing," Rosencrantz said. "That guy's name is John Fox. He said he was head of security for—"

Virgil and Becky finished the thought for him. "Salter Enterprises." They both said it at the same time.

Virgil looked at Rosie. "Okay, you guys are still going, but forget the district attorney. Put everything in a report and get it to Cora. We'll need the state AG to sign off on this one."

"You got it, Jones-man."

"Couldn't we use the Shelby County District Attorney?" Ross said.

Virgil shook his head. "No. We don't know him, but Sheriff Holden told me that Salter financed his campaign—the sheriff's—then leaned on him to hire Deputy Cooper, who was Salter's nephew. There's no way to prove it, but my gut tells me the Shelbyville DA might have his hand in Salter's pocket. I'm not saying anyone is dirty, but money from Salter could cause them to drag their feet, so I'd like to keep the county out of it as much as possible. So, the state AG."

"What about the Indian?" Ross said.

"What about him?" Virgil asked.

Ross took out his phone and handed it to Virgil. "With all this new information, I don't know how important it is, but we found him. He works the grounds for Salter."

Virgil sent the photos to his own phone before tossing Ross's back to him. "Becky, you still with us?"

"I was beginning to wonder if anyone cared," she said.

"Put together a composite and include the photo of the Indian I'm going to send you. I'll need it tonight, or first thing in the morning."

"You got it."

Virgil looked at Ross and Rosencrantz. "Patty will be able to ID the Indian. Include him as John Doe in the report. Becky, when you get the picture of the Indian, print it out and have it ready for Ross and Rosie when they get there for the report."

"Sure."

"Have you had any luck getting Delroy or Huma to answer their phones?"

"Don't you think I would have told you that?"

"Yeah, I guess you would have." Virgil thought for a moment.

"I can practically see your wheels turning, Jonesy," Becky said. "What are you thinking?"

"I'm thinking now that we know where they're staying, you could call the hotel and try them on their room phone. One of them is bound to pick that up eventually. They'll think it's room service or housekeeping or something like that."

"And if I get them?"

"Tell them to stay put. They're out of the way and out of danger."

"Will do. Are we done?"

"Looks like it. For tonight anyway. Just get me that spread."

"I will. Promise. But before I do, can Murton borrow your computer?"

"I guess so. How come?"

Murton took the laptop and began to walk away. "Electronic conjugal visit."

"Ah, Murt, c'mon man…" Virgil said.

"Relax Jones-man. I'll wipe it down before I give it back." They all heard Becky laughing as Murton walked away with the computer.

Virgil told Ross and Rosencrantz that he wanted them back as soon as possible. "Be waiting on the steps outside the AG's office in the morning. In fact, coordinate the whole thing with Cora. She'll have him there on time. I'll let her know to expect your call. Once you've got the paperwork in order, go pick up the owner of the tow truck and see if you can get anything out of him. If you do, arrest him for conspiracy, then get your butts back down here. Salter's big party is tomorrow, and from what I hear everyone and anyone is invited. That'll include us."

Rosencrantz assured him they'd do just that. They all pretended not to hear the sounds coming from the other room. Virgil decided he was getting a new computer, for sure. After a few seconds Ross cleared his throat.

"What is it?" Virgil said.

"I suddenly realized we don't have a car. We all rode down together."

Virgil looked at Murton's car keys on the table. He tossed them to Rosencrantz. "Drive it like you stole it."

Ross snatched the keys from Rosencrantz's hand. "I'll drive. I know the difference between forward and reverse."

Virgil gave Rosencrantz the eyebrow.

Rosencrantz looked at Virgil and said, "Ever heard of something called 'Three on the tree?'"

"Stick shift on the column? Yeah, I drove one as a kid. Why?"

"Because Rosie redefined the term," Ross said. He rubbed the back of his head. "I may need to put in for Worker's Comp."

Rosencrantz pushed Ross out the door. He looked back at Virgil. "It's not worth mentioning. Could have happened to anyone. See you tomorrow."

BECKY'S SYSTEM WAS CLEAN, BUT VIRGIL'S LAPTOP WASN'T. Not in any sense of the word. Wu and Nicky looked at each other and smiled.

"She bounced a packet through Ukraine," Wu said. He was impressed.

"Yeah, she's one to watch," Nicky said. "We'll have to be

more careful with her going forward." They'd heard and saw everything that Becky, Virgil, and the others had discussed. They forced themselves to stop watching during the conjugal visit.

When they told Nichole about the party, she began to work out a plan.

CHAPTER FORTY-TWO

Virgil called Patty and caught her right after she'd stepped out of the shower. "Call you back in twenty?" She asked him. Virgil told her that was fine. He made a mental bet with himself and took the over on Patty's twenty minutes, thinking the call back would be closer to forty-five minutes, maybe even an hour. He'd yet to meet the woman who could be ready in twenty minutes right out of the shower. When his phone rang fifteen minutes later, he checked his watch and thought, *Huh. Should have taken the under. Probably didn't dry her hair, or something.* Another reason Virgil never gambled…at least not with money. When he answered, the tone of his voice gave him away.

"Let me guess…you thought it'd take me longer," Patty said.

"What are you, a mind reader or something?"

She laughed at him, then said, "So, what's up?"

"I'm at the Esser house. I'm spending the night here and I'd like you to come by in the morning before you go out to the site. Do you know where it is? The Esser place?"

She didn't, so Virgil gave her directions. When she asked

why he wanted to see her, he gave her the low down. "My guys did a little reconnoitering today over at the Salter estate."

"There's a word you don't hear much anymore."

Virgil ignored her. "We think we've found the Indian who was in the field. The live one. Ross managed to get a picture and I'd like you to take a look and see if you can ID him."

"Uh, yeah, I guess I could do that."

"Try to contain your excitement a little," Virgil said, not bothering to hide his sarcasm.

"Sorry. My mind is working on about a hundred different things right now. Tomorrow I have on-site appointments with three different university archaeology department heads. Things are going to happen very quickly now, Jonesy."

"Wow, I guess so."

"Listen, can't you simply email me the photo? I could give you your answer right now."

"Nope. Doesn't work that way. We've got to put together a spread. If things go to court, we have to be able to honestly say we did it the right way, and the right way is with a spread."

"I don't know what that is. A spread."

"Ah...sorry. It's a photographic collection of different people. We'll put it together on the computer along with the shot we got today. You'll have to pick him out from the group on the screen. If we don't do it that way, a defense attorney could argue we steered you to a certain suspect because we only showed you the one photo."

"Oh, okay. I get it. Like an electronic line-up."

"Yep."

"Any reason you can't send the whole spread to me?"

"Yeah. Two reasons. The main one is this: I need to witness it. Doesn't have to be me specifically, but it does have to be an officer of the court. Simply part of the process. It's a procedural thing."

"Okay."

"So I'll see you in the morning. Eight o'clock work for you?"

"Yeah, that should work out fine. What's the other reason? You said you had two."

Virgil heard Becky squeal from the other room. "Trust me," Virgil said. "You don't want to know."

Nichole told her brother and Wu that she needed a way to access Salter's home network.

"As usual, Wu can do." He turned to his partner and said, "Nicky, find out who provider is."

Nicky ran a search of all rural internet providers in Shelby County. It took him all of thirty seconds to complete because as it turned out, the entire county only had one provider. The cities and towns had other choices, but the rural population only had one. He gave Wu the information.

"Only one?" Wu said with a chuckle. "Slice of pie, then."

"It's piece of cake, Wu."

"What?"

"The expression. It's piece of cake, not slice of pie."

"I know. Wu screw with you." He turned and looked at Nichole. "Your brother does not understand the complex alchemy of Wu's witticisms."

"I understand your witticisms. I just don't think they're very funny. Anyway, c'mon, chop-chop, Wu. We're waiting, here."

Wu looked at Nichole. "See? Again with the chop-chop."

Nichole looked at her brother. "Nicky…don't do that."

He waved her off. "Yeah, yeah. He secretly loves it."

"Not true for Wu."

Nichole gave them both a look, one they knew well. Time to quit playing. "How long will it take?"

"It will take approximately one hour to prepare," Wu said. "Unless Nicky does it. Then, who can say?"

"That's fine, Wu. That's better than fine. It's perfect." Nichole had it in her head it might take them all night. "Let me know when you've got access."

Nicky looked at his sister. "What are you up to?"

She bit into her upper lip, exposing her lower teeth. "I'll let you know the minute I figure it out."

Wu was working on hacking into the rural internet service provider's network when he happened to glance at Nicky's monitor. "Hey, look at that. It appears they are moving Carlos out of the Insensitive Care Unit."

Nicky turned in his chair and looked at the monitor. Then he said, "Wu, the 'I' stands for Intensive."

Wu looked at Nichole. "He fall for it every time."

"Make sure you get his room number," Nichole said. "And we'll need feeds from the hallway as well. We need to know how many guards they're going to have in place."

"Wu will do. So far, it has been only the one."

"Now that he's awake, that might change," Nicky said.

"I'll have a script for you, Nicky," his sister told him. "Nothing too complicated. You'll have to fill in the gaps."

"Gotcha," Nicky said. He knew what his sister meant. They'd been working hustles together almost their entire lives. Nichole would come up with a plan, and if a high-tech aspect was involved—and there often was—and Nicky had to speak with someone regarding something technical, she'd note it on the script. Nicky, who'd been a computer geek for most of his life, filled in the blanks. He could practically do it in his sleep.

AN HOUR LATER, THEY WERE READY. WU WAS IN THE RURAL network provider's system and Nichole had the script ready for Nicky. All they had to do now was hit the kill switch, then make the call. The only real potential problem was one they had no control over—who answered the phone when they called. If it happened to be a maid or someone like that, it might not work. Of course, if no one answered at all, that was a problem as well. If that happened, they'd keep trying until someone did. Wu hit the switch, then they waited about five minutes.

Nicky dialed the phone, and as it happened, they got lucky right out of the gate. The call was answered by Ken Salter on the first ring, and he didn't sound happy.

"Ken Salter." He spat his name out and it came through over the speaker so viciously that Nicky thought they might see actual spittle emerge from the phone.

"Hello, Mr. Salter. My name is Ken Mather." Nicky always used the same given name of the person he was scamming, and a very similar sounding surname. It triggered something in their brain...dropped enough distraction into their subconscious to derail any hostilities or suspicions. He'd read about it in a book on con artist techniques a long time ago and it had yet to fail him. "I'm calling from Rural-Net. We're your internet service provider. Are you by chance having any trouble with your internet connection?"

Ken Salter laughed and immediately changed his tone. "Wow, you guys must be psychic or something. I was just picking up the phone to call. Uh, listen, sorry about the way I answered…my tone of voice and all that. I was trying to do some work online and we lost our signal. I know it happens from time to time, but still, it pissed me off."

"Yes sir. I understand. I'd like to apologize for any inconvenience. I assure you we're doing everything we can to get your service back up and running."

"I appreciate it. How long will it take?"

"Unfortunately, it's a county-wide problem, sir, and an unusual one at that. I'll tell you something I'm not supposed to share, if you can keep it to yourself."

"Sure. What is it?"

"Well, believe it or not, one of the higher-ups made an executive decision that involved the installation of some new software. Nothing wrong with that, mind you, but no one bothered to check to make sure the update was compatible with the firmware on all the various routers on the client side. Now we have to call all our customers—or wait for them to call us—in order to get everyone back up and running."

"Sounds like a nightmare."

"It sure is. As you and your family are among our most valued clients, I wanted to reach out as quickly as possible to get your service restored. The process should only take a few minutes of your time. Would you like to proceed now, or should we schedule a more convenient time? I'd be happy to call you back whenever you'd like."

"No, no, let's do it now," Salter said. "What do you need from me?"

"Do you have access to your home's router, sir?"

"Yes, I'm standing right next to it. I've got nothing but a bunch of flashing red lights on the box. I've already tried the usual…you know, powering it off and then back on. It didn't seem to help."

"Well, you're one of the more knowledgeable ones then.

Most people don't even know to do that. They would if they bothered to read the user guide that comes with the router. It usually fixes about ninety percent of any issues, but in this case, we'll have to take a few additional steps."

"I'm ready."

"Very well, sir, and once again, I apologize for the inconvenience. I'd like you to unplug the router and then turn it over. On the bottom you'll find a series of numbers that include a serial number, version number, an SSID number and the factory password. Do you see all that, sir?"

Salter unplugged the box and turned it over. "Yes. Want me to read it all off to you?"

Do I ever. "Yes sir, if you would please. Let's start with the serial number."

Salter spent a few minutes reading all the information to Nicky, who typed it into his program, then read it back to him to ensure they had it right.

After he'd given away all the information, Salter asked, "Now what?"

"Please plug your router back in and let me know when the red lights turn green." He pointed at Wu, who typed in a command that would reconnect the Salter's internet service. "By the way, do you use a laptop or a desktop?"

"Both."

"Is your laptop nearby?"

"Yes."

"Perfect. Boy oh boy, I wish all our customers were as well prepared as you, Mr. Salter."

"Call me Ken, please."

"Ken it is, then. Hey, great name, huh?"

Both men laughed. Wu rolled his eyes and shook his head. Nicky wasn't only filling in the gaps, he was piling it on.

"While we're waiting for the router to connect—that'll only take a few minutes—I'd like you to open your email program. Once we've got you connected, I'm going to send you an email with a link. For security purposes, would you verify your email address for me, sir? Whoops, I mean, Ken." They chuckled some more.

Salter gave Nicky his email address and he entered it into his program as well.

"Okay, the lights on the box are all green now," Salter said.

"Perfect. Here comes the email. When you get it, simply click on the link."

"What's the link do?"

"It allows your browser to connect directly with our network's secure diagnostic data center, which automatically updates your router's firmware. That's a technical way of saying it's the last step in the process."

Salter clicked on the link. "Okay, I clicked it. Doesn't look like anything happened, though."

Oh, believe me, you idiot, something happened. "Yeah, it all occurs in the background. Tell me, are all the lights on your router box still green?"

"They are."

"Wonderful. Now, if you would, please go to the website of your choice and make sure everything is working properly."

Nicky and Wu knew everything was working properly because they not only saw what site Salter went to, they saw Salter himself through the lens of his laptop. They now had complete access to Salter's home network, all their computers, and their high-end home security system.

"Everything looks good on this end," Salter said.

"Perfect. Our end as well. Looks like you're all set, Ken. Once again, I apologize for the inconvenience. You've been very gracious this evening. You wouldn't believe the way some people talk to me on the phone. Half the time you'd have thought I personally cut the wires that connect them to the internet."

"I can only imagine," Salter said.

"Because of the inconvenience and especially your kind attitude, I'd like to credit your bill for one free month of service, with the hopes that you'll remain a satisfied customer."

"Don't have much choice, seeing as how you guys are the only provider for the rural areas."

Nicky laughed. "Well, you're right about that. Doesn't mean we don't care, though. I hope my level of service during this call demonstrated that, Ken."

"It did. But if you're offering a free month, I have to wonder, would you offer two?"

"Let me guess. Businessman, am I right? You guys really know how to hold someone's feet to the fire. Two months it is. Now I'm going to hang up before my boss fires me for giving away the company."

Salter laughed. "I appreciate the help. Thanks for everything."

"Have a good evening, Ken, and thank you for using Rural-Net."

Nicky hung up and looked at Wu. "Yes, I'm exactly that smooth."

"Smooth line of bullshit. What happens when he gets his bill?"

"Who cares? We'll be long gone."

"Yes, but then he will know he has been tricked. We may need long-term access."

Nicky frowned. "Huh. I didn't think of that. I guess I got a little carried away."

"That why Wu here for you." He spent several minutes typing away then said, "There. Wu take care of your customer service problem."

"You credited his bill?"

He held out his hands, palms up. "It's what Wu do."

"Good job. I'm going to let Nichole know we're in. See what she wants us to do."

CHAPTER FORTY-THREE

VIRGIL HAD ONE MORE CALL TO MAKE BEFORE HE TURNED IN for the evening. He didn't know if it'd work or not—he put the odds at even money after losing the last mental bet he'd made earlier in the evening. When the phone was answered on the other end, Virgil said, "How's life in the Wild West?"

"Depends on who's asking," Henry Stutzman said. After a brief pause, he said: "That you, Virgil?"

"Sure is. How are you, Hank?"

Henry Stutzman was a member of the Co-op, the only one of the group who'd actually done what he said he was going to do…sell everything off and move to Arizona to be closer to his grandkids. He still owned his Shelby County land, Graves and Mizner handling his acreage for him through the Co-op.

"Well, when I saw the number pop up on the caller ID, I about had a heart attack. Thought Charlie'd come back from the dead or something."

Virgil was on the landline at the Esser house because he had his cell phone plugged in to charge. He laughed. "Sorry about that. Didn't even occur to me that Esser's name would show up." *One more thing to deal with.* "How're the grandkids treating you?"

"Like an old fart who don't know nothin' bout nothin'."

"So, good kids, then. They sound smart too."

"I see you haven't lost what remains of your already mediocre sense of humor."

"Well you know how it is, Hank. Some of us still have to work for a living. We don't have time to sit on the front porch and whittle away at our wit."

"Shows how much you know about Arizona. It's only about eight hundred degrees out here. If I go out on the porch I'd burst into flames. I spend more money on my air-conditioning bill than I ever did on fuel and fertilizer."

"I heard it's a dry heat, though."

"Hold on a minute, will you? I've never heard that one before. I need to write it down." Virgil heard him mumble in the background, like he was actually writing it out.

"Seriously though, how are things going for you?"

"They're going good," Stutzman said. "Except I'm about bored right out of my goddamned gourd. You know what else? I'm sick of brown. Everything out here is brown. The grass is brown, the hills are brown, the houses are brown, the people are brown…it's brown, brown, brown. The only things that are green are the golf courses and the cactus. I don't golf and if you've seen one cactus you've pretty much gone and seen them all. Anyway, how about you? Everything good?"

"Ah, you know, all things considered…"

"Johnson taking good care of you?"

"Sure is. Don't know what I'd do without him."

Stutzman laughed. "Well you better figure it out pretty quick, like. You kill Mizner or Graves yet?"

"Not yet," Virgil said. "They are on my shortlist though."

"I don't doubt it," Stutzman said. "I heard what they did,

kicking you and Johnson out of the Co-op. Ain't right as far as I'm concerned. Told them as much, too. Not that they listened."

"Sort of why I called, Hank. I wasn't sure what I could do about it, but then I had an idea. I'd like to float it past you."

A little vim crept into Stutzman's voice. "Would it be dastardly? Beyond the pale and so forth?"

"Would you want it to be?"

"Hell yes. I need some excitement in my life, Virgil. The kids all sit around and don't do nothin' except play video games, the women are always off doing this and that, and I'm stuck here twiddling my thumbs and talking back to Fox News. Whatcha got?"

"You know that section of land of yours that butts up against mine?"

"The one north of the river, or the one by the access road, close to the Co-op?"

"That one…by the access road."

"Yup. I'm with you. What about it?"

"So, I met a guy by chance a few months back. Rick Said's his name."

"Saved his niece is what I heard."

"You *have* been keeping up."

"You ain't been listening. I don't have anything else to do *except* keep up."

"Anyway, he's got this new technology…" Virgil spent the next half hour and laid it all out for Stutzman. When he was finished, Stutzman asked if he could have the night to sleep on it. Virgil said that was fine.

"I'll call you first thing in the morning."

The next morning Patty showed up right on time. Virgil was running a bit behind though, still getting dressed, trying to get his mind to fire on all cylinders. He'd gone right to bed after speaking with Stutzman, the result being he didn't have a chance to tell Murton to expect Patty's visit. When she knocked, Murton opened the door wearing nothing except yesterday's boxers. "What's up, Pickle Chick?"

"Hi, Murton." She glanced at his boxers. "Hearts, huh?"

Murton looked down at his shorts, then back up at Patty. "Yeah, so what?"

"I don't know. I guess I sort of had you pegged as a skull and bones kind of guy. Or maybe daggers and knives. Something along those lines."

Murton shook his head. "Naw. The hearts are representative of my inner peace. C'mon in. I'll go find my pants."

"Don't hurry on my account."

Murton raised his eyebrows at her, then put his hand over his heart—the one in his chest—and said, "My heart belongs to another."

Patty looked at his boxers. "I'll take those hearts then."

Murton laughed. "You do know how to make a man feel good, I'll give you that." He knew Patty was simply flirting with him. He tipped his head toward the counter. "There's coffee if you want it."

"Thanks. By the way, what's that smell? It's atrocious."

Murton lifted an arm and sniffed one of his pits. "Not me. Close the door, will you? The offensive aroma to which you refer is, I believe, a result of Virgil's inattentive nature regarding all things septic. Don't look in the backyard. I'll tell him you're here."

Patty watched Murton walk away. She had been kidding about the boxers…mostly. *Bet he isn't a whiner,* she thought.

Her last boyfriend, Nate, had a constant whine that made him sound like a verbal alcoholic with a deviated septum.

Patty poured herself a cup of coffee and waited at the kitchen table. Virgil came into the kitchen and walked past her without saying a word. He grabbed a cup of coffee and sat down across from her.

"Good morning." When Virgil didn't respond Patty said, "Jonesy? You okay?"

He looked up from his mug and blinked a few times, slowly at first, then more rapidly, like he had something stuck in his eyes. He opened his mouth as wide as possible to relax his jaw, then gave his head a little side-to-side shake. "I'm, uh, not much of a morning person lately."

"Didn't Murton tell you I was here?" When he didn't answer she said, "Hey, Jonesy, you with me?"

"He, um, yeah, I guess. I asked you to come here, didn't I?"

Patty frowned at him. "Yeah. Last night. You called me, remember?"

Virgil did remember…now. He nodded, and blinked a few more times. "Would you mind if we sit quietly for a minute?"

Patty stood up and moved to the seat next to Virgil and put her hand on his forearm. "Take your time. PTSD isn't something that goes away by itself, Jonesy. You need to talk to someone about it."

"What do you know about it?"

Patty pulled her hand back. "That's a hell of a thing for you to ask me."

Virgil shook his head and waved an apology at her. "Ah,

I'm sorry. That's not what I meant. That's why I wanted to sit for a minute. My words don't come out quite right."

So they sat. After Virgil finished his coffee he looked at Patty and said, "I meant, how did you know that I'm having that kind of trouble?"

"Well, for starters, you just told me. And two, I recognize the symptoms because I've had them myself after everything that happened to me."

Virgil was starting to get his wits about him. He rolled his head and left his eyes closed for almost another full minute. When he opened them he said, "Well, you seem to be doing a hell of a lot better than I am. I told my doctor that when I wake in the morning it's like a junkyard of thoughts being tossed down into the basement of my brain…or something to that effect."

Patty nodded. "I know exactly what you mean. I told mine it felt like I was stuck in a thought tornado."

Virgil pointed at her with his coffee mug. "Man, that's it, exactly. But you're better now," Virgil said. It wasn't a question.

She moved back over to the other side of the table. "I am. Still going to therapy, but, yes. Much better."

Murton walked into the kitchen, this time fully clothed. "He back amongst the living yet?"

Patty shrugged. "Mostly…I think."

"I'm fine," Virgil said. And he was, the junkyard safely stored for another day. He looked at Murton. "Where's my computer?"

"Plugged in on the counter…right next to the coffee pot."

Virgil looked over at the counter. "Uh, yeah, I know. I misspoke is all. I meant to ask if it was all charged up."

Murton stuck his tongue in his cheek. "Uh-huh." He walked over and grabbed the laptop and opened it up.

"Why don't you go take a walk, man. Clear your head a little. Becky sent the spread last night. I'll go over it with Patty."

"I'm fine, Murt. Really. Let's see what she sent."

Murton looked at his brother like he had his doubts, but he knew better than to try to argue the point. He opened the email and clicked on the link to bring up the photos. Becky had done a nice job. There were six pictures on the screen in two rows of three. Every shot showed a Native American male, all very similar looking to the shot Ross had taken. Patty's Indian was in the middle of the bottom row. When she saw the spread she didn't hesitate. She pointed right at him. "That's him."

"And where did you see him," Murton asked.

"In the clearing, in Virgil's field. He was there and he was the one who shot Davis in the chest with his bow and arrow."

"You're sure?" Virgil asked. "This is very important. Take your time and look again."

"I don't need to look again. I'm one hundred percent positive that's him. And I know I've said this already, but I want to emphasize that it is my firm belief that his actions not only saved my life, but everyone else's as well. I'll testify in court to that fact."

"I understand, Patty," Virgil said. "That will all be taken into account." He took out his phone and called Ross. "You with the AG yet?"

"We're at his office, waiting. He's on his way. Should be here any minute now."

"I need you to amend your report."

"Jesus, boss. We typed the entire thing out last night. What kind of amendments are we talking about here?"

"I wanted the Indian listed as John Doe—and this is my fault—but I should have told you to leave a blank line parenthetically enclosed for an 'Also Known As' so we could write his name in."

Ross laughed with relief. "Then you'll be happy to know I did exactly that. Not my first warrant request, Jonesy."

"Okay. Good job. Rosie's with you, right?"

"Yeah."

"Okay. Get it signed and get over to the tow garage. Take care of business there, then get back down here."

"You got it."

Virgil ended the call and looked at Patty. She had her head tipped back. "What are you looking at?"

"The rooster wallpaper. Lot of cock in here."

Murton thought she may have brushed her eyes over him when she said it.

"What?" She said.

When neither man answered her, Patty said, "So we done? I've got to get out to the clearing."

"Yep," Virgil said, feeling more like himself with every passing second. "Do you need anything from me?"

Patty shook her head. "Not yet. As long as I have your verbal permission to work the clearing."

"Of course you do. But listen, before you go, can you sort of lay it out for me. I know you're meeting with some university people, but what's going to happen after that?"

"You want the long or the short of it?"

"Just the short for now."

"The short is this: You're going to be bombarded with offers to buy your land. All of it. They'll be coming in by the end of the week at the latest. I know you've got it on the market, but if I were you, I'd call the listing agent and tell them to be prepared for some phone calls. A lot of phone calls."

Virgil and Murton looked at each other. "Just like that, huh?" Murton said.

Patty nodded again. "Yeah. Just like that." She looked around the kitchen again. "I'll tell you something else…if you include this house as part of the sale, you'll get more out of it than if you try to sell it separately."

"Why's that?" Virgil asked.

"Because it's big enough to be used as a temporary office site and living quarters. And that out-building on the other side of the drive…is it empty?"

"Yeah."

"Dirt floor, or concrete?"

"Concrete."

"Perfect. They'll use it for storage and on-site examination. Get a septic guy out here and get the tank pumped though."

Virgil said he would. "I need to speak with your uncle. Is he going to be out at the clearing this morning?"

"Not until late this morning. Maybe early afternoon. He said he had a meeting."

"Have him call me when he has a minute."

Patty said she would. "Any message?"

Virgil hadn't heard from Stutzman yet. It was still early out west. "No, not yet. I'm waiting to hear from a guy."

Patty narrowed her eyes. "What are you up to?"

Virgil gave her a wicked smile. "Nothing. Thought I'd return a little favor, is all."

CHAPTER FORTY-FOUR

NICHOLE KNOCKED ON NICKY'S DOOR AND WHEN HE OPENED up, she did a little twirl in the hallway and said, "Whatcha think?"

He gave her the once over, and was impressed. She wore a dark blue woman's business suit, the blue so dark it was almost black. Under the suit, she wore a white blouse that revealed just enough cleavage to keep the eyes off her face. The male eyes, anyway. She wore sensible pumps, ones she could run in, if necessary, though no one thought it would come to that. The wig was a perfect fit...blonde, with dark roots, like she was well overdue for a trip to the stylist. The look said she was a busy woman who didn't have time for a three-hour session at the salon.

"Perfect," Nicky said. "You sure you want to go in alone?"

"I don't want to, but I don't see any other way. If we both go, it's one more person they can identify later on. Besides, you'll be parked right outside."

"Make sure to keep the connection open so I can hear what's happening."

"I will, I will," Nichole said. She loved her brother dearly, but he could stomp a plan to death. "You get my cards ready?"

Nicky nodded and handed her a stack of business cards. They identified her as Elizabeth McKesson, Esq., Managing Partner of McKesson, McKesson, & Cray. The tag line on the card simply read: Personal Injury Attorneys. The phone number went to a burner that Linda would answer should anyone want to verify her credentials. The cell number on the card went to the burner in her purse.

Their goal today was simple. Get to Carlos and let him know they would be taking him out of the hospital as soon as possible. The risk was minimal, but the visit was necessary. Carlos needed to know they were coming.

"What kind of car did you get?"

"Toyota Corolla. White. You ready?"

"Let's do it."

Nicky looked at Wu. "You know what to do if things go bad."

Wu nodded. "Do not worry. I will be ready."

Nicky knew he would. For as much grief as they gave each other, when it came time to run an operation, they worked well together. If Nicky told Wu they were in trouble, Wu would remotely set off the fire alarm system for the entire hospital. The chaos would be enough of a distraction that Nichole could get out of the building.

"A lot of risk for so little reward," Linda said.

"That's true," Nichole said. "But what choice do we have? He has to know we're coming."

No one had anything to say to that, so Wu and his wife Linda simply wished the twins luck and settled in to wait.

Rick Said turned into Salter's drive and made his way up to the main house. The activity was beginning to pick up, even this early in the morning. The annual party was a big deal for the Salters, and an even bigger one for the people attending. John Fox opened the front door and let Said inside. "May I have your keys, Mr. Said?"

Said looked a question at Fox.

"It's because of the party today, sir. With all the delivery people coming and going, we may need to reposition your vehicle."

Said handed over his keys, and let Fox lead him through the house. There wasn't much activity inside. The Salters wanted everyone to feel welcome, as long as they remained outside, where they belonged.

They made it to the back of the house and Fox took Said down a flight of stairs. "Mr. Salter is in the wine cellar." He opened the door and stepped aside. "After you, sir."

The room was one of the nicer wine cellars Said had ever seen. The temperature was perfect, the lighting soft and balanced, and the bottles of wine were perfectly tipped to maintain the integrity of their corks. Each bottle rested in its own space with brass labels indicating the year and type of wine. Roger Salter stood alone at the far end of the cellar, his back to the door, his head tipped just so, inspecting a bottle he'd pulled from its resting place.

"Is that you, Rick?" Salter said without turning around. "Come in, will you? I've something you must see."

Rick Said had made his fortune, big by some measures, small by others, by being able to—as he called it—read the room. He'd both made deals and walked away from others based on nothing more than his gut. Right now, his gut was telling him something, though he couldn't quite put his finger on what it was. At least not yet. "Quite a nice set-up you've got here, Roger."

"Thank you." Then to Fox: "John, close the door, will you please? I don't want to stress the French reds. You know how finicky they can be with the temperature variations."

"Of course, sir," Fox said. He stepped inside and closed the door. Said began to move closer to the back of the cellar. When he heard the door close, he turned, his thoughts on what Virgil had told him only yesterday. *Watch your back.*

Fox held a collapsible baton in his hand. When Said turned, Fox was right there. He hit him on the side of his neck with enough force to take him down to his knees. Salter walked over and squatted down in front of him.

"Do you know what kind of damage you and that niece of yours have done?" All of Salter's politeness was gone now, replaced with pure rage. "You were supposed to go out there, drill your goddamned holes and start pulling the gas out of the ground. But now, because of this discovery, that land will be sold, and the owner—a cop, of all people—will be wealthy and I'll be ruined."

Said was on his knees, one hand holding the side of his neck. His breath came in large gurgling chunks. His voice croaked when he tried to speak. "Other...land. Can get...another site."

"Not like this one. Not in my home state. Not in my county. There are issues at play you know nothing about." He took the baton from Fox's hand and delivered a blow that cracked Said's ribs. The bolt of pain caused Said to lose consciousness and he fell flat on the floor, blood trickling from his mouth when he exhaled, his breathing rough and ragged.

"It looks like he may have popped a lung, sir. I'll take it from here, if you like."

"Leave him locked up in here for now. We'll deal with both him and the Indian after the party."

Fox took the baton from his boss's hand before delivering the news. "I'm afraid I have some unpleasant information regarding Anthony, sir. It seems he's nowhere to be found. I've got Jakes out looking for him, but there's been no word. He must have left last night, which if true, gives him a lengthy head start."

Roger Salter was old, his body tired, but his mind was sharp. Why would the Indian leave? If anything, he should have stayed, expecting a reward for killing the man responsible for Cooper's death. Had he learned of the conversation he'd had with Kenneth over their plans? Kenneth wouldn't have said anything. That could only mean one thing: The Indian must have overheard the conversation on the veranda.

"Use Mr. Jakes. Allow him free rein. Whatever resources he may require. Tell him to do his best to make it look like an accident."

"Yes, sir. I'll get him on it right away."

"The gas under that ground was going to eventually put my son in the White House, John."

"I'm aware, sir. Perhaps there is another way."

Salter looked down at Rick Said. "There is no other way. Have Kenneth meet me in the study."

"Right away, sir."

"WE NEED TO BEGIN TRANSFERRING OUR FUNDS, KENNETH."

Ken Salter didn't understand. "Why is that, father?"

"I'm afraid the biggest pocket of natural gas we've ever

discovered is no longer available to us. Certain recent events have turned an already unstable situation into one that now threatens not only the future of our company, but our freedom, perhaps our very lives as well."

"What on earth are you talking about?"

"Aren't you listening? The Jones property is no longer available to us."

"*What?*"

Roger Salter filled his son in on the Indian burial site that had been discovered.

"But the commitments we've made…the funds we've already accepted. My political future…"

"Kenneth, listen to me. It's over. We've tried everything there is to try. I don't have it in me to keep trying. There are a few loose ends to tie up, things we need to do to cover our tracks, so to speak, then we're going to take the money and leave the country. I'm thinking the French Riviera would be nice. That list I gave you with the attendees for today's gathering? I know for certain there are a few who'd like to get in on our gas deal. We're talking the kind of people who can, with one phone call, transfer funds with amounts that contain more than two commas, all without batting an eye. They're going to be here this afternoon, and our job is to sell them the sizzle, not the steak. Do you understand?"

Ken Salter couldn't believe what he was hearing.

Neither could Wu, who sat at his computer and heard every word.

Nichole Pope walked into the hospital like she owned it and made her way straight to Carlos's room. An ICE agent sat in a metal folding chair right outside the door, his ankles crossed, his eyes half-closed, a magazine resting on his lap. When he saw she was about to enter the room, he stood and held out a hand to stop her.

"Sorry, Miss. No visitors."

"I'm not a visitor. My name is Elizabeth McKesson and I'm Mr. Ibarra's attorney." She handed the agent her card.

The ICE agent took the card and held it at the exact level necessary to look at both the card and her cleavage at the same time. His scrutiny appeared to have no boundaries. Nichole waited until he'd had a good long look at her breasts, then asked if she could see her client. "And let me be clear, officer, I'm asking out of politeness, not necessity."

The ICE agent shrugged. "I'm simply doing my job, ma'am. I'll have to check your bag though."

Nichole handed her purse to the cop, who gave it a perfunctory look before handing it back. "I'm afraid the door will have to stay open."

"And I'm afraid you are mistaken. Attorney-client privilege ensures us our privacy."

"He's a flight risk, ma'am."

"Take it up with the Supreme Court of the United States. It's their ruling, not mine. It also happens to be one of the oldest on the books." Then she softened just a bit, in both her tone and posture. She let one leg go soft in the knee and dropped a shoulder. The result was a subtle, seductive pose. "He's been shot in the leg and according to my records, he almost died on the operating table. The only flight he's at risk of taking is the stairway to heaven. Besides, I'm here to represent my client, not bust him out of the hospital. We're on the fifth floor. No one is going to be jumping out the window." She placed her hand on his bicep and raised her eyebrows just a touch. "The door stays shut until I open it, okay?" Nichole knew how to play her part.

The ICE agent knew he wasn't going to win this one, and in truth, he didn't care. The assignment was bullshit anyway…sitting in a hospital all day guarding an illegal who couldn't go anywhere without a wheelchair. He stuck the business card in his pocket and waved her in.

Nichole walked into the room and closed the door behind her.

Once the door was closed, the ICE agent took the card from his pocket and dialed the office number. It rang twice, then a female answered and said: "Thank you for calling the law offices of McKesson, McKesson, and Cray, personal injury attorneys. How may I direct your call?"

"Elizabeth McKesson, please."

"I'm sorry sir, Miss McKesson is out of the office. May I take a message?"

"Any idea where I can reach her?"

"She's at one of the area hospitals on a client visit. I'm afraid I'm not allowed to divulge any additional information, sir. May I ask what your call is about? Perhaps someone else could help you."

"No, that's okay, I'll try her cell later on." He hung up. Good enough. He looked at the card again.

Or was it?

The card had a website address at the very bottom. He pulled up the browser on his phone and typed in the address. When the site came up, it showed a picture of the woman he'd spoken to in the hallway, including a bunch of ambulance-chasing copy he didn't bother to read. Now he was good. The woman was legit.

Wu's computer dinged at him. He looked at his wife, Linda, and said, "The guard…very thorough. He went to the webpage. But now we have access to his phone, if need be."

"Let's take a look," Linda said.

"Wu cannot do. I am watching the Salters now. There is very much happening, most of which Wu not understand. But we may have an opportunity. You should watch Carlos's room. We will examine the Ice-man's phone when Nichole is finished."

CHAPTER FORTY-FIVE

Virgil took another call from Becky. "It worked," she said by way of a greeting.

So many things were happening all at once that Virgil didn't know which 'it' she was referring to, and told her so.

"I did what you asked. I called the hotel where Delroy and Huma are staying. It took four or five attempts, but they finally answered. Delroy feels bad about everything, Jonesy. He not only said so, you could hear it in his voice. He thinks everything that has happened is his fault."

"Ah, it's not his fault, Becks."

"I know that…and you know that, but tell me this: When have you ever won an argument with a Jamaican?"

Virgil chuckled. "Exactly never. So they're going to stay there for now?"

"Yes. I spoke with Huma as well. Although she's desperate to get back to the boys, they agreed to hang out down there a little longer. I caught them just in time. They had their bags packed and were getting ready to come home. I convinced them to stay until they heard back from us."

"And you're sure they'll go along with it?"

"As sure as I can be. Delroy is stubborn—I know you know that too—but he's smart and he's in love. He's not going to put Huma in danger. They'll stay until it's safe."

"Okay, good. Won't be that much longer now anyway. A day. Two at the most."

"I'll let them know."

"Tell Delroy I'm—" Virgil suddenly couldn't get the words out. They stuck in his throat, and Becky caught it.

"He knows, Jonesy. He knows. He said he's got a story to tell you. Wouldn't tell me what. Once they're back, everything will be fine."

I hope so, Virgil thought.

Ross and Rosencrantz had their paperwork in order. When they arrived at the service garage where the tow truck had come from—the one used to steal Delroy's car and kill Dobson—the owner pegged them as cops the second they climbed out of the car. He held a giant pry bar in his hands. He glanced over his shoulder like he thought about making a run for it, then thought, *screw it,* and tossed the bar back inside the service bay where it clanked around on the floor. Running wouldn't work. This wasn't the movies. He decided to put his fate in the hands of cooperation.

He lifted his shirt and turned a full, slow circle to show them he was unarmed. Then he sat down on the wooden bench outside the service bay. When Ross and Rosencrantz walked up, he said, "Hello, officers."

Then he began to cry.

After he'd calmed down and gathered himself together, he told them everything he knew about Fox, Jakes, their connection to the Salters, and how he'd gotten mixed up in the whole thing. "I'm barely making it here. I did it for the money, but I also did it because they made it clear if I didn't, they were going to kill my family. That Jakes guy? He's batshit crazy. I took the money because I needed it, but it was mostly to protect my family. I really didn't have a choice."

Ross called for a city unit to pick up the garage owner and they all sat quietly waiting for the patrol car to arrive. "If your story holds up," Rosencrantz said, "I'll make note of your cooperation in my report. You got a sheet?"

"A what?"

"A criminal record."

He bobbed his head. "Yeah. Juvie. About thirty years ago."

"What for?"

"Smoking weed." He choked out a snort. "First hit ever, if you can believe that. Some dickhead talked me into trying it. He lit up, took a long drag and passed it to me. We were standing in the alley and sure as shit, right as I hit it, a patrol car come along and turned his spot on me. First and last time I ever smoked the stuff."

Rosencrantz nodded. "That won't go against you. Those records are sealed." Then, "First hit, huh? Guess that would make you quit."

The city cops showed up a few minutes later and handcuffed him for the ride downtown. The guy was so honest and cooperative and heartbroken, Rosencrantz hadn't bothered to hook him up during their conversation.

"I'll see about getting you a decent public defender," Rosencrantz told him. "You might come out of this okay."

"I doubt it. I know how the system worked back then. Doubt that it's much better now. Gonna lose the shop. Probably my family too." He started to cry again.

Ross asked the city cops to follow them to the locksmith's place. The city guys said they would. When they got back in the car Ross looked at Rosencrantz and said, "That was cool, man. You gave that guy respect he probably didn't deserve."

"I think almost everybody deserves respect. The guy needed some cash and they threatened his family. What was he supposed to do? Tell them to piss up a rope. Sometimes this job really sucks, you know?"

"I hear you."

"I wish he would have run."

"Why?"

"Because then I could have chased him, cuffed him up and that would have been the end of it. I wouldn't have given it another thought once the paperwork was done. Now I'll be thinking about that guy for months, sitting there crying, stuck in a no-win situation. All he was doing was trying to protect his family. What he said is true. He's going to lose his shop, his wife will probably divorce him, and when he gets cut loose, the courts will say he'll only be allowed supervised visitation with his kids, if he gets any at all. His life is ruined, and all because we showed up here today."

"That's not true. It's because he did what he did." When Rosencrantz didn't respond, Ross said, "You okay man?"

Rosencrantz gripped the steering wheel so hard his knuckles were white. "I hope the locksmith runs."

The locksmith didn't run, which made for a very quiet ride out of the city. Ross hadn't known Rosencrantz all that long, but he'd never seen him so upset. He thought maybe some guy talk might help bring him around. "How about that Doyle, chick, huh? She's pretty hot. I might ask her out. What do you think? Would I have a shot with someone as nice as her?"

But Rosencrantz was locked in his own thought process. "Somebody better run today."

While Virgil and Murton were waiting for Ross and Rosencrantz, Virgil put a call in to Sheriff Holden—more as a courtesy than anything else—and told him they'd be picking up both Salter men and two of their security personnel, John Fox and Dale Jakes.

"Taking the man on the one day of the year half the damn county looks forward to, me included."

What is it with this guy? Virgil wondered. "Yeah, what was I thinking? Next time I'll call ahead and make sure he doesn't have plans before I show up and arrest them for murder, conspiracy to commit murder, and things like that. You do realize it's been Salter all along...all the way back to Charlie and Martha."

"Well, Lipkins, anyway," Holden said. "And how about you lighten up? I was simply stating fact, and the fact is the man knows how to throw a party. By the way, one of my deputies is over in Flat Rock right now. Apparently, Jakes has been over there kicking some of the Indian folk around looking for one of their own."

"What's his name? The Indian?"

"Deputy says Jakes is asking everyone—and by asking, I

mean kicking them around some—about a fellow who goes by Tony Hill. Full name is Anthony Stronghill. Supposedly he's a direct descendant of Little Turtle, not that I'd expect you to know who Little Turtle was."

"I know who Little Turtle was, Ben. I've lived my whole life in Indiana. Listen, let me call you right back. I need to check on the status of the warrant. If we've got time, we'll go over to Flat Rock to assist your deputy."

"Assistance from the state. Now there's a grand idea." He hung up.

Virgil looked at Murton. "I don't know if that guy really doesn't like me, or if he's just naturally cranky."

"Do the two things have to be mutually exclusive?"

Virgil ignored him and called Rosencrantz. He got Ross instead. "Why are you answering Rosie's phone?"

"He's driving. Plus, he's a little upset and not very talkative."

"Why's that?"

"We picked up the tow truck guy and the locksmith."

"Let me guess," Virgil said. "Nobody ran."

Ross was impressed. "Yeah. How'd you know that?"

"He pretends like he doesn't care, but he does. Your partner has a heart of gold, young man. How far out are you?"

"At least an hour. Could be closer to two. A semi-tanker blew a tire, jack-knifed across the median and rolled on its side. It's blocking both southbound lanes. At least that's what we're getting on the radio. They're saying two fatalities. We're bumper to bumper as far as the eye can see, and we can't even see the accident yet."

"Okay. Call me when you're getting close. The Indian's name is Anthony Stronghill, AKA Tony Hill. Write it in on the paperwork."

"You got it, boss. Listen, I'd like your opinion on something."

"Make it quick."

"You think I'd have a shot with that Doyle chick?"

"No."

"Well, Jesus Christ, don't put any thought into it."

"I won't, and neither will you." Virgil was almost as protective of Patty as her uncle was. "Call me when you're close." He hung up, then turned to Murton. "C'mon, let's take a ride over to Flat Rock."

"What for?"

"If nothing else, something to eat. Holden says one of his deputies is over there taking reports from some of the Indians. A guy matching Jake's description is pushing people around trying to find Stronghill. By the way, you ever heard of an Indian named Little Turtle?"

Murton gave him a lazy look. "Uh, yeah. And you would too if you hadn't slept through most of our high school history classes. Chief Little Turtle led about a thousand warriors against federal troops in the battle of the Wabash in the late seventeen hundreds. They essentially kicked the shit out of the US Army." Then, "Why do you always look at me like that?"

"Like what?"

"Like you're surprised I know things."

"I'm not surprised, Murt. I'm impressed."

"As you should be." When Virgil turned to grab his car keys, Murton cleared the browser history on the laptop. He'd looked up Little Turtle while Virgil was on the phone.

"You ready?"

"As usual, I'm waiting on you."

When they walked outside, Murton stopped and looked at

Virgil, who knew what was coming. "What, you didn't think I was going to let them drive my truck, did you?"

"At least Becky asked if we could borrow your laptop. You're familiar with the concept of asking, right? It's when you seek permission from another before taking or using their stuff."

"Yes, I'm familiar. But after what I heard last night, you can have that laptop. I'm getting a new one. Besides, I *own* my truck. Your car belongs to the state."

"Yeah, but it's *my* state car. You know I like to keep my shit squared away. Have you ever seen Rosie's car? It looks like he lives in it."

Virgil nodded, sort of sheepishly. "Yeah, you're right about that. Tell you what, when they get back, I'll clean it out."

"The hell you will. I'm taking it in for a full detail. On your nickel."

"Fine, fine, are you coming or not?"

"Yeah. How many times do I have to say it? I'm waiting on you."

Carlos was awake, but not quite as clear-headed as Nichole would have liked. "This is important, Carlos. Can you remember?"

He pushed himself up in the hospital bed. "I will try."

"You've got to do better than try, Carlos. You've got to actually do it."

"I do not see why. The medicine takes the pain away." His words were thick and slurred, like his tongue was thicker than normal.

"But we're going to need you to be alert when the time comes."

"Why? It is not like I will be of any assistance to you."

Nichole nodded at him, and it wasn't without sympathy. "I understand. I really do. But if you're bombed out of your mind and we need your help getting you out of here, we won't have it. Once you're out, you'll have all the meds you need."

Carlos sighed, then pushed the pain button that gave him a measured amount of morphine. "I will try, but it hurts very badly." The morphine hit him almost immediately and he went away for a little while. When he came back, Nichole was still there.

"See? That's what I'm talking about," she said.

"What? What are you talking about?"

Nichole sighed. She was getting impatient. She'd been in the room too long already. "Listen to me. Do this for your mother. She is going out of her mind with worry." She went over everything again. Carlos said he would do his best with the morphine. Nichole slipped him a burner. "Keep this hidden. I will send you a message when we're on our way. You must be ready."

"I will try," he said.

Nichole kissed him on the cheek and walked out of the room. Once the door closed behind her, Carlos pushed the button again.

The ICE agent didn't say anything to Nichole as she exited the room, but she could feel his eyes on her as she walked away. After she was on the elevator, the agent stuck his head in the room. The Mexican was asleep. He went back out to his chair and sat down.

Virgil and Murton arrived in Flat Rock and made a few passes through town before they found the deputy. He was on the southern side, just past a thoroughfare named Pope Street, of all things. "How's that for coincidence?" Murton said.

"I can never figure out if I believe in them or not," Virgil said. "Usually I do. I mean, it's only this little bit of happenstance, but then something like this pops up and it makes you wonder. Pope Street? *Really?*"

They sat in Virgil's truck and watched the deputy. It appeared he was taking a report from a male Indian. The man was waving his arms around as he talked, pointing first in one direction, then another. They didn't want to interrupt, so they sat in the truck and waited for the deputy to finish. Finally, after the man had hit all four cardinal compass points, the deputy put his notebook in his pocket and walked back to his car. Virgil rolled up next to him, his badge hanging out the window to let him know they weren't a threat.

He introduced himself and Murton, and the deputy told them his name was Norman Joy. Before Virgil or Murton could respond, Joy said, "And don't bother. I've heard them all. Yes, I'm a joy to work with. Yes, I enjoy my job, when I'm finished eating I'm joyful…"

Virgil interrupted him. "Speaking of eating, let's go grab a bite and you can fill us in on Jakes."

"You buying?" Joy asked.

"Sure," Virgil said. "Anyplace you'd recommend?"

"You want it quick or you want it good?"

Murton looked at Virgil and laughed.

"What?"

"Nothing. I was thinking that sounds like something you'd ask Small right before going to bed."

Virgil looked at the deputy and said, "How about someplace that's a little of both?"

"That'd be Nick's Kitchen. Follow me."

Virgil and Murton looked at each other. "Nick's?" Murton said.

"Ever feel like someone is trying to get your attention?" Virgil said.

CHAPTER FORTY-SIX

THEY TOOK A BOOTH BY THE WINDOW AND A WAITRESS brought them slippery menus and poured three cups of coffee without asking if they wanted it or not. She had a wad of gum in her mouth that snapped when she spoke. She called them all 'Hon.' When Murton—who was a fan of greasy spoons everywhere—asked who Nick was, she told them the backstory. Nick didn't own the place anymore. He'd sold it to a guy named Harry before moving to Florida where he lived for a little less than six months before dying of lung cancer.

"Why didn't Harry change the name?" Murton asked.

The waitress laughed without humor. "He did, about a year after he bought the place. He wanted to wait. A way to honor Nick and all that. After a year came and went, Harry called the sign maker and the transition, such as it was, got underway." Then she looked over her shoulder to make sure no one was listening. No one was, because they were the only customers at the moment. "Except Harry wasn't all that bright…and the sign guy was almost smart enough to make Harry seem like a genius. Anyway, the sign went up and it didn't say Harry's Kitchen. It said Hairy Kitchen." She spelled it out for them.

They all chuckled politely at the story. "Bet Harry wasn't too happy," Virgil said.

"No, he wasn't…"

Murton caught all the past tense. "The way you keep saying 'wasn't'…"

"Yeah…it's really sort of sad. Harry became the laughing stock of the town. He was on vacation when the sign went up. It was a week before he got back and saw it. Everyone said pretty much the same thing: No way they were going to eat food that came from a hairy kitchen. So Harry got good and drunk that very same night and went over to have a little talk with the sign maker. Things got ugly, Harry got his ass kicked so bad he ended up in a coma. Died about a year ago. The sign guy is still in prison, convicted of manslaughter."

Virgil and Murton looked at Joy, who shrugged. "Small towns. Shit happens. What are you gonna do?"

"So who owns the place now?" Murton asked.

"I do, Hon. Put the old sign back up and it's been business as usual ever since. What can I getcha?"

"What's good?" Virgil asked.

"Three specials, coming right up." She walked away without another word.

The three men made idle cop chit-chat for a few minutes before the waitress brought them their food. It arrived so quick, Virgil wondered if the term special might refer to whatever hadn't sold the day before. Maybe even the day before that. But it was hot, and it smelled good…turkey Manhattans with buttered biscuits, and green beans. They'd just gotten started when Joy took a swig of his coffee and happened to glance out the window as he set his mug down. He saw a small, wiry-looking guy across the street, holding an elderly Indian man by his ear, a picture stuffed in front of his face. "There's our boy. I'll be right back."

"Hold on," Virgil said. "We'll give you a hand."

Joy looked at them. "For that string bean? Give me a break. I'll get more kickback from this food." He walked out the front door before they could say anything else.

Jakes had his back to the deputy, but the old man he held by the ear gave him away when his eyes shifted over Jakes' shoulder. Jakes pushed the old man away and turned around. Murton and Virgil made it to the front door in time to see Jakes set his feet and throw three fast punches, the first to Joy's gut, the other two at his head as he doubled over. Jakes yanked the gun from the side of the deputy's holster and put it against the side of Joy's head.

Virgil took cover behind his truck, and Murton ducked low at the front of Joy's cruiser, their weapons drawn. Murton shouted at Jakes who turned his way. Then all of a sudden, before anyone could say or do anything else, Jakes fell to his knees, an arrow sticking through the side of his neck. His eyes went wide with shock as blood spurted from both sides of the wound. He dropped the gun and put his hands up to his neck.

"You see him?" Virgil shouted to Murton. He meant the Indian who'd fired the arrow.

"I've got nothing," Murton shouted back.

"I'm going for Joy. Watch my back, watch my back."

Murton looked up and down the street again but didn't see anyone. "Go." He stepped out from behind the cruiser, presenting himself as a target in case another arrow came their way. Virgil grabbed Joy by his vest and dragged him back behind the truck. Murton ran that way and all three men sat on the curb, their backs against the side of the Raptor. Joy was semi-conscious, his cheek swollen, and he was missing a front tooth. Murton popped up and looked out in the street. Jakes was on his hands and knees, trying to crawl away, but the blood loss was severe and he only made it about three feet before he collapsed. "I'm going for the gun."

"Hold on, Murt," Virgil said.

"I'm going. Keep an eye out."

Virgil stood eye level with the back of his truck and scanned the area. He didn't see anything at all. Murton scrambled out into the street, grabbed Joy's gun and took a very quick peek at Jakes before running back. He was dead.

They helped Joy back inside the restaurant where the waitress was waiting with a large, ice-cold, raw Porterhouse steak. They put Joy in a chair and she flopped the giant piece of meat across his face, then grabbed his hand and put it over the steak to hold it in place. He tried to speak, but the steak made it hard to hear what he was saying.

"What was that?" Virgil asked.

Joy pulled the meat away, tossed it on the floor and wiped the blood from his face. "I said I think I lost a tooth." It came out 'toot.'

Virgil looked at the waitress and said, "How about you toss the steak and grab a bag of ice instead?"

"I can get the bag of ice, Hon, but this baby here?" She picked up the steak from the floor and wiggled it in the air. "This is going to be tomorrow's special."

Murton was still watching the street. He didn't turn around when he spoke. "Small towns. Shit happens. What are you gonna do?"

Virgil put a call into Holden's office and told the sheriff what happened. "He okay?"

"Yeah. Lost a tooth. Got a black eye. Murt already left. He's got Joy in his cruiser. He's bringing him your way. That okay with you?"

"That's fine. You find the Indian?"

"No sign of him."

"What about Jakes?"

"He's still out in the street. I covered him with a tarp, but you need to get your crime scene people out here right away. The medical examiner too."

"They're already on their way. Five or ten more minutes, tops."

"Good enough. As soon as they arrive, I'm outta here. I'll get you my statement as soon as I can, but I've got to pick Murton up and get to Salter's place. My men should be arriving with the warrant any time, now."

"The party is already started out there. You better hurry. It's gonna get crowded."

"Thanks, Ben."

"You sure Joy is okay?"

"Yeah. Embarrassed more than hurt. He'll need to see a dentist. Kept saying he got his ass kicked by a string bean." Despite everything that'd happened, Virgil let out a chuckle. "Speaking of string beans, if you happen to be at Nick's Kitchen tomorrow, don't get the special."

WHEN THE POPE TWINS RETURNED TO THE HOTEL, NICHOLE told everyone about her visit with Carlos. "He's still not restrained," Nichole said. "I'm not sure how long that will last. I say we make our move tonight. If we wait any longer, I'm afraid he'll forget I was ever there. He's pretty doped up."

"What about the guard?" Linda asked. "He accessed the site, so we've got his phone if we need it."

Nichole thought about that for a few minutes. "I'm not sure what good that will do us. Maybe a distraction of some kind? I don't know. The truth is, I don't think he'll be a problem, the way we've got everything set up."

They talked it through, and eventually they all agreed they should go. "The later the better," Linda said. She'd worked in a hospital before she met Wu and knew how things worked. "They run tests at all hours of the day and night, so there won't be any suspicion there. In fact, they do more testing of the admitted patients at night than any other time. It's quieter, no family visitors waiting around and all that."

Nichole thought about it. "That may be true, but we don't want it dead quiet. We'll stick out like sore thumbs. We want some activity."

Linda nodded. "Then let's do it during the nursing shift change. The nurses are so busy coordinating the rotation that the patients are left alone for a while." She turned to her husband. "Wu, what time do they rotate the nursing staff?"

Wu, who had his connection to the hospital open, searched around until he found what he needed. "Ten p.m."

"That'll work," Linda said. "Nichole?"

"Ten it is. Nicky, get the pilots ready. Tell the nurse practitioner as well."

"You got it."

Wu turned to Nichole. "There is something else. Lola will want to hear this."

"What is it?" Lola asked. She'd been glued to the monitor that showed Carlos in his hospital bed and hadn't been listening all that closely.

"The Salters are preparing to move their money. They know they are in trouble and are taking the necessary steps to flee. If we act quickly, we can make an intercept. Lola will have her revenge."

Nichole shot Wu a look. She wasn't happy that he blurted out the news without telling her first. "Wu!" She snapped it at him.

Wu pretended not to notice. Nichole could get a little too bossy for his liking every once in a while. The problem was, she was usually right.

Lola looked a question at Nichole. The two women stepped out of the room for a few minutes. When they returned, Nichole told Wu she wanted to see the feed. "Back it up," she said, still with a little bite in her voice. Nicky hung up the phone and told them the pilots and the nurse would be ready and waiting.

"Good. Nicky, come over here and watch this. Tell me what you think." Wu backed the Salter feed up and played the entire thing for them.

"Who's the dude in the wine cellar?" Nicky asked. "He looks like he may need medical attention."

"It's not our problem," Nichole said. Then a thought occurred to her. It could buy them some good will. "Keep an eye on him. Let me know if they decide to do something with him."

"If he regains consciousness, I can release him," Wu said.

"How?" Nichole asked.

"The door is secured with a magnetic lock. Since we are in their system, Wu have code."

"Keep an eye on him, but sit on it for now."

"Wu will do."

Nicky looked at Wu. "How long would it take to prepare the intercept?"

"I did most of the work already. If we do it, we'll bounce the funds around Europe, converting chunks of it into Bitcoin as we go along. By the time it arrives at whatever destination the Salters have chosen, there will be nothing left."

"What are these bits of coin?" Lola asked. "I do not want a bunch of loose change."

Nicky sucked on his cheeks. "Bitcoin is a cryptocurrency, Lola. It's not regulated by the federal government. That means it is all but invisible. Once we have converted the funds, there will be no way to trace it back to us."

"Like the gold from the lottery?"

"Yes, only better. And safer for us."

"This is what we will do then, yes? Nichole?"

Nichole looked at Wu and her brother. "What's our exposure if it goes bad?"

"Cannot go bad," Wu said. "If something go wrong, I hit the kill switch and the money goes through like nothing happened."

"How long will it take?" Nichole asked.

"To finish the set-up or the actual movement of the funds?"

"Both."

"Another hour or so for set-up. Since the movement of the funds is handled electronically, the process itself will be over almost instantaneously…once it has started."

"And there is no risk? None whatsoever?"

"Absolutely none. It is like taking candles from a baby."

"It's candy, Wu," Nicky said. "Candy from a baby. You wouldn't let a baby have a candle."

Wu looked at Nichole. "Every. Single. Time."

"Do it," she said.

Nicky and Wu smiled and got to work. This was the part they loved. The women went off to work out the details of moving Carlos. They had to get that right above all else. If they didn't, the money wouldn't matter.

CHAPTER FORTY-SEVEN

ONCE THE SHELBY COUNTY CRIME SCENE CREW ARRIVED, Virgil left Flat Rock and went to pick up Murton. When he arrived, Murton handed him a form and told him to sign it.

"What's this?"

"Your statement on the Flat Rock incident. I did mine, and since you weren't here, I figured I'd type yours out as well."

Virgil tipped his head. "Oh, man, thanks a lot. One less thing to deal with."

"No problem. I misspelled a few words on yours so they'd know it was genuine."

"Very funny." Virgil glanced at the document, signed it, then walked the report over to the desk clerk with instructions to include it as part of the Flat Rock incident. The clerk gave him a lazy look, then dropped the form in a wire basket without replying.

They left the Shelby County Law Enforcement Center, then drove back to the Esser house. When they arrived, they discovered Ross and Rosencrantz still weren't there.

"What the hell is taking them so long?" Murton said.

"Ross said the accident was pretty bad, and the traffic was even worse."

Murton took out his phone and called Ross. "What's the hold-up? When I'm away from my woman for too long I start to get cranky. You don't want to be around me when I'm cranky."

"The semi was a tanker loaded with diesel fuel. The fire trucks couldn't make it through all the traffic in time to get the foam on it and the whole thing blew up. Because it didn't happen right away a bunch of people were standing around gawking, and now instead of the original two fatalities, they've got eleven, and a bunch of other cars blew up as well. The whole thing is a mess. We finally made it past, so it shouldn't take us that long now. Maybe another half an hour or so."

Murton relayed the information to Virgil.

Virgil didn't want to wait. "Tell Ross to call the A.G.'s office and have them email the paperwork to me. I'll pull it off my phone. They can meet us at the Salter's."

"You catch that?" Murton asked Ross.

"Yup. I'm on it."

"Ask him how Rosencrantz is doing."

"How's Rosie?" Murton said into the phone.

Ross hesitated a bit before answering. "It *is* a nice car. How long before I get one?"

"Can't talk, huh?"

"Okay, okay, I'm just asking, is all," Ross said. "I'll get the paper headed your way."

Murton ended the call. "Man, for a guy who likes to kick some ass, that Rosencrantz really lets the job get under his skin every once in a while."

"Look who's talking," Virgil said.

"I am," Murton replied.

A few minutes later Virgil's phone dinged. He printed off the paperwork and they headed for the Salter estate. With any luck, they'd be home in time for dinner.

THE PARTY WAS IN FULL SWING. ROGER SALTER WALKED among his guests, most of whom he didn't know, but since everyone was wearing a name tag—they were the blue and white stick-on kind that said, Hello! My name is—he addressed everyone by their name and made them feel as if the party had been thrown just for them. He thought there were at least two hundred people already present, with a steady stream still arriving.

He continued to move through the crowd, shaking hands, smiling, and encouraging everyone to have a good time. He saw his son, Ken, working one of the guests that he'd been assigned to wring as much money from as possible. He watched as the two men spoke for a while, the guest eventually taking his phone out and making a call. Ken Salter handed him a slip of paper with the wire transfer instructions and stood patiently as the guest spoke into his cell phone. When he was finished he put his phone away, pointed a finger at Salter—a friendly warning—then both men laughed and shook hands. Roger Salter timed his approach perfectly.

"Murphy, you tight bastard. How much did he ding you for?"

The man's name was Conner Murphy. He turned and shook the elder Salter's hand. "More than I wanted, and less than he did."

"That's usually the way these things go," Roger said. "Let me guess. A half?"

Murphy took a long pull of his scotch and said, "Three

quarters, God bless me."

Roger Salter put his arm around Murphy, then leaned in close like he was sharing a secret. "I'll tell you something, Con, and if you spread this around, I'll cut your left nut off, but if you make it an even million, I'll give you an extra half-point on the back end."

Murphy leaned away a little. "I'll tell *you* something, Roger. Make it a full point and I'll go up to one-five."

Salter dropped his arm and shook his head, like the request was completely out of the question. "Can't do a full point for anything less than two. Not even supposed to do it at one, but we're friends, so I thought I'd give you a shot, if you wanted. Don't worry about it. I wasn't aware that things were so tight for you right now." Salter put a little emphasis on the word 'tight.'

"Fuck you, Roger. Tight my lily-white ass." Both men laughed, then Murphy took his phone back out and made another call. "Yeah, it's me again. Hold on a second." He put the phone to his chest and the ball back in Salter's court, a serious look on his face now. "I'll go three…for a point and a half."

Salter put a pained expression on his face, then he squinted and looked up, like he was doing the math in his head. He pointed at Murphy and said, "Only for you. And I mean it, Con. If anyone hears about this, I'll take both your nuts."

Murphy smiled and brought his phone back up. "Change the amount to an even three. Yes, that's right, I said three." He paused, then said, "Yeah, yeah, just do it." Another pause. "Oh, that's right, I'd forgotten about that." He bit into his lower lip, then said, "Well, take it from the discretionary fund, then." He ended the call and looked Salter in the eye. "I'm going to tell everyone."

"Not fond of your nuts are you?"

"Wife took them so long ago I don't remember what it was like having them to begin with. Who do you think I was talking to?" Then he leaned in close and said, "It's her money anyway. I married into every goddamned penny." Then, "Spread that around and I'll have your nuts to replace mine."

Salter shook his hand and said, "Your secret…and your money are safe with me, Conner. Go get another drink. Enjoy the party."

Murphy wandered away and Ken looked at his father. "Jesus Christ, you took him from seven-fifty to three million. That was impressive."

Salter ignored the compliment. "Have you started the transfer yet?"

"No, there's one more person I want to speak with first."

"Good. And enough with the nickel and dime stuff. This is our future, Son. We don't want to have to dip into the principal, now, do we?"

"No, we certainly don't."

"Alright. Let's wrap it up then."

"When are we leaving?"

"As soon as the transfer is complete. The jet is ready. We'll be halfway across the Atlantic before the party is over. Let's get to it."

Salter's phone buzzed at him. He put it to his ear and listened, snapping his fingers at his son to keep him close. Ken Salter turned around and rejoined his father.

"Where are you now?" He said into the phone.

"At the main gate," Fox said.

"And you're sure the information is accurate?"

"There's no question."

"Very well. We're making preparations as we speak. Your account will be funded with enough to take you anywhere you'd like to go. I cannot overstate how valuable you've been to me over the years, John. Stay out of sight inside the gatehouse and let us know the moment they arrive. With all the activity right now, after they're in, you should be able to slip away without any problems."

"Thank you, sir."

"Let me know when they're here."

Salter slipped the phone back into his pocket. "Forget everyone else," he told his son. "Our friends at the A.G.'s office say that the authorities are on their way as we speak. Go to the house and see to the transfers. Put the three million that idiot Murphy released into John's account. The rest goes into the off-shore accounts. Go quickly now. I'll be on the back patio, near the pool. The helicopter is ready."

Nicky and Wu were ready. All they had to do now was wait. As it turned out, they didn't have to wait long.

"Here we go," Nicky said when his computer dinged at him. "You know what to do?"

"Of course," Wu said. "I'll mirror everything. He'll have no idea he's not at the real site. The only question is, how much of a delay do we want to put in once he hits the button?"

It was a valid question. The bigger the amount, the longer the delay. Of course, even the longest delay would be no more than ninety seconds. "He's logging in now," Wu said. "I need a number."

"Go with thirty seconds." Then, "Wait…how much is he moving?"

Wu tapped a few keys that changed what he saw on his monitor. "Huh."

"Huh, what?"

"He is making two transfers. A small amount of three million to Citi Bank, of all places."

"He's leaving it state side?"

"It looks like it."

"Okay. We can't touch that. Back away for a moment and let that one go through. How much is the other?"

"Just over one hundred million," Wu said.

"Okay, go with sixty seconds then. That'll be enough to make it seem real. That gives you enough time?"

"Of course," Wu said. "We only need to worry about the first bounce. Sixty seconds is a lifetime when it comes to this sort of thing."

Nichole walked into the room. "How's it going?"

"He's doing something weird," Nicky said to his sister. "He's splitting off three million and sending it to Citi."

"State side?"

"Yup."

"That is odd. And the rest?"

Wu began typing very rapidly on his keyboard, then sat back and watched the clock on the wall.

"Little over one hundred," Nicky told her. He glanced at his partner. "Wu's working the delay right now."

When the sixty seconds had passed, Wu began typing again. A few seconds later, he was finished. "Perhaps Lola would like to witness her revenge?"

Nichole hollered to Lola, who walked into the room.

"Yes?"

"You wanted your revenge. We thought you might like to actually see it."

Nicky stood from his chair and said, "Here, take my seat and watch the monitor."

"What will I be looking at?"

Nicky smiled at her. "I think it'll be pretty obvious."

As Lola sat down, Nicky pointed to the upper left side of his screen. "Hey look at this. That guy they knocked round in the wine cellar? He's awake. Looks like he's trying to find a way out."

Rick Said woke with a searing pain in the side of his chest and the taste of blood in his mouth. He spat on the floor and when he did, the pain from his rib cage flared like he'd been touched with a branding iron. He wiped the blood from his mouth that left a smear across the bottom of his face and all along the side of his right sleeve. He stood with great difficulty, one arm held tightly against his chest. He had to breathe with slow and shallow breaths to control the pain. When he tried the door to the cellar, he discovered it was locked. His cell phone had no reception in the cellar.

He beat on the door and tried to yell, but the pain was so intense his blows had no power and his voice came out no louder than a whisper. He couldn't catch his breath and knew that the blow he'd taken had punctured one of his lungs. He wasn't a medical expert by any means, but he thought if he didn't get medical attention, and soon, he'd die, his death a result of internal bleeding. Then, something completely unexpected happened.

CHAPTER FORTY-EIGHT

VIRGIL AND MURTON ROLLED UP TO THE SALTER ESTATE AND were stopped about thirty yards short of entering the drive, the inbound traffic backed up in both directions.

"So close, and yet so far away," Murton said.

They heard the beat of a helicopter's rotor blades, and when they looked up, they saw the state helicopter overhead. Virgil swore under his breath.

"Mac?" Murton asked.

"Looks like it. I had no idea he was going to be here."

"We should have known. A former US senator throws a party and the governor doesn't show? How often does that sort of thing happen?"

"Someone, like Cora, should have said something." Virgil pulled his phone out as they crept closer to the entrance of the property.

"Take it easy, Jones-man. We've been a little off the grid ourselves over the last few days."

"Yeah, yeah." Then into the phone. "Cora, it's me. Is Mac going to the Salter estate?"

"Good God, no. You guys are on your way to arrest them, are you not?"

"We are. But we saw the state helicopter fly overhead a few seconds ago. It's turning in to land right now."

"He told me he was going home for the day."

"I think he might have other plans in the meantime."

"If he's at that party, Jonesy…"

"I know, I know. We'll take care of it, Cora."

"Virgil…"

"I said we'll take care of it." He ended the call, then pulled out of line, hit his flashers and burped the siren. He passed the line of cars slowly—the road was narrow—and both he and Murton got their fair share of dirty looks, angry shouts, and a few middle fingers for jumping the line.

Fox heard the siren. He peeked through the window blinds of the gatehouse and saw the blue flashers behind the Raptor's front grill. He ducked down low in the gatehouse and pulled out his phone. When Roger Salter answered, he said, "They're here."

Murton happened to be looking at the gatehouse and saw the movement of the blinds. "Slow down, but don't stop. I'm getting out here."

"Why? What are you doing?"

As soon as you burped the siren, I saw someone peek out the gatehouse window."

"You think it's his security guy? Fox?"

"I'm about to find out. Once you're in, pull up past the gatehouse and stop on the back side. There aren't any windows there, so you'll be out of sight." Murton opened the door of the truck.

"Murt..."

But it was too late. Murton hopped out and ran ahead of the truck, his weapon held low against his leg. He beat Virgil to the gatehouse by thirty seconds. He crept around the back side, staying clear of the driver's side windows and put his back against the brick wall of the structure. As soon as Virgil turned in and passed the small brick hut, he pulled over in the grass, close to the trees that lined the drive.

Murton spun away from the wall and kicked the door in.

Said heard the click of the magnetic lock on the wine cellar door, but it took a moment for the sound to register with him. When he finally figured out the door was unlocked, he pulled it open and took a quick peek up the stairs. He was alone. Someone had unlocked the door, setting him free. But who? And why?

He let the questions go and began to climb the steps. He had to pause every third or fourth step to catch his breath. He was coughing and drooling, and the drool was filled with blood. It fell across his chin and covered his shirt. He kept one arm pressed tight to his side, the other on the stairway handrail, pulling himself up. The pain was so bad he thought he might slip and fall. He also knew if he did, it would probably kill him. He thought of Patty and what her ordeal must have been like. It gave him the strength he needed to continue the climb. He wondered what awaited him at the top of the stairs. He rested for a moment in thought.

Then he climbed on.

When Wu saw the man trying to get out, he unlocked the door.

"Why did you do that?" Nicky asked.

"He's hurt. He needs medical attention." Wu said.

"The distraction is good too," Nichole said, her hand resting on Wu's shoulder as she spoke. It was her way of an apology after how she'd sort of jumped on him earlier. Wu turned his head and touched her fingertips with his chin, acknowledging the apology.

"Look at this," Wu said. He had his screen split into sections, covering all the angles he could, because Lola was watching Ken Salter on Nicky's monitor.

"What is that?" Nichole said.

"Cameras from the gatehouse. This one," he pointed to one of the sections, "is the outside. The other is the inside." The cameras showed two things: Murton Wheeler pressed against the outside wall of the gatehouse…and John Fox waiting inside, his gun pointed directly at the door.

"That's Murton Wheeler," Nichole said. "He's about to be slaughtered. We need a distraction, Wu. And we need it right now."

Wu's fingers began to fly across the keyboard.

"What are you doing?"

"The only thing Wu can do. Call gatehouse."

The phone in the gatehouse wasn't a traditional one. It was more of an intercom, the kind that didn't have any buttons on the unit. It was a simple old-fashioned black telephone receiver that hung from a chrome hook. It didn't have a traditional ringer either. It had a loud sharp buzzer.

Fox had seen Murton's approach, the overhead camera

showed him standing with his back against the wall. Fox knew he was about to come through the door. He backed against the opposite wall, right next to the intercom, his gun pointed at the door. Half a second before Murton kicked the door, the intercom buzzed and Fox—already amped up and ready for what was about to happen—jumped and turned away from the door right when it burst open. By the time he got his gun back around it was too late.

Murton saw the gun swing toward him and fired a single shot that caught Fox center mass. Murton moved in and kicked the weapon from his hand. He checked Fox for a pulse and couldn't find one. He was dead. The intercom was still buzzing. Murton thought, *why not*? He picked up the receiver and said, "Gatehouse."

The voice on the other end said, "You owe Wu." Then the line went dead.

Virgil came around the corner, his gun out. He saw Fox and checked his pulse. "He's dead," Murton said.

"I can see that. Who was on the phone?"

"Some oriental guy. All he said was, 'You owe Wu.'"

Virgil put it together right away. He looked at his brother and thought, *thank you, Nichole, wherever you are*. "C'mon, man, we've got to get up to the house and find the Salters."

Lola began to laugh, but there didn't seem to be any joy in the sound that crossed her lips, nor was there any light in her eyes. It was the sort of laughter that sounded like it might be from a schoolyard bully.

They all turned their attention to the monitor in front of Lola and watched as Ken Salter frantically punched at his keyboard. He finally beat on it with both fists, then ran his fingers up through his hair. He pulled so hard they thought he might actually yank his own hair out.

Salter couldn't believe what he was seeing. There must be a mistake somewhere. He had his off-shore account pulled up, waiting for the transfer to go through. When the computer dinged, he looked at the screen expecting to see his balance listed at over one hundred and one million. Instead, it showed zero. He stood from his chair, knocking it over in the process. He stumbled backward, still pulling at his hair. Then he raced forward and tried punching at the keys again. He refreshed the screen multiple times, but the balance still showed zero. Both accounts—the origination and destination—were empty.

Nicky looked at Wu. "You're sure we've got it?"

Wu typed in a command and brought up a visual representation of the money. It showed the funds as they bounced around the European banking system, chunks of it being peeled away and converted into Bitcoin with every bounce.

Nicky looked at his sister. "Sis?"

She knew what he wanted. A little icing on the cake. "Is it safe?"

"It's better than safe," Nicky said. "It'll wipe his system like we were never there."

"Go ahead, then."

Nicky typed in a command and his voice came through on Salter's computer. "Hello, Mr. Salter."

Ken Salter was in shock. When he heard the voice coming from his computer, he thought he was imagining it.

"Mr. Salter. Ken? Can you hear me?"

"Who is this?"

"It's me. Ken Mather, from Rural-net. We spoke on the phone. You remember, don't you?"

"I don't…I don't understand."

"Of course you do, Ken. I know you're a little upset and

confused right now, so let me help you clear your thought process. First, my name isn't Ken. But that's the least of your worries, I would imagine. Also, I don't work for Rural-Net… another trivial fact, I know, but let's be honest, you're not very bright, so I'm thinking if I don't give you all the facts, you might not get a very good sense of what has happened."

"Who the hell are you?"

Nicky put a little edge in his voice. "Your worst nightmare, Ken. When you gave me all the information on your router, then clicked on that link, it gave me full access to your system, your network, your home security, everything. Once we had that, getting to your off-shore accounts was easy. Are you getting the message here, Ken? Seeing the big picture and all that sort of thing? Your money…all your ill-gotten gains? It's gone, Ken. Poof. Just like that, and just like me."

Nicky entered the command to destroy the code and disconnect them from the Salter network. There'd be no trace they were ever there. With that done, he turned and looked at Lola. "Happy?"

"I will be happy when we have Carlos and we are all back in Jamaica."

Nicky pushed out his bottom lip into a pout, then said, "Lola?"

She finally smiled "*Sí*. I am mostly happy." Even though the connection had been disconnected, Lola looked at the computer and said, "Take that, you gringo *hijo de puta.*"

Nicky raised his eyebrows and put his hands over his ears. "Lola!"

KEN SALTER GRABBED HIS COMPUTER AND FLUNG IT ACROSS the room. Then he screamed.

Said made it to the top of the steps and heard someone scream. The scream wasn't one of pain. It sounded like it was one of panic, fear, and rage. He heard a door slam, then nothing. He managed to get his cell phone out of his pocket—the pain so bad he felt like screaming himself—and called Virgil.

Virgil and Murton got back in the Raptor and were headed up the drive. It was slow going, because people and cars were everywhere. They got as close as they could before abandoning the truck in the grass.

When Virgil's phone buzzed, he put it to his ear without checking the display. "Jones."

"Virgil. Hurt."

His voice was so weak Virgil didn't recognize who was calling. He pulled the phone from his ear and looked at the display. "Rick, is that you? Rick?"

"Hurt. Bad."

"Where are you?"

"Inside."

"Inside where, Rick?"

"Salter's. Busted ribs. Bad lung. Bleeding…internal."

"We're on the property. Hang on, we're coming."

Virgil told Murton what was happening. Then they started to run toward the house.

CHAPTER FORTY-NINE

Ross and Rosencrantz pulled up to the gatehouse and saw a small crowd of people trying to get a look inside. Ross pulled out his badge and said, "State police. What's going on here?" A few of the onlookers heard the words 'state police' and wandered away.

One of the bystanders pointed inside the gatehouse. "Dead guy. Looks like he's been shot or something."

They told everyone to back off, then stuck their heads in the doorway and saw Fox lying on his side, the bullet wound right in the center of his chest. Another bystander walked up and said, "I'm a fireman and a paramedic. Anything I can do to help?"

Rosencrantz looked at him. "Not for that guy. He's gone. You sober?"

The fireman gave him a disappointed nod. "Yeah. I'm on duty in two hours."

"You're on duty right now. I need you to stand guard by this door and not let anyone in. Got it?"

He puffed up his chest and said, "Yeah, I can handle that."

Rosencrantz yanked the door shut. "Nobody gets in,

unless they've got a badge, understood?"

"Won't be a problem."

"Appreciate it," Rosencrantz said. When he turned to Ross he didn't see him right away. Then he heard the trunk of Murton's car slam shut and Ross was there with a scoped long gun in his hands.

"Does Murton keep his rifle dialed in?"

"What do you think?"

"That's why I'm asking. I don't know. "

"Me either," Rosencrantz said.

"Let's hope so. I'm going wide." He pushed through the tree line along the drive and disappeared.

Rosencrantz ran toward the main house.

KEN SALTER STUMBLED OUT OF THE HOUSE LIKE A DRUNK, HIS mind still trying to process the events that had occurred. He'd lost everything, the police were on their way…probably already here, and his father, once among the most powerful men in the country was now penniless. They were ruined, and it was all his fault.

The gun was a nickel-plated .380. He held it low against his leg as he watched the crowd. No one seemed to notice. The band was playing, the barbecue was smoking, people were talking and laughing, moving about, lost in an atmosphere of good times and free liquor. Ken Salter stood near the doorway, scanning the crowd for his father. He didn't know why exactly, but he wanted him to witness his son as he took his own life. Maybe then he'd realize how sorry he was for the mistakes he'd made. Mistakes that would ruin his father, his name, and everything he'd built. He'd tell him about the funds, then put the gun against his own temple.

With a single pull of the trigger, he'd be gone. Just like that. Just like the money.

Poof.

He couldn't see his father from his vantage point, so he left the doorway and took a few steps closer to the crowd.

Rick Said made it through the house, and walked outside through the same door Ken Salter had only seconds ago. After he'd stepped onto the back patio, he saw Salter, the gun held against his leg. He pointed and tried to shout, but he couldn't get any words out. He felt like he was drowning in his own blood, which, he was.

The band was set up on the far side of the pool, facing the house. The bandstand itself was elevated, and one of the musicians saw Said exit the house, covered in blood. He waved to the other musicians to stop playing, and the music fell away, a staggering totter of notes as the song died. The crowd groaned and the musician grabbed the microphone and shouted, "Hey, hey, we need a doctor. That guy is bleeding." He pointed at Said, who had made it as far as he could before he fell to the ground, unconscious.

The crowd turned to look and when they saw Said, a few of the women began to scream. Then someone looked at Salter and saw him holding a weapon. He shouted, "Hey, that guy's got a gun."

Most of the onlookers began to scatter, but a few of the men started to move in on Salter, their bravery fueled by their alcohol intake. Salter saw what was about to happen, so he raised the gun and started shooting. He hit one of the men who was moving toward him. After that, the rest of the men scattered too.

Salter began to run.

Since Cool couldn't drink, the governor told him to wait by the helicopter. "Not going to be here that long, anyway. Shake a few hands, get my picture taken, that sort of thing."

Cool gave him a nod. "Might grab a quick bite if we've got time," Cool said. "It smells like heaven coming out of that smoker."

"That's fine, but really, I'm talking ten minutes, tops."

"You got it, boss," Cool said. That'd be plenty of time. When the governor said ten minutes, that usually meant a half-hour, at least. Sometimes more. Much more.

Cool headed toward the food, and the governor made his way over to the bar. Mac knew the Salters liked their booze. That's where he'd find Roger Salter.

When they got to the house, Virgil and Murton decided to split up. "I'll take the west side, you take the east," Virgil said. Watch out for security. We don't know who's on the payroll and who's been hired as rent-a-cops for the party. Murton gave him a nod and they went off in separate directions.

Rosencrantz ran up the drive and saw Virgil and Murton go in opposite directions. He didn't try to think, he just went in the direction that felt right.

He followed Virgil.

Virgil had the odd psychic sense that most cops have, and when it spoke to him he listened. This time it told him he was being chased. When he rounded the first corner of the house he turned and waited. When Rosencrantz turned the corner a few seconds later, he skidded to a stop, the barrel of Virgil's gun pointed right at his forehead.

Virgil pulled his gun straight up, away from Rosie's face. "Sorry, man. I felt you coming."

Rosencrantz dismissed it. "Tell me what we've got. I already know about Fox at the gatehouse."

"Murt," Virgil said.

"Okay, now I know about the gatehouse."

"That's all I've got. Now it's just the Salters. We're going to hook them up and get the hell out of here. The governor is on the property. We've got to get him out too. Nothing else has changed."

Before Rosencrantz could respond, the music came to a clunky halt, then a few seconds later they heard some shouting, then the screams. A few seconds after that, they heard the gunfire.

"Sounds like things are changing."

They both ran toward the back of the house.

THE HOUSE ITSELF WAS SHAPED LIKE A FLAT-BOTTOMED V, the west end of the V much longer than the east. As a result, Murton made it to the back before Virgil and Rosencrantz. He heard the gunfire and when he rounded the corner he saw Said lying on the ground, covered in blood. The crowd was scattering in every possible direction and for a brief moment, Murton caught sight of Ken Salter, then lost him in the sea of people. He holstered his weapon and ran toward Said.

THE GOVERNOR WAS SPEAKING TO ROGER SALTER AT THE BAR when the gunfire erupted. Cool, who had kept an eye on the governor the entire time—not an easy task with all the people — pulled his weapon and ran that way. By the time he got there, the governor and Roger Salter were ducked down behind the bar. Cool looked at the governor and said, "Time to go, Boss."

The governor who had no idea what was happening looked at Salter and said, "I think your party is getting a little out of hand, Roger."

Salter himself wasn't exactly sure what was happening, but he knew it couldn't be good. He also knew that if the governor left, he'd be going to the airport, which is where he needed to be anyway. His jet was waiting. "I'm sure my security people will have the matter at hand dealt with accordingly. I'd take a ride out if you offered though."

"Of course. Let's go."

They peeked over the top of the bar and saw Ken Salter heading their way. He'd had the sense to put the gun in his pocket so he could blend in with the crowd of people who were still running away in every possible direction. Cool started to bring his weapon up, but felt Salter's hand on his arm. "It's okay. That's my son." He turned to the governor. "I'd like to bring him along too."

Ken Salter joined the other men behind the bar. His father looked at him without speaking.

The governor's patience was wearing thin. The sound of gunfire made him itchy. "Anyone else, Roger? Perhaps you'd like to put a proper manifest together before we leave." Then to Cool, "Let's go."

But Cool had his own plan. "Stay put, Sir. Let me go first. I'll get the engine started. When you hear the rotor come up to speed, be ready. I'm going to slide over this way. It'll make for a shorter run."

"Good enough," the governor said. "Quick as you can, now."

Cool took off toward the chopper, leaving the governor and the Salters behind the bar. A minute later they heard the sound of the helicopter engine begin to wind up.

"Nice party, Roger."

"It'll be my last, I assure you."

You've got that right, Ken thought. "Father, I need to tell you something."

"Not now, Son. Whatever it is, it'll have to wait."

"It's important."

"Here comes the helicopter," the governor shouted. Cool brought the chopper over, no more than a foot off the ground, crabbing sideways the entire way. He got as close as he could, but with the tables and chairs that sat scattered across the lawn, it'd still be about a fifty-yard run. "Let's go."

They ran to the helicopter, the Salters ahead of the governor.

"What in God's name is happening?" Roger Salter said to his son.

When he told his father about the funds, he did so with as few words as possible. When they stopped, the governor ran into them. "Why are you stopping? Let's go."

"What do you mean, gone?" Roger Salter shouted at his son.

Ken Salter reached into his pocket and pulled out the gun.

VIRGIL AND ROSENCRANTZ PUSHED PAST THE SEA OF PEOPLE moving away from the house. When they rounded the final corner, they saw Murton working on Said.

"Get Cool on the phone if you can and tell him to hold that chopper," Murton told Virgil. "Said's going to die if we don't get him out of here."

Cool set the helicopter down and was waiting for the governor and the Salters. He saw them all running his way, the Salters in the lead. He felt his phone buzzing and he pulled it out of his pocket and checked the screen. Virgil.

"I'm a little busy right now, Jonesy. The governor and the Salters are getting out. I'm their ride."

Virgil tried to keep his voice calm. "Cool, listen to me. We're here...on the property. I can see you. We're going to arrest the Salters and they know it. Do not let them on that chopper. Do you hear me? Where's Mac? Cool?"

When Cool heard Virgil say they were there to arrest the Salters, he dropped the phone and began flipping the switches to shut the chopper down. It only took a matter of seconds, but that was all the time that Ken Salter needed.

Ken Salter backed away and pulled the gun from his pocket, then put it against his head. "I'm sorry, father. I've ruined everything."

The governor jumped forward without thinking. He lunged at Salter and tried to swat the gun away from his head. Salter moved to side-step the governor, but their feet got knotted up and they both fell to the ground, the governor underneath Salter, both men struggling for control of the weapon. When the gun went off, the governor's eyes went wide with shock and pain.

CHAPTER FIFTY

THEY ALL HEARD THE GUNSHOT, AND VIRGIL TOLD MURTON and Rosencrantz to get Said to the chopper. Then he began to run that way.

THE SHOCK WAS REAL, AND SO WAS THE PAIN. THE GUN HAD been pointed sideways, the bullet taking the flesh from both men's chests, but neither of them were seriously injured. Salter jumped up, the gun still in his hand. His hearing was mostly gone and so he never really heard Cool or Virgil as they yelled for him to drop the weapon.

Salter turned and looked down at the governor. The gun wasn't really pointed directly at him, but it was close enough as far as Ross was concerned. He was one hundred yards away, the rifle resting atop a fence post. He hoped the scope was right. He exhaled and squeezed the trigger…ever so gently. He watched through the scope as the top right of Ken Salter's head blew apart.

Cool didn't know Ross was on the property. All he knew was another shooter was in the area. He took cover behind the chopper. Virgil ducked down as well more out of reflex than fear of being hit.

Ross reached up and quickly made a slight adjustment to the scope, but it gave Roger Salter enough time to bend over and grab the gun his son had dropped. Somewhere in the back of Salter's mind he heard his own voice asking why he was picking up the gun, though in his heart, he knew exactly why. They'd do the work for him. All he had to do was have the gun in his hand. What did they call it? Suicide by cop?

Roger Salter stood erect and pointed the gun at the governor. Ross had already begun his squeeze when Salter suddenly looked down and saw the feathers of the arrow protruding from his chest. He felt his heart seize up, then nothing at all.

Anthony Stronghill set his bow in the grass and laid the quiver next to it. He unstrapped his knife from his belt and put it next to the bow. Then he got down on his knees, placed his hands high in the air and waited.

Ross took his finger off the trigger.

Cool saw Murton and Rosencrantz carrying Said toward the helicopter. It didn't take much thinking on his part to figure out what to do next. He got the engine re-fired and they loaded Said on board. Murton climbed in to do what he could, which he knew wouldn't be much, given the nature of Said's injuries. Virgil hustled the governor on board as well, then grabbed the handle to close the door. He had his feet on the skid and Cool was already off the ground by the time he got the door shut. He jumped down and turned his back as the helicopter flew away.

Rosencrantz looked at Virgil. "You okay, man?"

"Yeah, I sure hope Said makes it." Then he looked over at the Indian. "I think someone is trying to surrender."

"Guess we better go let him," Rosencrantz said. He pointed at Roger Salter. "Did you see that? Suicide by Indian."

They walked over and Virgil said, "Are you Anthony Stronghill, also known as Tony Hill?"

Stronghill nodded.

"We need to hear you say it, sir," Rosencrantz said.

"I am."

"Please place your hands behind your back."

Stronghill did as he was asked and Virgil put the cuffs on him. "We have a warrant for your arrest. You have the right to remain silent. Anything you say can and will be used against you in a court of law…"

Virgil made a quick call to Cora and told her about the governor. Then he asked her to set up an escort. When he was finished with Cora, he called Patty, who was working out in the field. He gave her the bare minimum about her uncle, but told her to get up to the city right away.

Patty was shaken…he could hear it in her voice. "How bad is it, Jonesy?"

"I honestly don't know. That's the truth. Maybe it looked worse than it was."

"Okay, I'm going right now."

"I'll have a state trooper give you an escort. He should be waiting at the highway by the time you get there."

Patty hung up without replying. Virgil met Ross, Rosencrantz, and Stronghill back by the bodies of Roger Salter, and his son, Ken. Rosencrantz grabbed two table cloths and covered their bodies, then set up a temporary barricade by placing a number of tables on their sides in a tight circle around the dead men. Virgil sat Stronghill down in the grass outside the circle, then told them he was going for his truck. When he got to the gatehouse, he saw a man standing with his back to the door, his feet planted firmly, his arms crossed over his chest, a scowl on his face.

"Who are you?" Virgil asked.

"Shelby County Fire Rescue. Who's asking?"

Virgil pulled out his badge. "Virgil Jones, MCU."

The fire rescue guy relaxed. "Oh, okay. One of your guys told me to keep everyone out of here."

Virgil nodded. "Appreciate the help. Any trouble?"

He shook his head. "Naw. A couple of drunks wanted to see. I told them to beat feet."

They both turned when they heard the sirens out on the road. A steady stream of traffic was leaving the property, and the Shelby County cops were having a hard time getting through.

"Here comes your relief," Virgil said. "If you see Sheriff Holden, tell him I'm up by the house, back yard, close to the west side. He'll see us. I've got to get back and string some tape."

"No problem. I heard the gunshots. Everything okay now?"

Virgil wasn't quite sure how to answer. Finally he said, "No, not really."

The fire rescue guy nodded. "I hear you."

When he returned, Ross helped him move the tables out of the way and together they strung a roll of yellow crime scene tape around a wider area.

With that done, they all stood there for a moment without speaking. Virgil looked down at the cloth that covered Ken Salter. Blood from his head wound was seeping through the thin cloth. He pulled the covering back and looked at his head. Ross's shot had taken a large portion, and Virgil realized it wasn't with the body and they should find it.

They all looked around for a few minutes and when they found it, one of them put a little yellow evidence marker next to the skull cap, then covered it up as well, mostly because no one wanted to look at it.

With that done, Virgil turned to Ross—he was still holding Murton's rifle—and said, "Nice shooting."

Ross looked at the rifle. He had it cradled in his arms, the way shooters do, the bolt opened for safety's sake. "Are you kidding me? I damned near missed. High and to the right from one hundred yards? I'm almost embarrassed."

Virgil shrugged. "Maybe he moved at the last second."

Ross, who took his shooting seriously, said, "Ah...he didn't move."

"Anyway, you got the job done. Nice work."

"Thank you."

"You okay?"

Ross pulled his head back and gave Virgil an odd look. "Yeah, why wouldn't I be?"

Virgil looked at the bodies on the ground. "Just checking."

When Holden finally arrived, he hobbled over and took in the scene. Virgil expected his usual bad attitude. What he got surprised him.

"You and your guys okay?"

"Mostly," Virgil said. "The governor, of all people, got banged up a little. Nothing serious. He'll probably have a scar across his chest and a story to tell. Rick Said caught the worst of it. I'm not even sure what happened to him. Not yet, anyway. But he was in pretty bad shape. I think he's got some busted ribs and a punctured lung. Looked like he'd lost quite a bit of blood. To tell you the truth, I don't know if he's going to make it or not."

"Well, let's hope he does. Thoughts and prayers and all that. I see you got your Indian."

"Yeah. I'm going to run him up to Indy. My guys will give their statements whenever you'd like. I'll get mine to you as soon as I can."

Holden stuck his tongue in his cheek. "Your spelling is awful. Anyone ever tell you that?"

Virgil sort of bobbed his head. He told Ross and Rosencrantz to stay and assist the Shelby County cops, then loaded Stronghill in the Raptor and drove away.

Lola was worried. There was some disagreement about who was going to the hospital when they made their run for Carlos, and who was staying behind. Linda was going for sure. She knew hospitals, knew their routines, their lingo, and how things worked in general. Since Wu was staying behind to monitor the extraction and give them direction and real-time updates, that decision was a no-brainer as well. Lola wouldn't be going for obvious reasons, the obvious being her age, her lack of skills regarding covert operations, and her overwhelming state of general anxiety. That left the twins, and that's what the disagreement was all about.

Nicky wanted to go, and while his reasoning was valid, it bordered on the chauvinistic side of the equation. "There has to be a man there," he told his sister. "Wu can't go. He'll be our eyes and ears. That leaves me."

Nichole shook her head. "But I've been there already. I know the layout, I've seen Carlos, and he'll be expecting me. I've also seen the guard."

"And that's exactly why you shouldn't go. What if it's the same guard and he recognizes you?"

Nichole began to tick the reasons off her fingers. "First, I'd be surprised if it's the same guard. The guy isn't living there, for Christ's sake. They've got to have a rotation of some kind. You know that. Second, even if it is the same guard, I'll have on an entirely different disguise. You know I'm good with that sort of thing. And third…"

"Don't even bother with third," Nicky said. "I know what third is. We all know what third is. You like the action, the excitement. You live for it."

"So what? I'm good at what I do. Just like you are."

Lola stood up and said, "Stop this!" They all got quiet and looked at her. She sat back down then said, "I do not understand why all three of you do not go."

"Wu has been watching," Wu said. "When they move the patients, there are only two orderlies who do the moving. Three would stick out. It may cause superstition." He looked at Nicky, who refused to take the bait this time, mostly because Lola was in no mood.

Lola turned to Nichole. "You have always been our

leader. And you are very good at what you do. But I have a suggestion."

"What is it?" Nichole said.

"What if Nicky went too, but was there in another capacity. Perhaps a janitor or maintenance man? That way, he could be close by to assist if needed, but not part of the deception of Carlos's escape."

They tossed that idea around and decided it could work. They'd have to outfit him, which wouldn't be that big of a deal, since they had to outfit Nichole and Linda anyway.

In the end, they agreed. Linda and Nichole would be the patient transporters, and Nicky would be the janitor. Linda went off with Lola to a scrubs store, and from there they'd go to a fabric shop to get the necessary supplies and equipment to fabricate their disguises. Nicky had to go with them because they'd need the proper attire and a wig for him. Nichole didn't need a wig. She traveled with three or four of her own at all times.

Wu began looking at the various video feeds, watching the janitors, locating the supply closets and so forth. When the others were about to leave, he said, "Wu wonder something."

Nichole had her purse over her shoulder and her hand on the doorknob. "What is it?"

"The hospital has only one helicopter landing pad. We will need to create a situation to have the pad clear for our own."

No one had thought of that. "Can you get into their dispatch system?" Nichole asked.

"Yes, but to be on the side of safe, we will want our helicopter already in the air and very close by. The timing will be critical."

"Set it up, Wu," Nicky told him. "I'll talk with our helicopter pilot."

"Wu will do."

CHAPTER FIFTY-ONE

ONCE THEY WERE CLEAR OF THE SALTER PROPERTY AND THE traffic jam created by the mass exodus after the shootings, Virgil pulled over to the side of the road. He looked at Stronghill and said, "Stay put." He walked around to the other side of the truck and opened the passenger door. "Hop out."

Stronghill looked at Virgil for a moment, his face neutral. He slid out of the truck and faced Virgil.

"I'm going to ask you something, and depending on your answer, I'm going to do something I probably shouldn't do."

Stronghill raised an eyebrow at him.

"Good trick. I can do it too. Apparently it gets on people's nerves sometimes."

"What is your question?" Stronghill asked.

"When you were out in my field and saw the woman—Patty Doyle is her name—you witnessed her assault."

"That isn't a question, but it is a truthful statement."

"Fair enough. I'd like you to tell me what you saw, particularly when the Mexican mechanic came to her aid."

Stronghill took ten minutes and told Virgil everything he

saw. He wrapped it up by saying, "I believe the mechanic did the right thing. Although the workman was killed, it truly looked like an accident." He tagged a caveat on the end of his statement. "Make no mistake, he would have been injured very badly had the blow landed on his side instead of his head, but he was acting in defense of another. Also, I cannot provide or serve clear evidence of his intent had the blow landed where he was aiming, which was, without question, at the man's side…not his head. May I ask, how is the mechanic? He will survive?"

"It looks like it. He's in the hospital and I'm going to question him later today. His survival isn't the only issue, though."

"May I ask what the other issue is?"

"He will likely be deported. He's part of the DACA program. That's the Deferred—"

"I am familiar with DACA, Detective."

"I see. In any case, unless everybody's stories line up, I think ICE is going to send him back to Mexico. They may do so regardless."

"At least he will be alive. I believe he will tell you the same things that I have. Although I would not expect him to speak to his intent after the first blow."

"Nor would I," Virgil said. "Since you mentioned intent, let's talk about that. When you shot the other driver, there was no doubt in your mind of his intent? No other way of handling the situation on your end?"

Stronghill shook his head. "None whatsoever. The man was going to keep shooting. You could see it in his eyes. His mind was…not his own in that moment. If you ask the young woman, I believe she will back me up on this."

"She already has," Virgil said. "Adamantly."

"She speaks the truth."

"I know she does. If I unhook you, are you going to give me any trouble?"

"What purpose would that serve?"

"I'm looking for a yes or no."

"I will not give you any trouble, Detective. You have my word."

Virgil looked Stronghill in the eye for a full minute. "Turn around."

Stronghill turned around and Virgil removed the handcuffs. "You saved the governor's life."

Stronghill turned back toward Virgil and rubbed at his wrists. "Perhaps. Perhaps not. I know at the very least, I saved my own."

"What do you mean?"

Stronghill looked at Virgil's truck. "I like your ride. Does it have Bluetooth?"

"Yeah, it does. Why do you ask?"

"Because there is something I'd like you to hear."

They got back in the truck and Virgil hooked Stronghill's phone into his system. "The recording is not easy to hear, but if you listen closely, you will hear the Salter men speaking of my disposal, among other things."

Virgil listened to the recording three times during the drive back to the city. After the third time, he said, "A good attorney will be able to say that you were acting in self-defense."

"And a good prosecutor will be able to say that I was acting out of premeditation." He crossed his arms over his chest. "Either way, I am not worried."

"Is that the Indian way? It'll be what it'll be, and all that?"

Stronghill didn't answer. He simply stared out the window.

Virgil walked him into the Marion County Central Booking, gave a copy of the warrant to the jailer, then asked him to put Stronghill in a private holding cell. The jailer said he would. He knew Virgil from the bar—he was a regular there—so it wouldn't be a problem. Virgil looked at Stronghill. "We'll talk again."

"I am certain we will. Thank you for the consideration on the ride back."

Virgil turned to leave and thought, nice guy. *Hope the system doesn't get him.* What he didn't know was, the system already had him. His name was going to pop up the moment he was printed.

"When's Delroy coming back?" The jailer asked.

With the threat to Delroy and Huma taken care of they could come back whenever they wanted to. "Should be any day now," Virgil said. He nodded at Stronghill as they led him away. He spent ten minutes with the intake paper, then headed for the hospital. Something about the conversation he'd had with Stronghill on the ride back to the city was nibbling at his brain. Virgil couldn't quite get his mind around it, and decided to let it go…for now anyway. It'd come or it wouldn't.

He parked in the first spot he could find, well away from the valet parking. He'd learned that lesson the hard way. He called Murton to find out where he was and learned that everyone was still in the Emergency Department, with the exception of Said, who had been taken in for surgery. When

Patty saw him, she ran over and hugged him. "Tell me," Virgil said.

"He's got two broken ribs. They both punctured his lung. He lost a lot of blood. The doctor said they think he's going to be okay, but the look on his face when he said it wasn't very encouraging." She began to cry. Virgil wrapped his arm around her and she put her head on his shoulder.

He waited until Patty's crying had worn down, then looked at Murton. "Mac?"

Murton grinned. "Pissed off. And in a fair amount of pain. He's got a nice .380 groove across the center of his chest. Caught some muscle, so it must hurt like a bitch, but if it doesn't get infected, he'll be okay. Although Cora is ready to kill him."

Virgil grinned. "I bet. He told her he was going home for the day, then skipped out to go to Salter's party."

"That's what the doctors said about Uncle Rick. Infection. They're worried about it."

They should be, Virgil thought. He knew what that was like.

Cora and the governor came around the corner, his arm over her shoulder for support. They all stood up.

"How are you, sir?" Virgil asked.

The governor spoke slowly, as if he had to search for the right words. He was clearly medicated. "I'm okay. Don't know what I was thinking, going for that gun. Next time, I'm leaving the police work to the professionals."

"*Next time?*" Cora said through her teeth.

The governor rolled his head in her direction. "Every time, then." He looked at Virgil. "If you don't mind, I think we should push our get-together back a week or so."

Virgil nodded. "No problem, Mac. Go home. Follow the doctor's orders, will you?"

"He doesn't have a choice," Cora said.

"I don't have a choice," The governor said. He looked at Murton. "Thank you, Murt." Then he giggled, almost like a schoolgirl, and said, "Are we still divorced?"

"I think we can work it out," Murton said.

The governor gave him a big dopey grin, pointed a finger at him, and said, "In sickness and in health." Then he looked at Cora and said, "To the castle, M'lady."

Despite her troubles, Patty smiled. Cora took the governor away, then they all settled in to wait.

After a while, the waiting began to wear on Virgil. He told Murton and Patty that he was going to go try to speak with Carlos.

"Did you get your Indian?" Patty asked.

"I did," Virgil said. "He backs your part of the story up, practically word for word."

"I told you he would."

"He seems like a pretty good guy, actually. I hope everything works out for him."

"Is there anything I can do?" Patty asked.

Virgil shook his head. "Not that I can think of. Besides, you've got enough on your plate right now. I'll be back shortly." He looked at Murton. "You okay to stay for a while longer?"

"Of course. Me and the Dungeon Dame aren't going anywhere until we find out how our patient is doing. Then—on Becky's orders no less, this young lady is spending the night with us."

"Good. That's good." He looked at Patty. "You shouldn't be alone tonight."

"So I've been told." She pulled her feet up on the chair and wrapped her arms around her legs.

"He's going to be okay, Patty."

She didn't answer, so Virgil turned and headed for the elevators.

He waited for the elevator, then suddenly remembered he didn't know where he was going. He went to the information desk across the hall and asked what room Carlos Ibarra was in. The elevator dinged announcing its arrival, and the desk attendant finally found what she was looking for. She told Virgil, who then made a mad dash for the elevator and got there just as the doors slid shut. He thought he saw a young man inside give him a smug look as the doors closed.

When he got to Ibarra's room he was stopped by the ICE agent. When he showed his badge and identified himself, the agent said he could go right in. Virgil pushed the door open and found an empty spot where the bed should have been.

He walked out, looked at the agent, and said, "There's no one in there."

"They took him for tests. MRI or something like that," the agent said. He was reading a magazine article and started to tell Virgil all about it. The article depicted a detective in Minnesota who'd rescued a young girl after she'd shot and killed a crooked cop. The cop—the live one—ended up adopting the girl. The article was sort of a big deal, written by a different cop, a friend of the one who'd adopted the girl.

The photo spread had been done by none other than Annie Leibovitz. "And get this," the agent said. "The cop who wrote the story? His first name is Virgil."

"Yeah, yeah, great story," Virgil said. "Someone should write a book about it." He didn't care. "Where's the MRI room?"

The agent was a little offended. He was simply trying to make small talk. "What, I'm a tour guide now? The nursing station is right over there." He tipped his chin in the general direction of nothing.

Virgil thought he heard him mutter, 'asshole' as he walked away.

THE NURSING STATION SAT EMPTY AS NURSING STATIONS OFTEN do, so Virgil had to wait. When someone showed up, he identified himself and asked when Ibarra would be back in his room.

The nurse, a cute young female with black hair wrapped up in a bun looked at Virgil's ID, then his face. She repeated the process twice, then sat down and began to punch at the keys in front of the computer monitor. "He's down in imaging right now. They're going to do a full set. X-rays, CAT, and MRI."

"Well, shoot. I was hoping to talk to him."

"You can wait, but it's going to be quite a while. Everything is all backed up. Did you hear about that semi accident?"

Virgil nodded. "I did."

"Most of the injured ended up here. The burn victims were gone of course, but when that thing blew up, a lot of people got knocked around. We ended up with a boatload of non-fatal broken folks, almost all of them requiring some sort of imaging. So, like I said, things are a little backed up."

"What's your best guess when I could speak with him?"

"Later tonight."

"Later, like seven, or later like midnight?"

"Split the difference and you should be okay. Or wait until tomorrow."

Virgil thanked her and left. The ICE agent ignored him when he walked past.

When he got back to Murton and Patty, he found them speaking with a surgical assistant who'd come out of the surgical suite to give them an update. The surgery was going to take a little longer than anticipated. A bone fragment was still lodged in the lung and every time they tried to inflate it, they ended up with a slow leak.

"But he's going to be okay?" Patty asked.

"It certainly looks that way. We got his blood level back to where it needed to be. Once they've got that fragment out, they'll re-inflate him and close up."

"When will I be able to see him?"

"He'll be in post-op recovery for a while, then the ICU to make sure the lung keeps doing its thing. I'd say you could get a few minutes with him in the ICU, but he won't know you're there. If you want to speak with him, it'll be tomorrow at the earliest. I've got to get back in. The message is this: He's going to be all right. If I were you, I'd go home and rest. Get something to eat."

"Thank you," Patty said.

After the surgical assistant left, Virgil and Murton had to convince Patty to leave. It was no small effort and she only agreed to go if Murton promised to bring her back after dinner. He said he would.

"I might be coming back later myself," Virgil said. "Still need to get with Carlos."

A few minutes later they all piled into Virgil's truck. He'd give them a ride back to Murton's.

"Didn't park by the valet lot, huh?" Murton said.

Virgil ignored him…and his laughter. Patty asked what was so funny and Murton told her the whole story.

CHAPTER FIFTY-TWO

It was a fairly short run from the hospital to Murton's house, and Murton worked the story the entire trip.

"I was at a disadvantage, is all," Virgil said. "The kid had me over a barrel and he knew it. As negotiations go, it wasn't my best, I'll admit."

They turned into the drive and Murton said, "As negotiations go, it wasn't a negotiation."

Virgil gave Patty a squeeze. When she and Murton were out of the truck, Virgil said, "Call me the minute you hear anything." She told him she would.

"Any idea when I'm getting my ride back?" Murton asked him.

Virgil shook his head. "Have to call Ross or Rosie. They'll probably need a ride back to the MCU...or they could spend the night with you. I'm sure you'll negotiate something."

Then he hit the gas and drove away.

When he got home, Sandy had dinner waiting and Virgil—his last meal being the attempted special at Nick's—discovered he was beyond hungry. He was famished. He wolfed down his food like a starving man, saying little during the entire meal. When he was finished, he sat back, put his hands on his stomach and belched loudly.

"Nice one," Sandy said.

"Excuse you," Jonas added.

Wyatt simply looked at his father, his one green eye and one blue eye sparkling with innocent joy, a toothless smile on his face. He said, "Ack," then threw his spoon on the floor. Virgil bent over to retrieve the spoon and got a good look at all the food on the floor. When he spoke, his mouth was ahead of his brain. "Man, we need a dog."

Jonas looked at him, his mouth hanging open. "Are we getting a dog?" He turned and looked at Sandy. "Are we, mom? Are we getting a dog?"

Sandy gave Virgil a look, then put her elbows on the table and her forehead in her hands. She was already overloaded with both the boys. And with Huma gone, a dog was the last thing she needed.

The dog comment had sort of slipped out. Virgil wasn't even serious when he said it. But he realized he'd started something that wasn't going to go away very easily. He looked at his wife and said, "Uh, how about I clean up the kitchen?"

"Can we, mom?"

Virgil rubbed the top of Jonas's head. "We'll talk about it later, buddy, okay?"

"Can it be a puppy? I really want a puppy!"

Virgil looked at his wife and mouthed 'sorry' to her. She gave him a smile that landed somewhere between genuine and how could you? She took Wyatt for his bath, and said,

"I'll let you get started. C'mon, Jonas. Bath time for you too, buddy."

He followed her down the hall and Virgil could hear Jonas talking about all different kinds of puppies. He took a hard look at the kitchen, and discovered it was a real mess. He stood up and got to work.

Huma, please come home, he thought.

Two hours later the kids were asleep, the kitchen was fairly clean—Virgil had even gotten the Swiffer out—and he and Sandy finally ended up alone on the back deck.

"A dog? What on earth were you thinking?"

"I guess I wasn't. I'm really sorry. It just slipped out. I saw all the food on the floor, and thought, 'you know what would take care of all—'"

"Virgil?"

"Yes, dear?"

"Shut up."

"Yes, dear."

She put her hand in his and he wrapped his arm around her. They sat on a glider facing the pond and Virgil rocked them gently back and forth. "How bad was it today?" Sandy asked. "I caught some of it on the news, but it sounded like they were filling in a lot of gaps."

"I bet," he said, his voice thick with sarcasm. Virgil had issues with the news and the way it was reported. He thought the weather reporter was okay, though. "It was pretty bad." He gave her most of the details and wrapped it up by saying, "At least the bad actors are off the board and out of the equation. Delroy and Huma will be coming home, and if everything Patty says works out, we'll get the land sold. Then everything will be back to normal."

Sandy laughed. "Tell me what that looks like again… normal."

"Not sure I can. By the way, did the news mention anything about Mac?"

She pulled away so she could see his face. "Mac? No, why?"

"That's good. He wants to push our get-together back a week."

"That's fine. How come?"

"Well, he sort of got shot a little…"

Sandy was mad. They'd both had their differences with the governor, but through it all, he remained dear to them, his kindness, generosity, his strength of character, and the way he watched out for everyone all made him much more than their boss. He was a friend. He was one of *them*. "What was he thinking? I'm going to kill him."

Virgil laughed. "You better hurry. Cora might have beaten you to it."

"I can't believe he went for the gun."

"It was pure instinct, I'm sure. He's former military. You know that. So…"

"Yeah, yeah. Still."

Virgil didn't try to talk her down. He laughed to himself. Dinner next week should be fun. The governor was going to get an earful.

"I've got to go back to the hospital tonight," Virgil said.

"How's Rick?"

"I don't know yet, so I'm going to look in on him. That's

one reason. But I've got to question Carlos Ibarra. If something isn't done and soon, he's going to end up in the system for doing nothing more than saving Patty."

"At least the Indian—what's his name, again?"

"Stronghill."

"Right. At least Stronghill backs up what Patty said."

"That's true, but Stronghill has his own problems."

"From the way you tell it, it sounds to me like he should be okay. In defense of another and all that."

"There's something weird about that guy. Stronghill. I can't quite put my finger on it."

"Weird how?"

"I'm not sure. It feels like there's more going on with him than what he's saying."

"You think he's got a sheet?"

"We'll find out soon enough," Virgil said. "I hope not."

"When are you going?"

Virgil looked at his watch. "I should go now." He untangled himself from Sandy, who didn't make it easy.

"What are you doing?"

"Trying to get you to stay. Are you sure you have to go this minute?"

Virgil checked his watch again. "Well, not this minute exactly. I could give you the best sixty seconds of your life."

"I'll take it," Sandy said. "Plus, if you go the full sixty, you'd double your current endurance record."

"Hey…"

Wu was set up on the plane. When he asked one of the pilots for power, they wanted to know how long he'd need it.

"Wu not sure."

"Okay. No problem," the captain said. "We can run on battery power for thirty minutes, but if you want more than that, we'll get a GPU hooked up. Sounds like that might be the way to go. You'll have all the power you need for as long as you need it."

"What is GPU?"

"Ground power unit," the copilot said. "It's essentially a big generator that plugs into the aircraft."

"It is easy to disconnect quickly?"

"Yeah. Flip a switch and pull the plug." He cocked his head at him. "Why, we making a getaway or something?" He laughed at his own humor. Wu did not. He gave the copilot a flat stare and said, "I require privacy. When the helicopter arrives, be ready for an immediate departure."

The pilots nodded and went away. A few minutes later the interior of the aircraft lit up and Wu switched from his batteries and plugged the laptops in. He connected to the onboard WIFI and brought the hospital's systems up on one, his comms system on another, and the medevac dispatch center on the third. He put his headset on, and did a comms check with Linda, and the twins. They wore tiny earbuds that were wireless, and invisible. They were also voice-activated. If they spoke, they were transmitting, and Wu would hear everything. Everyone acknowledged the comm check. They were in place and ready to go at the hospital.

Nicky informed him that the hospital's helicopter was currently on the pad. "I'm looking at it right now. The pilots are in the lounge with their feet up."

"One moment, please." Wu typed in a series of keystrokes and then studied the screen for a few minutes. "Go back inside. I will clear the pad." He typed in a few more commands and said, "They will be departing momentarily."

"Where are they going?"

"To the Evansville airport to pick up a patient who doesn't exist."

Nicky heard a loud chime in the pilot's lounge. When he went in, he took out a screwdriver from his tool belt and began to tighten a door hinge. No one paid him any attention. A printer on the counter spat out a flight manifest and the crew grabbed their gear.

"Where we headed?" one of the pilots asked the other.

He looked at the paper. "We're taking a nice boring run down to the Evansville airport for a pick up."

"Wake me when we get there. Man, we only had one more hour before our shift ended."

They walked out the door, neither of them saying anything to Nicky. Why would they? He was nothing more than a lowly maintenance technician. *If you only knew,* Nicky thought.

Five minutes later the pad was clear. Nicky radioed Wu to let him know.

"Everyone please stand by," Wu said.

He took off his headset and exited the aircraft. He walked over to the medevac helicopter and spoke with the pilot. "You are ready?"

"Just tell me when to launch," the pilot said. He was strapped in, helmet on, and waiting for the signal to go.

Wu gave him a burner. "Watch for my message. Depart when you get it."

"Roger that," the pilot said.

He looked at the nurse practitioner. "You are ready as well?"

"I've been ready since we arrived," she said. "Let's get to it."

Wu re-boarded the jet and sat down next to Lola. "We are prepared."

Lola simply nodded at him. She was so anxious she couldn't speak.

Wu patted her shoulder. "Do not worry. This is what Wu do." He walked to the rear of the aircraft, took his seat, and typed in a command on one of the laptops. Then he put his headset back on and keyed his microphone. "Nicky, I have disabled the fire alarm control panel on the west wall directly across the hall from the nursing station. Go now."

Nicky was on the steps that led down from the helipad on the roof. "Got it. I'm on my way."

Disabling the fire alarm control panel would put Nicky only two doors down from Carlos's room. He'd be able to watch the guard, and maybe even distract him if necessary when it was time to move Carlos.

Wu zoomed in on the guard and took a screen grab and sent it to Nichole's phone. "Nichole, I have sent you a photo of the guard."

"I'm looking at it now," she said. "It's the same one who was there went I went in before."

Nicky said, "Sis?"

"Don't sweat it, bro. He's not that bright. I've changed my look. He won't even notice."

"And if he does?"

"Then we'll handle it. I'm ready."

The radios were silent for a few seconds. "Okay, it's your call. I'm at the doorway in the stairwell."

Linda and Nichole were in the stairwell at the opposite end of the hall. "Let's do it," Nichole said.

"Going in now," Nicky said. He pushed through the doorway and began to move down the hall. The nursing shift change was scheduled to happen in five minutes.

Wu sent the signal to the helicopter and fifteen seconds later he heard the turbines begin to spin up. Sixty seconds after that he heard the change in the rotors as the pilot pulled on the collective, changing the pitch of the blades. The change in pitch lifted the helicopter from the pad.

"Our helicopter has departed and is currently inbound. ETA at the hospital is seven minutes. I'm sending the order to the nursing station. Linda, Nichole, go now."

The women pushed through the door and headed for Carlos's room.

CHAPTER FIFTY-THREE

Virgil got to the hospital, asked the information clerk where he could find Rick Said, then went that way. According to the clerk, he was in ICU and Virgil wouldn't be allowed in. He decided he'd give it a shot anyway. At least talk with one of the nurses. Maybe get a read on how Said was doing.

The hospital—like hospitals everywhere—was a maze. He got turned around a couple of times, but he eventually found the ICU. The nursing staff wouldn't let him in, but Patty—God bless her—had put Virgil on the HIPPA list. That meant the nurses could answer his questions.

Nicky walked past the guard, gave him a polite nod, and saw the panel Wu had disabled. The guard tipped his head at Nicky, then said, "Long night, huh?"

"Aren't they all?"

"You look like the guy they call when something needs to be fixed."

"That's me," Nicky said.

"What's broken?"

Nicky pulled the screwdriver from his belt and used it as a pointer. He saw his sister and Linda headed his way from the other end of the hall. "Ah, it's that damned control panel over there. It keeps frying a circuit and blanking out the display. I'm trying to get it worked out."

The guard leaned past Nicky and looked at the panel. It was completely dark. "Huh." Then, "Remember the good old days when all they had was those little red boxes? All you had to do was pull the lever."

Nicky laughed. "Yeah, I do. I also remember getting my ass kicked once by my old man for pulling one. You'd have thought I launched a nuke or something the way he reacted, the drunk bastard."

The guard laughed right back. When he spoke, he put the back of his hand against the corner of his mouth. "Me too. On both accounts…pulling the lever and the drunk bastard. Hey maybe we're related."

They laughed some more, then Nicky said, "I don't mind working on this one so much, though."

"Why's that?" The guard said.

"Are you kidding me? With this kind of eye candy floating around?" Nicky looked down the hall and tipped his eyes at the women. He'd timed his comment perfectly, finishing right as Nichole and Linda walked up. Nicky looked at them, put a little perv in his voice and said, "Hello ladies."

Linda rolled her eyes and said, "Yeah, keep it up, Billy. I heard Karen from radiology is thinking about filing a report after that shit you pulled yesterday."

Nicky gave them an innocent shrug. "Ah, I was only messing around and she knows it."

"Uh-huh." She pointed a finger at him. "Well, let me tell

you this: She's a friend of mine and you better watch it. Grabbin' ass isn't messing around as you like to call it. Not anymore it ain't. And I saw the way you were looking at us." She turned to the guard. "What'd he say as we was walking up?"

The guard shook his head. "I'm not getting involved. I've got my own grief to deal with." He glanced at Nichole, then did a little double-take. "You look sort of familiar. Have we met?"

Linda stepped right in, keeping the charade going. "See? That's what I'm talking about, right there. What kind of bullshit line is that? *You look sort of familiar.* Where'd you get that, from a book? Let me guess, was it One-Liners For Dummies, or the Ultimate Guide For Picking Up Chicks?"

"Easy," Wu said over the comms. "Don't get carried away. Four minutes."

Nicky looked at the guard. "Good luck, dude. I'm outta here." He went to the panel and began to tinker with the panel.

The guard ignored him, his attention on the women. "It wasn't a line," he said. "Honest. She looks familiar is all. Christ, you can't say anything to anyone these days."

Nichole snapped her fingers and smiled. "Wait a second. I bet I know what it is. Have you been here all day?"

He nodded. "Yeah. Working a double. Why?"

She tipped her head at the door to Carlos's room. "The Mexican in there…we're here to take him down for imaging."

"Again?"

Nichole shrugged. "Don't know anything about again. The orders said take him to imaging, so that's why we're here. If he was down there already, someone must have taken a bad pic. It happens. Anyway, none of that matters.

What I was getting at was this: Does the Mex have a lady lawyer?"

"Matter of fact, yeah." Then he snapped his fingers, like Nichole had. "You look a lot like her. Different hair and clothes and all, but you guys could be twins."

"That's because if you're talking about who I think you're talking about, we are. Elizabeth McKesson, right? Nice clothes, blond hair with dark roots. Walks around like she owns the joint. Sorta bitchy."

The guard pulled the business card out of his pocket and nodded. "Yup. That was her. You're her sister, huh?"

"Yeah. Ellen McKesson. Lucky me. She got the brains and I got the guts." She slapped Linda's arm with the back of her hand and let out a snort. "Get it? I got the guts?"

Linda looked at the guard and rolled her eyes again. "Yeah, I get it. I get it about ten times a day. You need some new material, woman. Can we get on with it, already? I've got a date tonight and an early shift tomorrow."

Nichole winked at the guard. "I'm nothing like my sister, or my co-worker, for that matter, if you get my drift. What time are you outta here?"

The guard got the drift alright. "Midnight. Maybe we could grab a drink, or something." He put a little emphasis on 'something.'

Nichole took a Sharpie from the pocket of her scrubs and held out her hand. The guard gave her the business card. "I'm going to give you a number, but don't call it until after one a.m. That's when I'm done."

"That's no problem," the guard said.

Nichole gave him the card back. "I mean it. If my phone rings when I'm on duty, they'll hand me my ass." Then she leaned in close and whispered in his ear. "That'd mean no ass for you." She pulled away and looked at Linda. "You ready?"

Linda shook her head and walked into Carlos's room.

Nichole looked at the guard. "And you thought my sister was bitchy…"

Virgil got as much information as possible. Said was doing as well as could be expected. The lung appeared to be holding, and pending any further complications, they expected a full, albeit slow recovery. Virgil thanked them and asked if he could leave a note for Patty so she'd know he'd been there.

"You could," the nurse said. "Or you could tell her yourself. She's down in the cafeteria."

Virgil wasn't surprised. He went to the elevators and reached out to push the button. Up to speak with Carlos, or down to the cafeteria to see Patty. He was going to go down first—Carlos wasn't going anywhere tonight—but then he thought, if he didn't get to him now, he might not have the chance. Plus Patty would probably be here all night anyway. He'd talk to her after he saw Carlos.

He hit the up button.

They unhooked Carlos from all the equipment as quickly as possible, released the wheel locks on his bed and pushed him to the door. When the door opened, Nicky turned his head away and whispered into his shoulder. "Light the panel back up, Wu."

Wu tapped the command into the laptop and the panel lit up. "One minute," he told them.

Nicky snapped the panel back in place and began to walk

toward the elevators. He pushed the up button. Linda and Nichole wheeled Carlos out, and once they were clear of the door, Nichole hung back and let Linda push the bed. She looked at the guard and said, "I'll see you when we bring him back. Looking forward to later though."

"Me too," the guard said.

The elevator dinged and Nichole said, "Gotta run."

"Don't let that guy get away," the guard said with a chuckle. "They'd hang me by my ball sack."

"Don't worry," Nichole said. "I won't let him out of my sight. He'll be with me the whole time." She jogged to the elevator and slid through the doors as they began to close.

As soon as the doors closed, the other elevator dinged and the guard looked up. He thought maybe they'd forgotten something. When he saw it was the other car, he sat down. When he saw who stepped off he looked away.

Virgil felt the elevator begin to slow and when it stopped it made a little ding and he stepped off. He thought he heard laughter coming from the other elevator car.

He turned toward Carlos's room and noticed that the same guard was still there. He felt sort of sorry for the guy. Guard duty was about as boring as it got. Plus, if he was being honest with himself, he'd been a little dickish with the guy earlier. Virgil knew he could be like that every once in a while without meaning to. It was something he was working on.

He walked over and stuck out his hand. "Hey, listen, about earlier, I'd had a pretty rough day. I was sort of being an asshole…"

The guard waved him off. "Don't worry about it. I was a

little bent out of shape myself. But believe me, my night just got about one thousand percent better."

"Well, good for you. No hard feelings then." They shook hands.

"If you're here to speak with the Mex, you missed him again."

Virgil shook his head. "Jeez, maybe I should have your job. If I stand guard, I might be able to catch him."

"Ah, hang out for a while. He'll be back. They had to take him down for imaging."

Virgil frowned. "What? Again?"

"Yeah, I guess they got a bad picture earlier. The nurse, or orderly or whoever said it happens."

Virgil turned and looked at the elevators. "Imaging is downstairs."

"Yeah. What of it?"

He pointed at the elevators. "Then why are they going up?"

THE HELICOPTER TOUCHED DOWN ON THE PAD AS LINDA AND the twins rolled Carlos through the doors. The pilot kept the engines running as instructed, and the nurse practitioner slid the door open and manhandled the gurney out of the chopper all by herself. She rolled the gurney over to the doorway—they couldn't take the hospital bed near the chopper because of the sheets and other bedding. Didn't want to risk anything flying off the bed and getting caught in the rotors, or worse, sucked into the engines.

They parked the gurney right next to the bed and as carefully as they could—which given the situation, wasn't all that careful—got Carlos out of the bed and onto the gurney. The nurse unhooked the IV lines at their connectors, transferred the catheter bag, strapped him down, then released the brakes. "That's it. Let's go!" She shouted.

They all began to push the gurney toward the chopper.

The guard jumped up, and said, "C'mon, we better go check it out."

Virgil felt like his mind was in overdrive, almost like everything around him was moving in slow motion. He'd heard the laughter coming from the other elevator car and the more he thought about it, the more he realized it wasn't humor he'd heard in the laughter, it was relief. Carlos's mother, Lola, was a part of the Pope crew, and Carlos himself was about to end up in the system. Virgil knew the Popes would never let that happen. He also knew that if Carlos hadn't acted when he did, Patty would have been killed or at the very least, brutally assaulted.

His father's words were running through his head. *What I'm getting at is sometimes you have to do your job, and sometimes you have to do the right thing. They aren't always the same. Remember that.* What Virgil did next was something he never thought he would. He held out his hand and stopped the guard. "Hold on. I think I might be a little paranoid. Let me check with the nurse's station."

"Man, I don't know," the guard said. "What if they're getting away?"

Virgil looked at him like he was the paranoid one. "You've never pressed the wrong elevator button before? What, you think they've got a helicopter waiting on the roof or something? This isn't the movies." He laughed politely, clapped the guard on the shoulder, then walked over and got the attention of one of the nurses. "Could you check something for me please?"

"What is it, sir?"

Virgil had his badge out. "Do you have an order for a patient, Carlos Ibarra, to be taken down to imaging?" Virgil knew she'd probably try to throw some HIPPA bullshit at him, so he added, "I don't need any particulars, I'm simply asking if that's where he went." Then he leaned in a little closer and added. "I'm trying to avoid putting the entire hospital on lockdown." The guard had walked over to the desk and was listening now. He'd heard Virgil's last comment about a lockdown and knew he could trust him.

The nurse had been through a lockdown before and it was the last thing she needed at the end of her shift. She tapped at her computer keyboard and after a few seconds she nodded at them. "Yep. Full CAT series. Looks like someone screwed up the imaging from earlier."

"How can you tell?" The guard asked, a whiff of suspicion in his voice.

"The billing code," the nurse replied. "This one didn't go through to central billing. That means the error was on our end."

Virgil thanked her then turned to the guard, his elbows in, his hands turned palms up. "See? There you go. Crisis averted. Man, I can get myself wound up sometimes. I think I need to get some sleep."

The guard, who nearing the end of a double anyway and was very tired himself, had all the proof he needed. He looked at the nurse and said, "How long will a full series take?"

"Couple of hours. Looks like there's a few ahead of him, so it's going to be a while."

He looked at Virgil. "Want to grab a cup of coffee?"

Virgil shook his head. "Love to, but I can't. I've got paperwork like you wouldn't believe. You hear about that Shelby County thing today?"

"Yeah."

"That was me."

The guard knew about paperwork. "Oh boy. Good luck then."

They shook hands again and Virgil left, taking the stairs. As soon as the door closed behind him, he began to run, taking the steps two or three at a time.

He had four floors to go to make it to the roof. He only felt a little bad about the guard…if he was right, that is.

But he knew he was.

———

THEY HAD CARLOS ON BOARD AND SECURED WHEN NICHOLE, already buckled in herself, turned and grabbed the helicopter's door to yank it shut. That's when she saw Virgil burst through the hospital's door and onto the helipad. She cupped her hand over her ear so she could hear Wu, and he could hear her.

"Wu, give me a status on the guard."

Wu checked his monitor. "Guard is sitting in his chair by Carlos's room. You should be airborne by now. What is the delay?"

"We're lifting off in two minutes. Keep your eye on that guard and let me know if he moves."

"Wu will do."

When he pushed through the doors and ran out onto the helipad, he saw Nichole Pope inside the helicopter, her seatbelt fastened, her hand on the door, ready to close it up. When she saw Virgil, she held the door for a moment, her hand cupped over her ear. He could see her lips moving, but with the helicopter's rotors beating and the whine of the turbines, he couldn't hear what she was saying. Plus, she clearly wasn't trying to speak with him anyway.

Nichole unbuckled her belt and climbed out of the helicopter. She walked over to Virgil as if she didn't have a care in the world. "Hello, stranger," she said.

Virgil gave her the eyebrow, then said, "Hello, Nichole."

They looked at each other for a beat. Then Nichole said, "The last time we spoke I believe you said something to the effect of, 'I better not ever see you again.'"

Virgil nodded. "That sounds right." He looked away for a moment, then said, "But, you know…"

She tipped her head. "Time passes?"

"Does it?" Virgil said.

"What was that?" They had to speak louder than normal because of the noise from the helicopter.

"I said Carlos is a good man who did the right thing for the right reasons."

"I know that. It's why we're here."

"In all likelihood, you guys saved Murton's life today. Tell Wu I said thank you."

Nichole cupped her ear and listened. "He says you're welcome. He also says I have to go now, unless you plan on stopping me."

Virgil shook his head. "Not me. But I'll consider my debt paid in full."

"Not quite, handsome. I like to keep the books balanced in my favor."

Virgil was intrigued. "And how do you plan to do that?"

She smiled at him. "You'll see." Then she jerked her thumb over her shoulder toward the helicopter. "Thank you for this."

Virgil shrugged. "Go, before I change my mind."

"You won't," Nichole said.

"What makes you so sure?"

"Do you remember my hesitation when I walked out of your bar?"

"I do. I've always wondered about that. It looked like you were going to say something."

"I was."

"What was it?"

"Something I knew then, but was too mad to say." Nichole pulled him close and kissed him on the cheek. "You're a good man, Virgil Jones." Then she turned and walked away.

And this time, Virgil was sorry to see her go.

EPILOGUE

Thanks to Wu's meticulous planning, the jets touched down in Montreal within two minutes of each other. Carlos was taken from the Bombardier Global 8000 and loaded onto the Gulfstream G-5 for their trip back to Jamaica. The nurse would go as well. For the amount of money they were paying her, she'd stay as long as they wanted. The change in planes might have been overkill, were it not for two things: One, it was another broken link in the chain.

The other was nothing more than a way to keep the books balanced in Nichole's favor.

Virgil's phone buzzed at him at six in the morning. The text message came from an unknown number. When he pulled it up, it read: Million Air, IND - one hour.

He frowned at the phone, swore under his breath, then got dressed as quietly as possible in order to not wake Sandy or the boys. He hopped in his truck and headed out to 37 north, where he'd catch 465 over to Million Air, one of the fixed base operators at Indianapolis International Airport. He didn't know why he was going or what the text was about, but when he was about halfway there, he did notice that for the first time in a long time, his thoughts were clear, his mind at rest. It felt so good the feeling was almost foreign to him.

He turned into Million Air's parking lot and went inside the building. He was surprised by the level of activity so early in the morning. Any number of jets were lined up on the tarmac, where executives and other people of demonstrable wealth milled about, most with bored expressions on their faces. Just another day in the life. They were all dressed in business attire that left Virgil feeling a little like a field hand. He wore blue jeans, a plain white T-shirt, and his Timberland boots…without socks. *On the other hand,* he thought, *maybe I look like one of those tech billionaires.* Based on some of the nasty looks he was getting though, he had his doubts.

A young and very pretty woman with bright green eyes and long red hair dressed in a Million Air outfit walked over to him and said, "Good morning, Mr. Jones. May I offer you a coffee or tea? Perhaps something stronger, if you like?"

Virgil looked at the young woman. Her name tag read 'Sarah.' "Little early, isn't it? For something stronger, I mean."

"With this crowd? You'd be surprised. Anyway, how about a coffee?"

"Sure."

She disappeared, then returned a few moments later with a mug of coffee in a Million Air mug. "Here you go."

Virgil took the coffee, then asked a question. "Listen, Sarah, uh, can you tell me why I'm here?"

She gave him a bright smile and said, "Existentially speaking, or in a general, banal sort of way?"

Virgil sipped his coffee. "It's too early for a philosophical debate—at least for me—so how about the boring version. And how do you know my name?"

"Your party should be arriving...oh look, there they are now."

Virgil looked out the window and watched as a lineman in a bright orange vest vectored the aircraft to a stop right in the front row. Sarah put her hand in the crook of his arm and led him to the door. "I have to escort you out. Rules and all that. I hope you don't mind...Detective."

When Virgil shot her a look, she said, "We're very good at what we do."

"Clearly," Virgil said. "Lead on."

They walked out of the building and up to the nose of the large business jet. Once the engines were shut down, the door opened and lowered smoothly right at their feet.

A moment later Delroy and Huma walked out of the aircraft. Delroy stood on the top step and looked at Virgil, laughed his big Jamaican laugh, and said, "Yeah, mon. Welcome home."

Delroy and Huma told him the story on the ride back. "I did some asking around, me, while we were in Lucea. I can't believe how much everyting has changed."

"Asking around about what?"

"The Pope twins, what else? We spoke with them while we were there. You should see my hometown. There is a new library, a Jamaican cultural center, two new schools, medical clinics with doctors and nurses and all the modern equipment you'd find here, in da states. There's even an outdoor musical theater. The Pope's, Jonesy, day form a, uh..." he looked at Huma.

"A non-profit foundation to handle their philanthropic endeavors," Huma said.

"Yeah, mon. Dat's it. Delroy forgot, is all. The foundation, day name it *The Lucea Foundation*, and day pay for all of it. Churches have been renovated and everyting, mon. It's beautiful. People are working and eating and being cared for, all because of those two."

Virgil smiled and thought, *Way to go, Nichole.*

When they walked in the door, Sandy was prepared to give Virgil another talking to about disappearing without telling her where he was, but when she saw Delroy and Huma her irritation vanished. She threw her arms around them both. They laughed and smiled and cried and Virgil put on some music and everyone began to dance. Huma held Wyatt in one arm and Jonas's hand in the other. The world was right and it was only eight-thirty in the morning.

When Virgil's phone rang, he answered, then had to step outside so he could hear.

"I guess I'm also his personal secretary now, too," Cora said.

"Excuse me?"

"The governor would like me to inform you that he has to go to DC for a few days. As such, he's asked me to relay to you and Sandy that he has to once again delay your dinner engagement."

Virgil was fine with it. "Okay. Anything else?"

"No, that about wraps it up. *Is there anything else, he asks?* Jonesy, what the hell is he up to?"

"Mac?"

"No," Cora said, her voice thick with sarcasm. "The Pope."

Interesting choice of words, Virgil thought. "I honestly don't know, Cora. With God as my witness, it's a simple get-together for dinner. One, I might add, that doesn't seem to be too high on his agenda."

"Keep thinking that," Cora said. She hung up.

Virgil went back inside and rejoined his family.

A few days later Rick Said was released from the hospital and flown back to Kentucky for his recuperation. Virgil told Patty she could use the Esser house as her base of operations regarding the dig. "You might as well stay there, too. Keep the place alive and all that."

"You sure you don't mind?" Patty asked.

"Not at all. In fact, you'd be doing me a favor. If the place doesn't get used, it'll start to fall apart."

Patty assured him it was in good hands with her, and Virgil didn't doubt it. "Any word on the bids?" He asked.

"They're trickling in. Still not even up to market value yet, but that's normal for this type of thing. Give it a few more days. One of the professors down here, he's hooked up politically, and says there's something in the works, but he doesn't have any particulars…or so he says."

"Huh."

"Yeah, that about says it. Don't sweat it, Virgil. It'll happen."

"Hope so."

"Listen, I've got to get back to it," Patty said. "But I wanted to ask, have you heard anything about the Indian guy? Stronghill?"

"As a matter of fact, I haven't. I'll look into it. Let you know."

"Do that."

Virgil hung up and was about to dial the prosecutor's office when his phone rang. Mac.

"Hey, Jonesy, I know it's short notice, but I've put you guys off long enough. How's tonight work for you?" He was speaking fast, like he had about one hundred things going at once.

"Let me check with Sandy and get back with you. Six?"

"Yep." And then he was gone.

When Virgil called the prosecutor's office and asked about the status of Anthony Stronghill, he was rerouted to three different offices before someone finally spoke with him. "That file has been sealed."

Virgil frowned into the phone. "Sealed? By whom?"

"Oh, sorry. Thought you would have known, Detective. It was sealed by order of the governor."

WITH HUMA BACK, THE LAST-MINUTE INVITE WORKED FOR Sandy. They pulled into the governor's drive at exactly six and he greeted them both at the front door, a glass of scotch already in his hand. He turned on his galactic smile and led them through the mansion and out to the back patio.

He gave Sandy a hug, then winced a bit when she squeezed back a little harder than necessary.

"That's what you get for going for the gun. What in the hell were you thinking?"

The governor let his head hang down. "Oh, not you too. Please, I'm begging you. Cora…well, I'm not sure I'll ever hear the end of it."

"Good," Sandy said with a little bite. Then she softened and said, "I can leave the dirty work to her then. Seriously, are you okay?"

He waved it off. "I'm fine. Lost a little chest muscle. Got my pride banged up more than anything." Before she could say any more on the subject, he added, "Too bad the kids couldn't come."

"They could have," Sandy said. "But they were so happy Huma was back, I didn't think we'd have any peace if we brought them with us. Jonas especially. He'd just beg to go home."

The governor handed them each a drink, then sat down and looked at Virgil. "I understand you've been making inquires regarding Anthony Stronghill."

The question caught Virgil a little off balance. He'd only made the request a few hours ago. That meant someone had tipped the governor. "I have. Nothing out of the ordinary, Mac. I arrested him."

"Solid arrest, was it?"

"In what regard?"

The governor didn't answer. Instead, he said, "You spent some time with the man. Anything stand out about him?"

Virgil took his time answering. When he finally spoke, he said, "Yes. He's clearly educated. On the drive back to the city I indicated that due to corroborating witness statements regarding the shooting in the field, a good defense attorney could argue he was coming to the aid of another. He responded by saying something to the effect of 'a good prosecutor will be able to say that I was acting out of premeditation.'"

"I see."

"When I asked him about Davis—the guy who was doing the shooting before Stronghill took him out—he said: 'I cannot provide or serve clear evidence of his intent.'"

The governor nodded. The three of them sat and stared at each other for a few moments.

"Why'd you seal the file, Mac? And where is Stronghill?"

"Good questions, both. I had to fly to DC for a few days. That was the reason for the delay in our little get-together."

"I'm aware," Virgil said.

The governor reached into his pocket and pulled out a badge and laid it on the table. "Ever see one of these?"

Virgil picked up the badge and examined it. He hadn't. It was shaped like a traditional police badge, gold in color, but a few differences were obvious. The badge was topped with an eagle, its wings arched, its head turned to the side. In the center sat a portion of the American flag, overlaid with the face of a Native American in full headdress. Three olive branches encircled the decorative center. The top of the badge read Department of the Interior, and the bottom said, Bureau of Indian Affairs. Across the very bottom in large bold letters, it said: Special Agent.

"A BIA badge?" Virgil said.

"It is indeed," the governor said. "You know, out there at the Salter's, I'm sure Ross would have finished the job. Thanks to Agent Stronghill, he didn't have to."

"Agent Stronghill?"

The governor smiled and yelled into the house. "Tony, come on out, will you?"

Anthony Stronghill walked around the corner, a sheepish grin on his face. He shook hands with Virgil, introduced himself to Sandy, then placed the badge in his pocket.

"I hope you'll forgive the deception, Detective," Stronghill said.

"Call me Jonesy," Virgil said. "And I do." Virgil could feel his face turning red. "Uh, sorry I hooked you up."

Stronghill shrugged. "You had the decency to unhook me as well." Then he laughed.

"What's so funny?" Sandy asked.

Stronghill tipped his head at Virgil. "When your husband took me to the city, he dropped me off at central booking. He was very kind…concerned even, for my welfare. He stayed longer than necessary and made special arrangements for me regarding a private holding cell."

"I didn't want you in the general population."

"Nevertheless, I was out the back door and gone before you ever walked out the front." He laughed again. "I do appreciate it, though."

"Glad I could be of service," Virgil said, dryly.

"You were of great service, Jonesy, and now I intend to return the favor."

"In what way?"

He glanced at the governor, who gave him the go-ahead with a single nod. "Mac and I have been working together, behind the scenes, so to speak. As I understand it, not even his chief of staff was aware of our meetings."

Virgil looked at the governor. "That's why you didn't want Cora to know about this meeting."

The governor nodded. "We've put together quite a plan, Jonesy. Ironically, Ken Salter was a big part of it. Such a shame the way his father had him under his thumb. No one is either completely good or completely bad." He patted Sandy on the wrist. "Anyway, we're hoping you guys will go along with it."

Virgil and Sandy looked at each other. "Lay it out," Sandy said.

"The federal government—" Stronghill said.

"Along with the state," Mac interjected very quickly.

Stronghill winked at them. "Mac doesn't want to miss his piece of the pie. Anyway, yes, the federal government, along with the state, would like to use your land to bring back some cultural diversity to the area. The state of Indiana is a natural choice for a number of reasons, not the least of which is its name. It was named after the Indians. It's a chance to undo at least a portion of the original escheat…some would even say rapine of the native land."

"When you say cultural diversity," Virgil said, "You're not talking about using the land as…"

"A reservation?" Stronghill said. "No. Absolutely not. We've put together a plan that will take your land, all two thousand acres of it, and build schools, museums, hospitals for the poor and indigent, housing for the residents, the works."

"That sounds wonderful," Virgil said. "And I don't want to ruin anyone's parade, especially ours, but with the political climate these days…"

Stronghill waved him off. "All of it is going to be funded through a public-private partnership. Emphasis on private. *That* is the political climate these days."

"What, exactly does that mean?" Sandy said.

Mac got serious. "Two things. One, you'll have to give up the mineral rights." Virgil started to open his mouth to speak, but Mac held up a finger. "There'll be no fracking, whatsoever. The only way any gas will be pulled out of the ground is with Said's new patented technology. You'll get a percentage of royalties, but the vast majority of funds from the gas will go toward sustainability of the project."

"What's the other thing?" Virgil asked.

"You'll have to be willing to sell the land at an agreed-upon price that's already been fixed," the governor said. He slid a piece of paper over to Virgil and Sandy. "This is a letter of intent to purchase. Sign it, and the figure listed at the bottom will be deposited into an account of your choosing."

They both looked at the document and when Sandy saw the amount—exactly twice what the land was valued at on the open market—she looked at the governor and said, "May I borrow your pen?"

The governor handed her a pen and she signed the paper, then gave the pen to Virgil. He looked at the document and was stuck...not on the price, but from where the funds would come.

"Virgil," Sandy said. "Time to sign. Virgil? Hey, what are you waiting for?"

Virgil kept looking at the name of the foundation that was supplying the bulk of the funding. He couldn't take his eyes off the name.

The Lucea Foundation.

"Virgil," Sandy said again, a little worry in her voice. "Are you going to sign? Virgil?"

THE NEXT DAY VIRGIL WENT OUT TO THE FIELD AND MET with Patty and told her everything. "You and your hand-picked team will be in charge of the dig and all the artifacts for the museum that will eventually get built."

"So you took the deal?"

"I did."

She gave him a big hug. "I'm so happy for you."

"Thank you. I'm happy too. And I guess I'm rich."

"No, you're wealthy, Jonesy. You and your kids are set forever." Then, with a bit of worry in her voice she asked, "You're not going to stop doing what you do, are you?"

Virgil laughed. "Naw. I'll have to fight Delroy on it, but I'm going to keep going. Don't feel like my work is complete yet. Don't know why, other than I enjoy it. But my gut says to keep going."

"Gotta listen to your gut."

He tipped a finger at her. "That you do." Virgil checked the time. "I also have to listen to my watch. I've got a meeting at the Co-op, so I'm out of here. I'll be seeing you, Patty."

"Count on it."

Virgil pulled into the Co-op lot and saw everyone was already waiting on him. He went inside and found Graves and Mizner seated at the table, along with Carl Johnson. Virgil sat down and got right to it.

"Thanks for coming in, everyone. This won't take long."

"You ain't gonna change our minds, Virgil," Graves said. "I done told you before, it's just business."

Mizner was nodding right along with him. "He's right. End of the season, you're out."

"Not trying to. I simply wanted to let you fellows know that next spring, Johnson here is going to be the head of the Co-op."

Graves and Mizner looked at each other and chuckled. "I don't think so," Graves said.

Virgil hollered into the back. "Hey Hank, you back there?"

Stutzman walked into the room. "Howdy boys."

"What the heck are you doing here?" Mizner asked. "You're supposed to be in Arizona."

"I wouldn't miss this for the world. And to answer your question, I'm turning control of my land over to Carl Johnson."

Graves huffed. "Go ahead. Won't make no difference to me and Angus here."

"I think it might," Virgil said. "The final decision will be yours of course, but I think you'll come around."

"What makes you so sure?"

Virgil showed them the paperwork. "You see, Hank's land and mine butt up against each other. That's where the gas is going to be pulled from. The royalties from the gas are going to be…significant. The deal's already been made and Rick Said, the guy who owns the patent and the company has agreed to it. So, I'd think it over, if I were you."

"Think what over, exactly?"

"Put Carl in charge of the Co-op. He's already got Hank's land. If you do, I'll cut you in on the gas extraction. If you don't, you can keep the Co-op and keep planting your beans and corn and whatever else you want, while the rest of us, including Carl, here, make a fortune." Then he looked at Graves and Mizner. "It's just business, you understand. Nothing personal." Then, "Hank, Carl, let's go."

The three of them stood and walked out the door. Once outside Stutzman looked at Virgil and said, "Think they'll go for it?"

Virgil never got a chance to answer. They weren't yet halfway across the parking lot when Graves and Mizner came running out the door. They were both shouting at him.

"Hey! Hey Virgil. Hold up a second. Hey, c'mon, hold up there, Virgil…"

ACKNOWLEDGMENTS

Thank you for reading this story. I maintain that it is an honor to write for each and every one of you. I hope that means something to you, because you have no idea how much it means to me.

I'd like to thank the following people for their help, support, and encouragement along the way:

My editor, Linda Heaton. Linda's laughter is infectious, her eye is sharp, and her enthusiasm, dedication, attention to detail, and patience have proven to be absolutely invaluable. Any mistakes in this book are mine, not hers. Once again, I couldn't have done it without you, Linda. I am so grateful to have you in my life and on my side. You've become more than an editor, you've become a lifelong friend. Thank you.

My wife, Debra: Your rock-solid, unending, marvelous and mystical understanding of who I am and what makes me tick is the stuff that keeps me going. Many of you have asked where my stories come from. My answer remains the same: *Me, trying to figure myself out.* Debra knows me better than anyone else in the world and without her, I'm not sure I'd bother to try to figure myself out, much less write about it. In other words, without Debra, none of my books would exist. Thank you, sweetheart.

As a deeply sad aside, shortly after I finished this manuscript and put it in the hands of my editor, I learned my father had passed away. If you've been with me throughout the entire series, then you know that all of my novels have two basic underlying themes: One is that most everyone is not either all good or all bad. In other words, the good guys are sometimes a little bad, and the bad guys sometimes try to do good. The other is the complicated and often painful emotions that exist between fathers and their sons. My dad and I had a difficult, fragile relationship. Some of it was on him, and some of it was on me. As we both grew older—when we should have been wiser and kinder to each other—things got turned around and we went the other way. In short, we'd somehow managed to exile ourselves from each other.

But like Delroy and Huma in this story, fortunately we found our way home near the end of his life. We had a wonderful reunion…just the two of us, with the hope of many more to come. And even though it turned out there'd be no more, I'll be forever grateful for the visit we shared. It was open and honest, full of forgiveness and compassion, and it ended with a long, warm loving embrace and a kiss goodbye. We both smiled and laughed, and no matter how sad his passing remains, I'll never forget that perfect moment. After he was gone, my wife, Debra, my children, my editor, Linda, and her husband, Charlie, all propped me up and kept me going. Thank you, one and all.

And speaking of thanks: To every single one of you who have taken the time to leave a review on Amazon: Thank you! Your endorsement of my work remains one of the highlights of my accomplishments. I am humbled by your trust, encouraged by your support, and in awe of your generosity during our continuing journey together. Thank you so very much. Send me an email if you get the chance. I'd love to hear from you. I really would. Nothing lights up my day more than hearing from my readers. I wasn't kidding when I said it's the best part of the whole gig.

...and the story continues.
Virgil and the gang return in State of Freedom.

State of Freedom - Book 6 of the Virgil Jones Suspense Thriller series

Virgil Jones thinks he has it all: A beautiful wife and family he loves, a job he enjoys, a tight-knit group of friends and co-workers he trusts with his life, and more money than he could ever spend. But one of those friends has a secret, one they've been hiding for over a year...

The governor needs something from Virgil's wife, Sandy. When he tells her what he wants, she finds herself intrigued by the idea. In fact, she's more than intrigued. Sandy thinks she may have found a new purpose in her life, if, that is, Virgil goes along with the idea...

Except there's a problem. Ron Miles, Virgil's unofficial boss, has suddenly disappeared while working out of the Gary, Indiana field office. Miles, in charge of a task force to help stem the flow of illegal weapons into the city of Chicago, hasn't sent back one of his regular daily reports. And when one of the Major Crimes Unit detectives starts asking questions, the answers turn out to be not only mysterious, but deadly...

As Virgil and the rest of the MCU look into Ron's disappearance, they suddenly discover that not only will they be fighting for freedom, they'll be fighting for their lives.

> You've felt the Anger.
> You've experienced the Betrayal.
> You've taken Control.
> You've faced the Deception.
> You've accepted the Exile.
> Now...It's time to fight for Freedom!

Get your copy of State of Freedom today!

— **Also by Thomas Scott** —

The Virgil Jones Series In Order

State of Anger - Book 1
State of Betrayal - Book 2
State of Control - Book 3
State of Deception - Book 4
State of Exile - Book 5
State of Freedom - Book 6
State of Genesis - Book 7
State of Humanity - Book 8
State of Impact - Book 9
State of Justice - Book 10
State of Killers - Book 11
State of Life - Book 12
State of Mind - Book 13
State of Need - Book 14
State of One - Book 15
State of Play - Book 16
State of Qualms - Book 17
State of Remains - Book 18
State of Suspense - Book 19

The Jack Bellows Series In Order

Wayward Strangers - Book 1
Brave Strangers - Book 2

Visit ThomasScottBooks.com for further
information regarding future release dates, and more.

ABOUT THE AUTHOR

Thomas Scott is the author of the **Virgil Jones** series, and the **Jack Bellows** series of novels. He lives in northern Indiana with his lovely wife, Debra, his children, and his trusty sidekicks and writing buddies, Lucy, the cat, and Buster, the dog.

You may contact Thomas anytime via his website ThomasScottBooks.com where he personally answers every single email he receives. Be sure to sign up to be notified of the latest release information.

Also, if you enjoy the Virgil Jones series of books, leaving an honest review on Amazon.com helps others decide if a book is right for them. Just a sentence or two makes all the difference in the world. Plus, rumor has it that it's good for the soul!

For information on future books in the Virgil Jones series, or to connect with the author, please visit:
ThomasScottBooks.com

And remember:
Virgil and the gang are back and waiting for you in State of Freedom!

State of Freedom - Book 6 of the Virgil Jones Suspense Thriller Series

Grab your copy today!

Printed in Great Britain
by Amazon